Lyn Andrews was born and raised in Liverpool. The daughter of a policeman, she also married a policeman and, after becoming the mother of triplets, took some years off from her writing whilst she brought up her family. In 1993 Lyn was shortlisted for the Romanic Novelists' Association Award and has now written seventeen hugely popular Liverpool novels. Lyn Andrews divides her time between Merseyside and Ireland.

Also by Lyn Andrews

Maggie May
The Leaving of Liverpool
Liverpool Lou
The Sisters O'Donnell
The White Empress
Ellan Vannin
Mist Over the Mersey
Mersey Blues
Liverpool Songbird
Liverpool Lamplight
Where the Mersey Flows
From This Day Forth
When Tomorrow Dawns
Angels of Mercy
The Ties That Bind
Take These Broken Wings

My Sister's Child

Lyn Andrews

HEADLINE

First published in hardback in 2000
by HEADLINE BOOK PUBLISHING

First published in paperback in 2001
by HEADLINE BOOK PUBLISHING

10 9 8 7 6 5 4 3 2 1

ISBN 0 7472 6365 5

Typeset by Avon Dataset Ltd, Bidford-on-Avon, Warks

Printed and bound in Great Britain by
Mačkays of Chatham plc, Chatham, Kent

HEADLINE BOOK PUBLISHING
A division of Hodder Headline Limited
338 Euston Road
London NW1 3BH

www.headline.co.uk
www.hodderheadline.com

For my cousin Hilary Lawson who shared all my childhood days – the happy ones and the miserable ones and sadly for us the latter were more frequent.

For Grainne Walsh, Maria Lynch, Mary-Margaret Smythe and Keiron Nolan who helped me make our transition from one home to another less fraught in their professional capacities and the private hospitality and friendship they have given us.

Also for my secretary Peta Jane who relieves me of many burdens and is a treasure.

Lyn Andrews

PART I

Chapter One

1909

'Mam! Mam! Come quick! Come *now!*' Tom Ryan's young face was flushed and his breath was coming in short, painful gasps. He caught and held his mother's arm tightly, his fingers pincer-like around the firm, bare flesh below her rolled-up sleeves.

'In the name of God what is it?' Molly cried out in pain. 'What's wrong? What's the matter with you?' She prised her arm from her fourteen-year-old son's vice-like grip, anxiety filling her dark brown eyes, the muscles in her stomach contracting with fear. He was in a terrible state. Whatever could have reduced her normally stoic son to a gabbling, shaking wreck?

Tom had regained some of his breath and his face had lost the ruddy flush of exertion and was now unnaturally pale. 'It's what ... what Da was afraid would happen. Come *on*, Mam,' he pleaded, once more grasping her arm.

Molly suddenly realised what he was talking about and,

3

pushing Tom aside tore off her apron, flinging it across the kitchen table on which the dirty dishes from teatime still remained. She turned distractedly to her daughter.

'Ellen, go up the street and see how many men and lads you can get and then follow us down. Go on, girl, don't stand there with your mouth open like a cod on a fishmonger's slab!' Molly was already reaching for her heavy black shawl but didn't bother to wrap it around her dark, neatly coiled hair as she always did when she went out of the house.

Her daughter stood for a few seconds, totally transfixed and mesmerised by the scene unfolding before her eyes. At sixteen she was taller than her petite mother, her hair was lighter than Molly's, more of a chestnut colour, but she had her father's clear grey eyes which were now wide with fear. What they'd all dreaded seemed now to have happened and she could see all their recently acquired financial security evaporating. These days they had far more than any of their neighbours in Milton Street possessed in the way of money, food, coal and decent clothes, but they'd been just as poor and desperate to keep a roof over their heads until at least six months ago. Now it seemed that their good luck had deserted them and their former misery was about to return. 'One step forward, two steps back,' she muttered before gathering her senses and galvanising herself.

'Mam, shall I go and get the brigade too?'

Molly turned back, her thoughts racing distractedly around in her head. 'No! Get one of the young lads to go, better still, if you or anyone else knows where that young hooligan of a brother of yours is, send him.'

'Our Bernie's at the Cooneys'. When I ran up the street I saw him swinging on the street lamp with Teddy Cooney outside their house,' Tom supplied, his eyes filled with fear and impatience.

'I'll swing for *him*!' Molly said grimly. 'Ellen, go and get him and then for God's sake get on with finding help before your da loses everything and we all have to go on the parish!'

Ellen needed no second telling. Without even waiting to grab her own shawl, she followed her mother and brother out into the bitterly cold, frosty night. She didn't even pause to watch her mother and brother start to run down the street, instead she went immediately up the steps of number 16 and hammered on the door until it was opened.

'Is our Bernie here? Is he? It's terrible! Something terrible has happened and we need him, now!'

Gussie Cooney turned and yelled down her dark, damp lobby, 'Bernie Ryan! Yer sister wants yer! Now! Gerrout 'ere!'

Mrs Cooney took in Ellen's white face and fear-filled eyes. The girl looked half demented. It had to be something very bad.

'Is it yer mam, Ellen?'

'No, Mam's all right.'

'Then what's up with yer, luv? Yer look as though yer've seen auld Nick 'imself.'

'Oh, please, please Mrs Cooney, can Mr Cooney and the lads go down to the yard? Our Bernie's got to go and get the brigade and I've got to get as many men as I can to help.'

'Holy Mother of God! Is the yard on fire? Is that why yer need the fire bobbies?' Alarm now replaced curiosity in the older woman's eyes and her hand went to her throat.

Ellen nodded. 'Oh, please hurry them up!' she begged before turning away as her neighbour gave young Bernie a shove and told him to run like hell to the nearest police station. She muttered a sincere prayer that no one would be killed and the damage would be light. She had a lot of reasons to thank Molly Ryan these days, the food on the table and the fire in the range, just to start with.

Ellen went from house to house pleading desperately for help. Soon men and boys were rushing out from the decrepit old houses, some in shirt sleeves, some pulling on greasy, threadbare, often torn jackets. Crisscrossing the street, she finally reached the bottom. Thank God this was the last house, she thought as she hammered with what strength she had left on number 36.

Number 36 was the home of John Meakin and his family. The Meakins were not popular. They kept themselves to themselves, John Meakin saw to that. He ruled them all with a rod of iron and Mrs Meakin was terrified of her husband. Ellen had often heard her mam and Mrs Cooney discussing the woman's plight.

When the door was opened by Mr Meakin himself Ellen instinctively backed down to the second step.

'Oh, Mr Meakin! Please help! Please come quickly, there's a fire at the yard, everyone else is going up there! Look, all the men are going.'

John Meakin glanced briefly up the street then turned to stare at her. He was a small, dark, wiry man. 'Ferret Face', Tom and Bernie called him and she thought the description fitted him well. But this was hardly the time for such deliberations.

'Then you won't need my help, will you, girl, if half the street's gone already? It's nothing to do with me what goes on at that yard. I've heard it's not up to much anyway. I think he's got a nerve to call it a "business". Now he thinks he's better than anyone else, *all* you Ryans think you're a cut above. I remember a time not long ago when you used to come knocking here in rags, asking to borrow a bit of this, a bit of that, as if we were made of money. "The Cadging Ryans" I used to call you – still do. So clear off and let a decent man have some peace and quiet after a proper day's work.'

The door slammed in Ellen's face, leaving her stunned. Why was he taking that attitude? What he'd said about them having to 'borrow' bits of food was true but he didn't have to be so rude and nasty. It was as if he hated Da, and as far as she knew he had no reason to. She'd only asked for help. Suddenly tired, she leaned against the corner of the soot-encrusted wall of the next house where it joined the narrow alleyway that led into the darkness of number 3 Court. The property there was in an even worse state than the rest of the street. One standpipe and a single deep gutter ran down the middle, always clogged up with rubbish. The two privies that served nearly thirty people stank even in the depths of winter.

She caught her breath and, putting John Meakin's

collapses, it could go any minute!'

She realised he was right. The whole ramshackle building was ablaze, the flames leaping skywards from the roof. The horses' screams of terror, almost human in their pitch and intensity, became louder as did the sound of the pounding of hooves against wood.

Tears were running unchecked down Ellen's cheeks. 'You've got to go and get him out! Get him out from there, please? And my mam, don't forget my mam!'

'God Almighty! Your mam's not in there, luv.'

'Where is she?'

He set her down on her feet. 'At the gate. Look, one of the lads is holding her and your brother. Go on over to them.'

Before Ellen could move they heard the panels in the heavy wooden door splintering, followed by the ear-splitting crash as the door fell outwards and downwards sending a shower of sparks shooting upwards. She felt herself being caught up and swung around again as the fireman pressed her against the wall, his body protecting her. Over his shoulder she saw an enormous black shape, eyes rolling white with terror, huge white-feathered hooves thundering on the wet cobbles, the thick black mane on fire. It filled her entire field of vision and passed so close she could smell the burning horsehair. Then a figure, bent double, appeared from the wall of smoke and flames, and Ellen recognised her father.

'It's Da! It's my da!' she screamed and was instantly released as her protector ran forward and half carried, half dragged her father to the gate and away from danger.

Jack Ryan was in a state of collapse. Heedless of his own safety he'd plunged in, desperately trying to save the small business in which lay all his dreams. It had been the means of escaping the grinding poverty of the past and making a secure future for his family. It was all he'd thought about. It was all he'd cared about.

Molly cast off the grip of Tom and Bernie and fell to her knees beside her husband, not even feeling the jarring of the hard cobbles.

'Jack! Jack! Speak to me for the love of God, Jack?' Molly pleaded, placing her arm around his shoulders, feeling the warm, wet, charred cloth of his jacket disintegrating beneath her fingers.

The fireman helped him sit up.

'I'm all right,' he croaked. 'I'll live, Moll, but everything . . . everything I've worked for . . .' He couldn't go on. He began to cough and he was shaking.

Ellen put her arms around her brothers and drew them close. They too were shaking and crying and she herself was fighting back the tears. Da looked so . . . so beaten. 'It's all right, Da's not hurt and neither is Mam,' she comforted, trying to keep her own voice steady.

'What about Eddie?' Tom suddenly asked.

In all the terror and confusion their stepbrother, Eddie, had been forgotten, as had Annie, their stepsister, for Molly was Jack Ryan's second wife.

'I don't know where . . . where he is,' Ellen replied.

'Well, he's not where he should be and neither is that little madam. They should be here helping your da and me.' Molly's voice was shrill with fright.

A shot rang out and Jack Ryan covered his face with hands that were badly burned.

Molly crossed herself. 'Oh, Holy Mother of God, the poor beast.' Then she looked up to see a policeman towering above her. Another one was coming over to join him and was holding a revolver. Only the police and vets were allowed to put down horses and rabid dogs.

'I'm sorry about that, luv, you've got to be cruel to be kind. It was too badly . . . hurt. In a terrible state really. The only thing we could do was put it down but the other one doesn't seem too bad. In a real state of shock, but gradually calming down. There's a lad who is going to lead it away from all the noise and confusion. We'll call an ambulance to take yourself and your husband to hospital. Are the kids all right?'

'Yes! But we don't need an ambulance. We're not that bad and I . . . I'll tend to my husband.'

'Well, if you're sure, but I'd get someone to look at those burns. It'll take a while yet to get that out.' He jerked his head towards the fire and the still-burning buildings. 'They'll have to move all the coal bit by bit just to make sure it's not left smouldering, then restack it. It's bad luck it being a coal yard.'

Jack just nodded. It would probably take the best part of twenty-four hours to sort out what was left.

Ellen helped her mother to her feet. The crowd was melting away and, as the constable had said, a lad was helping to hold and calm the other shire horse. It was continuing to rear and plunge, its eyes wild, and there were flecks of white foam around its nostrils. Narrowing her eyes in the dark and the smoke, she realised the lad was Eddie. Ellen glared at him. Trust him, always too flaming late to be of any use, and there was no sign at all of Annie. She was probably still in town with her friends.

Molly tried to compose herself. 'Let's get you home, Jack.' She began examining his injuries as gently as one could. 'I've got some goose grease, that'll help ease the burns, but we'll get the doctor. You're sure nothing's broken?'

Jack Ryan shook his head slowly. 'Only my heart, Moll. Only my heart.'

Chapter Two

They walked home in the darkness, every beam of light cast by the moon and the street lamps catching the frost that was now covering every surface and making it glisten. Few front doors were open, it was too cold, but from dimly lit windows the figures of anxious women, awaiting news, were discernible.

Jack nodded and briefly thanked the men and boys who had turned out to help.

When he reached his own doorstep Arthur Cooney turned towards the little group. 'I 'ope it's not too bad, Jack. The fire bobbies arrived smartish, like, and we all did our bit for yer, lad. Get them burns seen to and get some sleep.'

'Easier said than done, Artie,' Jack said wearily.

'Just say ter yerself 'to 'ell with it until mornin'.'

Jack nodded. 'Thanks, Artie, I don't know what we'd have done without your help and all the others.'

'What are mates for?'

Molly managed a weak smile of thanks to her neighbour.

When the front door had closed behind them and Molly had put on the kettle, she went to search for the jar of goose grease in the scullery. Jack sat down, his shoulders slumped. He covered his face with his hands.

Gently Ellen put her arm around his shoulder. She was still shaking herself but her da looked terrible. 'Oh, Da, I'm so sorry. I'm so sorry. And look at your poor hands.' Tears filled her eyes again.

'Ellen, make the tea, luv, and put plenty of sugar in each cup. Tom, go down and see if the Dispensary doctor will come out. I know it's late but if you explain and tell him that we have the money to pay what he charges, he might come. Go on, lad, be quick.'

Molly squatted down before her husband and gently removed his hands from his face. He looked terrible.

His hair, eyebrows, eyelashes and moustache were all badly singed. His face was black from the smoke, as were his clothes – what there was left of them. The whites of his eyes were very bright in contrast to his face, but they were bloodshot.

He looked at her through tears.

'I know, luv, I know,' she murmured soothingly as she began to spread the grease over the burned skin. He had now begun really to feel the pain from his injuries but it was nothing to the desolation that filled his heart.

Ellen handed the tea around. Molly held the mug to her husband's lips but he shook his head.

'You've got to have *something*, Jack. Will I get Artie to go down to the Swan for a drop of brandy? It's supposed to be good for shock.'

'No, no thanks,' Jack gasped. The pain from his burned hands, arms, face and shoulders was becoming unbearable.

Molly looked at him, almost overcome with pity. He hadn't had a very good life. Born into the poverty and squalor of the Liberties – the slums of Dublin – he'd come to Liverpool as a very young child, like hundreds of thousands of others, to escape the Great Famine. As he'd grown up he'd worked at anything he could get. During his first marriage, which she knew hadn't been happy, he'd tried to provide the bare essentials: rent, food, fire and clothes, but the deceased Martha Ryan had been a feckless waster. And a bit of a slut to boot, so Gussie Cooney had told her once, after Gussie had had a bit too much to drink.

Her own mother, dead these fifteen years, had told her she was mad to take him and his two kids on when he was forty-four and she only twenty-eight. She'd waited for true love and at last she'd met Jack. She loved him then and she loved him now, even though he was now sixty and therefore classed as an old man while she was only middle-aged.

'The doctor should be here soon, Jack. He'll give you something for the pain.'

'If our Tom shifts himself,' Ellen remarked impatiently.

Molly turned to her. 'See to our Bernie, luv. Make sure he has a good wash before putting on his pyjamas and going to bed.'

She was proud of the fact that they had pyjamas and nightdresses, proper towels and gentler toilet soap instead of carbolic, but that thought made her heart sink. For how much longer? If everything had gone ... but no, she wouldn't think about that now.

Bernie went into the scullery without the usual litany of

complaints. Ellen stood, leaning on the doorjamb, her mug in her hand, watching him affectionately.

'See you fold your clothes up ready for school in the morning.'

'My shirt's all covered in smuts, Ellen.'

'No one will notice if you wear your jersey over it, but if they say anything tell them what . . . what's happened.'

The kitchen door opened but to everyone's disappointment it wasn't the doctor, only Gussie Cooney.

'I've just cum ter see if there's anythin' yer want? Artie told me it was shockin', smoke an' flames everywhere. 'Ave yer sent for the doctor fer 'im?'

Molly nodded, then bit her lip. 'Our Tom's gone to the Dispensary but these burns are more serious than I thought. Maybe you should have gone to hospital,' she said anxiously to her husband.

'I wouldn't trust the daylights in one of them places,' Gussie sniffed.

'If the doctor thinks he needs to go, then I suppose . . .' Molly shrugged.

'Yer should 'ave got them 'ands inter cold water straight away, I've 'eard that's the best remedy.'

Molly didn't want to be sharp with her neighbour but her nerves were frayed to the point of snapping. She took a deep breath before replying. 'I've heard that too, but I've already smothered his hands with grease.'

'God, would yer look at the state of 'is clothes, Moll! Fallin' off 'is back, burned ter bits.'

'I know, but at least they protected him a bit.'

Gussie sat down and accepted the mug Ellen passed

18

her. "'Ow did it start, like? Who told yer?'

It was a question Molly herself hadn't yet asked.

Jack tried to gather his wits. 'I don't know how it started, but I was just on my way up there to settle the horses and make a final check like I do every night when a bloke stopped me and said he thought he could see flames and smoke. We . . . we ran and he was right.'

'Who was this bloke? Do yer know 'im, like?' Gussie asked.

'No. No, I didn't know him. I asked him to go for help but then our Tom arrived, so I sent him down here to tell Molly.'

'What did yer do then?'

Jack frowned and tried to think back. It seemed like a month ago. 'I . . . I . . . unlocked the padlock and opened the gate.' He shook his head, trying to remember what he did after that; it had all been so chaotic.

'Do yer know what the damage is then an' what's 'appened to the other 'orse? Our Artie said they 'ad ter shoot one. Terrible it was, 'e said. The thing was mad with the pain, 'e said it was burnin' all over, God 'elp it.'

Ellen glared at the woman. A shudder ran through her as she remembered the stampeding animal. Did she really *have* to go on like this?

Jack didn't look up so it was Molly who answered. 'We won't know until morning what's . . . what's left—'

'And Eddie was going to see to the horse,' Ellen interrupted. 'Gossipy Cooney' is what the woman should be called, not 'Gussie' Cooney. Couldn't she see

19

she was upsetting Mam further?

There was silence in the kitchen and seeing there was nothing more she could learn or do, Gussie finished her tea, said 'Tarrah' and left, bumping into young Tom who was closely followed by Dr Jenkinson.

'Oh, thank God you've come, sir!' Molly cried in relief. 'If you'll excuse me for just a minute. Tom, get a good wash and then both of you go to bed. Ellen, you've work in the morning and if you don't turn up they'll dock your wages or maybe worse.'

'I'm all right, Mam. I'll be going in to work,' Ellen said with more confidence than she felt.

Dr Jenkinson examined Jack's burns while Molly watched in silence, wiping her hands on the piece of rag she kept near to the range for removing hot pans and dishes.

'So, Mr Ryan, what happened?'

Haltingly, Jack related the events of the night again while the doctor shook his head. Jack Ryan and his family worked very hard. The man was out in all weathers humping sacks of coal until late at night and lately he'd seen a lad of about twenty driving another coal cart. He admired the man. Looking around the room he thought Mrs Ryan kept her home as clean as was earthly possible in the crumbling, damp, vermin-infested hovels the people in this area were forced to live in. Oh, conditions in the slums had improved with Dr Duncan being appointed the first Medical Officer of Health in the country, and Kitty Wilkinson, who had opened her home as the first public washhouse, and Mrs Rathbone initiating the first District Nursing service, but there was still terrible overcrowding, poverty, disease and dirt.

'Did you clean these burns, Mrs Ryan, before you put on the grease?'

'Clean them?' Molly looked perplexed.

'Yes. Did you make sure there was no dirt or ash or charred material embedded in the skin?'

She was confused. 'I . . . I . . . don't know about that. I'd always thought . . . I mean I was always told that grease . . .'

'It is, but wounds should be cleaned first. Although now I don't think he could stand the pain. But I'm sure everything will be all right. You've all had a terrible experience. I'm going to leave you something to take for the shock and if you'll call and see me tomorrow morning, Mr Ryan, we'll see how you are.'

Molly held out the coin. 'Thank you, thank you so much for coming, sir. I know it's late.'

Picking up his black Gladstone bag he gestured that Molly should keep the money. 'The hospital wouldn't have charged you, Mrs Ryan, and it *was* an emergency. You did the right thing calling me out. Good night.'

Molly let him out and then leaned against the door for a second. Now she knew she would have to try and talk to Jack and it wouldn't be easy.

She went back into the kitchen and took a deep breath. 'Jack, what do you think will . . . happen?'

'I don't know, Moll, and that's the truth. You know how hard I worked for that little bit of extra money to get started.'

She nodded. She'd scrimped and saved too. She'd gone without food herself, had used oil lamps instead of lighting

21

the gas jet. Saved as best she could on fuel for the range, patching and darning and altering the clothes for all of them. They'd been as badly off as the neighbours. Sometimes there had been no coal and no oil and they'd made do with candles and rubbish picked up from the gutters, old orange boxes and bundles of wood from the cooperage that you had to queue for at the end of the day. Often they'd existed on just weak tea and bread.

Then had come the little windfall: a piece of luck they never in their wildest dreams expected. Old Ma Stebbins at number 4 had died and Jack had been astounded when he'd been told that she'd left him fifteen pounds. No one in the street had even known she'd got any money. She'd lived in Milton Street for years. She'd rented two rooms but after her kids had all grown up and left and Charlie Stebbins had died, she'd made do with just one. She appeared to live in poverty and want like everyone else. So where she'd got the money from was anyone's guess, although it was generally known that old man Stebbins liked to bet on the horses. Jack had always been good to her, doing whatever jobs he could, she being a widow and bent almost double with bad arthritis. And then Jack – the most prosaic of men – had revealed to her that he had a dream.

'So you told her you always wanted your own bit of work?' Molly had said. 'Something you've always dreamed about? I'd not have thought you'd be—'

'A dreamer of dreams, Moll?' he'd finished, laughingly. 'Aye, I've got my daydreams and my hopes for all of us.'

After that he'd worked fourteen, sixteen hours a day, sometimes all night too, going from one menial job to another until he'd earned the money that, together with the fifteen pounds, enabled him to see his dream become reality. He'd rented the yard, done the repairs needed to the stable, purchased his horse and cart and his first stocks of coal. And then he'd gone out touting for business. And that business had grown; now Eddie drove the second cart and in time Molly had hoped Tom and then Bernie would work for their father too. A family business, she'd reflected. People liked that. It sounded reliable and trustworthy. She pulled herself back to reality.

'I'll go down first thing in the morning to see . . . to see what's left,' said Jack.

'Oh, Jack, just when we thought things were getting better . . .'

'I know.' He managed a smile. 'Do you remember the day we got the cart, Moll? You said we should have a photograph taken of it with the big shire in the shafts and me standing beside it.'

'Jack Ryan and Sons: Coal Merchants. The family firm you can trust,' she said quietly.

'Aye, it was a proud day for us all. And then the second horse and cart for Eddie and more customers . . . Everything was going so well, we'd nearly got enough money to be able to move out of here. And now?'

'It might not be too bad. Surely all the coal won't have gone? Maybe one of the carts could be patched up and there's still old Betsy and our savings.'

'She'll be hard to handle after this. I won't be able to trust Eddie with her, she'd be prone to bolting. Where is Eddie?'

'He won't be long now.' She didn't want him getting even more upset. She glanced at the clock on the over-mantel and wondered irritably where the hell Annie had got to. She should have been in an hour ago. Still, she had more important things to think of than her recalcitrant stepdaughter.

The question of where on earth Annie could be entered Ellen's mind too as she lay in bed, her nerves still jangling. Oh, didn't Mam have enough on her mind without flaming Annie and her antics to contend with? Her mam had tried hard with Annie but the girl had always resented the woman who had taken her own mam's place. She'd never liked Mam and as she'd grown up she'd challenged her mother's authority time and time again, until Da had had to give her a good talking to – and the threat of a beating. 'I'll not have you behaving like a tart!' he'd yelled at her stepsister once.

Worry filled Ellen's mind, and not just about Annie. What if Da *had* lost everything? He'd have to go back to the docks or to whatever job he could find, and that wouldn't be easy, not at his age and anyway there wasn't much work at the best of times. Oh, they'd all worked and saved so hard. She too remembered the day they'd got the first cart. Both she and Mam had had tears of pride and happiness in their eyes. But Annie hadn't. She'd never said a single word.

Chapter Three

'It's all been too much for you, luv.'

'For you too, and Ellen and the lads.'

'Thank God no one was killed. When I saw Ellen and that fireman right in the path of that poor crazed animal, I honestly thought they'd be killed. And I was demented with worry until I saw you stagger out.'

'I *had* to try, Moll. I had to try to get those animals out.'

'I know, luv, but ... well, you got Betsy out,' she'd replied, trying to comfort him. The enormity of the loss really hadn't begun to sink in properly.

Molly had succeeded in persuading Jack to go to bed. She'd helped him to undress, wincing herself at the sight of the burns on his back and shoulders and his forearms.

'Thank God you had on your jacket and old overcoat, otherwise these might have been far worse.'

'They're bad enough, Moll.'

'Can you stand me cleaning them up a bit like the doctor said I was supposed to do? I'll be as gentle as I can.'

'Do what you have to,' he'd said and gritted his teeth the whole time she gently wiped the burned flesh with a piece of clean towel wrung out in warm water. Then just as gently she smeared the thick creamy fat over the burns. She extended the bandaging on his hands to his arms but he couldn't bear to have anything on his back and shoulders.

'God knows how I'll get any sleep.'

'You'll have to lie flat on your stomach with your arms stretched out. Take these,' she instructed, putting in his mouth two of the tablets the doctor had left. She held the glass of water to his lips. 'Now straight to bed, you're exhausted.'

'So are you, luv, and what about Eddie and Annie?'

'Leave them to me. I won't have you worrying yourself about them. In the morning we'll sort everything out.'

When he'd gone, she gathered up his clothes, shaking her head sadly. Oh, he'd driven himself to the limit to build up that business, and all so they'd have a decent future. One without the miseries of poverty. She'd even begun to look at houses in the more respectable areas of Liverpool, well away from the slums. That would have to wait. She'd put this bundle of charred rags into the bin.

She'd got to the scullery door when the back door opened and Eddie came in. 'Where's Betsy?' she cried, hoping that nothing had happened to their one remaining horse.

'I managed to get her a stable just for tonight. I stayed with her – she's used to me – I just kept talking to her and rubbing her down gently. It seemed to sort of, well . . . calm her. Her mane's badly singed and so is her tail, but we can hag her mane and dock her tail. She seems all right. There are no bad cuts on her legs; her eyes and ears are okay too. I saw she had water and her nosebag.'

'Thank God. Finding her somewhere permanent is another thing we'll have to do tomorrow.'

'How's Da?' the lad asked. The last time he'd seen his father was when he'd been lying on the ground with Molly and the fireman bending over him.

'He's shocked, burned, exhausted, what did you expect? Where were you anyway?'

'I was on my way home. I'd been to the Palais de Luxe in Lime Street.'

'What's your da told you about going up to Lime Street with all those tarts parading up and down! Brazen hussies that they are!'

'I don't go often,' Eddie protested. 'I hardly ever go, but there was nothing I wanted to see on at the Roscommon.'

'There's six picture palaces on Scotland Road to choose from. There must have been *something*.'

'No, Ma, there wasn't.'

'Well, never mind. Here, dump these in the ashpit, I'll put the kettle on.'

'Aren't you going to bed?'

'Not yet, your sister's not in. She's getting to be a right little madam but your da's got enough on his plate at the moment without trying to sort that one out.'

The lad returned from the ashpit and took off his smut- and smoke-stained coat, washed his hands and face in the scullery sink and then sat down at the table while Molly made a fresh pot of tea. She sighed heavily. She really didn't mind Eddie. Most of the time he was a good lad. He didn't hang around street corners smoking or get himself caught down the back jigger playing pitch and toss. As far as she knew he didn't lie about his age and go into pubs. He worked just as hard as Jack and had only a few pleasures: buying clothes and going to the pictures.

'What'll we do now, Ma?' he asked, his hands cupped around the mug she'd given him. She'd put three heaped teaspoons of sugar into it. Soon she'd have to ration that.

'We'll go up there in the morning with your da and see what's left.'

'Do you . . . do you think there'll be anything?' Eddie asked tentatively, gazing at his stepmother.

He'd always got on with her. When his da first told him he was going to marry her he'd been hurt, resentful and sullen, like Annie, but he'd quickly grown to like Molly. She was kind and understanding, and had tried to give them the same love and attention as his real mam had. Far more attention, in fact, he'd said to Annie, which had caused a terrible row between them. But then Annie really missed her mam – she was like her in so many ways.

'There's bound to be *something*, but the stables are useless, especially the empty one where the carts, traces and harnesses were kept. The loft with the straw and oats and sacks will have gone too.'

'What about the coal?' Eddie queried earnestly. 'Please let there be something,' he prayed.

'Didn't you hear the policeman saying it would all have to be moved? I don't know how much will be saleable, Eddie, and that's the truth. I just pray to God there will be enough for us . . . to go . . . on.' She was struggling to get the words out and the anxiety, so plain on the lad's face and in his eyes, seemed to make it worse.

'Da's not going to be able to do much, like, is he? With his hands in that state?'

'No, he's not, not for quite a long time, and that'll make him feel worse. He'll want to be doing everything himself.'

'Perhaps if there's things to do I could get a couple of the lads from the street to help? Pay them . . . not much, of course. Just a couple of coppers, like, and our Tom and Bernie can help too, after school, though it's nearly dark when they get home.'

She nodded her agreement. 'Just to sort it all out. Pull down what's left of it, clear up the yard. It'll be a start.'

'Maybe we could try to get another cart and I could do the rounds and hope people won't mind a bit of a wait for their coal? I'll work until midnight if I have to.'

'Oh, Eddie, I know you mean well, lad, but it's freezing out there. People won't . . . can't wait. We'll lose an awful lot of customers. There's plenty of other coal merchants. Still, no one was badly hurt, we have to thank God for that. There's some money we've managed to save – I've managed to save . . .'

Eddie bit his lip anxiously. 'I know, it was for another house. A better house. Ellen told me.'

'Well, that will have to wait, we've lived here for years so a few more won't hurt.'

They both fell silent until they heard the back-yard door creak on its hinges. Molly's expression became grim as Annie walked into the kitchen.

'This is a nice time to be coming home, milady. Just where have you been?' Molly demanded quietly but sternly.

Annie pursed her lips and glared at Molly defiantly. People often told her that she was the image of her poor mam, God rest her. That pleased Annie for she hoped it irritated her stepmother. But she repeated what they said frequently just the same, though never in her da's hearing.

She had a photo of her mam and dad on their wedding day. It was a bit faded and tatty now, but Mam had been young and every time Annie looked in the mirror she tried to smile the way Mam was smiling in the photo. Like her mother, Annie had blonde hair that curled naturally and large blue eyes. She was inclined to be plump, now that they had plenty of food. She knew she was pretty and that if she had the right clothes – fancy clothes – she'd be really good looking. Beautiful even. But she didn't have expensive clothes – although the ones she did have were far better than any she'd had in her entire life. She'd saved up for most of them. 'Cheap and cheerful', she called them and grudgingly she admitted to herself that where money for her 'keep' was concerned, Molly didn't demand an excessive amount.

'I asked you a question, Annie.' Her stepmother rudely interrupted her daydreaming.

'Me and Josie went to the pictures, then we got chips and ate them at her house,' Annie retorted. 'Does that satisfy you?'

'Don't be so hardfaced to Ma. She – we've all had a really bad night,' Eddie snapped at his sister.

Annie looked at them closely, noticing for the first time the smudges on her stepmother's face, the weariness and shock in both sets of eyes and the smell of smoke that seemed to float around the room – it wasn't the smoke from the fire in the range.

'What's up? What's happened?'

'There's been a fire at the yard,' Eddie said dejectedly.

'Your da's gone up to bed, he's shocked and he's got some nasty looking burns and I'm worried to death about both him and the business. But don't bother about us, we managed fine without you.'

'How was I supposed to know!' Annie demanded.

'You should have come home earlier, then you'd have been some help. Not much, but a bit. Thank God I had Ellen.'

At the mention of her stepsister Annie's eyes became as hard as two sapphires, and her lips set in a line. Oh, yes, Miss flaming perfect Ellen would be here, of course.

'Well then, if you had *her* you wouldn't have needed me anyway.'

Molly got to her feet, her dark eyes blazing with anger. 'Don't you dare speak like that to me, Annie Ryan. While you were off gallivanting with Josie Rafferty your da's business burned to the ground. One of the horses had to be shot; the brigade are still up there, damping the coal down. Your da could have been burned to death trying to get the horses out. Yes, milady, everything has gone and we'll be damned lucky not to be back where we were six months ago – with virtually nothing! So you can say goodbye to new clothes, the visits to the pictures and the chip suppers.'

Annie sat down beside her brother, the fear and regret plain now in her eyes. Her poor da! If what Molly had said were true it really was a disaster. She couldn't go back to those other days, which now seemed like a lifetime ago. Not enough food or heat. No decent furniture or clothes and not a single hope of buying any more. Now that she could wash with good soap and had a large thick towel to dry herself, proper bedding and nightdresses, good food, warmth, treats such as those Molly had mentioned, a bit of scent and lipstick even, she couldn't . . . *wouldn't* go back to not having any of those things.

'Did anyone know how it started?' she asked quietly, looking at her brother.

Eddie shook his head.

'Your da was going up to check everything when a man stopped him and told him.'

'What man?' Annie had poured herself a cup of tea.

'Just a feller. Someone passing,' Eddie replied.

'Fortunately Tom was going up that way. Your da saw him and sent him down.'

'What time was that?' Annie asked. Something was niggling at her memory.

'About half past nine. Why?'

Annie looked thoughtful. She hadn't been to the pictures with Josie Rafferty, she'd gone with Pat Cleary, but she'd met him outside. She now remembered gazing out of the window of the tram as it passed Freemason's Row on the way into town. The tram stop was very near to the entry and there was a street lamp on the corner so she'd noticed a man walking up towards the entry, then turn into it. The yard was at the bottom of it and unless you were going there, there was no other reason to be in the entry. That's what had made her remember. It was a small, thin man. Old like her da.

'I . . . I saw someone. I was on the tram—'

'At that time? I thought you said—' Molly interrupted.

'Oh, Ma, never mind what I said, let me *think*! I knew him. I'd seen him before.'

'Then who the hell was it, Annie? Don't start playing games now, it's too important,' Eddie demanded.

Annie concentrated hard, closing her eyes to help her recall that momentary sighting as passengers got on and off the tram. 'I know now! It was Mr Meakin. John Meakin.'

'Are you sure? It was dark,' Molly pressed.

'It *was* him. The tram was stopped and there's a street lamp there. I'd know old Ferret Face anywhere. It was definitely him and he was walking towards the yard. That's why I remembered.'

Eddie rose, the legs of the chair making a screeching noise on the lino. 'I'll sort him out! I'll go up there now!'

'No, wait, Eddie! I don't want you or your da going up there tonight. We all need our rest. We'll tell your father in the morning. Go on up now, the pair of you. I'll wash these things and then come up myself.'

Fortunately Ellen was awake since Annie didn't even try to open the bedroom door quietly or move carefully around the room.

'Did they tell you?' Ellen asked, sitting up but pulling the blankets around her.

'Of course they did. At least it took Ma's mind off why I was in so late.'

'Is that all you can think of?' Ellen was annoyed.

'No, it's not! I'm . . . I'm as upset as everyone else is. I *won't* go back to living the way we used to do.'

'You *won't* go back. God, you're so selfish, Annie. You should have seen the state of Da, of Mam, Tom and Bernie. Even Eddie managed to come and help. It was awful, really awful.'

'I *know*! Ma just told me so!' Both she and Eddie insisted on calling Molly 'Ma', not 'Mam' the way her stepsister and -brothers did. Their 'mam', their proper mam, was dead. Annie sat down on the bed. 'And I saw who did it,' she announced.

Ellen's eyes widened. 'Who? How?'

'I was going into town on the tram, late, like, and I saw him walking towards the yard.'

'Who?'

'Old Ferret Face. Mr Meakin.'

'You couldn't have.' Ellen was confused and suspicious. Annie shouldn't have been just going anywhere 'late'. 'It was dark, you must have made a mistake.'

'I'm fed up hearing that! Everyone's so flaming thick. There's the bloody street lamp! I saw him. I bloody did.'

Ellen was even more confused. 'I went and asked him to help. Everyone else in the street was going. He was *there*. He was at home and he was nasty, he wouldn't go and help.'

'He must only just have got back then. He'd have had time to get home and play the innocent.'

'The way he carried on you'd have thought he hated Da.'

'He does. He can't stand it that Da got that money and

34

started his own business. He was always lording it over everyone, especially us. Why us, for God's sake? We were broke like half the street. He wanted to go on being so bloody high and mighty, hardly passing the time of day to anyone in the entire street. His wife's terrified of him and there's definitely something wrong with that Lucy. She never speaks either, she scurries up the road like a scared rabbit and sometimes I've seen her in the back jigger crying.'

'Didn't you ask her what was the matter?'

'No. Why should I? She won't speak to me. Oh, I used to *hate* going to that house on the cadge.'

'So did I – and that's what he calls us: "the Cadging Ryans". Shall we tell Mam now?'

Annie looked thoughtful. 'Are you going to work in the morning?'

'Of course I am. I can't afford to lose my job now. Are you?'

Annie nodded. She didn't want to lose her job either, not if they were ruined.

'Then neither of us will be here.'

'Right, let's tell her now. Has she come up yet?'

'I haven't heard her.'

Ellen wrapped the quilt off the bed around her and they both went downstairs, Annie carrying the old paraffin lamp which was still used in the bedrooms.

Molly was sitting in the armchair, her head in her hands, her shoulders shaking with silent sobs. The sheer magnitude of the problems she now faced had overwhelmed her.

'Mam. Mam, are you awake?' Ellen asked quietly.

Molly looked up and dashed away the tears with the back of her hand. Now what? she thought, catching sight of Annie. She'd heard no raised voices from upstairs so there hadn't been a row.

'Annie was telling me she saw Mr Meakin, but he was there, Mam, when I called at the house. He opened the door to me. He was nasty to me. He said Da thought he was better than anyone else, that we all thought that. The way he said it, he sounded as if he hated Da.'

'So he'd have a good reason to set fire to the place,' Annie said.

'And he'd have had enough time to get back home,' Ellen added. 'Do you think we . . . Da . . . should go to the police?'

Molly looked thoughtful but then shook her head slowly. 'What good would it do, luv?'

'But I saw him! I bloody *saw* him!'

'Annie, don't swear, luv. It would be your word against his. Did anyone else on the tram see him?'

'How would I know that? How would we even know how to start finding out who the other passengers were?'

'We couldn't and he'd say you made a mistake, it was someone else. How could he be up there when he was at home – and hadn't he a witness to that in Ellen?' But despite all she was saying to the girls, Molly believed Annie's story. Her cheeks were burning with anger now. Meakin *did* hate them. He hated Jack's success, obviously so much that he was prepared to put Jack out of business.

'What about Mrs Meakin? She'd know he was out.'

Annie was exasperated. 'Oh, God, Ellen, are you stupid? Haven't I just said she's terrified of him? She'd never go against him.'

'Annie's right. The poor woman has a dog's life with him.'

Ellen was outraged. 'So is there *nothing* we can do?'

'No, luv, there isn't and I'm just as furious as you are.'

'There is something. It's not legal but someone would give him a hiding—'

'Annie, we don't want more trouble,' Molly interrupted.

'There wouldn't be any. You know what the fellers are like in this street, they all hate him and . . . afterwards . . . well, he wouldn't go to the scuffers and even if he did it'd be all their words against his. That Lucy and her mam would keep their mouths shut. They'd probably be made up to see him getting a good belting.'

Molly knew that if Jack asked or even hinted to the men to do to John Meakin what Annie had just outlined, then they would, but it wasn't the path either she or Jack would want to follow.

'I'll talk to your da in the morning. Go on up now, the pair of you.'

Annie turned towards the door but Ellen held her ground. 'Not until you come up, Mam. I'll not leave you down here on your own, worried to death and crying.'

Annie rolled her eyes and pursed her lips. If she had her way Jack bloody Meakin would be kicked up and down the bloody street like a football. He'd definitely done it. He'd been the one who'd ruined her life.

Molly smiled at her daughter, turned off the gas light

and, taking the lamp from Ellen, went ahead of the two girls up the stairs.

Chapter Four

Jack was still in terrible pain next morning. He'd spent a restless night and so had Molly. She'd lain beside him silent and still, wishing she could take some of the pain away. She'd gladly suffer herself if it helped him. She'd thought of everything both girls had told her, although she did wonder vaguely where Annie had been going at that time of night. But she was still sure Annie was telling the truth. She had no reason to lie, not about seeing John Meakin anyway.

When the first vestiges of dawn crept across the sky she got up.

Jack stirred and groaned.

'I'm sorry to wake you, luv.'

'I was already awake.'

'Well, you're not getting up. I know you've had precious little sleep. I'll bring you up a cup of tea and two more of those tablets. Did they work?'

'A bit. I suppose as the burns heal up the pain will go too.'

'It *will*, Jack,' she said firmly.

Molly raked out the ashes and clinkers in the range,

built up the fire and put the kettle on it to boil. Then she began the ritual tasks of the day.

Ellen was the first to come down, looking tired and pale. 'I couldn't sleep, Mam.'

'Neither could your da and I. Take this in to him and a couple of those tablets. I'll have the porridge done when you come back.'

The kitchen was warm and the porridge was ready in bowls on the table, along with a plate of bread and butter. The teapot was in its usual place too. She wanted them all to have a good breakfast. It was bitter outside and all too often in the past they'd had to go out with empty bellies. A good breakfast set you up for the day, her own mam had always said.

She saw the girls off to work. Annie had gone out in a huff because she wanted to go with her da to confront John Meakin. She'd be delighted to tell him to his thin ferrety face that he was a liar and a fire-raiser, and that was illegal. There was a fancy name for it but she couldn't remember what it was; Da would know. But Molly had been adamant. They were both going to go to work. Tom and Bernie had gone to school, quiet and uncomplaining. The usual moans and arguments, particularly from Tom, about 'having to have *him* tagging along', were missing. Eddie had had a bit of a lie-in seeing as there was no work for him. But after he'd eaten and had filled the coal scuttle he felt restless and in the way.

'I think I'll go down to the docks later, just to see if I can get a half-day. To help out, like. It'll be better than just hanging around here, getting under your feet.'

'That's good of you, Eddie, but don't get your hopes up, there's too many in this city without work and it's coming up to Christmas,' Molly had replied, as she tried to make her husband more comfortable.

So there were just the three of them in the kitchen when Molly told Jack the tale. She watched his face, pale and drawn with pain, change and flush red with anger, his eyes like two pieces of flint.

'So, that's it, Jack,' Molly finished and sat down.

'I believe you. I wouldn't put it past him at all. But, as you say, it'd never hold up in court.'

'*Should* we report it though?'

'No. I'll go and see him myself to see just what he has to say.'

'He'll have gone to his work.'

'Then I'll go tonight.'

'You know the fellers in the street would go with you, Da,' Eddie chipped in.

'I don't want anything like that, Eddie. I'll not sink to his level of hatred and envy.' Jack gave a short bark of a laugh. 'And he calls himself a Christian. He's nearly eating the altar rails at Mass on Sundays.'

'Then should we go and tell Father Healy? He might have something to say to that flaming no-mark.'

Jack shook his head. 'Let's leave the clergy out of it.'

'So, will we go to the yard with you then and see . . . see . . .' Eddie's voice tailed off.

They all knew it had to be faced sooner or later.

It looked even worse in the drab grey winter morning,

Molly thought, tears pricking her eyes. The huge puddles of water left by the Fire Brigade had frozen solid, causing another hazard.

'Be careful how you go, Eddie, we don't want any more disasters.'

The men from the Council had obviously removed the carcass of the poor horse but the smell of smoke, still drifting on the cold air, was overpowering. The back wall of the yard was made of brick, two thicknesses of it: it was blackened but still standing. The pieces of wood that had withstood the inferno, mainly heavy joists and spars, were black and twisted. The coal was stacked in small piles all around the yard amongst the other debris, objects rendered unrecognisable by the inferno.

In silence Jack walked around, kicking each pile with the steel-capped toe of his boot and shaking his head.

Molly felt she had to break the silence. 'How much of it is useless?' she asked quietly.

'About half, I'd say. I'll tell the Council to take the cinders to use on the road. They might save a few horses slipping, breaking legs, having to be . . . shot.'

'Well then, that's a good thing at least. And we've still got a fair bit of good coal.'

'Everything else has gone, Moll.'

'I know.' She felt so helpless.

'There's still Betsy, Da. I'll go and find a new stable for her later on.'

Jack cast a grateful look at his eldest son.

'And we've got a bit put by,' Molly added.

'We won't have a penny after we've bought a cart, sacks,

shovels, harness and paid livery charges for Betsy. It's going to be a long time before I can afford to rebuild.'

'But we'll manage, Jack. We'll do it, just to let John Meakin see he hasn't got the better of us.'

'Ma's right, we won't let him beat us. I'll do all the shovelling, humping, delivering and driving, Da, until your hands are better,' Eddie offered enthusiastically.

'Believe me, luv, everything will turn out fine. We'll show him.' There was anger mingled with determination in Molly's voice.

'And we'll tell him that if it happens again the fellers in Milton Street won't stand for it.'

Molly nodded, hoping that their encouragement had bolstered Jack enough to go and see Dr Jenkinson. She hadn't realised how much time was slipping by and the doctor had said he wanted to see Jack this morning.

She didn't manage to get him to the Dispensary until late afternoon. He had insisted that Eddie take him to see where the horse was now stabled and, finding it suitable, he haggled over a fair price for livery, saying that Eddie would see to the animal morning and night until it had settled down enough to put between the shafts of the cart he hoped to buy, along with all the other things necessary to get started again. After that they'd asked a couple of the lads in the street to start to clear up and stack the coal into just two mounds.

Molly had given him all the money they'd saved, and the housekeeping too, after failing to persuade him to go to the doctor. For the first time in months she would have to go to the pawnshop but there were plenty of things she could do without.

She met Gussie when she was halfway down the street on the way to Clarkson's.

' 'Ow is Jack now?'

'Still in a lot of pain. He *should* be seeing the doctor but you know him, stubborn as a mule. He's at the yard with Eddie.'

Gussie nodded gravely. 'Artie said things were bad, Moll.'

'Bad enough, but thank God some of the coal is all right, we'd a bit saved and Eddie will do the driving and the like until Jack's burns are better.'

'Is there any news on 'ow it started, like?'

Molly was very tempted to tell her but knew that it would be all over the neighbourhood in half an hour. Jack wouldn't have had the chance to tackle John Meakin yet.

'Not really, Gussie, but I don't think it got started by itself.'

Gussie gawped at her. 'Will Jack be goin' ter the scuffers then?'

'What for? There's no evidence. We'll just have to tighten our belts and that's something we're well used to.'

'Yer should get a few bob fer that lot.' Gussie looked pointedly at the things that were folded up in Molly's new coat. It was the first coat she had ever owned, recently purchased and much prized, kept for Sundays and special outings.

Molly swallowed as she ruefully patted the bundle. 'There's the coat itself, the clock, the two pot dogs and the brass candlesticks.'

'That's cleared the mantelpiece fer a start.'

Molly tried to be cheerful. 'There'll be less to dust now.'

'Don't yer go worryin', girl, yer'll 'ave them all redeemed before long. I just wish I 'ad them ter pawn.'

'Don't worry, Gussie, I won't see you go short.'

'You're a saint, that's what yer are, luv.'

'I know, though my halo's in danger of slipping a bit. But we've both been through worse times than this! We'll get through it, Gussie.' She'd tried to sound light-hearted as she turned away and resumed her journey.

Mr Clarkson didn't mention the fact that it was a long time since he'd seen her to do business with, but he'd heard of the fire and was sympathetic.

'Hopefully I'll be able to redeem them in about six weeks.'

'What will you do for Christmas, Mrs Ryan?'

He was unfailingly courteous to his customers. He knew it was always a blow to their pride to have to use the service he provided: why add to their misery?

'It looks as though it's going to be like last year and all the others before that. I had hoped, planned, that this would be a "real" Christmas, with all the trimmings.'

'I'm sorry. But look on the bright side, Mrs Ryan, you have acquired quite a lot of things, so I heard, and you know I'll give you the best price for them.'

'I'm grateful, Mr Clarkson, but hopefully I'll not have to pledge anything else. I hope we'll be getting on our feet again.' She smiled tiredly.

* * *

The Dispensary was always full. Dr Jenkinson was called the 'tanner' doctor, because that's what he charged, if he charged at all. All the others charged far more than sixpence, but Dr Jenkinson was known both for his kindness and generosity and for taking the City Fathers to task at every opportunity about the terrible conditions his patients had to live in. He didn't have fancy clothes or a car, nor did he live in luxury, but it was rumoured that he had a private income and he had no wife or children to make financial demands on him.

Neither Molly nor Jack felt in the mood to discuss their situation with anyone so they both sat on the hard wooden bench, leaned their heads against the wall and closed their eyes until Jack's name was called.

'I expected you much earlier than this, Mr Ryan.'

'I'm sorry, doctor, there was so much to do.'

'I *did* try to get him here this morning, sir,' Molly added earnestly.

'And how are things with your business?'

'We've enough to manage on and replace some things. We'll get by.'

'Right then, let me look at you.'

Jack was in agony although Dr Jenkinson was gentle, but he didn't cry out. When it came to looking at Jack's hands, the doctor's expression changed.

'What is it, sir, please?' Molly asked.

'I'm not very happy about these hands. I think they should be seen to in hospital.'

Jack shook his head. 'I'm sorry, sir, but I've more important things to do than sit in one of those places for hours.'

'You shouldn't have to wait long. I'll give you a note.'

'I don't want to seem rude or ignorant, or ungrateful, sir, but it's my living. I have to get it started again.'

'Well, there's nothing I can do to *make* you go to the hospital, but you are running a serious risk. I want to see you in two days' time. Keep those dressings clean, Mrs Ryan.'

'I will and I'll make sure he comes back too.'

'What time will you go to see John Meakin?' Molly asked on the way home. She insisted they walk; taking the tram for a few stops was a luxury they'd only recently indulged in anyway.

'After everyone's home.'

'Will you go alone or do you want me to come?'

'I'll go alone.'

She wasn't happy with this arrangement. They didn't know how John Meakin would react and if he struck out Jack would retaliate and he was really in no fit state to take someone on, even though the nasty little piece of work was small and weedy-looking.

'Take Eddie with you and maybe Annie. She *did* see him, after all.'

Jack shook his head. 'No, Moll, I'm not involving the kids. It's just him and me.'

She held her peace, but her heart was full of anger – and fear too.

Eddie, Annie and Ellen were all disappointed at not being included in the trip to number 36.

'But I saw him, Da,' Annie protested.

47

'And Ellen spoke to him at home but she's not going either. I'll hear no more about this.'

They all sat at the table and Molly ladled out scouse into bowls. A loaf had been cut up and placed on a dish in the middle of the table.

'This is blind scouse, Ma!' Annie protested after she'd taken her first spoonful.

'I know, Annie, but we can't afford meat every day now.'

'I don't like blind scouse either,' young Bernie said mutinously.

'It'll give you something else to talk about to your mates,' Tom cut in sarcastically. 'You should have seen him, Mam, he had half the school crowded around him and he was telling them all how daring *he'd* been. How *he'd* helped the fire bobbies, how *he'd* helped Eddie with Betsy.'

Bernie's cheeks flushed and he bent his head over his bowl. He'd got a bit carried away but for once he had been the centre of attention and it had felt great. Even Stanley Harvey, the class bully, had been envious.

'Well, we'll have no more of that, meladdo!' Molly reprimanded. 'Things are bad enough without you telling half the neighbourhood our troubles and lying into the bargain. Now get on with your meal.'

When Molly had cleared the table she helped Jack to put on his overcoat. He gritted his teeth at the extra weight on his burns.

'Da, are you sure you don't want me to come?' Eddie pleaded.

'I'm sure. I won't be long.'

He went slowly down the lobby and then they heard the front door close. They all looked at Molly with apprehension in their eyes.

He was in agony as he walked down the street. Each step jarred and his clothes were chaffing. The tablets the doctor had given him helped a bit but he could hardly bear the weight of his clothes and his hands, heavily bandaged, were throbbing fiercely. Only anger helped to take his mind off his injuries.

Maggie Meakin opened the door to him. She was a pale, timid woman with hunched shoulders and greying hair who looked much older than her years.

'Is he in, Mrs Meakin?'

She nodded.

'I've got a few things I'd like to say to him.'

'He . . . he's having his meal and I can't . . . I daren't . . .'

'Tell him you're sorry to disturb him but I threatened to push past you and come in anyway.'

She turned away but Jack saw real fear in her eyes. The man was a monster, the way he treated his wife and daughter. He'd seen the child, Lucy, once, crying her eyes out in the jigger, but she wouldn't tell him why. He'd suspected a severe beating. He'd gone and knocked on the door, intending to have it out with Meakin, but it had been Maggie who'd answered and she'd begged and pleaded with him to do or say nothing. He heard John Meakin's raised voice, then the kitchen door slammed and he came down the lobby.

'What the hell do you want, coming hammering on the

door when I'm having my meal? Clear off! You've no business here.'

'I'll go when I've told you a few things.' Jack's voice was cold and hard.

The other man's gaze didn't falter. 'Like what?'

'Like I know it was you who started the fire yesterday. Arson's an offence. It's worth three years' hard labour in Walton Jail.'

'What the hell are you talking about? I was here, at home, where any decent man would be at that time of night.'

'You were seen. You were walking towards the yard.'

Jack waited to see the impact his words would have. A flash of fear crossed the other man's face.

'Who saw me? Tell me that?'

'If you hadn't been out of the house why ask who saw you?'

Meakin tried to look uninterested. 'Just curious, that's all.'

'It was our Annie, she saw you from the tram. It was stopped to let people get on and off. She got a clear view, there's a street light on that corner.'

'Your Annie! That little slut! You believed her lies? That's what they are. The other one can vouch for that. She was here when I was trying to read my paper.'

'You mean Ellen? And if you call our Annie any more names I'll swing for you, so help me God!'

'You've no proof. I was here with Maggie and Lucy – anyway, who'd believe the likes of you?'

Jack's eyes narrowed. 'You hate me, don't you? You're

jealous as hell that we got that money and started up the business. It put us on a higher footing than you with your tuppence-halfpenny caretaking job and you couldn't stand that. Well, we'll manage. You'll see, after Christmas we'll have a second, then maybe even a third cart. You'll not get the better of me again, Meakin.'

John Meakin's face was puce; the veins at his temple throbbed. He lashed out, catching Jack on his shoulder.

The pain made Jack sway and stagger backwards and John Meakin came down the steps after him, yelling abuse. He usually avoided fights and arguments for he wasn't strong enough to hold his own, but what could Ryan do with bandaged hands? It gave him courage. He jabbed his finger into Jack's chest.

'Go on, get away from my door. And don't be sending your bloody kids down here cadging or I'll belt them too.'

A red mist of pain and anger swam before Jack's eyes but before he had time to shout back he heard a yelp. It was coming from Meakin who was being held by Ozzie Ogden, one of the biggest and toughest men in the street. The weasely little man's face was now turning blue, for the grip on his collar was choking him, and his feet weren't even touching the ground.

'Listen, youse, next time pick on someone else! You're an effin' coward and an effin' bully. We all 'eard about Jack's yard. Did 'e 'ave anythin' ter do with it Jack, la?' Ozzie's grip tightened; Meakin's face was going purple.

'Yes, but I can't prove it.' Jack's shoulder felt as though it were on fire again.

'Do yer want me ter take it out of 'is bloody little ferret gob?'

'No. No thanks, Ozzie, I don't want you getting into trouble with the law for the likes of him.'

'That's no problem, like, 'e's not goin' ter be in any fit state ter go whingeing ter the scuffers after I've done with 'im.'

'No, I really do appreciate it, Ozzie, but leave him alone.'

'Just as yer like, but listen, youse, if there's any more fires or beltin' anyone or name-callin', next time yer won't gerraway with it. Me and the lads will leave yer fer dead, an' I effin' well mean that!' He released the man.

John Meakin picked himself up off the floor quickly in case the big docker kicked out at him, ran up the steps and slammed the front door.

' 'E's just like a bloody tart! Shit scared! In fact I know some tarts who'd make bloody mincemeat out of 'im.'

'Thanks, Ozzie.'

'I meant it, Jack. Iffen 'e does anythin' else, *anythin'* at all, he'll pay fer it.'

Jack nodded.

'Are yer all right? Yer've gone a shockin' colour. Let's get yer 'ome, la.'

Jack was grateful for the strong arm and shoulder to lean against. Thank God Ozzie Ogden had been passing.

Chapter Five

Two days later Molly had an argument with Jack over his visit to the doctor.

'Jack, I promised him you'd go. I promised faithfully. What's he going to think of us after him being so kind, not even accepting the sixpence for coming out to see you in the first place?'

'It can't be helped, Molly. There's so much to do and not enough time and Eddie can't do it all by himself.'

'But, Jack, it's your health, for God's sake! Money can't buy that. Eddie *can* manage for a few hours on his own. He's a good lad, have you heard him complain about anything at all?'

'No, and he *is* a good lad, but I've a cart to buy, sacks to fill and the sooner I get back on to my rounds the better chance I'll have of keeping some customers. They won't wait, not in this weather. I can't leave Eddie to cope with Betsy, she'll be very skittish.'

'But, Jack, what could you do if she did bolt?' Molly pleaded. 'You couldn't haul in the traces, not with those hands.'

'But I could shout. She'd recognise my voice. And I

could tell Eddie just what to do. I'll get things going again as soon as I can, Moll, I promise, and then I'll go and see him.'

Molly knew it was useless to carry on when he was in this mood. She could argue until she was blue in the face and it would do no good at all.

'Just a couple of days then. And I won't be held responsible for you not going. You can go up to the Dispensary by yourself and explain to him.' He just grinned at her and despite her worries she had to grin back. 'Sometimes, Jack Ryan, you're half a fool and the other half's not sensible!'

'At least we've managed to keep our sense of humour, Moll.'

Over the following days life seemed to become so hectic that Molly felt she hadn't time to turn around, let alone sit and think and plan. Jack and Eddie were out at eight in the morning until sometimes ten at night. They were both exhausted. Tom had asked to help out after school and in the Christmas holidays for, as he told his hesitant father, he could shovel the coal into bags and weigh it at least.

'And our Bernie can help me,' he'd finished.

'That lad's far too interested in kicking a football around or playing Lally-O with Teddy Cooney and that tribe of hooligans he calls his mates.'

'So you see he could be doing something useful for a change.'

Molly had agreed. She'd taken more things down to Clarkson's and she was determined that it would be the best Christmas they'd ever had. The things she'd pawned weren't absolute essentials and she could economise. She'd go to St John's market late on Christmas Eve to buy her vegetables and a goose or a capon. She'd make a small pudding and two dozen mince pies, half of which she'd give to Gussie. She bought crêpe paper, and that only cost threepence, in red and green, which Bernie and young Teddy Cooney could make into paper chains to decorate the kitchen. It would keep them out of mischief and there would be enough for Teddy to take home to liven their house up a bit. She knew her neighbour would try hard to make it a good Christmas but Artie hadn't had any work for over a week. She'd take Ellen along with her to buy the holly, that too went for half of nothing on Christmas Eve, and there would be plenty to pass on too. There wasn't much use asking Annie to accompany her, the girl would be off somewhere with Josie Rafferty and her other friends. She sighed. She'd have to ask both girls to contribute more to the household budget soon and she had a good idea what Annie's reaction to that would be. Ellen would understand but would be disappointed.

She knew both girls were saving hard to buy a smart costume, hat and shoes for Easter. It was months and months away but for once they were in agreement. They really wanted to cause a stir at Mass on Easter Sunday. She'd told them both that Mass wasn't supposed to be some kind of fashion parade, but she knew that neither of them had taken any notice.

The girls, to her surprise, had been looking together in the *Echo* at the prices charged by Frisby Dyke's, Sturla's and Frost's on County Road. Shops like Cripp's, the Bon Marché and Henderson's were well beyond their means. Together they had animated conversations about colours and styles of hats and shoes and Molly knew Ellen had set her heart on a pair of dainty high-heeled button boots in pale grey suede. It always amazed her that at such times they behaved like natural sisters – friends even – when at most others they fought like cat and dog.

Business was holding steady; Jack was relieved and Eddie was working like a trojan, doing the job of three men, helped as much as possible by Tom and even Bernie. Betsy had, after a few scares, settled down and begun to respond to Eddie's voice. After Christmas he'd have enough to buy more coal and possibly another horse and cart. The carts were cheaper than the horses and he'd have to find somewhere to stable another horse. Working horses like their Clydesdales always got on better being stabled together.

With Molly's economies and the help of Clarkson's Pawnbrokers they were holding on to a semblance of prosperity. Jack, however, still kept putting off the visit to the Dispensary, which worried and infuriated Molly, but there was nothing she could do except change the bandages. She couldn't help noticing the burns on his hands didn't seem to be healing as well as those on his back and shoulders. However, as she told herself ruefully, you can lead a horse to water but you couldn't make him smile. And when it came to looking after himself, Jack was far more stubborn than any of his horses.

* * *

56

On Christmas Eve Jack, Eddie and Tom were out all day.

'What time do you think we'll finish, Da?' Eddie asked.

Jack looked at his eldest son. The poor lad was completely worn out. Tom, sitting behind them, leaning on a sackful of coal and trying not to fall asleep, was not much better. 'Not too late, lad, around four or five. Most of the orders have been delivered, except Mrs Pemberton's anthracite. We'll have to go down to the Salthouse Dock especially for that.'

It was top-grade coal and expensive, so he couldn't afford to keep it in stock. She was the only customer who asked for it. He sold it to her cheaper than other coal merchants, which was why she gave a regular order to them, but he made a loss on it. 'Put this sack over your shoulders, you're getting soaked,' he said gently, 'our Tom's got that old mackintosh and sou'wester.'

It had started to drizzle, needle-fine rain that soaked into everything. Already it was nearly dark; the brightly lit shop windows displaying every kind of food you could think of, and the goodnatured bantering between shopkeepers and their customers made Jack think back on so many Christmases when all his kids could do was peer enviously through the glass, noses pressed to the panes until they'd been moved on by the shopkeeper or a policeman. Sweets and toys had been beyond his meagre wage when they were young.

Eddie fastened the empty coal sack over his shoulders, pulled his cap down lower on his forehead and turned the horse's head in the direction of the docks. It would take half an hour to drive there, fill up two sacks and then drive to Mrs Pemberton's. He was looking forward to getting home. There'd be a good fire in the range and the smell of cooking. True, his mam and Ellen would be down the market but just a cup of tea, a slice of bread and jam and a seat by the fire would be heaven right now.

His head down, his cap protecting his face from the rain and cold, he didn't see the cart coming in the opposite direction until Jack yelled a warning. It was too late. Both horses shied and reared. Both drivers were thrown from their seats, as were Jack and Tom, whilst coal and timber littered the cobbles, bringing the busy traffic in the Dock Road to a standstill.

Eddie helped Jack to his feet. Someone was helping the other carter, two burly dockers were hanging on to the bridles of both horses to stop them from bolting and two policemen had arrived.

'He wasn't looking where the hell he was going!' the carter, shaken and bruised, yelled at Eddie.

'He was going too bloody fast! Hogging the entire bloody road!' Jack shouted back. By his side, poor Eddie looked terrified but didn't appear to be injured much.

'Well, we can sort all that out later. For God's sake, let's get this mess cleared up, then we can all go home and have a decent Christmas,' the older constable urged.

But Jack knew there was something wrong. He leaned over towards the other carter and sniffed. 'He stinks of ale! He's drunk! He shouldn't be on the road at all in that state. God knows how many people he could have killed!'

The policeman looked annoyed at the prospect of his 'early dart' slipping away. He'd been looking forward to a pint or two himself when he got off duty, which should have been in fifteen minutes' time. Now it would be much later.

'Then it's a night in the Bridewell for you!' he scowled. 'Drunk in charge of a horse and cart on the King's highway. Go on, get a move on, you'll clear this bloody road first! A fine way to spend Christmas Eve.'

Jack sat on an iron bollard by the dock wall and watched his sons, the carter and the two dockers clear the roadway. He was bursting with frustration. And he didn't feel at all well. What do you expect? he asked himself. He was too old to be getting flung on to the cobbles. He was shocked and bruised but apart from that nothing seemed to be broken. He was a bit light-headed, because he'd struck his head on the ground, but his hands were throbbing more severely than any of his joints. By God, if only he could find some evidence against John Meakin he'd see him sent down to serve three years' hard labour with great pleasure.

When at last the road was clear enough Eddie and Tom helped him back up on to the seat.

'What'll we do, Da? About Mrs Pemberton's anthracite?' Tom asked.

'Did you just shovel it up?'

'Yes, there wasn't time to put it in sacks,' Eddie answered.

'Go further up and then stop and we'll all bag it up to save time.' He couldn't let the woman down, even after all this. She paid top price, after all.

'But you can't, Da,' Tom said, worried by how terribly pale his father looked.

'I can sort of hold the sacks open for you. Let's get going or at this rate it will be Christmas morning before we get home.'

Molly was still up. She'd been to the market with Ellen and they'd come home with hemp bags full of vegetables, fruit, a goose and an armful of holly and mistletoe. Bernie and Ellen had gone to bed, but Annie was not in yet. As the time passed and there was no sign of Jack or the two lads Molly became more and more worried. He'd said he would be finished at five and after rubbing down and seeing to the horse they'd walk home. She grew increasingly anxious and angry as the minutes ticked by. She'd have a few words to say to Annie, Christmas Eve or no Christmas Eve. It was nearly half past ten and at her age she should be in too. Oh, this would be a fine start to the holiday and after all her planning and hard work.

The kitchen ceiling above her was criss-crossed with paper chains and there was holly on the bare overmantel and around the shades of the gas light. The range gleamed with blacklead and the room was tidy. Ellen, bless her, had helped with the cleaning.

Molly was finally dozing in the chair, worn out by the exertions of the day, when Jack and Eddie and Tom came in the back way.

She sat up with a start. 'What's the matter? You said you'd be earlier, much earlier.'

'We had an accident, Ma,' Eddie said, slumping down

on the old sofa, heedless of his coal-impregnated clothes.

'Jack! What kind of an accident? Are any of you hurt?' Molly cried.

'No, we're just shaken up and bruised. It was a bloody carter who'd been on the ale all afternoon by the state of him. He's been taken to the Bridewell but he, Eddie and Tom had to clear the road, then we had to deliver Mrs Pemberton's anthracite and she'd nearly given us up for lost. Still, she'll go on being a regular customer and she gave the lads two shillings as a Christmas box.'

'Are you certain you're all all right?' Molly demanded, jumping to her feet to get a good look at them. 'I don't want any heroics!'

'Just a few cuts and bruises, Mam,' Tom said, stripping off his mac.

Molly hurried through into the scullery where she kept the TCP lotion and then went to a drawer in the dresser and took out one of the pieces of clean cloth she used for Jack's dressings. In silence she dabbed and cleaned the cuts and grazes.

Jack lay back in his armchair and closed his eyes. He was so tired and his head was aching.

At the sound of the latch being lifted he opened his eyes and sat up. Molly, who had been on her knees cleaning the cuts on Tom's knees, looked round.

Annie grinned at them all. 'I'm sorry I'm late. Happy Christmas! Josie an' me, Josie an' me . . .' She dissolved into laughter.

'She's drunk!' Molly cried, getting to her feet, anger flashing in her eyes. 'You're a disgrace, milady! Drunk at your age, and while your da and your brothers have been out working and got thrown from the cart—'

'Oh, Ma, don't nag, it's Christmas.' Annie's speech was slurred. She'd been having a great time with Josie and the gang – they'd all been in Yates's Wine Lodge in Moorfields.

Jack was on his feet instantly, biting back the cry of pain as he gripped his daughter by the shoulder.

'You apologise to your ma! She's a right to nag, she's a right to be as flaming angry as I am. By God, girl, you'll go to the bad! And I don't want any excuses or lies and you can leave that Josie Rafferty and her like alone. She's a bad influence on you. Now go to bed!' His last words cracked with anger as Annie sullenly wove her way between the furniture to the kitchen door.

Jack sank back into his chair, his anger spent. 'What the hell are we going to do with her, Moll? I mean it, she'll go to the bad.'

Molly struggled to remain calm. 'No, she won't, Jack. We'll sort her out after tomorrow. Let's have a really good Christmas, everything's ready. Now all of you get washed and go to bed.'

'I'll just sit here for a minute or so, Moll,' Jack said, 'until I feel a bit . . . stronger.' His eyes closed wearily again as the two lads went into the scullery.

Molly was really concerned. He looked terrible. His face was almost grey and the whites of his eyes were very bloodshot. He'd banged his head and she knew that that could be very bad. She made up her mind.

'Jack, you sit there and rest, I've got to go out, just for a few minutes. I promised Gussie something.' She was lying. She didn't put on her shawl, knowing it would make him suspicious since Gussie only lived a few doors away.

He half opened his eyes. 'All right, luv.'

She ran all the way to Dr Jenkinson's and hammered on the door until he himself opened it, dressed in pyjamas and an old dressing gown and slippers.

'Mrs Ryan! In the name of God, what's the matter? You've no coat or shawl on, woman, you'll get pneumonia.'

'Doctor, please . . .' She fought for her breath.

'Is it your husband?'

She nodded.

'Has he got a fever?'

'I . . . I . . . don't think so, sir. He's been out with our Eddie, working like mad, but this afternoon there was an accident.'

He drew her into the hallway out of the cold.

'A bad accident?'

'Not really, the lads just had cuts, grazes and bumps, but Jack . . . he banged his head . . . He looks terrible, doctor. I know it's late and it's Christmas but—'

'Wait there, Mrs Ryan, I'll go and get dressed.'

She stood shivering in the hall until he reappeared, dressed and with his overcoat and bowler on, and carrying his black bag.

'Lead on, Mrs Ryan.'

They hurried through the darkened streets, past pubs from which came roars of laughter and tuneless singing until finally they arrived in Milton Street.

Jack looked to be asleep but on Molly calling his name

63

softly, he opened his eyes, which widened in surprise at seeing the doctor.

'I hear you've been in the wars again, Mr Ryan.'

'Collision on the Dock Road, sir.' Jack struggled to rise.

'Don't get up, man, just try and relax.'

'They were all flung out on the road,' Molly added.

Gravely the doctor examined Jack's head. 'Well, you've got a nice bump coming up there. Have you anything cold, really cold, Mrs Ryan, to use as a compress?'

Molly thought hard. 'There's ice on top of the washboard in the yard. Will I scrape some of that off and wrap it in a cloth?'

'That would be fine.' But Dr Jekinson still looked concerned. 'Let me have a look at your hands.' In silence he took off the bandages and his expression became even more serious. He held his hand to Jack's forehead.

'You've a temperature and I very much suspect that it's hospital for you.'

Molly stopped at the door as her hand went to her throat. Something must be very wrong to have to go to hospital on Christmas Eve.

'What . . . what . . . is it, sir?' she asked timidly.

'He should have gone to hospital on the night of the fire. I fear septicaemia has set in. Blood poisoning.'

'What . . . what will happen?' Molly was gripped by fear now.

'Oh, it will be dealt with. Could I have a word with you, Mrs Ryan, in private?' He turned to Jack. 'It's just to give her instructions on how to treat you.' Jack leaned back and closed his eyes again. He really *should* have gone back to the doctor's after the accident.

They went into the lobby. Molly felt as though there was ice water in her stomach.

'Mrs Ryan, what I said about dealing with it wasn't true. If it's septicaemia, as I fear it may be, there is no cure. The poison is carried through the body by the blood.'

She couldn't take it in. 'No! NO! You can't . . . you can't be telling me that he might . . . die?'

'I'm afraid so. If he'd gone to the hospital or come to see me when he was supposed to there would have been more of a chance. It would have meant amputation of both hands, but . . .'

Molly stared at him in horror. 'Amputation! He would never have consented to that, sir. Never!'

Dr Jenkinson nodded his agreement. It would have been devastating but in time he would at least have been able to work, supervising his sons. Now that seemed unlikely.

Molly fought down her tears and her disbelief. She would have to be calm and sensible. She could break down later, when she was . . . alone. 'I . . . I . . . want him to stay here, at home, sir. I don't want him to go to hospital. He'd hate it and he'd know. I'll look after him myself, I've the two girls to help and the neighbours are good.'

Again he nodded. They might live in hovels that were unfit for animals but when trouble came they all helped out in any way they could. He admired them, especially the women. It was the women who kept the home and family going, often taking a beating from a violent drunken husband at the same time.

'Get him to bed and keep him there. Make him as

comfortable as you can. I'll call regularly. There's no need to worry about payment.'

As something began to dawn on her she looked up at him with horror. 'Oh, my God! It was me! I caused it! I should have cleaned the burns on his hands right away! I . . . I've killed him! How am I going to live with that, sir?' She was crying, shaking, on the verge of hysteria.

He put his arms around her. 'You didn't know, lass,' he said gently. 'You just didn't *know*. You mustn't blame yourself like this.' He looked up to see a young girl standing on the top stair.

'Come on down here, child, your mother's upset. Your father is very ill.'

His words stunned Ellen. She'd been asleep until Annie had come in, banging doors and cursing. She'd heard the strong voice in the kitchen and had crept down to see who it was. She'd never seen her mam in such a state. And the doctor here on Christmas Eve? Slowly she came down the stairs and, reaching out, took her weeping mother in her arms.

'He's going to die, Ellen! Your da's going to die and I . . . it's my fault!'

Dr Jenkinson was very firm. 'No, it isn't, child! I'm the authority on such things. Your mother is very, very upset. I'm going to leave a sedative for both your parents. Can you manage?'

Ellen nodded. She felt cold, so very cold, and here was the doctor asking *her* if she could manage. He should be asking Annie; she was the oldest. But Annie was fast asleep and she reeked of alcohol. So she *had* to cope. Mam was hysterical and Da . . . Da was probably going to die. She knew in that moment that she would always hate Christmas. It would remind her for ever of this night.

Chapter Six

Ellen didn't sleep; she lay beside Annie whose snores in part kept her awake. She felt numb. Cold and numb. It was Christmas Day now, she thought, soon it would be getting light and she still hadn't made up her mind what to do. Poor, poor Mam, how she must be blaming herself even though the doctor had been insistent that it wasn't her fault. Ellen knew her Mam would feel guilty for the rest of her life. But she had to think of the immediate future. What would be best? To tell everyone and ruin Christmas, or try to keep up an act of being cheerful? Oh, she wished there was someone to talk to, to advise and comfort her. Annie would be useless, she'd get more sense out of Eddie but she couldn't go and wake him up, she'd disturb Tom and Bernie. She wished there was someone she could confide in, an aunt, or cousin, but the only relative she had was her da's brother, and he was still in Dublin. She was torn with anguish and misgivings.

The dawn was creeping into the room for neither she nor Annie had pulled down the paper blind, the cheapest form of decent window covering. It would be hours yet before her stepsister would wake. She fervently wished that when she did it would be with an almighty hangover. She deserved it – she seemed to have less and less respect for Mam these days.

She got out of bed, scarcely feeling the ice-cold lino beneath her feet, and got dressed. She crept down the stairs and along the lobby. The kitchen door was closed to keep in what warmth there was and she turned the knob very slowly and carefully for it squeaked and she didn't want anyone to hear it. She'd build up the fire, make herself a cup of tea, and try again to come to terms with the worries that bowed her down.

'Mam!' she cried. She was shocked to see Molly sitting by the range in which the fire was almost dead. Molly was dressed in the clothes she'd worn yesterday, so she obviously hadn't been to bed at all. Ellen went across and put her arms around her.

'Oh, Mam! Have you been here all night?'

Molly nodded. It had been the longest and most agonising night she'd ever known. She'd get over the shock – in time. She'd get over the fact that she was likely to lose the only man she had ever loved – in time, although she would miss him desperately. But she'd never get over the guilt she felt. It wouldn't change things, no matter how much Dr Jenkinson or Father Healy would tell her it *wasn't* her fault. No, she would never stop blaming herself.

'What will I, we, do without him?'

'We'll manage, Mam. We *will*!'

'I'll never forgive myself, never.'

'Don't think like that, Mam, please?'

'Oh, Ellen!' Molly leaned her head against her daughter's

shoulder. Ellen held her mother in her arms and Molly cried as though her heart would break. Ellen's own tears fell on to her mother's hair. All night she'd wanted to cry but she'd held back. She knew that if she'd given full rein to her grief Annie could well have woken from her stupor and demanded an explanation and then the whole house would be up.

She tried to pull herself together.

'Come on, Mam, the lads will be up soon. We'd better go and wash our faces. We . . . we'll not spoil the day for everyone, they've all been really looking forward to it.'

Molly nodded, gulping back her tears, getting up stiffly and going into the scullery.

Ellen looked around the room. The paper chains and the holly, symbols of what should be the happiest day of the year and of the fact that this was the first time they'd all looked forward to it with such high expectations, seemed such a mockery now. It was the day Jesus Christ had been born. Into her mind came a blasphemous thought that horrified her. Had there ever been a baby who'd grown up to be crucified for all their sins? Was there even a God in Heaven? And if there was, how could He let things like this happen? Surely they'd suffered enough? Her da was a good-living man and he'd worked all his life. He'd lost one wife and now he was dying. It wasn't fair. It just wasn't fair. Look at people like John Meakin: nothing bad seemed to happen to him. A slow anger began to burn in her. Indirectly, he'd killed her da! If there hadn't been a fire her da wouldn't be lying in the bed in the front room now, slowly dying, and on Christmas Day too.

Molly had come back into the kitchen. She'd washed her face and tidied her hair, and she was calmer.

'Mam, he's got to pay! That flaming man has got to pay for what he's done.'

Molly looked confused. 'What man?'

'Mr Meakin.'

Molly clenched her hands tightly. 'He will, but don't think about him today; we've got to put a brave face on things and that'll be hard enough. Will you put all those little bits and pieces in the dresser drawer into our Tom and Bernie's stockings for me?' She managed just a hint of a smile. 'Fancy, a big lad of fourteen wanting to put out his stocking.'

'He's never done it before, Mam. You know we never did because we knew it would be a waste of time,' Ellen replied sadly, remembering the presentless Christmases they'd had as children.

Molly built up the fire and boiled the kettle, watching her daughter fill the two socks with penny toys, glass marbles – 'ollies' as they were known – a shiny new penny and an apple and orange.

'Will you take this in to your da, luv? Try to smile and wish him happy Christmas.' She held out the mug of tea and two tablets and Ellen noticed that her hands were shaking although she looked and sounded fine. 'We'll have our presents when everyone's up.'

'We'll be waiting until this afternoon if we wait for our Annie!' As soon as the words were out Ellen was sorry she'd spoken. Molly's forehead creased in a frown.

'Leave that one to me. I'll give her what for, coming

72

home in a state like that.' Ellen just nodded her agreement.

The front room was cold and in semi-darkness, the curtains closed. In the big iron-framed bed, which took up most of the room, lay her father beneath a tangle of blankets. Ellen's hand too began to shake. 'I've got to be cheerful. I've just *got* to be!' she told herself firmly. She placed the mug and the tablets on the old chest next to the bed.

'Da, Da, happy Christmas,' she said quietly as she gently touched her father's forehead. She helped him to turn over and sit up and held the mug of tea for him.

'Happy Christmas, luv.' He smiled weakly. 'I didn't get much sleep and your mam didn't come to bed at all.'

'I know. It's all the work and the worry, but she'll be fine, don't you know that? Mam is great at coping,' she finished with a smile nailed to her face, fighting down her anguish. 'The kitchen looks really great and I'm going to get the others up now. I would have thought that our Bernie at least would have been down, prancing around with his sockful of pressies.'

Jack too managed a smile. He'd not felt well all night, but they'd been so looking forward to today that he was determined not to spoil it. All he really wanted to do was to sleep, but that was so selfish, he had to make an effort.

'That's a sight I'm going to enjoy,' he said. 'All of us together and with everything a body could wish for. It's going to be a great Christmas.'

It *was* a wonderful day. For long moments Ellen forgot about her da's illness. There were small gifts for everyone.

A pair of thick gloves for her da from Eddie. A woollen scarf which was her gift to him; new yellow oilskins to keep the weather out from Molly, who kissed her husband's cheek but refused to look him in the eyes for fear she'd break down. She'd paid quite a few visits to the pawnshop over the last few days. From Tom and Bernie there was pipe tobacco and from Annie, when she finally emerged, three big cotton handkerchiefs. For Molly there were inexpensive bits of jewellery, a nice scarf and a small bottle of Evening in Paris scent in a dark blue bottle. That was Jack's gift, bought for him by Ellen. She and Annie had similar things but from her mam and da there was a book, *Her Benny* by Silas Hocking, something she'd read and enjoyed once before when she'd borrowed it from the library. The tears she had been fighting almost tripped her up though, because it was lovely but so sad in parts. Annie, who was virtually illiterate, had skitted her about it, but she'd taken no notice. She knew she'd treasure this gift.

Her mother, though, hadn't been able to forget their situation even for a moment. As Molly had dished up and served the first proper Christmas dinner they'd ever had she'd thought bitterly how well they all looked, sitting around the table together: the lads and Annie and Jack all joking and laughing and Ellen telling them not to be stuffing themselves like pigs but to try and have some manners. That was a picture, an image she would always carry with her. It was a comfort of sorts.

After swallowing a short sharp lecture from Molly, Annie's day hadn't been spoiled. True, she hadn't felt so bad in a long time. Her head was almost bursting with the pain, her mouth was like a sewer and she felt queasy. It would be a while before she'd set foot in another drinking place of any kind. Thankfully, Ma didn't go on at her, nor her da either, but there was something odd in Ellen's behaviour, she thought. Something she couldn't put a finger on. Still, it was the best Christmas she'd ever had and she had some nice bits and pieces. And maybe Ma would let her put a spot of the perfume behind her ears – for really special occasions. All in all, Annie felt satisfied with their day.

By teatime Jack was so exhausted, pale and sweating that Molly helped him back to bed. Between them the two girls had washed, dried and put away the dishes. Bernie was with the Cooneys, Tom had gone to show his own mates his first collection of ollies, and Eddie was half asleep, sated with the warmth and good food.

Molly sat down and looked around her. The day was over. Now she would have to tell Annie and Eddie.

'I . . . I've something to tell you, Eddie, and you, Annie. Ellen knows already—'

'Isn't that a surprise,' Annie interrupted sarcastically.

'I'll ignore that, Annie, because you're going to need Ellen and Eddie's help in the weeks ahead.'

Annie, chastened, looked down at the table, suddenly afraid. Ellen plucked at the edge of her jumper whilst Eddie sat up, alert and anxious now.

'The doctor came last night. I went for him. Your da looked terrible and I was afraid that lump on his head was something serious. It wasn't, not really . . . it was . . . Well, Da . . . The doctor's almost certain your da's got blood poisoning. Oh, he gave it a fancy name but that's what it is.' She was trying hard to stay in control but was losing the battle. 'The burns . . . the burns on his hands . . .'

'Have turned bad,' Ellen finished for her.

'How bad?' Eddie asked.

'The doctor says it's too late even to . . . to amputate. He . . . he thinks he's going to . . . die.' Molly could no longer keep back her tears. She laid her arms on the table, dropped her head on to them and sobbed.

There was complete silence in the kitchen until Ellen got up and stroked her mother's hair. 'Oh, Mam, come on! Please don't get yourself into this state!'

Molly couldn't stop, not even for the sake of her daughter and stepchildren. Ellen turned to her shocked siblings. 'Da doesn't know and Mam's decided not to tell him, nor our Bernie and Tom. We . . . she didn't want to spoil the whole day for everyone, that's why we never said anything. She was up all last night. Just sitting here.'

Eddie sat as though carved from stone, tears running down his cheeks. Annie was stunned and white-faced. She was going to lose her da, just as she'd lost her mam. Her own lovely, lovely mam. Then she'd have no one except this lot and even Eddie didn't approve of the things she did or said. He always sided with *her*. She stared hard at the figure of her sobbing stepmother and anger flared up, intensified by shock and disbelief.

'Who let his hands go bad? Who didn't even think to clean them? It was *you*! It's all *your* bloody fault! You've killed him, you've killed my da every bit as much as that bloody Meakin feller!'

Eddie, now as white-faced as his sister, jumped to his feet, but Ellen was faster. The palm of her hand as it caught her stepsister across the cheek sounded like a rifle shot and Annie staggered back, her hand to her face, tears springing into her eyes.

Ellen opened her mouth to speak but Eddie jumped in. 'You bloody asked for that and if you don't keep your bloody mouth shut, I'll shut it for you, now! Da will hear you and want to know what's going on!' The full extent of Molly's words hadn't yet sunk in; Eddie's reaction was automatic.

Annie turned on him. Her face was flushed, her eyes were hard and she was shaking. 'You! You always take their side! I hate you! I bloody hate you! She took Mam's place and now . . . now . . .'

'Don't you dare say it, Annie!' Eddie's voice was full of menace. 'If you ever say that again, to anyone, I'll . . . I'll throw you out!'

'You an' whose army?' Annie jeered.

'Ellen, Ma and me, that's who,' Eddie retorted.

Annie snatched up Ellen's shawl from the hook on the wall and stormed out.

'There's no pubs open tonight!' Eddie called jeeringly after her. 'Go round an' see that Josie Rafferty. They'll all be half cut in that house by now. And don't bother coming back!'

'Eddie! For God's sake hush, Da will hear you!' Then Ellen opened her arms to her stepbrother and held him while he sobbed, his anger at his sister subsiding, to be replaced by the anguish they all felt.

'What'll we do, Ellen? What'll we do without him?'

'We'll manage, Eddie. Somehow, we'll manage. Let's hope it won't be . . . long.'

Molly raised her head and looked at Ellen. Her daughter was taking this far better than she could have hoped for and from that she drew courage.

'Eddie, go after your sister.'

'Why the hell should I?' he demanded. 'After the things she said to you!'

'She's upset. She's shocked and angry, as we all are.'

'No. I don't care if she never comes home. All she does is cause trouble anyway.'

'Oh, Eddie, what kind of a thing is that to say on this day of all days?' Molly said pleadingly.

'I'm still not going, Ma!'

'And don't ask me, Mam, I'll belt her again,' Ellen said quickly. She shared Eddie's opinion.

Molly sighed and wiped her eyes. 'We all need a drink. There's that little bottle of whiskey I got for your da. He didn't want any so we'll have a drop. Then, Ellen, will you go and bring Bernie and Tom home? We . . . we'll sort . . . things out properly tomorrow.'

Both boys were reluctant to come back from their friends' but they were told that it was time for bed and that was the end of the matter.

'Where's our Annie?' Bernie demanded, thinking it was grossly unfair that she could go out and stay out and they couldn't.

'I don't know and I don't care,' Ellen answered.

'There's no need to get all airyated about it. Have you

had a row with her?' Tom queried.

Ellen looked at Eddie. 'Sort of. We both have.'

'What's she done?' Bernie queried.

'Never you mind. I bet you had half the street green with envy at you having got ollies from Father Christmas,' Ellen said, changing the subject.

'Oh, yeah, but Franny O'Neill got a football. A *real* casey with laces an' all!'

Eddie glared at his younger brother, knowing just how many things Molly had taken down to Clarkson's just to get him anything, and how much more she'd have to take. 'Some people are never satisfied. You can bet your life that Father Christmas didn't bring *that*. His da's nicked it. They don't call him "Old Sticky Fingers" for nothing.'

Molly brought the argument to a close. 'Go on in and say good night to your da, the pair of you, and thank him for the great day you've had.

'Oh, how are we going to manage?' she said wearily when they'd left the room. She knew that from now on responsibility for the boys would fall solely on her.

They sat silently, listening to the two younger boys clatter up the uncarpeted stairs, each deep in their own thoughts. None of them heard Artie Cooney, Gussie's husband, come in.

Molly gave a sharp cry. 'Holy God! Artie! You near gave me a heart attack.'

' 'Ow is 'e, Moll?'

'He's had a good day, but he's . . . he's tired out now. It was good of you to call.'

'Aye, well, the kids are either out or in bed and Gussie's

'ad a drop too much stout an' is snorin' like a pig.'

'She's worked hard, Artie, it's not been easy for her.'

'Aye, well, that's as may be. But 'ow long 'as 'e got, luv?'

Molly's hand went to her throat and her eyes widened. 'How . . . how did you . . . know?'

'Your Annie. She said she was going to tell 'alf the flamin' street that it's your fault. I gave 'er a right ear-bashin', I can tell yer, girl.'

Molly groaned. 'Oh, Artie, that's just what I didn't want to happen. He doesn't know and neither do the two lads and that's the way I want it to stay.'

'An' that's the way it'll be, girl, no one will 'ear about it from our 'ouse, except Gussie, of course. Yer can't keep somethin' like that away from 'er. But I made your Annie promise to keep 'er gob shut!'

Ellen was on her feet again. 'Mam! I *hate* her! I *hate* her! She knew she'd upset you but she's determined to do it, and give them all something to jangle about – and it's not true! It's just not true!'

'You're dead right there, girl,' Artie nodded. 'What's yer mam done? Given 'im an 'appy 'ome, tended 'im night an' day, that's what. She's not supposed ter be a bloody doctor.'

'Ma, if she carries on like this I'm going to see Dr Jenkinson and get him to tell her off,' Eddie cried angrily.

'There won't be any need fer that, lad, no one will 'ave a word said against yer ma, especially not our Gussie after the way yer've treated us all so well, like. I'll send 'er in termorrer ter see what she can do ter 'elp, like.'

'That's good of you, Artie. I know . . . I know the women will be glad to help out until . . .' She choked.

'They will, Mam. You know that,' Ellen said comfortingly.

'Was there any sign of our Annie when you came in here?' Eddie asked.

'No, but she was determined ter go an' see Ozzie Ogden ter find out what they all intended doin' to sort Meakin out.'

'Oh, my God!' Molly exclaimed.

'Don't worry, luv, Ozzie'll be fallin' down drunk by now. I 'eard he was in the pub till past four o'clock an' 'is dinner was ruined an' didn't their Tessie march in with it all on the dish, threw it at 'im an' say, " 'Ere's yer bloody dinner what I's been savin' up fer fer bloody weeks! Yiz can eat it off the bloody floor! Share it with yer mates whose wives are sittin' at 'ome with ruined meals! You're all the bloody same, the lot of yiz!" There was nearly murder, I can tell yer. So, don't worry too much about Ozzie Ogden an' 'is mates.'

Molly felt exhausted. 'Oh, isn't that all we need, a flaming fight with the Meakins on our hands. And I wanted it to be such a wonderful day.'

'She'll have to come home eventually and I'll be waiting for her,' Eddie said in a voice no one had ever heard him use before.

Molly looked into the flames in the fire. That's how all this had started, with a fire. Now she was facing an insecure future with a business to run, five children to care for, animosity between herself and her stepdaughter, and a growing rift between the sister and brother she'd tried so hard to love and care for, even though she knew she could never take the place of their own mother. Ellen wasn't the only one who from now on would shudder at the thought of Christmas.

Chapter Seven

Eddie had waited downstairs, numb to all feelings except exhaustion and anger. Eventually he gave in to tiredness and went to bed, past caring about his sister. There was always tomorrow.

So the house was in complete darkness when Annie at last opened the back-yard door. For the past couple of hours she'd walked the streets. There were any number of 'do's' she could have gone to. Nearly every street had at least one. Even though it was a slum area, rife with poverty, money was always found from somewhere to buy ale. They deserved a bit of pleasure this one day in the year. She'd walked on in silence, her head down, not really seeing anything, ignoring the good-humoured invitations showered on her. She hated them all now. Why was God so cruel as to take both her mam and da? It wasn't fair. If that's the kind of God there was up there then she wanted nothing more to do with Him or His flaming Church. She even hated her brother, although it wasn't as deep as her hatred for Tom, Bernie and Ellen. And of course *her*. What kind of a future did she have now, stuck there with *them*?

The jibe Eddie had shouted after her about the drunken

Raffertys was true. A big, obstreperous, rowdy family, one member or other of which was always serving time in Walton, they had all been roaring. She hadn't been able to get any sensible conversation out of Josie and after helping herself to two glasses of beer she had left. She was cold, tired and miserable, and had no choice but to go back home.

There was still some semblance of a fire in the range and she stirred up the ashes and put more coal on. She was freezing; she needed warmth and a cup of tea. She looked around the tidy room. Her gaze rested on the small bottle of whiskey on the dresser. Well, why not? Hadn't she had a shock? Too bloody right she had. She took a mug from the dresser and emptied the contents of the bottle into it and then, when the kettle had boiled, she added the hot water and sat as near to the fire in the range as she could without setting herself alight. Oh, the next weeks were going to be awful. She didn't want to have to see her da slowly slipping from life. It would be too hard. She didn't want to be here at all. She'd go to work and then spend as much time as she could out with Josie and her mates. She knew the money she was allowed to keep would soon be diminished, so why not spend it while she had it? She'd go into town at the first opportunity and spend the money she'd saved.

She sat with the mug cradled in her hands. Just what would life really be like after Da was gone? She didn't enjoy her job much. In fact she'd really come to hate it over the last weeks. Picking okum ruined your hands and nails. It was dull, dirty work and the air always seemed to be full of dust. Nearly everyone who had worked there for any length of time had a cough. Trust bloody Ellen to have a better job. It was factory work but in the much cleaner bagging room at Tate & Lyle's Sugar Refinery at the bottom of Burlington Street. All her life she seemed to have been at the receiving end of everything that was dull and dirty. She'd always been undernourished, badly clothed and lived in overcrowded, rat- and bug-infested shacks, and now she was sick of it.

She sat staring into the fire, sipping the hot toddy and contemplating her future. Maybe if she got married it would be a way out. She knew plenty of boys but when she thought about it there really wasn't one she could spend her entire life with. They were all the same, or so it seemed: no money, no steady jobs, no prospects. What kind of life would she have? She'd be a drudge, a downtrodden, worn-out skivvy, old before her time with constant childbearing. No, she'd stick to her job, much as she hated it. There seemed no way out.

Gussie came in the following morning looking pale but concerned. Molly was thankful that everyone was out. Jack was in bed, mercifully asleep. He seemed to be getting weaker.

Gussie sat down in an armchair. ' 'Ow are yer, Moll? I couldn't believe it when Artie told me that that little trollop, sorry if I's givin' yer offence, came in an' started rantin' and ravin' that 'er da was dyin' an' it was your fault an' that bloody Meakin feller's.'

'I know, Gussie. She was upset, that's all. I suppose it was her way of dealing with it. I came down this morning and she was sitting in the chair by the fire, asleep. She'd been there all night.' Molly didn't say that she'd almost trodden on a mug that smelled of whiskey and seen the empty bottle left on the table.

'Aye, well, that's as may be but she got no change out of us. What'll yer do, luv?'

'I don't know, I haven't really thought . . .' Molly was so weary.

'It's a terrible shock, "desperate" as me old mam, God rest her, would 'ave said. Will yer give up the coal, like?'

Molly shook her head. 'No. No, he worked too hard to get it started and then up and running again after the fire for me to just let it go.'

'The lads'll be up ter it. Eddie's a good, steady lad. Your Tom will 'elp, seein' as 'e's just left school, an' even Bernie can do somethin'. Oh, God, I can tell you I'm goin' ter 'ave trouble with that bloody young 'ooligan of mine, I can feel it in me bones!'

'Which one?' Molly asked tiredly, not really concentrating.

'Our Teddy. Them Rafferty lads will 'ave 'im in the Reformatory an' I'll not be able to 'old me 'ead up in this street! But never mind all that. Will the girls 'elp yer, like, with money an' other things?'

'Yes.'

'Well, luv, yer know yer can count on us all to 'elp with the washin' an' shoppin' an' seein' ter the kids. 'Ow long will it be? What did the tanner doctor say?'

'He didn't, Gussie. He just said keep him comfortable and he'd call in regular. He wanted him to go to hospital but I said I'd sooner have him at home.'

'Yer done the right thing there.' Gussie looked around the room, noticing the things that were conspicuous by their absence.

Molly caught her gaze and interpreted it. 'Mr Clarkson's going to be seeing a lot of me in the future. But thank God I've got it to pawn. I'll have to sell some of it though – I'll never be able to redeem everything. We can manage with one pan, the kettle and just a few dishes.' Her eyes moved appraisingly round the room. 'There won't be much food so that press can go and the glass bowls and the gas mantles from the bedrooms. I've already taken the bowl and jug sets and he came for the washstand.'

'Oh, Moll, all yer good stuff.'

'I'd go barefoot begging in the snow if it would give Jack back his health, and I wouldn't complain about it either.'

Gussie shook her head. It was a tragedy. Jack Ryan was a rarity around here: a man who worked hard for his family, and always had done. Most of them just worked for beer money, and their women, after years struggling with everything, often gave up and took to the bottle themselves, especially in times of crisis. Then the kids ran riot: dirty, barefoot and hungry, begging or stealing, usually a bit of both. It was very hard on the women; they bore the brunt of everything.

'I think I'll have to get some kind of a job, for a while anyway, until I see how things go.'

'What'll yer do?'

Molly shrugged. 'Cleaning. Minnie Jones cleans at that place Cunard have to keep the immigrants in until they get the ships to America. She says it's not bad.'

'Well, I've 'eard different. Them foreigners 'ave filthy 'abits, don't know what a toilet is for, go messin' all over the place. Dirty heathen lot.'

Molly frowned. 'I didn't know that. I'll wait and see.'

Gussie sniffed. She could see she wasn't going to get Molly to change her mind. She decided to move on to another subject. 'Well, at least your Annie would have got no joy out of Ozzie Ogden last night. Artie said he was blind paralytic drunk. So there won't be a fight. Tessie's got her work cut out as it is though, but she's well able to stand up to him. An' she often goes off on the ale too.'

Gussie knew that Tessie Ogden was one of the wives who had given up but she didn't blame her. It didn't seem right to criticise the woman. If she didn't nag the daylights out of Artie she'd have given up herself years ago. She heaved herself out of the chair.

'Well, I'd better be goin', that 'ouse looks like the wreck of the *'Esperus*. Just remember all yer need ter do is ter send one of the kids down if yer need 'elp. Anythin' at all, Moll.'

'I will, Gussie, thanks. It's what will keep me going, knowing I can count on you all. We've good neighbours in this street.'

Gussie left and Molly went back to her task of clearing up the kitchen. Afterwards she would go and see if Jack were awake and if he needed anything.

Dr Jenkinson called after lunchtime.

Molly, startled, dragged off her stained pinafore and

tucked the stray wisps of hair into the bun. 'I didn't expect to see you so soon, sir.'

'I said I'd come, Mrs Ryan. How is he?'

'Oh, he seems to be getting weaker. He won't eat anything. He just picked at his Christmas dinner. Now he's starting to sleep a lot. He . . . he couldn't sleep before with the pain. Last night he never stirred.'

They both went quietly into the front room. Molly drew back the curtains and watched the doctor check Jack over. Her husband opened his eyes once, looked vaguely surprised and then drifted off again. Her heart was in her mouth when Dr Jenkinson finished.

'It's the beginning of the end, isn't it? How . . . how much longer?'

He shook his head. 'Hard to tell but only a day or so at the most.'

'Oh, so soon!'

'I'm afraid so. It's no use me telling you a pack of lies or offering you empty platitudes.'

She didn't understand the last word but it didn't matter.

'Your family? Your neighbours?' he asked gently.

Molly nodded and squared her shoulders. 'I . . . I'll have all the help I'll need and I'll sit up with him all night.'

Watching her courage, he felt so helpless, so frustrated. The poor woman was labouring under the twin burdens of guilt and sorrow and it could all have been avoided if she had known the very basics of medical hygiene, but he wouldn't add that to her burden. He reached into his bag.

'Here, put a few drops in a cup of water or tea, it'll help. He'll be more sleepy, more at ease.' He wanted to say give

him the whole bottle and let the man go quickly, with some
dignity, instead of letting things drag on. It would bring the
poor woman some relief too. God, you'd shoot an animal
rather than let it suffer, he thought, but he'd sworn an oath
and euthanasia – mercy killing – was a criminal offence.
'One or two drops wouldn't hurt you either, Mrs Ryan.'

'No. No, I'll manage, thank you.'

'Send word to me any time of the day or night and I'll
come.'

'Thank you, sir. When . . . when the time comes to send
for you, should I . . . should I call in the priest?'

He nodded and fastened up the buckles on his bag. It
was one of the things that always amazed him, they put so
much trust and belief in their Church and its priests, who
told them they would be sure of getting into Heaven
because they were all so poor. As if poverty were some kind
of virtue, some sort of passport. Better to suffer here or
some such nonsense. He knew that if his patients realised
he was an atheist they would never come to him for help
and advice. He'd long ago abandoned the belief that there
was a God. Merciful or otherwise.

It was three o'clock when someone knocked quietly on the
front door and, tying on a clean pinafore, Molly went to
open it. She was startled to see Tessie Ogden standing on
her step.

'Tessie, come in.' She had never really had much to do
with Ozzie Ogden's wife but she wouldn't keep her standing
on the step.

Tessie was older than herself – not that much older, but

she looked like an old woman of sixty. Her face was lined and drawn, her hair almost uniformly grey. She was big by anyone's standards, well able to stand up to her formidable husband, which she frequently did. Molly certainly wouldn't like to cross her. Tessie was dressed in the uniform of the poor: long black skirt, old blouse and equally old black shawl and coarse calico apron. A pair of black men's boots without laces protruded from the hem of her skirt.

' 'Ow is 'e?' Tessie mouthed as Molly led her to the kitchen and quietly closed the door.

'Very bad. The doctor came this morning and he said . . .' She couldn't go on. All day she'd been holding herself in check ready to be calm and rational when everyone came home, but her neighbour's enquiry unnerved her.

'Oh, yiz poor woman! Is 'e goin' ter die soon, like?'

Molly could only nod and make a futile gesture with her hand.

Tessie's expression became grim. Oh, like the rest of the street she'd been envious seeing how well the Ryans were doing with their coal business, the money for which had come out of the blue, but Jack and Molly Ryan had never been boastful or flaunted their new-found prosperity before them, and she knew there was many a woman in the street that had knocked on Molly's door for a 'loan' of something or 'a penny for the gas' and none had ever been turned away. Moreover, she'd always treated Tessie with friendliness and respect and to someone like herself, with her lifestyle, that respect was much appreciated.

'Yer know we'll all 'ave a whip round, like, fer the flowers fer the funeral.'

'That . . . that's kind of you, Tessie.'

'Are yiz in a burial club, luv?'

'Yes, with the Co-op.' Molly was wondering why she suddenly felt so disconnected, sitting here discussing funeral arrangements. But it was the thing that the women of the slums all dreaded, not to have the money for a proper funeral. A pauper's affair was so degrading.

'Well, yiz can't beat them, I always say. I pay me penny a week even if we 'as ter go without a sup of milk an' 'e 'as ter go short in 'is boozin' money! The useless, lazy, idle get!'

Molly tried to be fair. 'There's not much work around, Tessie.'

The other woman shrugged. 'What I cum ter tell yer is that 'imself an' a couple of the other fellers will be callin' on that Meakin feller ternight. Late, like.'

'Oh, Tessie, no! Please don't let them. I don't want any trouble.'

'There won't be no trouble, girl. Just a warnin', like. This is all 'is fault, the lying, snivellin' little toe-rag! 'E's a right no-mark when yiz look at 'im properly. All gas and gaiters. Don't go upsettin' yerself. Now, is there any washin' ter be done? I'll be goin' down the bag wash myself later on.' She was one of the many women who took advantage of the public washhouses, for with a big family it was virtually impossible to wash everything at once at home. They all sweated and strained with the heavy washing, dragging it from the coppers into the shallow rinsing troughs and finally to the big mangles. Then it was folded, parcelled up in a bundle and carried home, balanced on the top of the women's heads, a remarkable skill that Molly had never mastered.

'That's really kind of you, Tessie. I just don't seem to be able to get myself organised. I'll put it in a bundle and give you the money for it. You're so kind.'

Tessie, an argumentative woman known for her fierce battling, looked on with trepidation and fear by her peers, put her arms around Molly and gave her a hug. 'Yer'll all get through somehow,' she said comfortingly.

Chapter Eight

Everyone was so good, Molly said to Ellen. Even the neighbours she didn't know well all offered help and she was glad of it. She really felt sorry for people who had no such support: people who lived in the middle-class suburbs of the city. She could devote all her time to tending Jack knowing full well that the rest of the family were being cared for.

She marvelled at herself. Somehow she managed to keep going. Where had she got the energy from? She'd sat up with him these last two nights and not even felt drowsy. Perhaps it was because she *didn't* have much time left to share with him.

She'd sat in the small dark room with only a nightlight on the chest beside the bed so the harsh glare of the unshaded gas jet wouldn't disturb him. All night she'd held one of his hands, her gaze resting on the face that was so dear to her. Sometimes she prayed, but not for him – his place in Heaven was assured. No, her prayers were for herself to have the strength to cope. As the hours passed she forced herself to think of all the happy times they'd had together. No matter how bad things had got they had always pulled together: working and suffering together, crying together – and laughing too.

All the children came in to sit for a while with their semi-conscious father. Ellen had insisted on telling Tom and Bernie.

'Mam, they'll *have* to know soon. We can't keep it a secret. It's not fair on them. They think he's got a chance of getting better, they really do. It will be a terrible shock for them, they might even accuse us of telling them lies.'

'We've never told them lies.'

'But we've not actually *said* anything, we've just let them go on thinking what they like.'

Molly was hesitant. 'Oh Ellen, I don't know.'

'Mam, I'll tell them if you can't face it.'

'I can't face it, luv, and that's the truth. I only seem to be able to concentrate on your da. Is that wrong of me?'

'There's nothing at all wrong in that, Mam,' she'd replied and then later she'd taken her two mystified brothers up to their bedroom, sat them both on the bed and told them as gently as she could that their da wasn't going to get better and that soon he'd be going to Heaven.

Tom concentrated so hard on trying not to cry that Ellen feared he was going to faint. He looked so pale. Bernie clung to her, weeping. He didn't want his da to go to Heaven no matter how great it was supposed to be. His da wasn't an old man and only old people or little babies died and went up there, he sobbed.

Now that she'd broken the news Ellen didn't know what to say next, to either of them. When Eddie came into the room relief flooded through her.

'I think Tom is going to pass out or be sick – look at the colour of his face – and as for this one . . .' She was near to tears herself, it had been such an ordeal.

'Go on down, Ellen, I'll see to them.'

Gratefully, she'd gone, pausing for a minute at the top of the stairs to wipe away her own tears.

She and Annie were both still working and there was even more hostility between them than usual after the row they'd had after Annie's outburst. It had been a very bitter argument and Ellen had fought back with such strength and vigour that she'd surprised herself. She'd found she wasn't shaking in the slightest after Annie had slammed out, calling her a string of names. Now they hardly spoke, not that Annie was around much, and Molly was too preoccupied to notice the underlying tension that at times threatened to erupt into a shouting match again.

On the third day, another grey and miserable winter morning, Gussie came in bringing a cup of tea and asked Molly to give her all their clothes.

'I'll take them along to Johnson's to be dyed for yer, luv.'

Molly nodded her thanks. It was just another of their kindnesses. Someone had realised they would soon need mourning clothes. She'd have to make sure – later – that they were paid. No one could afford to be out of pocket on her behalf.

At eight o'clock, the nightlight had burned low on the chest beside the bed. Jack's eyes were closed but they seemed to have sunk back into deep sockets. His skin was taut, he looked like a complete stranger or worse still like a picture she'd once seen of the Grim Reaper. She'd never forgotten that picture because it troubled and disturbed her for weeks afterwards.

She picked up one of his hands and held it between her own. You could feel the fever. He was struggling now for breath. It had arrived at last, this moment they'd been dreading since Christmas Eve. It was time to send for the doctor and the priest. She went into the kitchen and asked Eddie to go for the doctor and Ellen or Annie to go for the priest. Annie made no comment and didn't attempt to move, so Ellen went. The two young boys said nothing. Both men arrived almost simultaneously and Eddie and Ellen showed them into the front room and then closed the door behind all of them.

'Shouldn't your sister be here?' Father Healy asked of Eddie.

'I'll go and ask her, Father, but . . .'

'Do you want them all in here, Mrs Ryan?' Dr Jenkinson asked, knowing from all-too-frequent experience the rituals that accompanied a Catholic death and funeral.

'No, no . . . not the two young ones,' Molly answered, watching the doctor take Jack's hand to feel for a pulse, then raise one of his eyelids and nod to the parish priest. They all knelt while the Last Sacrament was given to Jack Ryan, but both men were fully aware that the man had breathed his last and was beyond all suffering.

The neighbours were in and out all night and Ellen often felt like screaming or throwing something. It was a long, emotionally draining, confusing night. No one went to bed. Eventually Tom fell asleep on one of the two battered armchairs, while Bernie sobbed in Ellen's arms, his tears soaking her blouse, until, exhausted, he too fell asleep. Ellen kept on gently stroking his hair.

The women whose task it was to wash and prepare the body of the deceased had come and gone, as had the doctor who had left a small bottle of laudanum for Molly to administer to all of them if necessary. Father Healy remained and from somewhere four candles in brass candlesticks appeared and were placed at each corner of the bed. Other neighbours brought white sheets with which to cover the walls. Black crêpe was draped across the windows and front door and in every house but one in the entire street the curtains remained closed and would do so until after Jack Ryan was buried. The Meakins were the exception.

Endless cups of tea were made and drunk, the quiet buzz of sympathetic voices rose and fell as dawn came and more people arrived. At last Ellen could stand it no longer. The house was like a bear pit. She eased Bernie into the unoccupied armchair; he was in such a deep sleep that he didn't stir. She looked around, then began nervously.

'I'm . . . we're . . . so very grateful for . . . everything but we are all exhausted, so please . . .' Her voice trailed off. She couldn't say it. She just couldn't utter the words which would sound so ungrateful.

Tessie took everyone in hand. 'Right, the lot of yiz, go 'ome ter yer own 'ouses. We've all done as much as we can do. Let's give them all a bit of peace ter rest, like. When yiz feel up to it, Moll, send one of the lads down an' we'll come and sort out the arrangements.' And then suddenly the house was empty.

'What did you have to go and do that for?' Annie said, wiping her eyes and glaring at Ellen. 'It was better to have all the noise and people around than . . . this . . .'

'Don't you start. Everyone's upset enough,' Eddie said acidly to his sister.

'Oh, shut up, you! I hate you! I *hate* you!'

Molly pulled herself out of the trance-like state that she'd been in for so many long hours. 'That will do, the pair of you! Your poor da is lying in there and all you can do is fight! For heaven's sake, let's try and act with a bit of decency and sense. Life has to go on.' As she spoke she felt the burden of responsibility settle heavily on her shoulders. If only she could lay her head down and sleep forever, but that was impossible. 'We have to eat. I don't know how long it is since we had anything. Ellen, do you think you could set the table, please? Annie, could you boil up the kettle, Eddie, will you fetch in some coal and Tom, luv, go and fetch the water from the standpipe. We've all *got* to make an effort.' And herself most of all. They all depended on her now.

'Mam, I'm not going in to work today,' Ellen said and her mother nodded. Tomorrow would be soon enough. Tomorrow would see the return of some semblance of normal, everyday life.

The funeral was terrible. It was far, far worse than Ellen could have imagined. It was a bitterly cold Saturday morning with flurries of snow on the strong east wind. The time in between her da's death and this day had passed quickly and she'd felt as though she were in a dream most of the time, but now reality hit her. She would never see her da again. She'd never hear him laugh or rebuke her. He'd never know how much she had loved him. He'd gone into a coma before she'd had time to whisper it to him.

They walked to church behind the hearse. Molly had insisted on it. They would have a long journey from the church to the cemetery: they'd need the extra money to pay for the carriage to take them, wait and return. Ellen supported her mam; Eddie, with an arm around each, followed with his stepbrothers. Annie had insisted on walking alone and kept her head bent. The rest of the neighbours followed. When they all turned on to Scotland Road the traffic halted to let them pass, men doffed their caps, women bowed their heads and crossed themselves. It was the custom in that part of the city. There was a small wreath from the family and an even smaller one from the neighbours in the street, all of whom had given a halfpenny or a penny they could scarcely afford. Not to contribute, however, was to commit a grave social error. No one had even bothered to go to the Meakins' house. They were now to be completely ostracised.

She'd thought the Mass, even though the prayers, hymns, candles and the all-pervading odour of incense were familiar, was terrible. But nothing had prepared her for the burial in the Catholic Ford Cemetery. It had begun to snow in earnest now, thick white flakes were blotting out the contours of the cemetery, settling on the black plumes in the horses' bridles and their black shiny coats. It rested on and then soaked into their clothes. It was the worst thing that she'd ever had to cope with. She leaned against her mother's shoulder, bent her head and broke down completely.

Molly was struggling herself. She was cold, so very, very cold. A coldness that had nothing to do with the weather. She felt totally drained and her legs had begun to buckle. She could give no strength to her children. It was Gussie who came quietly to her side and guided Ellen away to the back of the silent crowd, while Doris Henshaw caught Molly around the waist to stop her from falling. 'Keep yer 'ead up, Moll, it'll soon be over,' she murmured and Molly felt the dizziness recede. Tessie, who had become a frequent visitor, and two of the others had stayed behind to heat up the soup and set out the sandwiches for the mourners when they returned. There was no money for the traditional wake.

'They'll get tea an' flamin' like it!' Tessie had said to Gussie. 'We're organisin' this, not the bloody fellers who'd eat an' drink yiz out of 'ouse and 'ome.'

They were all glad of the hot soup after the long and harrowing journey, which had been undertaken in silence, broken only by the occasional sob from Bernie, but people stood awkwardly around, unsure what to do or say. Father Healy was talking to Molly and Ellen; Dr Jenkinson who, to everyone's astonishment, had turned up for the burial, was talking to Eddie, trying to give the lad some support, asking about the business and what plans he had for the future.

Annie sat alone upstairs in the room she shared with

Ellen. No one could ever comfort her for her loss and she didn't want anyone to try. She hated this house now and she'd made up her mind she would go into service. She would be away from *them* and Milton Street. She'd live in a decent house, have good food, be fairly well dressed. The pay was half what she was getting now, but that wouldn't bother her. It wouldn't be easy to get a place though. She was a factory girl and as such was looked down on by girls in service who gave themselves all kinds of airs and graces. Still, she'd go and speak to Father Healy – if she could get him away from her stepmother and -sister.

'Annie, girl, where've yer been?' Tessie asked as she pushed her way into the kitchen.

'Upstairs. I couldn't stand it down here.'

'Well, everyone ter their own ways, I suppose.'

'I want to talk to Father Healy.'

Tessie looked at her closely.

'What's up with yiz? I mean apart from yer da an' everythin'?'

'Nothing. Is it a crime now to want to talk to a priest?'

'Well, that's a nice way ter speak ter anyone, I must say. You just watch yer mouth, girl!' Tessie said tartly.

Annie turned away and went to the priest's side, waiting until he turned to her.

'Annie, is there something you want to say to me?'

She nodded. 'Can it be somewhere . . . a bit more private?'

He wasn't surprised. He knew full well from the Confessional Box that she was more than a bit of a handful.

He beckoned her towards the lobby where a few people

lingered but, seeing the priest followed by Annie, they moved into the kitchen.

'What is it, child?'

'Father, I can't . . . won't . . . stay here. I'm so miserable. They don't like me and now that Da has . . .' She sniffed and he passed her his handkerchief.

'So what do you intend to do, child?'

'Go into service. I know it will be hard but if you could give me a reference it would help. Please, Father? I'm really unhappy here.'

He looked concerned. There were very few Catholic households he could recommend her to. And she was right, it would be hard. She knew nothing of the ways and manners of the better off. Her speech was rough and she was ignorant of many things that a prospective employer would assume she knew.

'I'll try, Annie, but don't put too much hope in it.'

'I don't care what kind of family it is.'

'Well, I do. It's very important that your spiritual as well as your moral and bodily needs are looked after.'

She looked down at her feet. She'd known he'd take this kind of attitude. 'But you *will* try, Father, please?'

'I will and in the meantime try and tidy yourself up a bit. Go into town to one of the better cafés and watch the waitresses; listen and learn.'

'I . . . I haven't got the money to spend on going to cafés. I bought new clothes for . . . for today.'

For the first time he noticed that her black coat was new, as was the hat she wore, and she had gloves, stockings and high-buttoned boots. He delved into the pocket of his soutane and produced a coin, a silver shilling. 'Here, take this then. Make good use of it, Annie, and I'll see what I can do.'

'Oh, thank you, Father! Thank you!' She pocketed the coin. It would only buy a couple of cups of tea and cakes in one of those places but it was a start. She felt so much better. Now she'd decided to leave this house as soon as possible the future didn't look so bad after all.

Chapter Nine

It having been a 'dry' funeral, as soon as enough time had passed to satisfy convention, Ozzie Ogden and two of his mates left and went to the pub on the corner for a drink.

'I'm spittin' feathers, I could do with a good bevvie,' Georgie McFadden – known to everyone as the 'Rocket Man' because he was always saying he had to 'shoot off' somewhere – said with enthusiasm.

'I'll second that, la,' Wilf Henshaw agreed. 'Wouldn't yer think they'd 'ave 'ad just a couple of bottles, like?'

'Yiz can thank our Tessie fer that. 'Er and Gussie Cooney done all the arrangin'.'

Georgie tried to be fair. 'What yer've got ter remember is that the woman 'asn't gorrany money any more. Just enough fer the burial, like.'

'Believe that an' yer'll believe anythin',' Wilf said scornfully.

' 'E was a good skin, was Jack Ryan. Stood me many a pint when I 'ad no brass, like. It's a bloody shame,' Georgie retorted.

'Well, yer know whose fault it were, don't yer?'

'Oh, aye, Ozzie, we know that all right, but Molly doesn't want no trouble.'

'She wouldn't 'ave ter know, would she?' Ozzie said, lowering his voice as they entered the smoke-filled pub. After briefly passing the time of day with the few other patrons of the establishment, they went and stood at the other end of the bar counter.

'What's yer poison, lads?' the barman asked.

'What's up with youse? Yer bloody well know by now what we drink, we've been puttin' hard-earned money across this bar fer years.'

'Just tryin' ter be friendly, like. Not much trade at the moment, as yer can see.'

'Well, it's 'ardly likely, is it? Molly 'as just buried their Jack,' Georgie informed him.

'An' norra drop of anythin' decent in the 'ouse,' Wilf added.

'Shurrup, youse!' Ozzie rebuked him and then watched in silence as three pints of ale were placed before them.

The barman drifted into the back leaving them on their own in the half-empty bar.

Wilf broke the silence. 'I think we should go and give that Meakin feller a good hidin', fer Jack, like. 'E'd be 'ere with us now, laughin' and havin' a bevvie if it wasn't fer that little gobshite!'

Ozzie nodded slowly. He and Tessie had had a few rows over just this subject but if it was done now there would be nothing she could say. Nothing he would take any notice of anyway.

'Finish yer ale, lads, an' we'll go,' he advised.

The other two drained their glasses and they all left.

It wasn't far to number 36. They cut down the jigger in

case someone saw them, then went into the yard. Ozzie hammered on the back door with his fist.

Wilf looked around. 'Jeez! Yer could eat yer dinner offen these flags.'

'Christ! Will yiz keep yer bloody gob shut! Iffen 'e 'ears yer 'e won't open up.'

Wilf was nonplussed and continued to marvel at the yard. There was nothing in it except the dolly tub, washboard and dolly peg, used to 'stir' the clothes being washed in the tub. A tin bath hung on a nail on the limewashed wall. The Meakins didn't have to share a privy: a luxury in itself. That too had been limewashed and was probably scrubbed out every day. Their own back yards were like rubbish tips and the shared privies were none too savoury.

Eventually they heard the sound of the doorlatch being lifted and the door opened. John Meakin stood in the entrance, a look of annoyance on his face. But by the time he recognised them it was too late.

Ozzie grabbed him by the front of his shirt and woollen cardigan. 'We'se cum ter pay a debt, yer sneakin', lyin', yeller-bellied murderer! We 'as just cum from Jack Ryan's funeral!'

John Meakin cried out in terror but was silenced by a hefty blow to his stomach. He doubled over with the pain and was clouted so hard across his head by Ozzie that he fell to the ground. Wilf Henshaw yanked him to his feet and punched him hard in the face. The blood spurted from his nose and then he was systematically beaten until his face was covered with blood and he lay groaning on the flags he made his wife scrub every day.

'All right, lads, tharrel do, we don't want ter kill the little bastard. 'E's not worth dancin' at the end of a bloody rope fer, even if he did do fer Jack. Will one of yiz knock and gerrer out ter see ter 'im?'

'She'll go to the scuffers,' Georgie said.

'Are yiz bloody thick or somethin'? No one goes ter the scuffers, not even 'er.'

There was no need for anyone to knock; the back door was still open and in the doorway stood Maggie, pale-faced, her eyes wide with fright.

' 'E needs a birrof cleanin' up, like, girl. Do yiz understand?'

Maggie nodded.

'When 'e's recovered, an' iffen 'e takes it out on youse or the girl, send word ter me,' Ozzie said firmly.

Maggie found her voice. 'I . . . I'll do that, I will, Mr Ogden.' Maggie looked straight up into the big docker's face. 'Thanks. Thank you.' Her voice was barely audible and she stood and watched them leave before making any attempt to help her husband.

'I told yer, there'll be no trouble from 'im,' sniffed Ozzie, 'and she was made up, the poor little woman.'

Twelve-year-old Lucy Meakin stood at her mother's side, clutching her skirt and shaking with fright. The girl was like her mother, small in stature and slim. She had Maggie's reddish-brown hair and brown eyes that always had a look of fear in them, and her complexion was very pale.

'Mam! Mam, what'll we do?' she whispered. She was terrified of her da but she was also terrified of the three big men who'd come to the back door. She'd watched in horror as they'd beaten her da up, and then, astonishingly, her mam had thanked them for it!

Maggie turned to her. 'Don't worry, luv. He . . . your da will be all right, eventually.'

'Will I go for an ambulance or the doctor or someone?'

'No, Lucy. I'll see to him,' Maggie answered in a voice Lucy had never heard her use before.

It was one that Maggie actually hadn't used before. She was glad, positively *glad* to see her husband lying in the yard in a pool of his own blood. Somehow it helped to make up for all the years she'd suffered. He never hit her where it would be seen and commented on. Sometimes he didn't hit her at all but he had a cruel and vicious tongue and would take his temper out on Lucy. Although he was a small man she was no match for him even when she tried desperately to defend her child.

They had always had more than anyone else in the street, apart from when Jack Ryan had started his own business and it had prospered. He'd hated that, to see the poor Ryans earn more, have more things than they'd ever had before, even hold a position above him. It burned him up with jealousy inside. Oh, his temper had been vile that night and she was almost sure that what Jack Ryan had accused him of was true. He *had* gone out that night with a small parcel wrapped in brown paper and string and returned in less than twenty minutes without it, sat down and studiedly picked up his newspaper. She had known better than to voice her suspicions. Still, now he had paid for his wickedness and she thought that justice had in part been done.

She sighed heavily as she went into the yard to help him. Would this beating be a good or a bad thing in the long term? She didn't know and she certainly wasn't going to think about it, but she knew now where she could go for help. To the Ogdens. It made her feel much better.

Ellen knew that Annie was up to something but just what she couldn't guess. Her stepsister seemed preoccupied, even smug.

'I just hope that whatever it is that you're up to doesn't cause Mam any more worry and grief,' Ellen said to her one morning as they walked to the tram stop to go to work.

'That's all you ever think about, your precious mam. Well, now you know how I've felt all these years,' Annie replied spitefully.

'Yes, I do think and worry because I love her.'

'And you don't think that I loved my mam?'

'I never said that. Anyway, I'm not going to start an argument.'

'And I'm not going to waste my breath on you or your mam, but you won't have to worry about me soon. I'll be away from you, all of you.'

Ellen stopped and stared at her hard. 'Just what's that supposed to mean? What are you up to?'

'You can take it any way you like but you're getting nothing more out of me.' Annie quickened her steps, leaving Ellen to follow, a frown on her face. Oh, how Annie longed to tell them that she was getting out, but she couldn't do that until she actually had a job, otherwise she'd be too humiliated.

Ellen walked behind her, feeling very apprehensive. She didn't need Annie causing more problems. Mam was having a hard enough time just coping.

A week later, on Friday night, after they'd eaten and Ellen had washed up and Eddie, worn out by his early start, was falling asleep on the sofa, there was a knock on the front door. Both girls looked up.

Molly was surprised. 'Who's that? No one comes to the front door this time of year.' Front doors were always open day and night in milder months, but in winter they were barely used.

'I'll go!' Annie cried, jumping up and leaving the room.

Molly and Ellen looked at each other, full of surprise and speculation. Annie returned followed by the parish priest.

'Oh, Father, it's kind of you to come,' Molly said, getting up. 'Will you have a cup of tea?' she enquired, thinking he'd come to pay a visit to see how they were all managing.

'No, Molly, but thank you. I won't take up much of your time: I'm sure you're tired. To your credit you all work very hard and I hear that even young Bernie is doing better at school.' Then he turned to Annie who felt she was about to burst with excitement. 'Well, Annie, you'll be glad to hear that I've managed to get you the job you want, as a kitchen maid.'

'A kitchen maid!' Molly cried.

The priest looked perturbed. 'Did you not know she wanted to go into service?'

'No, no, I didn't,' Molly replied, taken aback. She sat down again.

'Did you not think to mention it, Annie? Something as big and important as this, a change of living?'

Annie shook her head, but nothing, not even being taken to task by the priest, could spoil her happiness and excitement.

'Where is she going, Father?'

'Ah, not too far away, Molly. A family that belongs to Father Taylor's parish. He's a good friend, we were at the seminary together many years ago. They have a place for a scullery maid and we both asked if Annie could be considered for the post. Mrs Yeates takes good care of her staff, there'll be no need to worry about Annie missing Mass or Confession.'

Molly didn't speak. She wished the girl had told her, it was hurtful and humiliating of Annie to go behind her back.

'Is it definite, Father?' Annie asked, her blue eyes sparkling. 'Do I start right away?'

'No, you'll have to go and see the Housekeeper first. She is responsible for taking on the more menial servants. But if you smarten yourself up and answer any questions truthfully and respectfully I'm sure she'll take you on. A scullery maid doesn't need the same qualities or qualifications as a parlour- or ladies' maid.'

'Where do they live, Father?' Molly asked.

'In Newsham Park.'

Annie gasped. They must have pots and pots of money to live up there for the houses actually in the park were huge. It was a very select and wealthy district.

'You've to present yourself at number 40 at half past five tomorrow evening – and don't be late. The family dine at eight-thirty, everyone will be busy getting ready.'

'Oh, I won't, Father, and I'll wear my new things.'

'Good girl,' he replied with a smile. It could be the making of her. He sincerely hoped so.

Annie excused herself and ran upstairs. She was going to get everything ready; she might even pack the few things she had right away.

In the kitchen the priest turned to Molly, who was still sitting at the table looking subdued. 'I think it will be a blessing.'

Molly nodded and sighed. 'It might, Father, she is a handful and since Jack's . . . Jack's death, she's been . . . difficult.'

'She was never easy, Molly, was she?'

'No, she wasn't, but I *did* try.'

'Ma, you did everything you could do,' Eddie said firmly.

'It wasn't enough, though. I could never take Martha's place in Annie's heart. But why didn't she tell me about this? About wanting to go into service?'

'I don't know. I assumed she had,' Father Healy answered.

She just wanted to cause more of a rift, more worry, more fights, Ellen thought, but she didn't say so aloud.

'Well, I have it on good authority that Mrs Yeates is a good, caring, devoutly Catholic woman. She'll come to no harm there.'

'But will she be happy, Father? She's a factory girl and

the others'll look down on her. It's a well-known fact.'

'Not too much, I hope, but she'll just have to accept it, endure it and try to rise above it. She'll have to earn their respect, it's something that can't be bought or sold. Don't worry, she'll be fine. And she'll get time off to come home and see you.'

Molly rose. 'Thank you, Father, for everything. I know Annie must be grateful. I'm only sorry that she is so unhappy here that she feels she has to go.'

'Take it as a step up in the world for her. It's a blessing, Molly.'

'I'll try, Father.'

When she returned from seeing him out, Eddie and Ellen were sitting silently gazing at each other.

'I didn't know a thing about it, Mam,' Ellen said firmly.

'Neither did I, I swear.' Eddie was just as emphatic.

'To be truthful, I did think she was up to something,' Ellen said. 'I asked her what it was and she told me I'd find out soon enough.'

'But service! She'll not be happy. Your life's not your own: they have so many rules and different ways of going on. And the pay is terrible, so I've heard.'

'Ma, don't worry about her, she's a born survivor is that one. If she fell into a midden she'd come up smelling of roses!'

Ellen felt relieved. The atmosphere in the house would be far better without Annie. She was very awkward and disruptive at times and the strain was beginning to take its toll on all of them.

'I'll go up and see if she wants anything.'

'No, let me go, Mam. She wants everyone to be upset and annoyed that she's going. That's why she's kept it a secret. Well, for once I'll go along with her. It'll make *her* feel happy at least.'

'Take her a cup of tea, Ellen.'

Ellen poured the tea and then lit the oil lamp to go upstairs. She knew Annie must have lit the gas jet in the room they shared despite the fact they were trying to economise on everything.

'I've brought you a cup of tea,' she announced as she entered, placing the lamp and mug on the old trunk under the window and then reaching up to turn off the gas.

'Don't think you can get round me now with your cups of tea,' Annie remarked scornfully.

'I'm not. I want to know why you didn't tell *someone*?'

'Why should I? No one's interested in what *I* do or what *I* want or what *I* say.'

'Annie, you know that's not true! All right, we've had our fights but everyone does. It doesn't mean that we're ignoring you or that we don't care about you.'

'Oh, shut up, Ellen, for God's sake. Miss Prim and Proper! You can do no wrong. You've never had any time for me and neither has *she*. No one liked me or my friends.'

Ellen was relieved at the mention of Annie's friends. At least Annie would be away from Josie Rafferty and the others. 'Well, you've got to admit that Josie Rafferty's nothing but trouble. The whole family are. Someone's always in the Bridewell or Walton Jail, or going before the Magistrates.'

'She's all right, is Josie. She can't help the rest of them.'

'So you still intend to see her then, on your days off?'

Annie shrugged. 'Why not?'

'Won't the people you're going to work for object?'

'How can they? Who'll tell?' Annie narrowed her eyes. 'Maybe you'd be going up there to tell them?'

'Annie, I'd never do something like that and you know it!'

'Well, don't expect me to be spending my time off down here. And don't start about me not sending money home. I won't earn as much so I won't be able to spare more than a couple of shillings a month.'

'I won't.' Ellen sat down on the bed. 'Do you think you'll like it? I expect it'll be hard work.'

'I'm well used to that and what's not to like about it? Good food, a nice warm house with lots of comforts we don't have, and some wages.'

'What about the others? You know, the servants.'

'I couldn't care less if they're all toffee-nosed snobs. There's bound to be other kitchen maids: I'll make friends of them. Don't you worry about me: I'm glad to be going. I hate this house now.'

'And us?' Ellen asked quietly.

Annie just shrugged. 'Think what you like.'

It was a cold but clear January evening when Annie, in her best clothes, got off the tram and walked through the huge iron gates into Newsham Park. The road was wide and went around in a big circle and it was lined with trees and lampposts. In their light she could vaguely make out the shapes of flower beds and shrubberies. Above the lights a pale corona shimmered and it was very quiet. In Milton Street there was always noise of some kind. Mangy dogs barking, babies and small children crying, fretful men and women yelling at each other, men and lads scrapping. Here you could hear a pin drop. Even the air smelled different: cleaner, fresher. The house was so big that she could only stand and stare at it in amazement, but eventually she took a deep breath and walked around to the back entrance and rang the bell.

'I've come about the job,' she said nervously to the young girl who opened the door to her.

'The scullery maid?'

Annie nodded. She was so nervous now that she just wanted to run away back to Milton Street.

'Come in then. She's expecting you,' was the terse command.

Annie followed her and began to stare around.

'Shut your mouth, you look like someone soft in the head.'

Annie didn't know what position the girl held in the household, but she was obviously unimpressed and her words and tone of voice were sharp and far from welcoming. Annie followed her down a dark passageway until they came to a door.

'Is this the kitchen?' she asked in a whisper.

'No. Don't you know *anything*? It's the Housekeeper's sitting room, it's like the pantry butlers have.'

Annie was smarting at her ignorance.

'You'll leave the way we've come, after she's seen you.'

The girl rapped on the door, waited until she heard a summons and went in.

'The girl's here about the job, Mrs Hinchey ma'am,' she said and then left, closing the door behind her.

The Housekeeper was a plump woman dressed entirely in black and her dark bird-like eyes quickly assessed Annie. Any hopes Annie had nursed were quickly dismissed. She was used to large women being jovial and kind. This one looked to be neither.

'You are Anne Ryan?'

'Yes. Yes, ma'am.' Her voice was very unsteady.

'Fathers Taylor and Healy spoke for you which ought to count for something, but I believe you've never been in service? You work in a factory.'

Annie quailed. The woman had managed to make the word 'factory' sound like a brothel on the Dock Road. Again she nodded.

'Well, have you nothing to say, girl?'

'I . . . I . . . want to get out of factory work, ma'am, I *really* do.'

'Who wouldn't indeed,' was the sharp interruption.

'I'm very willing, like, and I want to learn.'

'You go to Confession and Communion and Mass each week?'

'Oh, yes! Father Healy could tell you that.'

'Just what exactly did you do in this . . . this factory?'

'I picked okum. It's a sort of rope-like stuff. They use it to fill the gaps between the planks of the decks on ships, but only on sailing ships, I think. It's used for other things but I . . . I can't remember what.'

The woman raised her eyes to the ceiling. 'Merciful God, a weak-minded cripple could do that!'

Annie hung her head. This was far worse than anything she'd expected – she felt so humiliated. She knew she should have prepared herself, though. Enough people had told her she wouldn't be welcomed with open arms.

'Well, you appear to be strong enough to carry out the duties and tasks that will be required of you. No doubt you'll have to be shown how things are done. It's only because *two* priests have recommended you that I've made my decision. Don't expect to be paid anything like the amount I believe you earn in *that* place. Five shillings a week is what you'll get. You'll live in, be provided with your meals and your work dresses.'

'You . . . you mean . . .?' Annie was confused.

'Yes, you can start next Monday at six o'clock in the morning and be prompt.' Mrs Hinchey turned away to indicate that the interview was over and as quietly as she could Annie left the room. She stood in the dark corridor shaking. She'd got it! She'd really got it. She would work her fingers to the bone just to live here. There was no one to see her out but she didn't care.

Chapter Ten

February 1910 for many years went down in the history books as the worst month for snow, ice and freezing east winds. Hundreds who lived in the slum hovels died for lack of food, clothing and warmth, particularly the old, the sick, babies and young children. It was the coldest Lucy Meakin had ever experienced and yet as she walked to school, muffled, her eyes watering from the bitter wind, she really didn't mind the weather at all. She was just glad to be out of the house. If she'd somewhere else to sleep she would never go home at all. But then she felt guilty even thinking that – she couldn't leave her poor mam.

For weeks her da hadn't been able to work and each day her mam grew more and more worried about making ends meet, particularly as a good fire was now essential. But his temper was very short, shorter than usual. At least her da could do the repairs the house always needed. Now the wind didn't come through the gaps in the window- and doorframes. There were heavy chenille curtains behind the parlour and the kitchen doors hung on runners he'd put up, which kept the heat in, although the parlour was never used. He'd nailed pieces of biscuit tin lids over all the holes in the skirting boards to keep the rats out and poison was laid on bits of bread for both rats and mice.

Her mam was strictly forbidden to take anything to the pawnshop and Da only gave her half of what she used to have to run the household on. Before his beating she'd never have believed life in their household could have been more miserable. Now she knew just how bad it could really be.

In the days that followed his beating, Maggie had said nothing to her husband at all, except when she changed the bandages, and then it was only a formal apology to the effect that she was sorry if she hurt him.

'I'll have the bloody lot of them behind bars! They won't get away with this,' he'd said through gritted teeth as she'd bound up his ribs. His body was a mass of bruises.

She'd kept silent.

'You saw it all, Maggie. They nearly left me for dead. You at least can testify even if they say Lucy is too young.'

'It's your . . . word against theirs,' she'd said quietly.

He'd turned on her. 'What the hell do you mean by that, woman?'

'Just what I said, John.'

'You'll bloody well come with me to court and swear that you saw them beat me up.'

Again she said nothing, yet inside she was quaking. Old habits died hard, but he had to rely on her these days for nearly everything and she took courage from that.

'Well?'

'I . . . I didn't really *see* it. I only came to the door when they were leaving.'

'You lying bitch! You saw everything and by God you're going to tell—' His words ended in a cry for his broken ribs caused a knife-like pain whenever he moved.

She'd gone to great lengths to find excuses why Dr Jenkinson couldn't come out to see him. It was better to go without financially if it meant he remained incapacitated and incapable of lashing out in the way he did when he was fit. He was so busy with everyone falling ill with the weather, she told her husband. She knew he wouldn't go to the hospital: it was degrading, he'd said, the way they treated you in those places, most of which had started out as workhouses and some of which still were. John Meakin would rather put up with her clumsy ministrations than end up in one of those places.

Maggie was out shopping, leaving Lucy at home with her father since the school was closed for the day. During the night a pipe had burst in the boiler room so there was no heating. Lucy stood tracing the pretty patterns the frost had made on the window with her index finger.

'Haven't you got anything better to do with yourself?' Meakin asked irritably as he came slowly into the kitchen and eased himself down on the sofa.

She looked sideways at him from under her lashes. 'Yes, Da,' she answered timidly, going to the table and opening one of her school books.

'Come here, I want to speak to you,' he demanded.

Lucy froze. The colour drained from her cheeks and she

began to tremble but she went and stood beside him.

'You were with your mam the day that lot came. Your mam won't testify, at the moment anyway, but just wait until I'm better, I'll deal with her.'

Lucy began to pluck nervously at the edge of her jumper. Oh, now what?

He reached out, groaned and slapped her hand down. The habit always annoyed him. 'But you'll go into the court and tell them, won't you?'

She became confused. 'They . . . they won't let me, Mam said so. I . . . I'm too young.'

He seized her wrist. 'You'll do as you're bloody told, girl, or you'll get the hiding of your life as soon as I'm fit! It'll be with the buckle end of my belt too.'

There were tears in the child's frightened eyes. 'Oh, please, please, Da! I *didn't* see everything. I was hiding behind Mam. I had my face pressed against her. I was frightened, I really was.' His grip was hurting her arm but she didn't try to pull away.

'You'll *say* you did, won't you? Won't you!'

She nodded. The old fear was paralysing her; she knew what was coming next but then to her intense relief he released her.

'Get back to your books or you'll end up in some bloody factory like the rest of the slummies in this street!'

Annie's first morning was a nightmare. She'd been so nervous and excited that she hadn't slept well. She'd been up at five o'clock, having packed all her things, except for those she'd wear, the night before. She'd made herself as presentable as she could and when she was having the last cup of tea she'd ever have in this house, Molly had appeared.

Since Jack's death Molly had not been able to face sleeping in the bed in the front downstairs room so it had been moved into the girls' room and now Ellen shared it with her. Annie still had her own single bed.

Her stepmother smiled. 'You're ready, I see, and you look very smart, Annie. They can't find anything wrong with your clothes at least.' Molly poured herself a cup and shivered. 'It's freezing in here and the roads will be slippery. Take care you don't fall.' She paused. 'I'm really sorry, Annie, that you don't feel happy here any more.'

'I never did.'

'Of course you did.'

Annie shrugged. 'I don't remember.' She put her cup down. 'Well, I'd better be going.'

'Take care of yourself and come home to see us whenever you can. You'll always be welcome but you know that.' Molly knew her stepdaughter's visits would be brief and infrequent, if she bothered to come at all. She hoped she would, if only to see Eddie. It worried and saddened her to see brother and sister drifting apart.

Annie didn't reply. She buttoned up her coat, put on her hat and picked up her small holdall. Then she looked around the room, shrugged and left.

Her nervousness increased as she got off the tram. In daylight the park looked huge and very beautiful. The frost was heavy on the bare branches of the trees and, as the first weak rays of winter sunlight broke through the darkness, everything seemed to shimmer like crystal. But there was no time to stand gaping so she'd hurried on.

The door was opened by the same girl as before, this time wearing a grey dress, white apron and cap. Her face wore a pained, irritable expression.

'I've come . . . I've arrived . . .' Annie said timidly.

'I can see that. Well, don't just stand there, get inside, it's freezing with this door open.'

Annie did as she was told. 'Where do I have to go?'

'To see Mrs Hinchey first off, then into the kitchen, and seeing as they had friends round last night, there's a huge pile of washing up that'll have to be done before breakfast. What's your name?'

'Annie. What's yours?'

The girl raised her eyes to the ceiling. 'I meant your surname, no one will call you "Annie" here.'

It was all too obvious that this girl wasn't going to become one of Annie's new friends. 'Ryan,' Annie answered.

'I'm Collins, one of the parlour maids.' And without another word she left Annie outside the Housekeeper's room.

Annie took a deep breath and knocked on the door. She was surprised when it was opened immediately.

'At least you're punctual!'

Annie was glad she'd made the early start. 'Thank you, ma'am. What . . . what will I do now?'

'Collins will take you to your room so you'll be able to unpack – although I shouldn't think that will take long.' She looked pointedly at the small grubby canvas bag. 'Then come down and I will explain your duties to you and introduce you to the other members of the staff.'

'Thank you. Are . . . are there many others?'

'Nine, including yourself. Now go and find Collins. She'll be in the kitchen.'

'Which way is the kitchen, please?'

'Through the door at the end of the corridor.'

Annie's stomach began to churn. As she walked into the enormous kitchen everyone turned and looked at her and she went bright red with embarrassment and fear. She looked down at the floor in panic. There didn't seem to be a single friendly face at all.

At last a large woman, also dressed in grey but with an old-fashioned mob cap over her hair, spoke.

'Collins, don't have her standing there like a great lump of wood. Didn't Mrs Hinchey give you your instructions? And don't be long, there's not a single fire lit upstairs yet.'

Collins pursed her lips but Annie was relieved to be led away.

She cheered up a little when she was shown where she would sleep. It was only a tiny room, right at the top of the house, and it was freezing, but she wouldn't share it with anyone. It was all hers and that was a luxury in itself. The bed was a narrow, iron-frame one but there were plenty of blankets and a heavy patchwork quilt. There was a wash-stand with a jug and bowl on its rather stained wooden top. A three-drawer chest and a single narrow wardrobe completed the furnishings. There was lino on the floor and a rag rug by the side of the bed.

'Unpack, then go back and see her.'

'I don't think I'll be able to find the way. Will you wait, please?' Annie begged.

The other girl sighed and watched as Annie took off her coat and hat and unpacked her shabby clothes, conscious that they were further evidence of how inferior she was in this household. Already she was terrified of going back into the kitchen to face all those people.

Most of them had disappeared by the time they got back, for which Annie was very thankful. Mrs Hinchey was sitting at the table discussing a menu with the woman who had told the parlour maid to take her to her room, who it seemed was the cook. Annie stood silently and waited until the Housekeeper had finished.

Finally, she turned to Annie. 'Right, Cook will inform you what's to be done. She is in complete charge of the kitchen. If you have any problems she will deal with them.'

Cook also turned to her. 'Well, Ryan, you can start by washing up and then wash the vegetables and peel the potatoes. You will be the first person down in the kitchen every morning, washed and dressed, mind! The floor is to be scrubbed each day, early, and you will rake out and then set the fire and see there is a good blaze too. I want no complaints about a cold kitchen. Then blacklead the range and set the table. It's been done this morning so you'll have an easy day to start with. I want those dishes washed, dried and put away before the breakfast dishes start to come down, and be very careful with them, they're Spode china and very, very expensive. If you break anything the cost will be deducted from your wages.'

Annie had never seen so many dishes, and they *were* very

beautiful and fragile. Was she expected to do them all? To do everything by herself?

'Ma'am, can I ask . . . something, please?'

Cook looked at her with annoyance. 'What?'

'Am I . . . am I the only kitchen maid?'

'Yes. That's why there was a position vacant. Mullins was hopeless – a lazy, slovenly girl. I couldn't keep her on. I hope you haven't come here thinking it will be easy work, because it isn't. It's not a rest home, not for us. Now roll up your sleeves and get on with that lot. I'll inspect everything and if there's a stain or grease mark on anything, then you'll do them again – and again if necessary. I'll have nothing slapdash in my kitchen. There's a calico apron on the chair, put it on and make a start. I haven't got all morning to be wasting.'

Annie did what she was told to do and there were a few salt tears mingled with the washing-up water. Maybe she'd get used to it, but she had thought that a house of this size would have had two kitchen maids at least. She'd counted on it, thinking to make new friends. Maybe this was the usual way a kitchen maid was treated. She didn't know. She realised there were quite a lot of things she didn't know, but at least the place was warm and the smell of bacon frying reminded her that she was starving, though she didn't have the nerve to ask about something to eat. Silently she applied herself to her mammoth task.

Although it was bitterly cold, Eddie found that the weather conditions were really no help to the business. The coal trade was very, very competitive. The horse, even though she had frost nails in her shoes, often slipped and slid, which could have disastrous consequences. So far this week he'd seen three having to be shot as they'd writhed in pain with badly broken legs. People put ashes and cinders out on the roads to help but they weren't much use: the frost was so severe that it hardly melted even during the daylight hours.

By the time he'd finished his rounds and returned home he felt as though he were a solid lump of ice himself. These days he was always tired, always cold, always hungry, as was Tom who worked beside him now he'd learned the right way to hoist a full sack of coal on to his shoulders without either spilling some of it or wrenching his back. But they'd lost a lot of custom since Da's illness and death, and once people got their coal from someone else they seldom went back to their original supplier. Day by day, week by week, Eddie saw the takings dwindle and the expenses grow. The horse needed more feed, more bedding and a heavy blanket to cover it these bitter nights. He knew he wasn't very good at getting a decent price for his stock from the supplier. He just couldn't argue or bargain. The future seemed fraught with worry.

Their meal was on the table as usual when he and Tom got home after grooming, feeding and watering Betsy and making sure the horse blanket was tied on securely.

'You must both be famished,' Molly said sympathetically as they came into the kitchen.

'Ellen said she nearly fell a few times herself, it's like a skating rink out there.'

'It is. Everton Valley is the worst. Going up we had to

lead Betsy by hand and we were all slipping and sliding. I was afraid the load would fall off the back of the cart and we'd lose it. Coming down is just a nightmare, it's so steep. We've done a lot of walking today. There've been accidents there all day, especially at the bottom of the road where the copper stands directing the traffic.'

'There were three of them today, it was that bad,' Tom put in.

'It's a busy enough junction already,' Eddie added. Three major roads merged at that particular point.

Molly looked concerned. 'I don't want you taking any chances. Couldn't you have gone along Walton Road? At least it's flat.'

'Martingales have got all around there boxed off,' Tom said gloomily. He knew it was supposed to be a 'family business' but he'd never been keen on the idea. All he wanted was money to go to the pictures and have some clothes like Eddie would have done. He certainly hadn't envisaged humping sacks of coal around all day in the freezing cold and not getting a penny for it. But they just couldn't afford a wage for him and that was that.

Molly sat down. 'I know you are both working yourselves into the ground, but business is very bad, isn't it?'

'We lost so much time, Ma. It couldn't be helped but we lost half of our customers after the fire and now we're down to about half of that, and there's the bills, and there's rumours about the price of coal going up.'

'There's always someone who takes the opportunity to raise the price when times are bad,' Molly said. She was managing, just. They were down to the absolute basics now and she didn't have Annie's wage to help out. She was making drastic economies, as was every woman in the street, probably in the entire city, because of the extreme cold. She never used gas for lighting now. There were oil lamps for downstairs and candles for upstairs. More than ever she needed to keep a good fire going, to keep one room warm and to cook on. There were still enough blankets and quilts on the beds but they slept in old clothes it was so cold. If things didn't look up, they could well be sleeping on ticking mattresses on the floor and in here, in the kitchen. They'd done it before, years ago when the children had been young and winters such as this were killers.

'I'll have to find work of some kind, just for a few months, until the really bad weather's over.'

'Doing what, Mam?' Ellen asked. She too was worried about their precarious position.

'Anything I can get.'

'Ma, everyone's out looking for work. Looking to earn even a few pennies. I've seen little kids, blue with the cold, with bare feet, around the stations and the dock gates and the Landing Stage, trying to sell bootlaces, matches, bundles of firewood, anything. When I see them I'm thankful I've got a warm home to come back to and a hot meal.'

'I'll try for cleaning. I'll go and see Minnie Jones about work in that Immigrant House Cunard have.' She shuddered as she remembered Gussie's description of the place but she couldn't afford scruples. She needed the money.

Chapter Eleven

Next morning, reluctantly, Molly made her way to the Pier Head and to the big square building known to everyone as 'the Immigrant House', where the great tide of suffering humanity, the poor and persecuted of every country in Europe and from farther afield, was housed. They were fed and cared for in a manner which to many of them seemed miraculous as they waited for a berth in steerage on the Cunard ships sailing to America and Canada every day.

She stood staring at it and thought how dark and forbidding it looked against the icy blue winter sky. It looked more like an army barracks or a jail or a workhouse. Inside she would find people who were as badly off as half of Liverpool, but they at least had hope in their hearts of a new and better life.

Well, she'd better get on with it, she thought. She pushed open the door and the smell hit her. It stank of every odour imaginable, a foul and noxious mixture. She had to fight down the bitter bile that rose in her throat.

A clerk dressed in a shabby, shiny suit was sitting on a high stool behind a wide, wooden canteen and studying a large ledger.

'Show me the docket they gave you and I'll stamp it and send you along to the receiving area. Do you understand?' He recited the words parrot fashion and without interest, without deigning to look up.

God help them if this was the reception they received. It certainly wasn't welcoming and to many it would be incomprehensible, Molly thought.

'I'm not a passenger, I've no "docket".'

He looked up and scrutinised her. 'What are you here for then?'

'Work. I was told that I could get something here, cleaning.'

'I dunno, missus. Not my department. I just check them in and out.'

'Oh, please. I'm worse off than many of these immigrants. I'm a widow with a family to keep.'

He was regarding her with suspicion. 'Where do you live?'

'Milton Street, off Scotland Road.'

'I know where it is.'

'Please? I need the work so much and I'm a good worker. Never late or not turning up at all.'

He relented. 'All right, at least you can try. Go through that door and along the passage a bit, there's a door on the left. Try there.'

'Who . . . who should I ask for?'

'Immigrant Welfare woman, name of Clarke. Mrs Clarke. She sees to the women, there's a feller sees to the men.'

'Thank you so much.'

He nodded and returned to his book.

The stench got worse the further along the corridor you

went and she was glad to reach Mrs Clarke's door.

When she entered she found a woman and a young man both sitting at desks covered with paperwork.

'The man at the desk sent me. I'm hoping to get work, ma'am, any kind of work. I'm desperate. I'm a widow with a family.' Oh, how she hated having to grovel like this and endure the woman's cold look of appraisal.

'If you've come looking for work in the kitchens you're out of luck. Everyone wants to work in the kitchens, no one wants the hard work in the laundry or the cleaning. Always the kitchen.'

Molly took hope from her words.

'No, I don't mind what I do. I'll work anywhere.'

'Have you any experience of *any* kind?'

'I've kept house and in a two-up, two-down in Milton Street that's not easy.'

'So you're used to the vermin and bugs. You'll be scrubbing floors and such like.'

Molly nodded. Oh, please, please let the woman give her *something*.

'Then we'll take you on for a week's trial period. You'll help the others scrub out every room, every day. I warn you, these people are mainly ignorant illiterates, they have no sense of decency or hygiene. But I expect you're used to that.'

Molly ignored the insult. 'Yes, ma'am.'

'Then start tomorrow morning at six sharp. Buckets, brushes, mops, disinfectant will be provided. Bring your own aprons, substantial ones. The pay is five shillings a week.'

Molly was so relieved. 'Thank you. Thank you so much, ma'am.'

'It won't be a picnic, Mrs—?'

'Ryan. Molly Ryan.'

The woman nodded, her name was entered in a large book and the interview was over. Molly could hardly wait to get out into the fresh air. God alone knew how she was going to put up with the smell and the dirt, but it was work and she needed it very badly.

It was a long, cold walk home. She didn't have money to waste on tram fares. She picked her way cautiously along the icy pavements, thankful at last to get to Milton Street without falling. Gussie saw her coming.

' 'Ow did yer do, Moll?' she called.

'I got cleaning work, scrubbing floors mainly. Five shillings a week. It'll come in handy.'

Even though it was bitterly cold Gussie leaned against the doorpost, arms folded. 'Was it as bad as I've 'eard, with all them dirty foreigners?'

'I only saw the entrance hall and an office but the smell, it was terrible. The whole place reeked of filth and sickness and . . . and . . . poverty. But I'm sure it's because the people living there don't know any better. They can't help being poor and ignorant.'

'Well, there's bad enough poverty and ignorance round 'ere an' I 'ope ter God we don't smell like that.'

'Maybe we do but we just don't notice it. You've got to admit, Gussie, the privies stink even in winter and they're unbearable in summer, with the stench and the flies. And there's all the rubbish in the gutters.' She shivered. 'Anyway,

I'm frozen. I'm going in to make a drink, do you want one?'

Gussie never turned down an opportunity. 'God bless yer, luv. I'm all out of tea until Artie gets 'ome with some brass, like.'

'He got work?'

'Sent word ter say 'e'd got a full day and maybe another tomorrer, thank God.'

Molly had often wondered why, if they were so desperate, didn't Gussie herself go out and find work? She'd mentioned it once.

'It'd be too much, Moll, seein' ter this lot,' she'd said, 'then goin' on wearin' meself out. I'm not fit. I'm not young like you. You're just a spring chicken, girl, I'm an auld woman.' People made their own choices, Molly thought, but she'd work her fingers to the bone if she could help her family.

Gussie settled down close to the range. ' 'Ow's business, Moll?'

'Terrible and getting worse. I just hope this weather breaks, it won't be so hard on the lads then.' All of a sudden Molly was almost overcome with worry and weariness. 'And I'm terrified of Betsy slipping and falling. We can't afford to buy another horse, it's bad enough keeping that one in food and shelter, to say nothing of us.'

'Amen ter that, luv, I've never known it be so cold. If the river freezes that'll just put the top 'at on it all! There won't be no work for anyone.'

Molly had managed to get some vegetables that were almost ready for the dump and a bit of scrag end and was stirring

139

the scouse when Ellen came home, blue with cold.

'Oh, Mam, it's terrible out there. I wish it would get a bit warmer, just a little bit.'

'So do I – so does most of the city. I got work though.'

'At the Immigrant House?'

Molly nodded. 'It's only five shillings a week but it's better than nothing.'

'When do you start?'

'Tomorrow at six. She didn't say what time I'll finish and I didn't ask. I was just so thankful for a job.'

'Will I set the table?'

'Please, luv. I wish I could afford a whole loaf to go with this, but I've only got half and that's got to do for the lads' carry-out for tomorrow. All I've got to go on it is dripping.'

'At least it's a hot pan of scouse, Mam. That'll warm everyone up.'

The kitchen door opened and Tom, covered in coal dust, came into the room.

'What has Mam told you about coming in here in those dirty clothes,' Ellen rebuked him.

'Oh, leave him, Ellen, it's bitter in that scullery and he's frozen stiff as it is. Come over here by the fire, Tom, till you warm up a bit. Where's Eddie?' Suddenly she noticed the boy's face was full of fear and anxiety. 'What's the matter?'

'We decided to try and collect some of the money people owe us. We hadn't sold much all day and there's a lot owing.'

'So?'

'You know the McNallys?'

'From Hopwood Street?' Molly asked.

'Well, they . . . them two fellers started on our Eddie.'

Molly turned abruptly, panic in her eyes. 'What do you mean "started"?'

'They belted him. Told him to come for the money next year and laughed.'

'Oh, dear God, where is he?'

'He's following. He's not too bad, Mam, honestly.'

'I'll go and get him home, Mam,' Ellen said, grabbing her shawl and running out of the back door.

'What about the horse and cart?' Molly asked Tom.

'I drove home, then I just put the nosebag on her and took her to the stable.'

'With the cart?'

The lad nodded uncertainly and Molly could see he was afraid. 'It's all right, luv, don't worry. We can get that sorted out after I've seen to Eddie and we've all had something to eat. Go and sit by the fire and warm up.'

Molly gave a cry as Ellen, supporting Eddie, came into the room. His face was cut and bleeding and he was leaning on Ellen for support, near to tears.

'Oh, Eddie! What have they done to you, luv? Come over here to me.'

'He's hurt his leg, Mam, and his shoulder, but I think he did that when they knocked him down.'

'Ellen, luv, see to the tea.' Molly looked searchingly at her stepson's face. 'Sit down there, Eddie, while I clean up those cuts. You're going to have some terrible bruises. Is your leg bad?'

'Not too bad, only when I try to walk, Ma. I don't think anything is broken.' His words were spoken thickly from lips that were already beginning to swell.

'Mam, will I go for the police?' Ellen asked.

'What good would that do, Ellen? If they arrested those two, the others would come down here and smash up the place,' Eddie said, fear evident in his voice.

'He's right. Oh, I wondered about letting any of that lot have coal on the slate.'

'We collected a few shillings, Mam, but not much,' Tom added. 'Shall I go and see Mr Ogden?'

'No!' Molly said firmly. 'He and the others did enough damage to Mr Meakin. I don't approve of violence in any form. We'll manage.'

They'd all eaten and Tom had stoked up the fire until it was roaring up the chimney. It was the one thing they did have – coal. And, as ever, Molly shared it with her neighbours. She really couldn't afford it now but how could she sit by and let others freeze?

Ellen sighed and looked around. There wasn't much furniture left now but Mam had insisted on keeping the heavy curtains. They helped to keep the room warm. By the light of the oil lamps it didn't look so bad and it *was* warm. Few other kitchens would be as warm and reasonably cosy as theirs. She just wished business would get better.

Bernie was working hard over his school books, an oil lamp on the table. He'd promised Mam he'd do well and he meant it. Anyway, he consoled himself, it was just too cold to play outside. By the time he left school perhaps things would be better. Maybe he'd get a decent job. He might even be lucky enough to get an apprenticeship. The pay was terrible while you were learning, but there was a trade at the end of it and that meant steady work for the rest of your life. That's what both Mam and Ellen had said and it was something to aim for. He didn't want to be like the others, out in all weathers, humping sacks of coal around and maybe getting beaten up by the likes of the McNallys when you asked for payment. No, he certainly didn't want that. It had been his da's dreams, not his, and Mam understood.

Despite his aches and pains, Eddie was trying to doze. Gradually his cold limbs were warming and the scouse had made him feel a lot better. Over the last month his fears had been increasing. He was afraid of so many things. There was his supplier, a bad-tempered man at the best of times who always shouted down requests and arguments. Then there were the customers who were reluctant to pay and found a hundred excuses not to do so. The fears nagged at him day and night and had changed him from being a careless lad to a serious, anxious youth. These days he felt like a man in his forties. Today had been so completely terrifying that he was thinking of finally telling his step-mother how afraid he'd become. Then he felt guilty. No, he couldn't tell her, she had enough on her plate. He dreaded tomorrow when he'd have to go out again. He'd heard that one coal merchant had had his horse, cart and entire stock taken from him by a desperate crowd.

All evening Molly, as she'd unravelled an old woollen jumper to utilise the wool to knit up again, had been fretting too. About Eddie, about the business, about their lack of money. She had caught the quick flash of fear in Eddie's eyes when the boys had come in, and she wondered if this was the first time they'd been threatened. Eddie was no match for the McNallys. She sighed heavily. It was becoming clearer and clearer that her stepson wasn't coping well with the business. She, Ellen and Tom had gone to where Betsy had been left and had unyoked her, spread fresh straw in the stable, broken the ice on the bucket of water and filled her nosebag. Tom had tied on the blanket.

Ellen too was worried. 'Mam, what *are* we going to do?' she asked when they finally returned from the stable. Things couldn't go on like this. There was only her wage and Mam's five shillings to keep a roof over their heads and food in their stomachs, never mind keep the business going through these lean times.

'Should we sell Betsy and the cart and the coal?' Tom asked quietly. He was afraid of going out again on the roads.

It had been in Ellen's mind but she was glad she hadn't been the one to mention it.

'I don't know and that's the truth,' Molly replied.

'But what if things pick up again? Without the stock we won't have any business,' Bernie interrupted.

They all turned to look at him, surprised that he was mature enough to even think about such things. His father's death had changed them all. Bernie flushed as they all stared at him.

'The money would see us through the next months and Eddie and me can get jobs,' Tom urged.

Eddie hadn't spoken. He'd willingly get another job,

especially after today, but he didn't want to admit to his fear and weakness.

Molly was clearly flustered. 'Oh, I just don't know. I keep thinking of what your da wanted for you, all of you, but things have become so bad and he couldn't have foreseen them.

'Eddie, is this the first time you've had trouble with customers?'

Slowly and reluctantly he shook his head.

'Why didn't you tell me?'

'I didn't want to worry you, Ma. It's getting worse and worse. People just *haven't* got the money and . . . and . . .'

'They take it out on us,' Tom added.

'Then this can't go on. I can't let you go out again.'

'If we could get in the money everyone owes us and sell up, could we manage, Mam?' Ellen asked, breaking into her reverie.

'I suppose so.'

Eddie was thankful.

'You know your da had always wanted his own bit of a business, and to sell up now . . .' Molly shook her head sadly. It would seem like a betrayal. If only she had someone to turn to for advice. Someone who could go and collect the debts. Then a thought came into her head.

'Conor. Conor Ryan,' she said aloud.

They all looked at her quizzically.

'Your da's brother. He could run the business. He'd be well able to sort out those McNallys and their like.'

'But, Mam, we don't know him. We've never met him even,' Ellen stated.

'Do you know where he lives?' Eddie asked, seeing a ray of hope. If Da's brother could take over the business, that would leave him free to get a job and that would be another wage coming in, and he'd have no one to fear.

Molly tried to recall what Jack had told her about his brother. He'd never been over-complimentary, she seemed to remember, but then he'd never said anything really damning. At least she knew the area her husband had grown up in, where his brother, to her knowledge, now lived.

'The Liberties, in Dublin.'

'Is that all? How will we find him?'

'I'll ask Father Healy to find out who the parish priests are in that area. I'll find him.'

'Do you think he'll come, Mam?'

Molly nodded. 'It's work, it's a business, and he's family.'

'It would solve some problems, Mam,' Ellen urged.

'Then it's agreed? I'll go and see Father Healy after work tomorrow.' They all nodded their approval and relief. It seemed they'd found a solution.

Chapter Twelve

Things hadn't got any better, Annie thought as she came down into the cold kitchen. At least it was getting lighter these mornings, and now spring was here, warmer. She could switch off the electric light at six o'clock. She still marvelled at the fact that you could flick a switch and the light came on instantly. No messing or fussing with the gas. There was gas, a big gas stove, although Cook mistrusted it and insisted on using the range for nearly everything. Tomorrow it would be a new month, which meant pay day. That thought should have cheered her up but it didn't. No one bothered with her. No one asked her if she was getting on all right.

Everything was so very different to what she was used to. The cleaning was very thorough, although compared to home the place was already immaculate. She'd lost count of the number of times she'd had to rewash dishes and pans in the first week she'd been there. She'd cried into the greasy dishwater every day. It was all work from five in the morning until nearly midnight and by that time she was dropping. She was very thankful the Yeateses never went to bed late. Every night she fell exhausted into her narrow

147

little bed in the freezing attic. Everyone else worked hard too, all except Mr Mansfield, the Butler, who seemed to hold such a high position that he hardly ever soiled his white-gloved hands.

She had really thought things would get better. That the other servants would become more approachable. That *someone* would befriend her. She took her meals with everyone else at the big table but still no one spoke to her. She sat at the very far end and she was glad of that, for she had no table manners to speak of. But she watched and tried to learn, conscious all the time of what they thought of her. A factory girl. A slummie with no manners and a thick accent, only fit to scrub floors and vegetables. She'd never before come across such snobbery.

On her first afternoon off she had gone down to see Josie, relieved and delighted to escape. She could have a real good moan and bitch with Josie; she couldn't do that with anyone else. To her dismay when she was halfway down the street she remembered that her friend would be at work and only when she was returning to Newsham Park would Josie be coming home.

She was determined not to go to Milton Street so she'd taken a tram into town and spent hours window shopping, trying to cheer herself up by choosing what she would buy with her first month's money. Soon she'd have a collection of clothes – new clothes – then maybe she'd go and see that lot in Milton Street. She'd tell them how well she was doing and they'd believe her because she would be dressed up to the nines. She'd have that smart costume and hat for

Easter Sunday. Ellen wouldn't and that gave her some satisfaction.

After that, on her next few days off she went back to town to window shop and have a cup of tea and a sandwich in the Kardomah Café in Bold Street no less. Bold Street was Liverpool's most expensive and exclusive street, but it soon paled as a diversion. It cost the earth for what they called 'Afternoon Tea' and she was so lonely she was even beginning to think of going back to Milton Street.

Today Mrs Hinchey gave her her pay in a small brown envelope. She should have been delighted but she wasn't. It was her day off too and she was going to buy a nice lemon and white dress and jacket and a white picture hat, just right for Easter. Then she'd sit in the park, somewhere well away from the house. She'd find one of those little arbours that had benches in them. In summer the roses and honeysuckle ran riot over the trelliswork, but even without the flowers it would be secluded, and it would be nice to sit and feel the warmth of the spring sun on her face.

'I see you've spent up,' Collins remarked as she returned later with her parcels.

'I've been saving up.'

'So what did you buy?'

Annie was rather taken aback by the other girl's interest. 'A new dress, jacket and hat, for spring.'

'Have you ever had anything new before? You know, chosen by yourself?' Collins asked in a patronising voice.

Annie glared at her. The bitch. 'I *have*. There's my black coat and hat, neither of those were hand-me-downs!'

Collins shrugged and took her cup to the draining board for Annie to wash later with all the other dishes.

Annie was consumed by anger and humiliation as she went to put her new things away in her room. She sat on her bed and looked around miserably. She *hated* it here. She'd thought it would all be so different. Oh, the meals were good and the place was warm but she'd never even been upstairs and probably never would. Finally she admitted to herself that she wished she could go back to Milton Street and to the factory. You had a good laugh with the girls and women there. But here she was, in this rich, posh household, in her own room, with new clothes, and all she wanted to do was to go back home and she couldn't. Her pride wouldn't let her. Oh, it was no use just sitting here feeling sorry for herself. She went down to make herself a cup of tea. At this time of day there was hardly ever anyone in the kitchen.

It was in fact completely empty, though as warm and tidy as usual. She was just putting the kettle on to boil when she heard the bell to the back door jangle. She went to open it, wondering who it was. Now she'd have to find someone to deal with whoever was standing on the step.

She gave a shriek of joy as she saw Josie, grinning at her.

'Josie! Josie! Am I glad to see you!'

'Well then, can I cum in?'

Annie's mood changed instantly as she ushered her friend into the kitchen, heedless of the fact that she might get into trouble over it.

'God, isn't it big an' isn't it warm! Yer fell on yer feet 'ere, Annie.'

'I didn't, Josie. I bloody hate it. I hate all of *them* too!'

'Oh, gerroff, you're just 'aving me on. I've never seen a room as big as this. So what are the people like? You know, who owns this lot?' Josie fingered the fringe of the cloth that was kept on the table when it wasn't being used.

'I don't know. I've never flaming been upstairs.'

'Never?'

'Never. And none of the servants speak to me either. Half the time I don't think they realise I'm here at all. All they talk about is the posh people who come here for dinner. Oh, Josie, I'm so miserable!'

'Well, I'll purra stop ter that, Annie. Get yerself changed an' come 'ome with me; we're 'avin a birrof a do, like.'

'A do? What for?'

''Cos our Freddie's 'ome.' Josie had picked up an orange from the fruit bowl on the big dresser and was staring longingly at it.

'Oh, go on, eat it, they'll never miss it.'

Annie thought hard. Who was Freddie? There were so many of them and there were even more cousins. Which brother was Freddie and why the party in his honour? 'Where's he been?'

'Away at sea.' Josie had peeled the orange deftly and the rest of her words were spoken through a mouthful of fruit. 'Me mam's dead proud of 'im. 'E's just a couple of years older than me an' he's the only one who's never been up before the stipe or a judge an' jury.'

Annie knew she should be shocked at such a revelation and the off-hand, matter-of-fact way it was delivered. She wasn't. She'd heard it before.

'Has he been away long?' She was trying to remember what he looked like. The Raffertys' comings and goings were confusing.

'Yeah, nine months.'

'That's a long time, no wonder I couldn't place him.'

'They went ter some dead faraway place. Months and months it takes just ter get there an' then they went up some river, the Am— Am— something. South America, me da said it were. 'E went an' looked it up. Imagine that, me da readin'. I never knew 'e could. Well, are yer comin' or not?'

'When is it?'

'Ternight, that's why I cum 'ere. I should be at work but I said, "Ah, ter 'ell with it! Yer brother doesn't see much of yer." '

Annie's expression had changed from one of excitement to dejection. 'Josie, I can't. I have to be back here by seven at the latest.'

Josie threw the orange peel into the fire and wiped her fingers on her skirt. 'God, it's not worth 'aving a day off! Can't yer get someone ter cover fer yer, like?'

'No. I told you they hardly speak to me.'

'Then to 'ell with them all! Come on, Annie, 'ave yer lost yer nerve?'

'No. But I'll get the sack and I don't want to have to go back to Milton Street.'

'Yer'll get the sack fer one bloody night? Fer a few hours? God, you've changed. You're as bloody miserable and po-faced as your Ellen.'

That did it. It was only a few hours extra, she could be

back here by half past ten. She'd say Ma had taken a bad turn while she was there and that's why she was so late. They'd probably dock her wages, but she didn't care. It was the first bit of fun she'd have had in months. She'd explain away her new outfit when the time came.

'All right, I'll come. But I'll have to leave with you now before anyone sees us both. I'll run up and get my things and for God's sake don't touch anything in here because if you break anything there'll be murder.'

Josie pulled a face but sat down at the table.

The Raffertys' house was like a three-ringed circus, Annie thought as she and Josie went down the lobby. She'd changed into her new clothes but thought the outfit didn't match her black coat and hat. She'd shrugged; Josie only wore a shawl. Even this early there seemed to be people everywhere and kids of all ages were running in and out of each room screeching with excitement or rolling around the floor fighting.

'I'm goin' up ter get dressed, Mam. I've brought Annie,' Josie called to her mother who was in the kitchen. It resembled the bar of a pub – through the open door Annie caught a glimpse of beer barrels and numerous bottles. 'Just don't ask where it all cum from,' Josie said, following her friend upstairs. Her mother's screams rocked the ramshackle house. 'Gerroff, yer bloody little swine! Gerrout of me kitchen!' she yelled.

'Oh, God, what's it going ter be like later when the fellers come back from the alehouse?' sighed Josie as they entered the cluttered untidy bedroom.

'What time do you think that'll be?'

'Well, Mam says they can stay there all bloody night and we'll 'ave a great time without them, but our Freddie's got some feller in tow, offen the ship, like, and 'e looks dead 'andsome. I'd like a closer look! But they'll come back when the money's run out or someone remembers that there's ale here. God, fellers are thick sometimes. Why spend when you don't need to?'

Josie was right. It got steadily more crowded and more noisy as the evening wore on and the menfolk poured in. Their number seemed to include most of the men in the street, as well as Rafferty uncles, cousins and nephews. Annie felt great in her new outfit. Her only regret was that she couldn't wear her new hat too.

'Follow me, Annie, while we gerra drink!' Josie urged.

She obediently followed her friend who was ruthlessly elbowing her way through the press of people to the kitchen which was a complete and utter shambles. Beer seemed to have been spilt everywhere. The table was sticky and so was the floor and Josie's da, who always looked drunk no matter what time of day it was, was holding his half-finished glass of beer at such an angle that she drew her skirt aside. She certainly didn't want her dress ruined the first time she wore it.

'Josie, who's yer mate?' a male voice yelled above the din.

'Annie. Annie Ryan, don't yer remember 'er?' Josie yelled back.

'Not very well.'

'This is our Freddie.'

The lad came and stood near to her, a glass in his hand, while Josie made a beeline for his friend and shipmate.

'Well, you've certainly changed since I last saw yer, Annie Ryan.'

'Thanks. So have you,' she shouted back. He was a handsome lad, she thought, with the dark hair and blue eyes that characterised all the Raffertys. Because his face was tanned his eyes seemed bluer.

'Will yer gerrus a drink, fer God's sake?' Josie interrupted. 'It's like Fred Carno's in 'ere! An' 'aven't yer gorrany manners? Whose yer mate?'

'That's Dave. This is me sister, Josie.'

Josie pursed her lips at the offhand introduction.

Mrs Rafferty, determined to give her favourite son the best do the street had ever seen, had managed to get a piano from somewhere. Even more miraculously she'd found someone who could play it. Not very well, but he produced something which nearly resembled a tune. Oh, this was far better than being stuck up there in Newsham Park with all those snobs, afraid to open her mouth or even look at them sideways. Annie accepted the drink Freddie had brought her and his invitation to try and 'trip the light fantastic' in the parlour.

'Oh, ger*rim*! The "parlour" now!' screeched Josie, overhearing her brother whilst she hung on to the arm of Freddie's mate. ''Asn't 'e come up in the world!'

Annie felt flushed and hot but her eyes danced with enjoyment. This was where she belonged. They were people like herself. Working class – well, there wasn't really much in the way of work – but they were her kind of folk and they knew how to enjoy themselves.

She accepted another three drinks and began to feel very light-headed. Nothing seemed to be real at all. It was like being in a dream and she lost all sense of time but she didn't care. Freddie was holding her tightly and she felt somehow excited. She'd never felt like this before but maybe it was the drink. When he bent his head to kiss her she didn't pull away as she knew she should have done. And she enjoyed it. She'd never been kissed before, certainly not like this. Whole new worlds seemed to be opening up before her.

When she awoke she felt terrible. Her head was thumping. Each movement sent excruciating pains through it. She remembered the sea of laughing faces, the thumping of the piano, Freddie's arm around her waist propelling her upstairs, but after that – nothing. A great blank. She felt sick but she felt far worse when she saw that her dress and jacket were on the floor and her chemise was open right down the front and beside her Freddie Rafferty lay snoring and without any clothes on at all.

She sat upright and groaned in agony at the movement. Oh, God! Oh, Jesus, what had she done? Just what had she let him do to her? She felt even more nauseated. And what about her job? What time was it anyway? Well, she'd done it now. It was the end of everything.

Father Healy himself came around with the address. Conor Ryan lived in the Coombe.

'Do you want me to write to him, Molly?'

'No. No thank you, Father. I'll explain the situation and I'm sure my brother-in-law will come.'

'Father Doyle at St Bridget's wrote and told me about conditions there. Your brother-in-law might not want to swap one slum for another, Molly.'

'I know but surely running a business, his own brother's business, will appeal to him? It might be so successful that we could move.'

The priest looked serious, as if he were contemplating something.

'Is there something else?' Molly asked.

'I suppose I should tell you. Father Doyle informs me that he's fond of a drink and that he is not a well-educated man. He can neither read nor write, which is why I offered to write to Father Doyle.'

Molly bit her lip. Conor Ryan didn't sound a very promising candidate to run a business. But then there were hundreds of people in Liverpool who were illiterate. Did he *need* to read or write? Eddie, Tom and herself would look after the paperwork, such as it was. All he'd have to do was get to know the area, collect the money, see to the horse.

'I presume he can deal with money?' she said.

'I'd say he could. In my experience people who are illiterate can always cope with addition and subtraction at least.'

'Well, then I'll give him a try. I've nothing to lose.'

'That's all you can do, Molly. Now, if there's anything else . . .?'

She smiled at the elderly priest. 'I know, Father, I've only to ask. You're very kind.'

'It's one of the joys of my calling, to see people get on in life despite the dreadful conditions and circumstances they find themselves in. Believe me, it doesn't happen very often.'

After he'd gone she sat at the table to write to the brother-in-law she'd never met. She'd have to be firm over the drinking. There would be enough men in the street who'd encourage him to waste money. Money they couldn't spare.

'He . . . he doesn't sound as if he is anything like Da,' Eddie said, when she'd read out what she'd written so far.

'Da was never one to go drinking,' Ellen said thoughtfully. None of them liked the sound of this uncle but there was nothing else to be done. Not if they weren't to end up in the workhouse.

'We shouldn't compare them. Look at you, Ellen, and our Tom, totally different but you get on well together.'

Eddie and Annie didn't, though, and they're brother and sister, Ellen thought.

Molly tapped the end of the pencil on the table. Oh, she really wasn't sure about this at all. She had serious misgivings. What should she say next? She didn't want him to think he was only being approached after all these years of being ignored because they were desperate. But neither did she want to give him any idea that the business would belong to him. 'I don't even know what he does, if he has work at all.'

'Just make it brief, Mam. Tell him about Da and you're sorry you didn't inform him but you were so upset and had no address. Ask him if he will come over and help out with the family business. That times are bad and you need help but once the business gets going again you could make him a partner or something.'

Molly stared at her daughter. 'You know, Ellen, you'd make a good businesswoman yourself. You see things clearly and then go and get them done.'

'Oh, Mam, I'd be no use at all.' Ellen laughed while Molly returned to her task. She'd have to send him his fare at least. It would cut into the budget but that couldn't be helped. They needed him. It was as simple as that.

Chapter Thirteen

Annie had got dressed. It had taken her ages because her fingers were trembling so much that she had difficulty fastening all the tiny buttons on the dress. Each movement was an effort – a painful one – but she *had* to do it and quickly in case anyone woke and found her in this room and in this state. She wished she could just curl up and die, she felt so awful. She refused even to think about what had happened to her, albeit with her agreement. Her cheeks burned with shame.

She made her way slowly and cautiously to the adjoining door and found Josie with Freddie's shipmate on the floor in the other bedroom. The bed was already occupied by four other people judging by the number of arms and legs she could see. She knelt and shook her friend hard.

Josie stirred and tried to open her eyes. 'Oh, Jesus! Me 'ead!'

'Josie, I need your help. I need to talk to you now.' Annie shook her again.

'Fer God's sake, Annie, will yer stop that, me 'ead is bustin'!' Josie groaned but she did drag herself up on her elbow. All she had on was her chemise.

'God, would you look at the pair of us! Josie, I'm going to be murdered! I mean it! I'll be killed! I can't go back but then they'll tell Father Healy and he'll tell Ma. Oh, God! I wish I was dead!' Annie was near to tears.

'Yer will be iffen yer don't stop shakin' me like I was some kind of bloody rag doll! Fer Christ's sake, pack it in!'

Annie tried again. 'Josie, it's different for you. You know what they're like at home.'

Josie leaned her head back against the wall and closed her eyes. She wanted to be sick. God, how much had she had? How much had they both had? She certainly couldn't remember the last time she'd seen Annie the night before and, what's more, at that particular moment she couldn't care less.

'Josie, please help me?' Annie begged. Slowly Josie tried to unscramble her brains. 'First off, fix yerself up then go ter Father Bunloaf.' She didn't even register that if her mam heard her using the local slang for a Catholic priest she'd get belted. 'Tell 'im yer want ter confess; 'e'll 'ave ter fergive yer. Tell 'im, oh, tell 'im whatever yer like as ter 'ow come yer didn't go back. 'E won't be able to tell anyone 'cos it will be all told in the Confessional, like, and yer'll get absolution.' Josie, like many people, assumed that once you confessed your sins you were instantly forgiven and usually got only a decade of the Rosary or some such as your penance. 'Then go back up there an' tell them whatever story yer decided on. Now will yer leave me in peace, fer God's sake?'

Annie frowned. 'Josie, I can't go to Confession and then tell more lies right away.'

'Oh, Annie! Sod off, will yer!'

Annie stood up and had to lean against the wall herself until the dizzy feeling faded. Her friend, as usual, had found the way out of one of her dilemmas. She'd have to lie during Confession and after it. It wasn't the best way but there *was* absolutely no solution to the other one. She wished she'd never set eyes on Freddie Rafferty.

Confession had been terrible. When she'd knocked on the door of the Parish House, she'd looked so awful that the Housekeeper – a sour-faced woman – had taken her arm and ushered her into the little room that was used for private business. She'd found it terribly hard to tell the priest about it. She stuttered and stumbled and at the end she'd received by far the most awful dressing down in her life. Now she still had to go to the house in Newsham Park and tell more lies. Oh, she'd never be able to face Father Healy again. She'd have to go to Confession again but she'd make sure she didn't go to him. All the way on the tram she tried to rehearse it in her mind. It helped to distract her from how ill and upset she felt.

As soon as she opened the kitchen door she knew it was going to be very bad. Both Cook and Mrs Hinchey were busy and there were dishes and trays everywhere. Collins was at the sink, up to her elbows in dirty washing-up water. She glared murderously at Annie.

'Well, the Prodigal returns! Just *where* have you been, miss?' Mrs Hinchey's voice was full of anger and the look she gave Annie made her quail.

It was all too much for her. She felt so dreadful and so

desperate she just burst into tears.

'For heaven's sake, girl, sit down and stop the hysterics this instant. Now, where have you been? You are my responsibility while you live under this roof and I will not stand for kitchen maids – or any kind of maid for that matter – just taking it into their heads to stay out all night!' A warning look was cast at Collins.

Between sobs Annie told all her lies about being summoned home because her ma had been taken very ill and that she'd just rushed off, still wearing the new outfit she'd been trying on at the time.

'Would it have been too much to ask that you tell someone?' was the acerbic question.

'Ma'am, there was no one here and I . . . I . . . didn't think.'

'Could you have not left a note then?'

'Ma'am, I was so upset and worried.'

'Well, not half as much as we were. If you hadn't turned up at lunchtime Mrs Yeates would have had to be told and the police called in!' Cook's tones were as sharp as the Housekeeper's.

'I'm so sorry, ma'am, please, please don't sack me. I'll never do anything like that again. I didn't realise . . . I didn't mean to cause so much trouble. I'm sorry. I swear it.' And she meant it.

The two women looked at each other while she tried to stifle her sobs. Even after all she'd said would she be sent packing?

Cook at last passed her a handkerchief. 'Here, blow your nose and pull yourself together, girl!'

'I will give you one more chance and, believe me, that's not normally something I do, especially with a scullion, but Cook has informed me over the weeks that you work hard, are quiet and have upset no one – until now. But put one foot wrong and you're out. Do you understand?'

The relief was so intense that Annie had to use the handkerchief again. 'Yes. Yes, I understand. Oh, thank you, ma'am. God bless you both. I'll never give cause for worry again.'

'Yes, well, that's the end of it. Go and take those things off and get down here and do some work. Your absence has put extra strain on the rest of the staff so you won't be the most popular person here below stairs.'

Annie almost ran from the room. It had worked! Oh, thank God it had worked, though she really shouldn't be saying 'Thank God' after telling a pack of lies. She still felt ill and ashamed, but she'd never go out again on her days off. She'd stay in and do some extra work. That would be bound to show them that she really appreciated the second chance.

In Milton Street they all waited with eager anticipation for the reply from the priest in Dublin. Eventually the morning came when the postman called, something he rarely did in this street. The night before there'd been much speculation and debate. They were sure that they'd be getting some kind of response to their letter soon and Ellen had wondered how much they should tell their neighbours about their plans.

'I'll *have* to tell people he's coming, if he agrees,' Molly had answered her daughter's query.

'Why?' Ellen demanded.

'To stop everyone gossiping and making up stories of their own. You know what they're like in this street.'

'I know what *some* of them are like. You'll only have to tell Mrs Cooney and it'll be all round the neighbourhood by teatime.'

'Ellen, that's enough. I know she's got her faults but she's been good to all of us.'

'I just wish we didn't have to have *him* to run the business. It's sort of admitting failure.'

'It *is* a failure on our part but I can't leave it all to poor Eddie. He's too young and not aggressive enough. But I can't be sorry for that. Sometimes I feel guilty about him going out on the rounds, but what else can I do?'

'Mam, don't worry. I know *we're* desperate but soon our Tom will have to go down to the docks.'

Molly looked shocked. 'I hope not. He's only just fifteen.'

Tom had managed to get himself the job of a messenger boy for the *Liverpool Daily Post and Echo*. It didn't pay much but it was regular, fairly secure and the bike was provided. And every penny counted these days.

It was Molly herself who found the letter the next day on the floor of the lobby. She'd returned tired, hot and with a headache from work which she hated more and more with every passing day. She pitied the immigrants: some had terrible tales to tell, others were so eager to have a kindly person to talk to that sometimes the women would actually help her. They'd be down on their knees beside her and she was grateful. But the work was exhausting.

It was so stuffy inside the house that she started to cough but the bout didn't last and she sighed as she opened the letter, thinking of Ellen's words about their 'failure'. She scanned the lines of neat copperplate written by the priest in Dublin and then nodded slowly. She had more or less known Jack's brother wouldn't refuse. It would be a golden opportunity for a man who had nothing.

In an attempt to get some air into the house she opened both front and back doors wide and pushed all the windows up. That wasn't easy as the wood in the sashes was rotten and she began to cough again. God help them all in number 3 Court – in all the courts, she thought as she went for a drink of water. The court, down the narrow alleyway near number 36, never caught a bit of wind or sunlight. It'd be stifling – and as for the two privvies, shared between nearly thirty people . . . Molly didn't even want to think about the state they'd be in this weather.

Just because she had finished one job it didn't mean she could sit down and relax for a bit. There was plenty to be done here. She began, wearily, to see to her own house and family.

Molly waited until they were all in and had had their meal before mentioning the letter. They had all complained of the heat.

'Oh, I do hate it when it's hot,' Ellen had grumbled.

'There's no pleasing us, is there? Winter is too cold, summer is too hot and the worst is to come – wait until July!' Molly grinned ruefully.

'Oh, Mam, don't even mention it!'

'All right, I'll change the subject. I had a letter today. From Father Doyle.'

'What did he say, Ma?' Eddie asked eagerly. He'd been praying that the answer would be 'Yes' and he wouldn't have to go back on the rounds, although now the first warm days of May had arrived people wouldn't be needing as much coal and the work would be lighter. Summer was always a slack time, except for people who had to keep a fire going to cook on. It was usually a time when they actually paid what was owing, if they could. But he preferred the work at the docks. He loved the river and all the shipping. Ships from every country in the world docked in Liverpool and their crews were of every colour and creed. Sometimes he wondered just what it would be like to sail on one of them.

'He says he'll be very happy to come and help out. He's sorry about poor Jack, he was always fond of him and he wished he'd known sooner but that that was nobody's fault. He also says he hasn't any money and would be grateful if I could send him his fare.'

'Does he say just when he'll be coming?' Ellen asked.

'No. I suppose he'll go straight to get a ticket and then come. I'll send the money, care of Father Doyle and ask will he let us know the exact day.'

'Is that all? He doesn't say much about himself, does he?' Tom mused.

'I don't suppose he wanted to burden Father Doyle with having to write his life story,' Ellen replied.

'We don't even know how old he is,' Eddie said.

'He's younger than your da was.' She didn't say that she'd remembered Jack had once told her he was a bit of an eejit, a word that seemed to cover a variety of unsuitable characteristics. She was beginning to have very serious doubts about Conor Ryan but it was too late now.

He arrived a fortnight later and they all went down to the Pier Head to meet him. The June morning was warm and without the hint of a breeze. The turgid grey waters of the Mersey were like a millpond, disturbed only by the thin, dirty cream wakes of the ferries and a couple of dredgers that worked constantly keeping the channel and the Landing Stage clear of silt so the big liners could tie up alongside.

A mist seemed to hang over the waterfront and it was, as always, busy, with the Isle of Man ferry, the Belfast ferry and a Canadian Pacific ship alongside, as well as the Dublin ferry.

'I'm glad it's a Saturday otherwise we wouldn't have been able to come and meet him ourselves. I really do want to see him,' Ellen remarked determinedly as they walked down the floating roadway.

The ferries were always packed. They sailed twice a day from Liverpool and Dublin but most people travelled on the overnight boats. At least then you could get some sleep although you had to lie on the deck if you didn't manage to get a seat.

'We don't even know what he looks like,' Eddie said.

'Look out for someone who looks a bit like your da,' Molly said. How she hated to have to say that. It was like searching the rails for Jack. No matter how long she lived she would never forget his face.

Eventually the hawsers were secured around the capstans and the gangway was lowered. There was the usual surge and crush but finally Tom pointed to a man who had detached himself from the crowd and was gazing around him, looking mystified.

'I think that's him. He looks a bit like Da, doesn't he?' Tom said.

'He does. Do you think we could push forward?'

'No sooner said than done,' Eddie replied and elbowed his way through followed by the rest of them.

'Are you Conor Ryan?' Molly asked tentatively while the others eyed him up and down. He looked all right, Ellen thought. He was as tall as Da had been, his hair and eyes were the same colour. He wore an old jacket over a collarless grey shirt, moleskin trousers and boots, and under his arm was a parcel, probably – certainly – everything he owned that he wasn't wearing.

'Molly, is it yourself?' He smiled and held out his hand.

'It is and you're very welcome, Conor.' She relaxed a little at his manner and the lilt in his voice.

'Aren't I the fortunate man indeed. Now you'll have to tell me who is who among this grand-looking bunch.'

The introductions were made and Ellen had to admit that he seemed friendly and surprisingly nice.

'We'll go straight home and discuss things properly. Get to know more about each other. This place is always like this, not room to swing a cat.'

'Sure, there's plenty going on to keep a body entertained all day, if he hadn't the work to go to.'

'There's eight miles of docks, and ships from all over the world. And there's the overhead railway,' Bernie pointed out proudly as they left the crowds and crossed the cobbled expanse of Mann Island.

'Did you have a good crossing? I've heard people say it can be terrible.'

'Wasn't it like a mirror all the way. It was fine but there was a feller after tellin' me how desperate it can be if it's rough.'

'There's always someone who looks on the bad side of everything.' Then Molly smiled. Like everyone else she thought that on first impressions she liked her brother-in-law.

'Would you look at all the traffic and the trams and the motor cars,' Conor marvelled. 'It's like Sackville Street — that's Dublin's finest street,' he added for their information.

'It's a much bigger city than Dublin, I gather, but I'm sure you'll like it here,' Molly said.

'Oh, I know I will, Molly. Why wouldn't I with what you're offerin' me? Haven't my prayers been answered.'

'I hope you feel the same way when you start to collect the debts. They've a hundred and one excuses.'

'Ah, I'll be well able for them all. You don't live your life in the Liberties and know nothing about people and their ways of going on. Don't you worry about that, Molly. Don't you worry about anything.'

Molly grinned. It had been a long time since someone had told her not to worry and she'd allowed herself to even half believe him. Maybe today she'd give herself the luxury of doing so.

Chapter Fourteen

Molly had watched Conor's expression as they'd travelled home and wondered if the slums of Dublin were worse than those in Liverpool. He seemed to be taking an interest in everything. Young Bernie was pointing out all the fine buildings and shops but Conor didn't comment much.

'There's a bed for you in the front room,' Molly informed him when they arrived back. 'The lads all share one bedroom and myself and Ellen have the other,' she continued as she filled the kettle and he looked around the room.

Even though there wasn't much in the way of furniture and home comforts, it was a damned sight better than the one-pair front he'd shared with four others out of work, carters and dockers. Life in the Dublin tenements was bad – really bad – and he'd been glad to get out.

'That'll do me fine. All of this will be grand altogether. Aren't you a generous woman.'

'Our Annie, that's Jack's daughter by his first marriage, is in service and lives in.' Molly was then silent. She was worried about Annie.

'And we don't see much of her. Well, we don't see

anything of her if the truth be told,' Ellen added.

Conor Ryan was a man who had all his wits about him all the time. Sure, there were times when he acted the eejit, the halfwit, but that was only when it suited him. He sensed immediately there was some reason why herself in service stayed away. She was bound to have at least one day off in a week. But he was wise enough not to comment.

Molly changed the subject. 'We haven't got much, as you can see, and this *is* a slum, but we all hope to move out one day if the business does well. What did you work at in Dublin?'

'I was on the docks for some of the time. Have they the same system here? You turn up for work and hope to God the feller in charge looks favourably on you and gives you a half-day's work.'

'It's the same here,' Molly replied.

'Well, it won't be like this for ever. There's bound to be trouble over it one day. Hasn't your man Jim Larkin already started to organise the Unions, and he a Liverpudlian too.'

'I work on the docks when I can,' Eddie informed him.

'Is that a fact? Well, if you've nothing to do can't you drive the cart with me? But don't be worrying your head about that now,' he added quickly, seeing the expression on the lad's face change.

'I like working down there. I love to see all the ships.'

'It must be a grand sight all right. Will you bring me out to see it all?'

'Tomorrow after Mass we'll take a ride on the overhead railway. You get the best view from there. We'll all go,' Eddie promised.

'Overhead, is it? Isn't that a wonderful contraption altogether. And you go to Mass, too, all of you?'

'All of us,' Molly said firmly.

'Well, sometimes I do and sometimes I don't but I'm after thinking that the Good Lord will forgive a working man if he misses now and then.' They were a devout family. He'd suspected as much. He didn't often cross the doorstep of a church these days but it might well be necessary to do so for a while, until he settled in.

'So, when will you be wanting me to start, Molly?'

'On Monday, if you don't mind. Eddie kept a book of all that's owing and people tend to have money on Mondays when they've taken things back to the pawnshops.'

'So you have that custom here too. There doesn't seem to be many things that are different over here.'

'We do. It's necessary. I've had to pawn a lot of things over the years and I've been grateful for the money. Sometime tomorrow one of the lads will take you up to where Betsy's stabled and sort of . . .'

'Show me how the contraption works. I'll be honest now, I've never had much to do with horses.' Except for the kind that ran in the races at Leopardstown and Fairyhouse and the like, he thought, and most of them were running yet.

'It's dead easy, even our Bernie can put her in the shafts.'

'I could do *that* when I was young,' the lad answered, stung at the insinuation.

'He's the one with the brains in this family. We have high hopes for him,' Ellen informed him.

'Good lad yourself, Bernie. You get the hell out of these

Godforsaken slums as soon as you can,' Conor advised, beaming at the lad.

'Well, we'll have tea and then I'll introduce you to some of the neighbours – if that's all right with you? If you're tired it can wait.'

'Not at all, Molly. What are they like then?'

Ellen laughed. 'You'll see that soon enough. Do I call you Uncle Conor? You *are* Da's brother.'

'I am so. But less of the formality, everyone calls me Con so it'll be Uncle Con, does that suit you, Ellen?'

She nodded and handed him a thick slice of bread and jam, bought specially for the occasion.

Molly and Eddie accompanied him into the street where they went from door to door introducing him. He declared them to be as 'grand a set of lads you'd ever meet in a day'. He took Ozzie Ogden's offer of an introduction to the landlord of the Swan pub seriously and they went off together chatting like brothers.

'Well, that didn't take him long, did it?' Ellen remarked caustically, when Molly and Eddie returned without her uncle, and with the news that he'd gone to the pub.

'I thought he had no money?' Tom said.

'He must have a few coppers,' Eddie added.

'He probably won't need money, they'll all stand him the price of a pint, if they've got it, and it *is* his first day.' Molly tried to sound optimistic but she was concerned that he'd gone off to the pub so readily and quickly. She really would have to be firm about that.

'Shall I put his things in the front room, Mam?' Ellen

asked, indicating the parcel. He'd not even opened it.

'Just put it on the bed. I hope it'll be comfortable enough, it's the best I can do.'

'Don't worry, Mam. He's probably slept in worse beds than that. It *is* a bed, not just a donkey's breakfast of mattresses on the floor. I'm sure he's well used to sleeping on the bare boards. He hasn't even got a cap and *everyone* has a cap or a hat.'

Molly chewed her lip anxiously. 'I do hope it's going to work out, Ellen. And I'm so worried about Annie.'

'Mam, she'll be fine.'

'I know but, well, I would have thought that by now she would have paid us a visit, just to see you and Eddie.'

'Like Ellen said, Ma, she'll be fine and I don't want her coming here and showing off about the way they live up there, lording it over us all. I'll bet she's picked up their snobby ways already. She'll be wanting her tea in a cup and saucer instead of a mug.'

'Perhaps I should ask Father Healy if he's heard anything.'

'Oh, Mam, leave it. She won't thank you for going round asking about her, checking up. She'll turn up one day.'

Molly nodded and sat down at the kitchen table. Maybe she should concentrate on what was going on beneath her own roof. 'Eddie, luv, give me that book with all the names and amounts in it and I'll try and work out how much is owed, how much we think we *will* get back and just how much it's going to cost each week to keep Betsy and get supplies of coal. I want to know that much at least before we start handing things over to Conor.'

'You'll have to *tell* him what's what, he can't read, remember.'

Molly sighed. 'Really, I could do with one of you to go out with him on Monday to help out with the figures and that.'

Tom and Eddie looked at each other.

'Mam, we'd both be better going to work,' Eddie said.

'I can't miss a day either,' Tom added urgently. 'It's not a bad job and I don't want to lose it. One of the other lads was telling me that you can get transferred into the office if they think you're good enough and then it's really interesting and pays more.' Tom was enthusiastic. That's where he wanted to be, where you knew things first from the reporters, before the paper went to press. If he was moved inside then he was determined to go to night school. Most of all he wanted to be a reporter himself one day.

'Mam. Tom and Eddie are right, they need to go to work. He'll be able to remember everything you tell him. He's not a fool. But he *is* another mouth to feed and I expect he'll want some money for cigarettes and clothes and a pint.'

'You're right, Ellen. We'll need all we can get.'

Conor arrived back an hour and a half later, very merry.

'They're a grand bunch of lads, all of them. That Ozzie even offered to "help out" as he put it if I had trouble getting them to pay up.'

'Mr Ogden's helped in the past, Con, but his methods are a bit extreme.'

'I don't really think I'll be needing much help at all.

There can't be all that many people who'll give me lip.'

'No, but some of them are hard men,' Molly warned grimly. 'I mean that.'

'Hard men, how are yez! They won't be when I'm done with "persuadin' " them!'

Molly thought it was now or never to broach the subject of drink. 'I know a lot of men in the street like a pint or two—' she began, tight-lipped.

'And more than two,' he interrupted.

'Yes, well, Jack was never one for going to the pub every night and as I know you'll understand, we haven't got money to spare. I'm not saying I object to drink, I don't, a man's entitled to a pint after a day's work, if he can afford it, but ... well ... things are going to be difficult for a while yet.'

'You're asking me not to come home roaring drunk and breaking everything before me after being on the batter with the lads when I've been paid what's owing.' He smiled winningly at her. He'd have to play his cards close to his chest if he wasn't going to let the best opportunity life had ever thrown his way pass by. He'd need to learn how to handle Molly.

His elder brother had seemed to be a bit of a misery, he'd always thought, though in fact he had barely known him. His da and the mammy had returned to Dublin before he was born – God himself only knew why – leaving half the family scattered in England. Jack, who had been far older than himself, was one of those left behind.

'I'll work hard, I promise you that, Molly, and if we've the money to spare I'll stick to the one pint.'

179

Molly relaxed. Thank God he seemed to understand what she was saying. Now for the question of wages.

'Con, will you come into the front room, while we talk privately about . . . about other things?'

Now what, he wondered as he followed her.

'This is where Jack died,' she said quietly.

He crossed himself. 'God rest him and God bless the mark afterwards.'

'You won't mind?'

'Why should I? Wasn't he me own flesh and blood?'

'I really wanted to talk to you about money – wages.'

He looked at her eagerly. So, now they were getting down to it. He was prepared to be grateful for anything – for the moment.

'When we get in the debts and custom picks up again, I'll be able to pay you a proper wage. But until then I'm afraid all I can afford is money for tobacco and one pint per night.'

He nodded. It was a start. 'That'll be great, Moll. Haven't you given me a home and my meals. That'll do nicely.'

She was relieved and smiled at him.

'Thanks, Con, I was a bit bothered about . . . about that.' She began to cough.

'That's a fine cough you have there, Molly. Shouldn't you go to the Dispensary for something for it?'

'If it hasn't gone in a week or two I will. I think it's all the dust in the air.'

'Well, you take care of yourself,' he said solicitously, 'you take care now.'

* * *

Conor did work hard, and in two weeks all the debts were paid, even the ones owed by the McNallys.

'Did you have any trouble with them?' Molly asked.

'Divie a bit! Didn't I give them the choice? "Pay up," I says, "or you'll be after getting a visit from meself and me brothers. We've come over to help out." '

He didn't have a pint until the first week was over and then he'd had to stand a couple of the lads a drink. 'They were a bit short and didn't they all set me up on the first night I was here,' he said to Molly and she'd had to agree. With the money he'd collected, her wage, Ellen's and the cash coming in from the two lads, plus a few new customers, life had begun to improve again.

Slowly she began to replace the things she'd had to sell and none of them went hungry any more. Their clothes improved too. But no matter how much you tried to do up the house, it was still an insanitary slum property. The heat as the summer progressed didn't help, and there was a rumour that cholera had again struck the city.

By July Conor had begun to come in later and later, showing all the signs of drink.

'Oh, Mam, he's going to have us on the Parish,' Ellen said fearfully, one afternoon.

'I know. He's got the business going again and we've got as many customers now as we had just before your da died but he's spending more and more of the profits. I'm really going to have to say something.'

'It's partly that Ozzie's fault, he encourages him. He's always saying Ozzie's done this and Ozzie's done that,' Ellen said.

'I know that too, luv,' Molly agreed.

'Do you think if you had a word with Mrs Ogden?'

'I can't see that doing much good. I know she stands up to him but she often gets a belt. But I suppose I can try.'

Molly decided to go and see Tessie first, before tackling Con when he came in later.

As usual Tessie was standing in her doorway, waiting to have a word with anyone who passed. And as usual there was a gang of scruffy lads camped on the doorstep, all of them hers.

'Tessie, can I have a word? Inside?'

'Come on in, Molly. The place is a pigsty, what with all them bloody kids, that's why they're all sittin' on the step,' Tessie complained as Molly followed her down the dark, fetid, airless lobby that smelled of old vegetables and urine. 'I 'ate the school 'olidays, they'd drive yer ter drink!'

'That's just what I've come to talk about.'

'Well then I must be a bloody expert. Sit down an' tell me what's up.'

Molly looked around for somewhere to sit and Tessie gathered up a pile of what looked like rags, but which Molly knew to be clothing, and dumped it on the floor in a corner. The room was stifling; a fire burned in the range.

'Con is what's up. He's drinking us into debt.'

'An' I'm an expert on tharran all.'

Molly was choosing her words with care. Tessie was a formidable woman and she certainly didn't want to get on the wrong side of her.

'He seems to have become great mates with your Ozzie and, well . . . Tessie, you're a reasonable, tolerant woman and you know I've got respect for you and I'll always be thankful for how you helped after Jack's death but . . .'

'I know what you're sayin', girl, an' I agree. Ozzie's leadin' 'im on, straight ter the bar of the Swan. I 'aven't 'ad more than a shillin' offen that feller all week, an' I'm gettin' ready for a bust-up meself. What do yer want me ter do, Moll?'

'Could you have a word with Ozzie, ask him – for Jack's sake, and ours – not to encourage Con?'

'Oh, I'll 'ave a word, burrit won't do no good, it's like talkin' ter a bloody wall. God knows I've tried meself.'

'I know you have, Tessie, he's led you a right dance. But this is a bit different, it's not family, it's us. Stress that, and that it's for all our sakes?'

Tessie nodded. 'I'll try, Moll. Didn't yer keep us in coal all bloody winter? We'd 'ave froze stiff but fer yer kindness. God luv yer.'

'Thanks, Tessie. I'm going to have a talk to Conor tonight when he gets in.'

'Well, the best of luck to yer. By the way, Moll, 'ow's your Annie? I haven't set eyes on 'er fer months.'

Molly sighed. 'She's another problem. *We* haven't seen sight nor sign of her since she went up there to live. She does get time off but she's never once been home. I wish she would, for Eddie's sake.'

'Count yer blessin's, I wish 'alf of this lot would clear off and not come back. I'll not gerra bit of peace out of them until they've got me six feet under. Maybe then they'll be sorry, when it's too bloody late.'

'I know. Maybe I will ask Father Healy if he can find out if she's doing all right.'

'If it sets yer mind at rest then ask. Kids! They're nothin' but trouble an' heartache an' what do yer get out of them when yer've fed an' clothed them? Nothin'. Bloody nothin'.'

Molly didn't share Tessie's view but she nodded her agreement and went home.

Chapter Fifteen

As Molly walked back she tried to think of what she could say to Conor. It was still hot even though the heavy summer dusk was falling. The pavements seemed to hold the fierce heat of the sun and flies buzzed and hovered around the rubbish in the gutters. She wrinkled her nose in distaste. Even at this distance she could smell the privies in number 3 Court.

'Ellen, Eddie, do you think that when Con comes home you could find something – anything – to do so I can talk to him?'

'Yes, but don't you think it best if Eddie or me stays with you?' Ellen was concerned.

'No, luv, I don't. If there's to be a row then I don't want you getting involved.'

Reluctantly they'd agreed, promising to get Tom out of the way too. If they stayed in the house they would hear everything, the walls were so thin.

They were as good as their word. Molly was alone, apart from Bernie who was already in bed, as she leaned against the framework of the front door and looked up and down the street. The lamplighter was working his way towards her and she could see other women and girls sitting on their doorsteps where it was marginally cooler than in the oppressive houses.

As she caught sight of him she went indoors to the empty kitchen and waited for him to join her.

'You're late again, Con, I've had to keep your meal warm so it's a bit dried up.' She didn't look at him as she removed the plate from the oven.

He frowned. He was getting a bit fed up with her dictatorial manner lately. She'd probably given Jack a dog's life. That was probably why he'd never gone drinking. You can bet she wore the trousers in this house, he thought irritably.

'It's very warm and working with the coal gives you a fierce thirst.'

'I know,' she said, quickly but firmly. 'Jack always said he didn't know which was worse, winter or summer.'

He looked down at the dried-up mince and potatoes with distaste.

She caught the look. 'If you'd have come home from the pub earlier it wouldn't be like that.' This annoyed him even more.

'Oh, for God's sake, Molly, don't start giving out to me now. I'm hungry and tired.'

'But not thirsty, I notice. *I'm* tired working in that place all day, coming home and having to cook and clean. Ellen and Eddie are tired – and Tom. Even Bernie's gone to bed without the usual performance. You promised, Con, that you'd only have a pint on your way home.'

He stared at her, his eyes narrowing. 'I did not. I said I

wouldn't be coming home roaring drunk and breaking everything before me. *That's* what I said and I'm not doing that.'

'No, you're not, Con, I'll give you that, and it's just what I *don't* want you to do because the business is picking up. I want to get another horse and cart for Eddie. He used to go out each day with Jack, driving the second cart.'

'Doesn't the lad like his work? Isn't he always going on about the ships and the foreign fellers on them? He might not *want* to be after driving a horse and cart.'

'He does like the docks but I can't forget that Jack always dreamed of a family firm.'

'Well, Jack's not here, is he? So leave the lad alone!'

She shook her head. 'No. We'll have another cart, but I won't be able to afford it if you keep on drinking the profits!'

She was greedy, he thought. He was happy enough to go on like this, but obviously she wasn't and it was greed and social position that drove her. A family firm, would you believe! Those ambitions were bad enough in a man; in a woman they were terrible.

She was going on still. 'I want you to promise me you'll go back to your one or maybe two pints, please? It's for all our sakes, Con.'

He was losing his temper with her. 'There wouldn't *be* any profits but for me!' he burst out. 'You'd be in the workhouse.'

Molly too was becoming annoyed by his attitude. 'No, we wouldn't! I would never, never have allowed us to get to that level.'

'It was you who wrote pleading with me to come over. Saying you couldn't manage.'

'We couldn't, but I was also offering you more than just a job. I was offering you a home and a business.'

He laughed derisively. 'You call this . . . this hovel a home?'

'It's far better than the one you had in Dublin, I'm sure. You shared a room with four other men.'

'I see you've been talking to Tessie, otherwise you wouldn't be knowing that,' he snarled. 'Now you just listen to me, I'm not taking any orders from you, though Jack probably had to. *I'll* do as *I* please.'

Molly's temper grew. 'Not while you're living under *my* roof you won't, and not while you're frittering away *my* business. I'd thought I might eventually make you a partner in it, but now . . .'

He roared with laughter. 'Begod, you're a desperate snob of a woman. Wouldn't you think it was some big fancy firm you had already. All it is is a creaking, rickety cart and an old nag that's ready for the knacker's yard to pull it.'

'It keeps a roof over your head, food in your belly, clothes on your back and money in your pocket!'

He got up, his face red with fury. '*My* roof, *my* business! Here, take *your* bloody dinner, I don't want it!' He threw the plate at the range and it broke. The remains of his dinner stuck to the oven door. 'You're a miserable old bitch, but don't think you can order me around the way you obviously did Jack. I'm off to the Swan for last orders.'

The whole room seemed to shake as he slammed the door behind him.

Molly stood pale and shaking, not knowing what to do.

'Mam, are you all right? What was he yelling for?' Ellen asked as she came in from the back yard.

'Oh, Ellen, I think I've made a very big mistake.'

'Why?' Eddie looked very concerned.

'He . . . he's going to do as he pleases, so he says.'

'It might only be a row, Ma. He might cut his drinking down. He's never been like this before.'

'I know, Eddie. All we can do is wait and see.' She tried to sound hopeful but her heart was heavy. Just what could she do? She couldn't physically throw him out. She couldn't go down to the bar of the Swan and order him home. Well, she could but she dreaded to think of the consequences. She was not Tessie Ogden. 'It . . . it . . . may all have been an act, this hard-working, good-tempered joking man.'

'Oh, Mam, I hope not,' Ellen said fearfully.

'Put the kettle on, luv, please. I don't feel very well.'

'You don't look very well, it's all the upset. Sit down, Mam.'

Molly sank gratefully down on the only easy chair and leaned back. She felt exhausted and this weather was not helping. She sat up again as she began to cough.

'Mam, please will you do something about that cough? You've had it for ages now.'

'It's just the weather, Ellen, it'll go when it gets cooler.'

'Mam, you should go and see Dr Jenkinson, he'll give you something for it. And give up that job. It's too much.'

'I wish I could, Ellen, but how can I with him drinking?'

'We managed before, Ma. We've all got jobs.' Eddie too was concerned.

'That's not the point. Oh, I know you mean well, Eddie, but it's the business. Your da's business that he wanted us all to benefit from. A better life for us all, that was his dream, and I can't give it up. Somehow or other I'm going to have to try and get Con to see that.'

'Drink this up, Mam, I'll clean up the range. Then go to bed. You're worn out now and you've to be up at five.' Ellen shook her head despairingly. 'I really wish you'd give that job up.'

'Well, I can't and that's that.'

Molly went to bed but she couldn't sleep. Ellen came up but even after her daughter was asleep she still listened for Conor to come back in. Eventually she heard the yard door slam. Then she heard him moving around the kitchen and then there was the crash of dishes. She couldn't just lie here and let what bit of a home she had managed to build again be destroyed. She got out of bed, careful not to wake Ellen, and went downstairs, her bare feet silent on the wood and lino.

He was slumped across the table. It was the clean mugs and plates that he'd broken. They lay in fragments on the floor. Ellen always set the table for breakfast before she went to bed.

Anger surged through her. She wasn't going to stand by and do nothing. She caught his shoulder and shook him hard.

'Con! Conor! Wake up! I'm not standing for this, do you hear me?'

He raised his head and looked at her with bloodshot eyes. 'Bugger off an' leave me alone, woman!'

'No, I will not! You'll cut this drinking out or—'

He got to his feet very unsteadily. 'Or you'll what?'

The smell of beer on his breath made her lean backwards and avert her head. 'You stink!'

He caught her by the arm. 'I said, "Or you'll what?" ' He laughed. 'There's nothing you *can* do. I'll do as I please!'

'Take your hands off me, Conor Ryan! The men in this street have been good to me.'

He laughed again. 'So you're going to ask them to give me a belt or two to keep me in line, is that what you're thinking? Well, I've got news for you. They all think I'm a grand feller and that you're nothing but a greedy, nagging, whining old cow.'

Her cheeks burned. 'Then I'll go to the priest.'

He let out a roar of laughter. 'The Father is it? And what'll he do? Fine me six Our Fathers and six Hail Marys? I hate the bloody clergy! Sitting in their Parish Houses, stuffed with food and drink, roasting themselves in winter by a big fire and waited on hand and bloody foot by the Housekeeper. What do they know about poverty? What do they *do* about it? Nothing. Go and tell the Father, I couldn't care less!'

She was fuming. So, this was why Jack had never bothered with his young brother. 'Then I'll go to the police.'

'I haven't broken the law and setting the police on me won't go down well with the lads. Oh, no it won't! Not a bit.'

Molly cast off his grip. 'Oh, go to hell!'

'I probably will but you can sit there while I tell you what I intend to do.' He caught her arm again and pushed her down on to a wooden chair.

'You take your hands off Mam.'

Conor looked up to see Ellen standing in the doorway with Eddie and Tom behind her.

'Begod! It's a deputation!'

'You're drunk. You're disgusting.'

'You mind your mouth, girl.'

'Touch her and Ma and I'll go for the scuffers,' Eddie warned.

'Ah, to hell with the lot of you!' he yelled and pushed past them into the lobby and his own room.

'Mam, why did you come down again?' Ellen demanded. 'Why didn't you just leave him?'

Molly pointed to the broken crockery on the floor and sat down. She felt terrible. She was sweating, yet she felt cold and she was shaking. Her heart was thudding in her chest and she had the beginnings of a headache.

Ellen got a brush and dustpan from the scullery and started to clear up. 'You're not going to that place tomorrow, Mam. You're ill and all this doesn't help.'

Molly could only nod. The way she felt she couldn't face the Immigrant House.

She slept badly and Ellen made her stay in bed the next morning.

'I can see to the breakfast, Mam, and I'll make Eddie get *him* out of the bed you paid for.'

She sighed with gratitude. 'You're a good girl, Ellen.'

'Well, I'm not having him upset you like this. Try and rest now.'

Ellen was surprised when Bernie informed her that

Con had already left the house.

'Did he say anything?' she asked.

'No. He didn't look very happy though. I don't think he was feeling very well.'

'Good!' Ellen said with satisfaction. 'Right, seeing as you're the only one ready, you can take this tea up to Mam. I'll have to get some more mugs today to replace those *he* smashed.'

'Did he break the dishes? I didn't hear it.' Bernie was disappointed to have missed a row that included throwing dishes. He could have told his mates about it.

'Yes, he did and be thankful you didn't hear it,' she replied, trying to get her own things together.

Once the family had all gone out and the house was quiet Molly felt she couldn't spend any more time in bed. Unless you were desperately ill it was sheer idleness.

She began to tidy up the kitchen but kept having to sit down. She felt exhausted, and was having difficulty breathing.

'Are yer there, Moll?'

Gussie's voice forced her to get up.

' 'Aven't yer gone ter work, luv?'

'No.'

'God, yer look terrible! Sit down an' give me that brush.'

'Oh, I don't know what's wrong with me, Gussie. I think it's the heat.'

'I know. Our 'ouse is like a bloody furnace an' the sweat's drippin' off me already an' it's only nine o'clock. I wish ter God it would break. Is everything all right? I couldn't 'elp but 'ear, luv.'

'You mean the rows?'

'Aye, the rows. What's that feller me lad been up to?'

'Drinking the profits, Gussie, and when I told him I wasn't going to stand for it he started yelling and then went back to the pub. It was when he came back that there was the second row, but at least he's gone out today.'

'I never really trusted 'im, Moll. 'Is eyes is too close tergether fer a start.'

Molly wondered what on earth her neighbour meant but further deliberations were cut short by the appearance of Tessie Ogden in the scullery doorway. Tessie was a more frequent visitor these days and real friendship had grown between herself and Molly.

'I seen your Ellen, earlier, like, an' she said yer were took bad.'

'Oh, I'm not that bad, Tessie, but thanks for calling. Come in. Gussie and I were just talking about meladdo.'

'Aye, well, it's 'im I've cum ter talk about an' all,' Tessie said.

'Molly 'ad high ding dong with 'im last night and if yer ask me 'e's a flamin' no-mark an' I don't care where 'e cum from. 'E fell on 'is feet 'ere all right,' Gussie informed her.

'Our Ozzie cum home near paralytic last night. Said Con 'ad bought 'im ale an' whiskey.'

Molly groaned.

'E's drinkin' 'er out of house, 'ome an' business,' Gussie stated.

'Then what I've cum ter tell yer will only make things worse. I'm sorry, Moll, yer a real good neighbour an' friend.'

'Yer are indeed,' Gussie added.

'Well, like I said, Ozzie was shootin' 'is gob off, 'e were that bevvied. An' 'e was tellin' me that that feller 'as been bettin' on the 'orses, dead heavy too.'

'Who with?' Gussie asked.

'That little cross-eyed feller from the court, yer know 'im, Gussie.'

'Yer mean Tommy Grady?'

'That's 'im. 'E's a runner for Big Jim Sampson!'

Molly's hand went to her throat. 'Oh, God! Is he in debt, Tessie?'

'Yeah, afraid so, girl. It's not shillin's either, it's pounds.'

Molly wiped the beads of sweat from her forehead with the back of her hand. 'Oh, Tessie, what am I going to do with him?'

'I'll tell yer what *I'm* goin' ter do. I'm goin' round ter see that Sampson feller an' tell 'im iffen 'e takes any more bets for meladdo I'll leave 'im fer dead. I'll take the bloody poker to 'im an' I'll be beltin' 'im where it really 'urts iffen yer get my meanin'.'

' 'E's terrified of yer, Tessie, that'll fix 'im,' Gussie said with satisfaction.

'Thanks, Tessie, but won't he only go and find another runner, another bookie?' Molly pointed out.

'I suppose 'e will, but it'll give yer some time ter sort things out, like.'

Molly sank back into her seat. 'I don't know if I'm ever going to "sort things" as far as he's concerned. I wish to God I'd never got in touch with him.'

'God, yer look terrible,' Tessie said, suddenly concerned.

'Yer do, Moll,' Gussie agreed.

'It's just the shock and I'm worn out. I'll be fine when I've . . .' The rest of her words ended in a bout of coughing and the two women looked at each other.

'Pass 'er that birrof cloth, Tessie. Gerrit up off yer chest, Molly. 'Ere, 'ave this.' Gussie passed the makeshift handkerchief to Molly who pressed it to her mouth, nodding her thanks.

'Will I go fer the tanner doctor?' Tessie asked.

Molly shook her head but when she took the cloth away she stared at it in horror and then looked up at her neighbours.

'Oh, Jesus, Mary an' Joseph!' Gussie cried, crossing herself. There was blood on the cloth.

'I'm goin' fer that doctor feller,' Tessie said firmly.

'No! No, please, Tessie!' Molly pleaded.

'Yer can go to one of them nice places an' get better.'

'I can't. When have the likes of us ever been sent to one of those hospitals? Please don't tell anyone. Not a single soul. Promise me? Promise me?' she begged.

'Rest easy, Moll, we promise, don't we, Gussie?'

'We do an' if there's anythin', luv . . .'

'I know.'

'It's that bloody place up at the Pier Head. That bloody Immigrant 'Ouse. That's where yer caught it. Yer shouldn't 'ave gone near them dirty foreigners. They shouldn't be let in 'ere, we've gorrenough diseases around 'ere without them bringin' more.'

Molly lay back and closed her eyes. The spasm had tired her even more and she realised that Gussie was right. She had picked up consumption and there was no cure for it.

She'd known, deep down, that this was the truth but she'd put off telling anyone for as long as she could. She couldn't hide it any longer.

Chapter Sixteen

Annie wiped her mouth with her handkerchief and leaned against the bedframe. She'd never been so sick before. She'd have to empty the chamber pot before she went down. She stood up but the dizziness overcame her again and she lay down on the bed, wishing she could just stay there. But she couldn't, she'd have to get dressed and go down and start her work.

She sat up and the nausea swept over her again. She must have caught something or maybe eaten something. She would see if anyone else was complaining of being sick.

The kitchen, as usual, looked bright and clean in the slanting rays of the sun that streamed in through the basement window. This was a basement she'd never seen the like of before. All the others she'd known were dark, damp and occupied by a large family. Thank God there was no range to clear out although she did still have to blacklead it. The weather had become so hot that Cook had given in and now used the gas cooker regularly although she continually complained about it.

She filled the kettle and then started to lay the table.

She was beginning to feel a bit better, and it was her half-day today. She had the afternoon to herself but it was so hot that she thought she might just rest on her bed. She'd just picked up the lacquered tea caddy when the realisation hit her so hard that she had to lean against the table for support. She'd always been a bit irregular with the 'curse' and she'd put it down to the miserable life she led. Oh, Holy Mother of God! There had been nothing for months and now the sickness. She was pregnant! She didn't want to believe it but she *had* to. She sat down, the tea caddy clutched tightly to her chest. Oh, it was the end of everything. Her world was falling down around her. Everything had gone. Her job, her reputation, her youth! She didn't want to be a mother. She was only just nineteen. She hadn't done anything with her life. There'd been precious few exciting experiences so far and now this. Oh, it was the worst thing that could happen to a young unmarried girl. She felt sick again and the perspiration broke out on her forehead.

Over the months she'd refused to dwell on the night of the party. She'd pushed it to the back of her mind . . .
'Haven't you even made the tea yet?' Collins's voice broke through her stunned reverie.

'No, I . . . I . . . don't feel very well.'

'You look awful. I hope you've not got anything contagious.'

'Who's contagious?' Cook demanded as she entered and caught the end of the parlour maid's statement.

'Ryan might be.'

'What's up with you, girl?'

'I . . . I feel sick and hot and cold and I'm sweating.'

'Perspiring,' Collins corrected. 'Only men and horses sweat. Ladies perspire.' Although you couldn't call a slummy a 'lady', she thought spitefully. Once a factory girl, always a factory girl.

'How long have you felt like this?' Cook demanded.

'Only since I got up, ma'am.'

'You don't look well, I'll say that. We'll see how you go this morning and then Mrs Hinchey and I will decide whether the doctor should be called in.'

'Yes, ma'am. Thank you.' Annie fervently hoped the doctor wouldn't be called. He'd know for sure what was wrong with her. She'd have to pretend she was well and this afternoon she would go and see Josie's mam, because she knew just who had got her into this state. Freddie Rafferty. She'd never known for sure just what *had* happened that night. When she'd mentioned it to Josie her friend had laughed and said it was a known fact that you never got caught the first time you did it and was amazed that Annie thought that she and her brother's mate had 'gone all the way'.

'Jesus, Annie! Don't yer know nothin'? I wouldn't let any feller do *that*, me mam'd kill me! A bit of messing about all right and I do get all excited, but I always stop before . . . that.'

She remembered Josie's words now. She began to shake but tried to calm herself and think. He'd have to marry her, that was the only solution. He'd *have* to.

She managed to pull herself together and at lunchtime she was so hungry she ate everything put down before her.

'Well, Ryan, you seem to be much better now,' Cook remarked.

'I am, thank you, ma'am.'

'I don't think we need to trouble anyone.'

'No, no, I . . . we don't,' she agreed hastily.

She finished her meal in silence, ignored – as usual – by everyone and after she'd washed the dishes and tidied everything away she went to her room to get changed.

'Off out, I see? Not much wrong with you now,' Collins remarked acidly as Annie went through the kitchen. Annie ignored her.

All the way on the tram she was trying to think how she could put it. She didn't even know if Freddie was at home or away. She'd never asked Josie for she didn't see much of her friend now. In the weeks after the party she'd stayed in. She'd not once been into town. She'd helped out wherever she was needed and she did it gratefully, thankful that she'd been given a second chance.

Freddie wasn't so bad, she told herself. He was handsome, he had a steady job, and as his wife he'd leave her a monthly allotment, a sum of money deducted from a merchant seaman's pay by the company and paid out to the wife or mother or anyone else he designated. She hardly knew him though. Face it, she thought, she didn't know him at all. He was a stranger and that made it far worse. Oh, God, what a mess! Why had she even gone to that flaming party and why oh why had she drunk so much?

The hot August sun beat down on her when she got off the tram. It was so hot that the tar on the pavements was bubbling and kids were taking great delight in bursting the bubbles with a stick to which the tar would stick fast. 'Tar Babies', they were known as and they were the bane of every mother's life as the tar stuck to clothes and hair as well.

She was rapidly losing her nerve and the heat and the stench were making her feel sick. Since living in Newsham Park she'd forgotten how these narrow streets of back-to-back houses stank and just how filthy everything was.

The Raffertys' door was wide open, as was every door of every house in the street, and she didn't bother to knock. She looked around. The paint was peeling and flaking. There were big patches of damp, even though it was summer. The banister rail was missing, as were some of the stair treads. Used for firewood, no doubt. There was a collection of accumulated junk in the space under the stairs and the whole house smelled. God, what a contrast to Newsham Park, she thought as she went down the lobby. She saw Josie's mam in the kitchen sitting on an old upholstered tub chair, fanning herself with some folded pages from the *Echo*.

'Well, look who it is! We 'aven't seen yer around 'ere fer months, Annie. Our Josie's at work.'

'I know that, Mrs Rafferty.'

'Sit down before yer fall down, girl, yer look shockin'. What's up with yez?'

Annie was thankful for the support of the chair for her knees were trembling. She was so nervous she could barely speak.

'Is . . . is . . . Freddie home?'

'Yes, 'e's due ter sail on Friday. 'E's out now. Gone ter

Greenwood's fer a new set of Tropical Whites although they won't stay bloody white fer long on that bloody auld ship. What did yer want 'im fer? Anything special, like?' It had to be special to bring the girl down here from the big posh house she worked in.

'Sort of.' Oh, how could she go on? But she *had* to. Maybe it would be better if she waited until he was home.

'How long do you think he'll be?'

'Dunno. 'E might 'ave a bevvie on the way 'ome, like.'

She couldn't sit here for hours. What if he didn't come home until late and was drunk? She'd get no sense out of him, and she had to be back by five o'clock. No, she couldn't wait.

'Oh, Mrs Rafferty, I'm in terrible trouble.' Tears brimmed over and ran down her cheeks.

'What's up, Annie?'

'At the party for . . . for Freddie . . . well, I had too much to drink.'

'Didn't we all, girl. Isn't that one of the points of 'aving a do in the first place?'

Annie nodded. 'Well . . . when . . . when I woke up, I . . .' She stopped and bit her lip. God, it was awful! Her cheeks were burning.

'Go on then, Annie. 'As the cat got yer tongue?'

'When I woke up I was in bed. In bed . . . with . . .'

'With our Freddie? Is that what you're tryin' ter tell me?'

Annie nodded.

Mrs Rafferty's attitude changed completely. 'Yer little tart! Yer bloody little 'ussy!'

'I don't remember anything! I passed out!'

'Oh, I see, it's all 'is fault, is it?'

'I . . . I don't know, but now . . . now I'm . . .'

'You're in the club an' you're blamin' it on our Freddie?'

'It's got to be him!'

'How the 'ell do I know that? It could be anyone's. Iffen yer fell into bed with 'im 'ow many more 'ave there been? An' you with all the airs an' graces. Blamin' my lad, the only decent one amongst all of them. Oh, I can see what yer game is. 'E's a 'andsome lad with a good job and 'e's away fer most of the year so yer wouldn't really 'ave ter purrup with 'im for long. Yer could do what yer like, an' with an allotment too. I didn't cum over on the last boat, girl! I've cum across the likes of youse before. You're nothin' but a little whore! Out for what yer can get, latchin' on fer a good thing. Well, yer'll get no joy out of 'im or me. Clear off! Go to buggery! You an' yer bastard!'

Horrified, Annie fled. As she ran down the street she couldn't see where she was going. Blinded by her tears, she wanted to get away from here as quickly as she could. But where could she go? She stumbled on a tram to the Pier Head and then managed to buy a return ticket for the ferry to Birkenhead. As the *Iris* drew away from the Landing Stage she stood on the top deck, gripping the handrail and sobbing out her despair. 'You an' yer bastard.' It was like a refrain, she couldn't banish it from her mind. Her child would be a bastard, shunned by everyone, and she'd be an outcast. He wouldn't marry her, not if his mam told him that she doubted the baby was his. She'd tell him they didn't know how many other lads there had been. Her sobs racked her. She'd lose her job. How would she manage? She knew there were women who 'helped' girls in this state but she had no money to pay them and besides it was murder, so the priests were always saying, and she couldn't do that.

She looked over the side and saw far below her the sluggish water of the river. It was deceptive, there were currents and tides. It would be over soon: she couldn't swim. But again the Church's view rang out in her mind. It was a sin. A mortal sin. Only God had the right to take a life. There was no way out there.

When the ferry boat docked and the passengers got off and a new set got on she was still standing, clutching her ticket, the tears running down her cheeks. In the distance, across the Mersey, the buildings of the waterfront seemed to shimmer in the heat haze. It was a beautiful day for a sail but to her the world seemed desperately dark. She stood motionless until they arrived back at the Landing Stage. She knew there was only one thing she could do. She crossed to the tram terminus and sat down on one that would take her back to Milton Street. She was utterly devastated.

Only Molly was in when Annie walked through the kitchen door and she was shocked by the change in her stepmother. She looked ill herself. She'd lost weight and she looked old and haggard.

Molly looked up from her chair. 'Annie! This is a nice surprise. Come and sit down, luv.'

Annie did so gladly but wondered how much longer it

would be before Molly's attitude changed to outrage and hostility.

'How are things at work? Do you like it any better than the factory?'

'No, I hate it. They still treat me like a . . .' She was about to say 'common tart' but stopped herself. It was too apt a description. 'They don't like me at all.'

'Oh, that's such a shame. You're a good worker and a pleasant girl. They must be very snobby.'

'They are.'

'Haven't you made any new friends? Or does Josie come around?'

Annie felt her stomach tie into a knot. 'No, I've no friends and I don't see Josie much at all. She's at work when I'm off and I'm at work . . .' She couldn't go on with this polite conversation. She broke down. 'Oh, Ma! Ma! I'm in terrible trouble and it wasn't my fault! It *wasn't*! I . . . I . . . swear it on Mam's grave!'

Molly got up and took the weeping girl in her arms. 'What is it, Annie? It can't be that bad. Why have you got yourself into this state? Is it something to do with Josie? Has she been calling at the house and making a show of you?'

'No. No, it's nothing like that.'

'Then what *is* it, luv?' Molly pressed.

Haltingly, Annie told her. Molly listened with growing despair to the all-too-familiar story. The girl was a fool but she felt that she herself was partly to blame. She should have made more of an effort with Annie after Jack died. She should have gone up to the house to see how the girl was getting on but there was always something else to be done. Something more deserving of her time, but there should never have been anything more important than Jack's daughter. She'd not known how desperately lonely Annie had been and most of all she should have kept a very watchful eye on that little madam, Josie Rafferty.

The girl clung to her as Molly tried to soothe her. 'It's all right, Annie, hush now, you mustn't get all upset, it's not good for you.'

Annie's sobs subsided gradually and Molly sat her down and put the kettle on.

'What . . . what will I do?'

Molly sighed. She was shocked and she was angry, but not with Annie. The girl's only sin was that she had been foolish.

'Don't say anything to anyone in Newsham Park until it becomes noticeable. Then you can leave and come here.'

Annie gazed at her with astonishment. She was so calm. There had been no shouting or yelling. 'You mean . . . ? You mean you won't send me away?'

'No. I'll be honest, Annie, I am shocked and disappointed and it won't be easy for you to hold your head up around here, but these things happen. It'll be a nine-day wonder.'

'But what about the others? Ellen?'

'Ellen will learn a valuable lesson,' was the terse reply.

'Will I be able to come and . . . visit on my days off?'

'You've always been welcome in this house, Annie. It was your mam and da's home before I came along.'

Now that some of the terrible dread about her future

had been removed, Annie began to notice how often Molly had to stop to get her breath.

'Are you sick, Ma?'

'No. It's just this heat. Everywhere is so dusty and it's getting on my chest. Have you heard that your Uncle Conor, or Con as we call him, is living here now and building up the coal business again?'

'No. I didn't know that. What will he say? About me?'

'Nothing. This is my house. I pay the rent, with my wages.'

But Molly wasn't very sure at all how Con would take this news, and he'd have to be told. Especially since Annie would now be visiting regularly.

After a much-relieved Annie had gone, Molly decided she would tell Ellen. There was no need for the lads to know yet. When her daughter arrived home she sent Bernie down to Gussie's so they could be private. The meal was ready but, as always, she'd have to put Con's in the oven. Things were very strained between them but at last, for some reason, he had curbed his drinking. Maybe because of his gambling. He didn't stay in the Swan until all hours any more, but Molly still worried about his gambling debts. She knew no more about them now than what Tessie had told her. She tried to not even think about them.

'I had a visitor this afternoon,' she told her daughter.

'Who?' Ellen was setting the table.

'Annie.'

'So, she finally landed up.'

'Ellen, don't take that attitude.'

'What did she want, Mam? Why the sudden visit after all this time?'

'She's in trouble. Ellen, I want you to promise that you'll tell no one what I am about to tell you.'

Ellen was mystified. Mam was very serious yet she'd spoken of Annie with sympathy in her voice.

'I won't.'

'She's going to have a baby.'

Ellen's hand flew to her mouth. 'A baby! Oh, God!'

'I know. It was a terrible shock to me too. She was very foolish. She was so lonely that she let Josie Rafferty take her to a party in their house. Annie had too much to drink and Freddie Rafferty took advantage of her.'

'Oh, Mam! They're a terrible family. Is he going to marry her?'

'He's not going to marry her and in one way I'm glad. They *are* a terrible family. Your da would turn in his grave if he knew she was living with one of them.'

'So what is she going to do?'

'Stay at work as long as she can and then she'll come home. She can make up her mind then whether to keep the baby or have it adopted.'

'She can get the hell out of here! There've never been any bastards in our family yet and I'm not after starting now!'

Both Ellen and Molly turned, shocked to see Con standing in the doorway. He had heard everything.

'I won't have you talking about her like that!' Molly snapped. 'She's Jack's daughter and he loved her.'

'*You* won't have it! Who is it who will have to work to

keep the bold rossi and her bastard? I'll tell you who. *Me*.
She's not setting foot over this doorstep or I'll sell the cart,
horse, the stock and goodwill and go back to Dublin with
the proceeds. That's what I'll do. You can all stew. You can
live off what you get from that Immigrant House and
manage as best you can.'

Molly went pale. Dear God, what was she to do? He was
deadly serious, she could tell. But she'd promised the girl,
although she knew what everyone would say. They'd side
with Con, who was asking – no, demanding – that she
choose between giving Annie and her baby a home and the
business Jack had held so dear and for which she'd made
so many sacrifices. The hardest one of which was putting
up with Con . . .

Chapter Seventeen

There was no time to reply to Con's demands for Eddie
had come into the kitchen followed by Tom.

'Have you washed?' Molly asked tersely.

Both boys nodded.

'Then sit down and have your meal.'

'Mam, was that you and Uncle Con fighting?' Bernie
asked.

'No, it was not. It must be Artie and Gussie, the walls
are so thin.'

Bernie opened his mouth to remonstrate, then, seeing
his mother's expression, thought better of it. Both Molly
and Ellen concentrated on serving the meal.

Con sat at the table, still in his dirty working clothes but
for once Molly said nothing.

'So, what are you going to do with her?' Con persisted.

Molly's temper flared. Why did he insist on pursuing the
subject? She wanted time to think, to decide. It would be
one of the hardest decisions she'd had to make for a long
time and surely she'd made it clear she didn't want the
boys to know yet.

'Do with who?' Eddie asked, reaching for a slice of bread.

'With that bold strap of a sister of yours.'

The lad was mystified. 'Ellen?'

'I said your *sister*.'

'Our Annie? What's the matter with her? Has she been here?'

'Oh, she's been here all right, but she won't be coming back.' Con looked malevolently at Molly.

'Does she want to come back? Does—' Tom began, but subsided when he caught a warning glance from Ellen.

'Ma, what's going on?' Eddie pleaded.

'I'll tell you what's going on. Your precious bloody sister is up the spout, that's what!'

Young Bernie looked mystified.

'Bernie, finish your tea and then take your books upstairs. You'll be going back to school soon, you'd better try and remember all the things you learned.' Molly spoke quietly, glaring at Con, daring him to speak.

They all concentrated on their meal and eventually the lad got down from the table and left the room, followed by Tom who wanted no part of the row he could see was brewing. Rows were sometimes interesting, especially at work, but not when they involved your own family.

'Annie came to see me this afternoon. She was very upset. She's been so lonely up at that place that she went to a party at Josie Rafferty's house, got drunk and . . . Freddie . . .'

'Now she's up the spout, in the club, call it what you like, the little slut is pregnant! But she's not bringing herself or her bastard here.'

214

My Sister's Child

Eddie had gone very pale and Molly looked at him anxiously.

'I wouldn't have let her marry Freddie Rafferty even if she wanted to. Your da would turn in his grave.'

'Sure, he must be spinning in it now that you think she'll be coming back here. She won't!'

'Oh, Ma! What'll happen to her?' Eddie cried, real concern mingling with the shock.

Molly shook her head and passed a hand over her aching head.

'She'll be out on the bloody street, that's what'll happen to her.'

Eddie jumped to his feet, sending the chair crashing backwards. 'She won't! I won't let her be thrown out! You've no right to say things like that. This is Ma's house. You're only a lodger!'

Con let out a roar of anger and grabbed the lad by his shirt front, then he cuffed him hard across the side of his head twice. He was about to do it a third time but both Molly and Ellen were on their feet.

'You leave him alone! Leave him alone! You're nothing but a drunk and a thief and a liar!' Ellen screamed at him.

'Don't you touch him again, Con Ryan! Let him go!' Molly felt faint but she summoned up all her strength and grabbed Con's arm.

He shoved her away as if she were merely a fly, and she fell against the table, banging her head on the back of a chair.

Ellen began to shake with temper. 'Get out! Get out of this house!' she screamed at her uncle.

Releasing Eddie he turned on Ellen – but backed off because she held the heavy brass poker in her hand. He could see by her eyes that she would use it.

'Put that bloody thing down, girl!' he commanded but there was a note of fear in his voice.

'I won't!' She was seething with fury, a force so strong and totally unexpected that she herself marvelled at it. How dare he? How dare he throw her mother across the room like that!

'I said put it . . .' His words died away and he stepped back. She'd raised the poker and was across the room like that! He'd never seen eyes so cold and hard. Like pale grey pebbles they were. He had never seen such an expression on her face – or any woman's, come to that. It was pure ice-cold fury.

Then everything happened at once. Molly screamed, Eddie yelled, Con put up his arms to shield his head, tripped over his chair and staggered just as she brought the poker down, missing him by inches.

'Ellen, for God's sake, leave him! Leave him!' Molly screamed.

'Ellen, give me the poker! Give it to me!' Eddie demanded.

Suddenly Ellen's shoulders slumped. The burning flame of anger had died.

Eddie removed the poker from her hand.

Ellen turned to her mother. 'Oh, Mam! Mam! I . . . don't know what happened to me. Something inside just . . . just snapped. I didn't mean to . . . hit him.'

Con had got up clumsily, having hurt his back as he'd

fallen. But he was clearly afraid of her. 'You're a raving bloody lunatic, you should be locked up!' he shouted. He would never forget the way she'd looked. It had to be some trait of madness in the family. She was just a slip of a thing but he had the feeling that she could have killed him.

Molly tried to calm the situation.

'It's all right, Ellen. Go and wash your face now. I'll tidy up. Eddie, go up and see that Tom and Bernie are not upset.'

'You're all mad! You belong in an asylum! I meant what I said. If the other one comes then I'm off. She's probably crazy too if the truth be known. I'm going for a sup of whiskey. I need it.'

'Mam, what are we going to do?' Ellen, trembling, whispered after he'd slammed out.

But Molly didn't hear. 'Ellen, what came over you? I could see you meant to hurt him. If you'd brought that poker down on his head you *would* have killed him and then you'd hang for it.' She was very shaken.

'I don't know what it was, Mam, really I don't. I didn't think about what would happen to me. When he started to hit Eddie I was so angry, really, really angry. And then when he went for you . . .'

'I don't know where you got such a temper from. I was furious with him but I'd never have gone that far, Ellen.'

'Well, at least it might do some good. But what will you do about Annie?'

'I don't know. I can't just abandon her, your da would never forgive me, and yet . . .'

'Could he really sell everything and go back to Dublin?'

'He could. He's so crafty that one morning we'd get up and everything . . . everything would be gone. I believe he'd do that. I think it was his intention all the time.'

'Mam, is the business really worth it?' Eddie asked. He was still shaken.

'I like to think it is, Eddie. Keeping it is sort of looking further ahead, going beyond the dream your da had.'

'Mam, you've suffered enough to keep it going, but we can't . . . we've *got* to help Annie,' Ellen pleaded.

'I know, luv, but it's a terrible decision.'

'Oh, I *hate* him! I really *hate* him!'

'She's right, Ma. I hate him too.'

Molly nodded. She couldn't help but agree. But she still had to find a way out of this terrible dilemma.

Later, when Con had come back and silently gone to his room and she'd sent both Eddie and Ellen to bed, Molly was still undecided. She sat staring into space. She couldn't abandon the girl. She'd promised. But just what *was* she to do? She sat there for a long time until the solution came to her. Annie could go to one of the homes run by the nuns for girls who had been foolish enough to believe the lies men told them. It wasn't the perfect solution but at least it would stop Con leaving, although she realised that one day he *would*. After she'd had the baby Annie could start her life again. Maybe she'd learn some kind of skill in there and have better prospects of a job when it was all over. But Molly was still dreading telling the neighbours. Her family'd be the main topic of all their gossip. Oh, what a terrible day it had been, and she still had to drag herself to work in the morning.

★ ★ ★

Molly made sure she finished early the following Wednesday for it was Annie's half-day. All week she'd been dreading it. A big black cloud seemed to have descended on everyone, except the irrepressible Bernie. She and Con barely spoke and he gave Ellen a wide berth. Eddie was very subdued, obviously shaken by that terrible night. Molly did feel a bit better, however, because the weather had broken abruptly in the form of a terrific storm, and it was now much cooler. September was upon them, summer was almost over.

'I . . . I'm here.'

Annie came hesitantly into the kitchen, wondering if her stepmother's views had changed. She had been so relieved by Molly's acceptance of the situation; in fact she could still hardly believe it.

'Come on in and sit down, Annie.'

Annie scrutinised her stepmother. 'No, you sit there, you don't look well at all.'

'Oh, I've had a lot on my mind since I saw you last. Sit down for a minute, Annie, please.'

Annie's heart sank. Something was wrong. She'd changed her mind. That *had* to be it.

'I . . . we . . . Con has put me in a terrible position.'

Annie's eyes widened. 'You won't take me in! You've changed your mind! I knew it! I knew it!' There was a sob in her voice.

'Annie, please listen to me. I haven't got much choice. He said he'd sell the business and go back to Dublin.'

'The business! The bloody business, that's all you care about!'

'That's not true! I'll take you to that house in Gambia Terrace when you have to finish work.'

'A house for fallen women! They treat you worse than you'd be treated in jail! Oh, I should have known you wouldn't take me in! I should have *known*!'

'Annie, please, it won't be that bad and I'll come and visit you every week, more if you want me to, and when it's all over you can come back. You can come home and begin your life again.'

Annie was on her feet. 'Home! Home! I'll never set foot in this place again! This is not my home! I hate you! I hate you!' And, turning, she fled along the lobby.

Molly laid her head on her arms and cried. Oh, Holy Mother of God! What would happen to the girl now? She was so weary, so afraid of the months ahead, so terrified that her cough would become worse and there would be no disguising what was causing it. She knew how it would end. With a haemorrhage. She'd seen it often enough. It would be violent and bloody and there'd be no way she could protect her children from the horror, no way.

Chapter Eighteen

As usual it was to Ellen that she turned. Never had she missed Jack so much. If he'd lived there would have been none of these catastrophes. When she'd finished unburdening herself Ellen looked at her with sympathy. She hated to see Mam so worried.

'Mam, what else could you do? He . . . he's turned out to be terrible and as for Annie, it was her own fault. She shouldn't have gone and got drunk. There's plenty of things she could have done with her time off.'

'Ellen, don't be uncharitable. Most of it's my fault.'

'No, it's *not*, Mam!' Ellen stressed. 'You tried with her, you really tried.'

'Not hard enough. I should have taken more time with her after your da died. She never accepted me as a mother and I can't blame her for that. Then losing her da and going to that place where they treat her so badly . . . I should have talked to her. Oh, Ellen, I just feel so helpless and so tired.'

'Mam, you're not well. That cough hasn't got better and the weather's changed. It's been pouring down all night. Please, Mam, give up that job?'

Molly nodded slowly. It had been harder and harder to drag herself up there and find the energy to brush and scrub. Often she had to stop and fight for breath.

Ellen sighed with relief. They could manage without the measly five shillings they paid Mam for working herself to death. There would be no more getting up at five o'clock, doing nearly a full day's cleaning, then coming home to more work.

'We'll manage, Mam. He's got more customers and at least he does give you most of the money now.'

But for how much longer? Molly thought. She knew he was still gambling and probably losing, and when he owed the bookie too much he'd sell up and leave, and then what?

Ellen was so pleased at her mother's decision that at the first opportunity she told Eddie. To her surprise the news didn't seem to cheer him at all.

'Well, what's wrong with you?' she asked, puzzled. 'It's making her ill, you can see that.'

He nodded. 'It is. Some days she looks terrible. But, Ellen, I can't stand it here any more.'

'What do you mean?' she demanded, her heart sinking.

'I've made up my mind, Ellen. I'm going away to sea.'

She was horrified. 'Eddie, you can't! You *can't* just up and leave!'

'It's something I've been thinking of doing for a while now. I want to travel, I suppose it's in my blood. Half the men in this city have salt water instead of blood in their veins and go away to sea. I love watching the ships but I'm always wishing I was on one of them.'

He looked so wistful that Ellen softened. 'What'll we

do? Even with your allotment Mam will feel she's got to go back to work and I'll . . . miss you so much and I'll have *him* to contend with.'

Eddie began to feel guilty. It wasn't fair on Ellen – on any of them – but he *had* to go. He just *had* to or he'd be as miserable as sin every time he watched a ship leave Liverpool and that meant all day, every day. 'He's scared stiff of you, Ellen. He really does think you're mad.'

She smiled ruefully. 'I suppose you could call that a good thing, though I doubt if I could do it again.'

'I'll miss all of you . . .' He twisted his cap nervously in his hand. 'You won't tell Ma, please, Ellen?'

She shrugged. 'No, it'll only make her more upset than she is.'

'I'm not like you, Ellen. I'm afraid of him, you're not.'

'Oh, I am afraid. I just don't know what came over me that night. I can't remember feeling very much at all, not after he hit you and pushed Mam. I think it was when she fell that I . . . I . . . snapped. I've often thought about it but I can't explain it.'

He realised that she'd already accepted his decision by the tone of her voice.

'When will you go?' she asked.

'As soon as I can get a ship. Any ship, but I'll try for something decent. I'll go down to the Flag of All Nations. That's where you get picked and sign articles.'

Ellen looked at him with a heavy heart. She'd miss him so much. Despite being only stepbrother and -sister there was a bond between them. Even as children they'd never fought, nor had he picked on her the way Annie had. They'd all miss him. Perhaps it would be better if she waited until he'd gone before telling anyone, at least *he* couldn't do anything to stop Eddie then and Mam couldn't beg and plead with him. Eddie wouldn't be able to bear that. He'd give in and not go, then be miserable for months, maybe years. She could understand what she'd heard described as 'the call of the sea'. He was right. Nearly all Liverpudlians made their living from the river, one way or another. It was in his blood.

Next morning Molly was so relieved not to have to go to work. She knew she was getting worse. Both Tessie and Gussie were now doing a lot of the chores for her and both of them begged her to go to see the doctor, but she refused.

'What good would it do?' she'd asked.

'I don't know, but there must be *something*, Moll.'

She'd shaken her head. 'You know there isn't, Tessie. How many people in this street have died of it? I know what's going to happen and I'm afraid. I'm so afraid, especially during the night. I think of Ellen lying beside me and know she's going to have to cope with everything. She's only just seventeen.'

'Ah, Molly, luv, don't talk like that. When the time comes, she'll have all of us to rely on, I promise.'

'But how is she going to cope with *'im*? That's what's really worrying me.'

Tessie had sighed. Ozzie would be no good at all. He wouldn't hear a thing said against bloody Con Ryan. But she had her own methods. 'I'll sort 'im out, Molly, don't yer worry about that. And she's not as 'elpless as she looks, is she? Oh, we all 'eard about the row and the poker an' all. She should 'ave given 'im a belt with it. It wouldn't 'ave done 'im any 'arm.'

'Tessie, I don't want things to get that bad again. Oh, what's going to become of them all? I've been up to that house in the park three times but Annie won't see me.'

'Then I wouldn't worry about her, Moll. Selfish, 'ardfaced little madam.'

Molly hadn't told anyone about Annie; they could see for themselves now. By October, not far off now, Annie would be showing and she'd have to give up her job. But where would she go? Oh, there were so many things to worry about. She prayed she'd be spared long enough to sort some of them out.

'Are yer there, luv?' Gussie's voice echoed down the lobby.

'Come in, Gussie, I've put the kettle on.'

'Not gone ter work then?'

'No. I've given it up. I sent our Tom with a note to deliver on his travels around town. I don't feel well enough to carry on.'

Gussie frowned. 'You're not. Now give me what washin' yer want doin', I'm goin' to the bag wash this mornin' and I 'ope the flamin' rain keeps off or I'll never gerr anythin' dry. Once it flamin' well starts it forgets ter stop an' I 'ate 'avin' it all draped around the place. After them kids 'ave finished with it, it needs doin' all over again and Artie says he can't do with the smell of wet wool!'

With some difficulty, Molly had gathered up the washing when Tessie arrived.

'I'm goin' inter town ter the market, is there anythin' yer want, Molly?'

'No, thanks, Tessie.' She almost toppled forward as a spasm of violent coughing overwhelmed her.

'Quick, Tessie, give me that tea towel!' Gussie cried as the rag Molly held to her mouth was instantly covered in blood.

'Sit down, luv, an' use this.'

Molly took the cloth. She was fighting for breath and she could feel the blood rushing up and into her mouth.

At last the spasm passed and the blood stopped coming. She stared white-faced at her neighbours. 'Oh, God help me, it's never been like that before.'

The two women exchanged glances.

'Molly, yer can't keep it from them much longer.'

'I know but . . . but I just want a bit more time.'

Gussie shook her head sadly as she added the stained cloths to the pile of washing.

Eddie had been completely overawed by the crowd of men who were packed into the Flag of All Nations. They looked so tall and so strong and he felt useless. They all seemed to have some kind of record book which they waved in the air when the name of a ship, its destination and pay were announced. But he was determined and so he worked his way to the front of the crowd and when the *Windsor Castle*, a Castle Line ship bound for the West Coast of Africa carrying the mail was announced, he waved his arms in the air and shouted his name.

'Any O.S. among you?' the man who seemed to be in

charge shouted and for a few seconds Eddie was confused. Then he remembered, they were looking for ordinary seamen not A.B.S. – able-bodied seamen – who were experienced men: stokers; trimmers; and grease monkeys, who kept the winches and other equipment in working order.

'Yes! Here, sir! Here!' he yelled as loud as he could.

'Right, get over to see the Bosun.'

He was relieved but now he had to explain away the fact that he'd never sailed before.

'Where's your Discharge Book, lad?'

'I . . . I'm sorry, sir, I don't have one.'

'Lost it? Had it stolen? The usual excuses for idle layabouts.'

'No, sir, I meant I've never had one.'

'You've never sailed before?'

'No, sir, but I really want to go. I'll do any job, anything at all. I'm a fast learner. Please, give me a chance.'

'Do your mam and dad know?'

'My da's dead, sir, and Mam, well . . .'

'All mothers are the same. They never want to let their lads go away to sea. What's your name and how old are you?'

'My name's Edward – Eddie – Ryan, sir, and I'm nearly twenty-one.'

'That's what they all say. But I'll give you a try. Turn up tonight at eight at the East Waterloo Dock. She sails at ten on the tide. Get yourself some sea boots and oilskins, a plate, mug, knife and fork. She feeds well but she's not a floating palace! Here, take this and sign it.'

He held out the coveted Discharge Book: a sailor's passport and record of achievement – or lack of it. It would be stamped by an officer when the voyage was over.

When he was outside he could have danced for joy! Tonight! By tonight he'd be away. Off on the big adventure. Then he began to think more clearly. He'd have to get all the things that the older man had mentioned. Oh, the mug and things he could take from home, but boots and oilskins? He'd have to take the afternoon off. That wasn't unusual. Some afternoons he didn't get picked for work anyway. He suddenly remembered that he'd not asked what the pay was or who the Allotment should be left for.

He had a few pounds saved up so he went first to Greenwoods, the naval outfitters, and bought the boots and waterproofs, plus a thick, heavy navy blue woollen jumper and socks. He would have to leave them in the yard and hope no one noticed them.

He was already in when Ellen came home from work. She looked at him hard. He was bursting with something.

'Mam, just let me wash my hands and I'll help you,' she said, staring at Eddie and jerking her head in the direction of the scullery.

'What now?' she whispered.

'I've got a ship.'

'Already? Where is she going?'

'Africa. She's one of the Union Castle boats, carrying the mail.'

'How long will you be away?'

'About two months, I think.'

'Oh, Eddie! That long? When do you sail?'

'Tonight. I've to be down at the East Waterloo Dock at eight!'

'*Tonight!*' Ellen forgot to whisper.

'Hush! I know it's short notice, but I was lucky to get it. I've got my things in a parcel in the back yard but I'll need my clothes and a knife and fork, plate and mug.'

'What am I going to say to Mam?'

'Tell her I'm sorry I left in such a hurry but it's something I've wanted to do for a long time and it's a decent ship. I forgot to ask how much the pay is or about the allotment, but I suppose I can do that when I'm aboard and then they'll get word to the office in the morning.'

'Oh, I just wish we'd had more time.'

'Will you come and see me off? I'd like our Tom to come too. We sail at ten.'

'What kind of an excuse can I make for being out until that time of night – and our Tom too?'

'Well, can you just come down with me at eight then?'

'I suppose so. I don't know about Tom though, but I'll try.'

Ellen turned to more practical matters. She'd think about excuses after tea. 'What will you use to carry everything?'

'I got a second-hand seabag.'

'Well, at least that's something. Come on now or Mam will begin to suspect something.'

All through the meal Ellen was desperately trying to think of an excuse.

'Mam, a bit later on I'm going to try and see our Annie. She might listen to me.' Oh, she hated to use her unfortunate stepsister, who so far had refused any of them, as an excuse, but she couldn't think of anything else.

'I'll go with you, Ellen,' Eddie chipped in, 'maybe I can talk her around.'

'I don't think it'll do much good, but I suppose it's worth a try,' Molly replied wearily, feeling the choking sensation that preceded a bout of coughing. She excused herself and went upstairs as quickly as she could.

It was a fairly mild night and the sky seemed full of stars.

'Just think, Ellen, I'll still be able to see those stars but I'll be miles away.'

She didn't answer. Now that he was going she felt lost and unhappy. They walked along the Dock Road in silence until they turned into the East Waterloo Dock.

'The *Windsor Castle* please, sir?' Eddie asked of the policeman on the dock gate.

'Straight down there, lad, but you'd better not go on board, girl.'

'I won't. I'm his sister and I've come to see him off.'

'It's my first trip,' Eddie said by way of explanation. He didn't like the expression on the policeman's face. He thought Ellen was a tart.

'Then I hope you're a good sailor because I've heard there's some bad weather coming in.'

'He'll be fine,' Ellen answered.

The ship was ablaze with lights and cargo was still being loaded. A bored A.B.S. was leaning against the bottom of the gangway and Eddie showed him the Discharge Book. He shrugged, passed it back and jerked his head upwards.

Eddie turned to Ellen. 'I'll have to go now.' Despite the

fact that he was about to realise his dream he bit his lip and felt tears prick his eyes. God, he'd have to hide those or he'd be the laughing stock of the entire crew.

'You will, it's nearly eight.' She hugged him. 'Take care of yourself, Eddie. I'll write. I'll find out where to send the letters to.'

'That'll be great, Ellen.' He turned away and began to ascend the gangway with all kinds of mixed emotions. It had happened so fast that he'd not had time to dwell on it. When he reached the top of the gangway he turned and waved and then disappeared from sight.

She sighed; there were tears in her eyes. Now she had to go home and break the news, she wasn't looking forward to it at all.

Chapter Nineteen

Ellen felt desolate as she caught the tram home. She relied on Eddie so much. She knew Mam wasn't well and she hoped Molly wouldn't take the news too badly. She didn't care what her Uncle Con thought or said. As far as she was concerned, he wasn't really family. He'd been no one to them until a short time ago and she wished she'd never met him.

The wind was fresh and smelled of autumn dampness, she thought as she walked down the street. Had there been trees in the neighbourhood she knew that the leaves would have begun to fall. A child passed her going in the opposite direction and she stopped.

'Hello, Lucy? Are you all right?'

'Yes. Yes thanks, Ellen. I . . . I'm just going to the shop. Mam forgot something.'

Ellen was puzzled. She'd never seen Lucy Meakin out at this time of night on her own or even at all and Mrs Meakin wasn't a person who would forget some item of shopping. As usual Lucy looked pale and frightened. But she soon dismissed Lucy from her mind; other things were weighing heavily on it.

'Well, how did it go, luv?' Molly asked when she went into the kitchen. Unfortunately Con was just finishing his meal. For once she'd hoped he'd be in the pub.

Ellen shook her head.

'Where's our Eddie?' Tom asked.

Taking off her shawl, Ellen sat down. 'Mam, I've something to tell you. I . . . I lied about going to see Annie and so did Eddie.'

'Ah, isn't she going to turn out like the other rossi? It's lyin' she's doin' now, the young bucko, too.'

Ellen turned and glared at him and he looked away.

'I went to see Eddie off. Oh, Mam, I promised him I wouldn't tell you until he'd gone but I expected it to be weeks away.' This was awful, she thought.

'What would be weeks away?'

'He's gone away to sea, Mam. I went to see him off. He's on the *Windsor Castle*, going to Africa. He . . . he'll be away for two months.'

Molly felt as though she'd been poleaxed. 'To Africa? Ellen, why? Why did he go? I thought he was happy enough here despite . . . everything. I was thinking of buying him his own horse and cart.'

'He never wanted that. He's been wanting to go for a long time, to travel, to see the world, and after the other night, well . . .'

Molly turned on her brother-in-law. '*You!* It's all your fault! He was so unhappy here that he wanted to get away from *you*! Oh, dear God, I rue the day I ever tracked you down!'

'Ah, so it's my fault now that another one has gone! I

work myself to death for a pittance and what thanks do I get? I'm accused of driving everyone out!'

Ellen got to her feet. 'Well, you have. It *is* your fault, but don't think you'll drive me out! This is my home, it's my da's business and I'll fight you every inch of the way because you're no good and never have been!'

He pushed back his chair. 'I'm not staying here to listen to her giving out to me. A bit of a girl too! Go to hell, the pair of you, I'm off for a jar.'

Molly was so shocked and worried she barely noticed him slamming out. 'Oh, Ellen! What's going to become of you all? First Annie, now Eddie and . . . I . . .'

Ellen put her arms around her mother. 'Don't worry, Mam. Eddie will be fine and I don't blame him. He's wanted this for ages, he never wanted the business, neither does Tom. He wants to be a reporter. Eddie will leave an allotment so you won't go short of his wages.'

'It's not the money, Ellen. My whole world is crumbling. Everything your da and me planned and worked and sacrificed for. Now it's slipping away.'

'No, it's not, Mam. I won't let it.'

Her words tore at Molly's heart. Ellen had been better than Eddie at coping with life's cruel ties, but she didn't blame her brother for that. But could she cope? How could a mere slip of a girl control Con and keep an eye on the business, run a house and keep her job? There was so much responsibility and she was so young. She should be out, enjoying herself the way Annie used to. She should meet a nice lad who'd treat her well and get married. She shouldn't have to end up being a skivvy and an old maid.

Molly couldn't hold back the tears. She was afraid. So very, very afraid. The sobs became a cough and she couldn't control it. It was just like it had been that morning. She pressed the cloth to her mouth, praying hard that it wouldn't be as bad, that it would stop soon. But it just wouldn't. First the piece she had covered her mouth with, then the edges of the cloth were covered with the flow.

'Mam! Mam! What is it?' Ellen cried, panic-stricken.

Molly turned her head away but not before Ellen had seen the bright scarlet stain saturate the cloth and spread and spread. She stood rigid with shock for a few seconds and then she ran. She had to get help and fast for she knew what it was now only too well. She hammered on Gussie's door until it was opened.

'Mrs Cooney! Quick! Come quick, it's Mam . . .' she gasped.

'Mother of God! Is there much blood?'

'Yes! Oh, yes, please come quickly!'

'Teddy Cooney, gerrout 'ere an' go an' get Mrs Ogden. Ellen, shift yerself: go and get the tanner doctor! Go on!' She pushed Ellen hard and the girl broke into a run.

She didn't see where she was running. Instinct overtook her. Consumption! Consumption! The word battered around in her head with every step she took and she ran as she'd never run before, her heart hammering against her ribs, fear driving her on and giving wings to her feet.

She almost fell into the hall of Dr Jenkinson's house when the door was opened.

'Ellen Ryan?'

'Please come quickly! Please, sir!' she gasped. 'It's Mam.

She's coughing up blood! A lot of blood! It was everywhere!'

He grabbed his bag, jacket and hat and followed her until they reached the main road. There he got a cab and bundled her inside.

'I don't care which way you go but Milton Street as fast as you can,' he ordered the driver who cracked his whip and urged his horse into a trot. It sounded like the later stages of tuberculosis, but why had the woman never been to see him?

When they both ran down the lobby they found Tessie and Gussie cleaning up the kitchen with old cloths and newspapers. Molly was lying on the sofa, her head propped on a rolled-up coat. She looked deathly pale, her skin almost translucent but with the tell-tale pink patches on her cheeks.

'I've sent our Teddy for Father Healy,' Gussie informed them.

'Why did no one notify me sooner?' he demanded.

'She asked us not to, an' we swore we wouldn't tell,' Tessie replied.

'How long has she been like this?'

'She . . . she's had a cough for months but . . .' Ellen shrugged.

'This mornin', sir, she 'ad a very 'eavy attack. She must 'ave caught it up in that Immigrant 'Ouse.'

He listened to Molly's chest, and took her pulse. It was very slow and faint. How she'd managed to conceal it he didn't know but he did know that she was dying.

'Mrs Ryan, how do you feel now?' he asked gently.

'Tired, sir, very tired and breathless.'

He nodded and looked at Ellen. She couldn't be more than seventeen or eighteen but now she was going to have to keep the home going and bring up her brothers. This family had seen too much trouble and heartache, he thought bitterly, but then which family in this vermin-, disease-ridden area hadn't?

'Where's the other girl?'

'She . . . she doesn't live here now, sir. She's in service in Newsham Park.'

'Then I suggest that someone goes and brings her home.'

'She won't come,' Ellen answered in a frightened voice.

He looked at the two older women. 'Do you want to . . . or shall I?'

'Iffen you don't mind, sir, would you . . .?' Gussie asked, wiping her eyes with the corner of her apron. 'She's a saint, that's what she is, sir. All through the bad times she never saw us go without a fire or food, even if it were only a loaf an' some tea. Last Christmas she even baked me a dozen mince pies. Oh, merciful God! Why must it be her?'

Ellen stared around. Dr Jenkinson looked very perturbed. Gussie was frankly crying and Tessie, the hardest, the loudest-battling woman in the street, had tears in her eyes.

'What is it? What's the matter?' Her voice was weak. She felt as though there was a hand around her throat choking her.

'Ellen, your mother is very ill. She is in the last stages of pulmonary tuberculosis, consumption as it's more commonly called. I'm afraid she hasn't got long, child. I'm so sorry, so very sorry.'

She couldn't believe it. No, Mam couldn't be . . . dying! She'd been sitting here when she'd come in. She'd looked tired and pale but . . . not dying! Never dying! It wasn't true. It *couldn't* be. But she could see by the doctor's face that he was speaking the truth. She felt dizzy and clutched Gussie's arm for support.

Tessie held out the sixpence to him. He shook his head and sat down, his head in his hands. The woman was probably right. She would have caught it working in insanitary conditions, in daily contact with people who had, or were carriers of God alone knew what diseases. But around here it didn't matter where you contracted it. He'd seen so many die from it. He'd stay until the end – he wouldn't have long to wait. But it wasn't an easy death.

Gussie took Ellen in her arms. 'Oh, luv, I'm sorry too. She *was* a saint an' I'll never believe otherwise an' I know Tessie feels the same.'

'You knew, both of you. Why didn't you tell me?'

'Because like we told Dr Jenkinson, we promised, Ellen.'

Ellen dropped her head on Gussie's shoulder and broke down. It wasn't true! It wasn't true!

Molly was drifting in and out of consciousness. She was aware that there were other people in the room but they were just shapes, their voices coming from far away.

Dr Jenkinson got up. 'I think it would be better if she were taken to bed.'

'I'll go and get my feller,' Tessie offered.

'Where's that usless no-mark?' Gussie demanded.

The doctor looked at her quizzically.

' 'Er brother-in-law, sir, 'e cum over ter run the business when poor Jack, God rest 'im, died, but 'e's been nothin' but trouble fer 'er. 'E'll be proppin' up the bar of the Swan.'

'I'll bring the pair of them along,' Tessie said grimly. After poor Molly died she'd get her hands on Con Ryan and he'd rue the day he ever stepped off the Dublin ferry.

Tessie soon returned with both men who fortunately were reasonably sober.

'You must be the brother-in-law?'

'I am so,' Con replied. He'd been shocked by Tessie's revelations.

'Then lift her gently and carry her up.'

Con did as he was asked, but sullenly. He didn't like the man's attitude but weren't they all full of their own importance? He'd never suspected she'd got it at all, never mind that she was dying. He left the bedroom with Ozzie while Gussie started to see to Molly.

Tessie caught him by the arm on his way out.

'Just you listen to me, youse. Yer'll wait in that kitchen until she's . . . gone. Iffen yez go to the pub, the pair of yer, I'll bloody swing fer yer an' I mean it!'

Neither man answered but went quietly downstairs. Father Healy arrived and passed the two men on the staircase.

'Oh, thank God you're here, Father!' Gussie exclaimed, relieved.

'How bad is she?' he asked the doctor.

'Hours, less maybe.'

The priest shook his head and began to carry out the ritual of Extreme Unction, the Last Rites. He too was thinking of Ellen and he prayed to God that He'd give her strength. They were good people, all of them, and it was tragic that again he'd been called to administer the Sacrament of the Dead.

When Molly had been made comfortable Gussie went to get Tom and Bernie who all this time had been sitting in their bedroom, sick with fear and confusion.

'Come in now an' see yer Mam. She's not got much longer on this earth, she'll be going to 'Eaven soon, to be with yer da.' The two lads looked pale and shocked. 'Go on now, sit on the edge of the bed but don't go messin' around an' disturbin' 'er.'

Ellen knelt by the other side of the bed, holding one of her mother's lukewarm hands. She could only see despair and darkness ahead of her without her mam. If only she'd known. If only someone had told her, she could have looked after her mam. Made her give up that job much sooner. The job that had killed her. This was the end of her world, the only world she knew. First Da, now Mam. How could she cope? And there was Annie and . . . 'Oh, God!' she cried aloud.

'What's up, Ellen?'

'Eddie! Eddie won't know! He's gone! He's just sailed for Africa!'

Dr Jenkinson shook his head sadly. He hated his profession at times. Well, if he was honest these days he hated it all the time.

'The Company will get word to him through their agents

241

when he docks, but he won't know for quite a while.' He didn't know just how long the lad had been a merchant seaman, but this voyage certainly wasn't going to be a good one.

'Ellen, luv, she's trying to say something.'

Ellen got up and bent over Molly. 'Mam! Mam, what is it?'

Molly's voice was very low. Each word was an effort. Suddenly, in a crystal-clear moment, she'd known she was dying. She wasn't afraid for there seemed to be a bright light in the corner of the room. Like a tunnel it was and it seemed to be drawing her towards it and it was comforting. It was giving her strength.

'Tom, Bernie . . . look after them, Ellen.'

'I will, Mam, I promise.'

'And Annie?'

Ellen was fighting down the sobs. 'Yes. Oh, Mam, don't waste your breath, it's so hard for you, rest a bit.'

'The business . . . Con . . . don't let him . . . ruin it.'

'Oh, Mam, I don't care about the business! I just don't want you to leave us!'

'You have to care, Ellen. Your da's dream . . . make it happen. Go beyond his dream, Ellen.'

A noise like gurgling water rose in Molly's throat.

'Mrs Cooney, Mrs Ogden, quickly, help me lift her!' Dr Jenkinson cried and Ellen caught both her brothers in her arms and clasped their heads to her chest. She didn't want them to see the bright red tide that quickly covered her mam's nightdress, the sheets and the quilt.

She bent her head. 'Mam, oh, Mam! What'll I do without you?' she sobbed.

With tears streaming down their cheeks Gussie and Tessie helped the doctor lay Molly's head down on the pillow which seemed very white against the crimson sea of bedclothes, the scarlet flood that had robbed Molly Ryan of her life.

'She's happy now, Ellen, she's with yer da an' she won't know sufferin' an' 'ardship no more.' Those were the only words Tessie could find to comfort them.

Nothing seemed real, Ellen thought. It was as if she were watching a play through a window. A play in which she had no part. She felt quite calm after she'd cried for half an hour by the bedside. Everything had been done by the neighbours, the doctor and the priest. Even Con seemed subdued. But it had been so sudden, that was the worst part. She'd never known. She'd promised Mam she would look after Annie too, but she just couldn't think of her stepsister at the moment.

'Will one of us go an' see Annie?' Gussie asked. Obviously Ellen couldn't go, she was far too upset. They all were, except *him*.

'I . . . I don't know if she'll come.'

'Why wouldn't she?' Tessie asked. 'Yer mam was good to 'er an' she never even bothered to visit. The ungrateful little bitch.'

'Please? Please, I don't want another row,' Ellen begged.

'There'll be no row. Tessie'll just go an' tell 'er, like, an' then she can suit 'erself.'

Ellen agreed. She was really too upset now to think of

Annie's predicament. She'd see her stepsister didn't want for anything.

The following morning Tessie went to Newsham Park. She looked around her at the big houses and the open parkland, the paths already covered in fallen leaves. Over on the other side a man was brushing them all up and emptying them into a wheelbarrow. She sighed. How the other half lived, but in the end, rich or poor, everyone died. Then there were no class distinctions.

The back door was opened by Annie herself and Tessie thought the girl looked very well.

'Can I come in, Annie? I mean, not really *come* in,' she added, seeing the look of horror in Annie's eyes, 'just step in for a minute, like.'

'Just a minute then.' Annie held the door open wide and wondered what had brought the likes of Tessie Ogden here. She hoped she wouldn't stay long.

'It's yer ma, Annie. It's Molly. I 'aven't come with good news, luv.'

'What's the matter?' Annie was suspicious.

'She . . . she died last night. I'm sorry, girl, she 'ad galloping consumption.'

Annie stared at her, her eyes wide with shock. 'I . . . I . . . never knew.'

'None of us did until just lately an' she swore Gussie an' me ter secrecy.' Privately she thought if the girl had come to Milton Street she might have seen some sign, some indication, but Ellen had begged her not to berate Annie for not coming.

'The funeral is on Tuesday at Holy Cross at ten o'clock,

iffen yer want to go, an' I think it'd be a flamin' disgrace if yer don't come. She was good to yer.' She sniffed. 'Well, I'm sayin' no more. I'll be goin' now, I've things ter do, like.' Tessie turned and walked out.

Annie gazed after her in panic. Ma dead! Dead! Now what was she to do? She had intended to leave soon and go back and see her stepmother to try to get her to talk to Con or to change her mind about the flaming business. Now what could she do? She'd sooner die than go to that place for fallen women! She'd have to leave, get a room somewhere and try and make the best of it. She couldn't go to the funeral. That Con would start on her and would tell the entire neighbourhood of her condition. She couldn't bear the shame of that. And no one would stand up for her. Eddie, who was her own flesh and blood brother, sided with the rest of them. She was the black sheep; she always had been. Well, when she left here she'd live up to her name. She'd make her way in the world by other means.

Chapter Twenty

Da's death had been sudden and so had her mam's. Ellen was still trying to come to terms with life without Da and now this. Fate was too cruel. Father Healy said, 'These things happen to test our strength, our faith and our trust in God,' but her faith, which had once been so strong, seemed to have deserted her.

Molly's funeral brought back so many bittersweet memories, Ellen thought. The only difference today was the weather. It had been cold and snowing the day they buried her da, now it was a beautiful autumn morning. There was a thin mist that was gradually being dispersed and the air smelled damp and sweet. Everything looked golden and mellow, bathed in the shafts of sunlight that penetrated the half-bare branches of the trees that bounded the cemetery and fell on the flowers on other graves and headstones.

She'd dragged herself around like an automated doll and she hadn't had the time or the inclination to be angry about Annie until now. Her stepsister hadn't come, not even to the church, and that was something she knew she would never forgive Annie for. Nor was she the only one who thought like that.

'It's a disgrace, a downright shockin' disgrace, it is!' Gussie hissed to Tessie.

'I've a good mind ter 'ave a word with Father Healy, tell 'im that he should go up to that house an' tell 'er, tell the whole flamin' lot of them that she couldn't be bothered to go to a Mass for Molly. They're supposed to be good Catholics so that wouldn't go down well.'

'Wouldn't yer 'ave thought they'd 'ave *made* 'er come?' Gussie speculated.

'Well, iffen she ever shows 'er face in Milton Street again she won't be gettin' no sympathy from me!'

Again a couple of the neighbours hadn't gone to the cemetery; they'd gone to the house instead to set out the tea for the mourners. The rest of the day went by in a daze for Ellen. As soon as they'd got back Con had disappeared, off to the pub, Ellen knew.

'Iffen 'e comes 'ome rotten drunk 'e'll feel the back of me 'and!' Tessie said darkly.

Ellen had given her two brothers the money to go to the pictures. Tessie and Gussie had raised their eyebrows but said nothing.

'I know it's not "decent" but they need something to keep their minds off . . . things,' had been Ellen's unasked-for explanation.

She drew the heavy curtains and tidied up, wishing she had Eddie here to comfort her, but there was no one. Now she would have to be a mother to them all. From somewhere she would have to find the strength to deal with her uncle and help Tom and Bernie get over their loss. She'd have to make everyday life as normal as possible. She sat down at the table with a pad and pen. It had to be done but it was the hardest letter she would ever have to write. How was she to tell Eddie that Mam had died? How could she find the right words? She leaned her elbows on the table and covered her face with her hands. What kind of an existence was facing her now? She didn't have much of a social life anyway. Trips to the moving picture shows, the occasional church dance with Edna Rooney and that crowd. Girls she'd been at school with and now worked alongside. And like other girls of her age she dreamed that one day she would fall in love, get married and have babies. She loved children. She loved the way tiny babies held tightly to your finger and nuzzled into your neck and chest when you nursed them. She loved watching them grow. But there seemed no room, amidst the responsibilities she was about to shoulder, for any such dreams of her own. After a few minutes she sat up straight. She would *have* to do it all, there was no use sitting here feeling sorry for herself. Mam had found the strength to go on after Da's death and so would she. She would have to set aside her grief and get on with life, face up to the tasks it had chosen for her.

The following morning, after she had cried herself into a deep exhausted sleep, she told Con she wanted to speak to him after work.

'What for?' he asked warily. What was she up to now? If it wasn't for her he'd be having the life of Riley now. Why sell up and go back to Dublin when he had all he wanted here?

'I'll tell you tonight, after you've had your meal, so I'd like you to be fairly early,' had been her abrupt reply.

Jesus! She'd only buried her mother the previous day and already she was beginning to act like Molly, he thought.

She'd deliberately kept herself busy for the whole of the day. Tom had gone to work and Bernie to school. The neighbours came in for a few minutes to see if she wanted anything and how she was coping. She'd surprised them all. She appeared to be doing a spring clean even though it wasn't the right time of year.

'She's doin' well, isn't she?' Tessie marvelled.

'I'd never 'ave thought it,' Gussie replied.

'She's like 'er mam. She's got a strong will an' she'll need it ter keep up with that feller!' was Tessie's ominous reply.

When they'd had their meal Ellen sent Bernie off to play with Teddy Cooney and she gave Tom money for the pictures again.

'Are we made of money now? That's two days on the run,' Con commented.

'So what? Do I count how many times you go to the Swan in one week?'

He ignored that. 'So, what's the great mystery?'

'There's no mystery. I just want to get things sorted out.'

He was instantly suspicious. 'What things?'

'Mainly money. If I'm to keep house I'll have to give up

my job.' And, she thought ruefully, her friends. 'I can't do both.'

'Your mammy did,' he shot back at her.

'Yes, and it killed her. I'm not going back to Tate's. There's Tom's money and what we make from the business.'

'We don't make a fortune from that.'

'Not yet, but I'll need at least half of it to run the house and keep everyone in clothes and boots, especially now that winter is on its way.'

'So how much am I to have?' he demanded, annoyed that he had to even ask.

'Whatever you take out now.'

'Ah, go away with you! It's little enough for what I do. I work hard.'

'So did Da and Mam,' she said coldly. 'I also want to save some so we can expand. Mam had managed to put some money by, but most of that went on the funeral.'

'And who will you get to "expand" with you?' he asked sarcastically. 'Tom won't work at it and why should he when he's a grand job with the prospects of getting on. Meladdo has run off to sea and God knows when we'll see him again – if ever – and Bernie's too young.'

'There's plenty of men around here who would be only too glad to drive a second cart and get regular wages. It's what everyone wants.'

He stared at her intently. 'You're a hard little rossi.'

'It's not just boys and men who can get on in the world. I promised Mam I'd do my best for the business.'

'Says you. Just don't be bringing that slut here to live.

She couldn't even come to the Mass. Too ashamed to show her face.'

'I've no intention of bringing Annie here. I can't forgive her for that.' For once she agreed with him, but she *had* promised Mam she'd look after Annie. She put the matter out of her mind. 'So, we're agreed then?'

'I'll have a few shillings more for being a sort of boss seeing as we're expanding.'

'How many?' she demanded.

'Ten.'

'Five.'

'By God I wouldn't want to be the feller that gets you. He'd have to be a complete eejit!'

She ignored the remark. She'd have to keep a close eye on him.

'We keep books so it won't be hard to keep track of everything: feed, new harnesses, livery for Betsy, stock and other things. Proper businesses always keep books.'

He was suspicious. She knew damned well he couldn't read or write. So he'd have to try and remember everything he'd spent money on and over a period of months that would be hard if he wasn't to trip himself up. Where the hell had she got this idea of writing everything down from? It was a bit beyond the simple records Eddie, and then Molly, had kept.

'Are there any debts I should know about?' she asked, looking him straight in the eye.

'Like what?' he hedged, feeling uncomfortable.

'Like how much you owe the bookie?'

God, she was getting worse. Where did she find out

about such things? The bloody neighbours, of course, he thought irritably. There wasn't anything that went on in this street that was private for very long. He'd have to tell Ozzie to keep his mouth shut in future. It was one of his failings: when he was drunk he talked too much.

'It's only a few shillings. The last two horses came good. I won. So I cleared most of what I owed.'

She said nothing, hoping he was telling the truth.

'Well, if that's it, I'm off, that is if you give your permission,' he finished sarcastically.

'I don't mind as long as you don't run up a slate.'

He glared at her and left, slamming the door behind him.

She passed a hand over her forehead. It had been a long, tiring day but at least she'd sorted him out. She was determined about one thing. She wouldn't let the business go down the drain.

Eddie was very pleased with himself. He hadn't been seasick despite the fact that they'd gone through some rough weather. He didn't mind scrubbing decks and cleaning out messes, he even helped out in the galley without being asked to and he took his turn on the watches which were incredibly boring. Oh, some of the men had played tricks on him, but he'd accepted that as part of the ritual of a first trip and because he'd been good-natured about it it had stood him in good stead. When they'd 'crossed the line' they'd thrown flour all over him and then he'd been dumped in a homemade swimming pool by someone dressed up as King Neptune. He'd felt more confident after that. It made him feel like a proper sailor.

The voyage had been long and rather tedious but as they sailed towards Lagos the weather was beautiful. It was warm, as was the breeze, and the sky was a clear cornflower-blue. At night the sky seemed vast, with far more stars than he ever remembered seeing at home. One of the old men who'd stood watch with him had explained how you could navigate by the stars. He'd spent all his life on sailing ships and had fantastic tales to tell, although Eddie wondered sometimes if they were all true.

'What are you going to do when we arrive, lad?' an enormous stoker from Athol Street, nicknamed Blanco, asked him as they stood and ate their evening meal. There was nowhere to sit down.

'Dunno. Have a drink, look around a bit.'

'Well, that's dead boring. A young lad like you, I'd expect you to be off with the girls. Some of these women are real lookers.'

'I don't think I'll bother.'

'You've never been with a girl, have you?'

Eddie became embarrassed. 'Well, I sort of . . .' he stammered, feeling his cheeks getting hot and the sweat stand out on his forehead.

'You haven't! Well, lad, we'll soon remedy that. You stick with me and Charlie. We only go to clean houses, some of them you wouldn't cross the door, never mind anything else. You'd catch all kinds.'

Eddie felt nervous, but it was an excited kind of nervousness. When he arrived back home, with money in his pocket, he'd be a man of the world. He'd have experience of being with a woman. He'd have crossed the Equator and sailed to the other side of the world. He'd have many a tale to tell and he'd know he knew more about life than his ignorant, oafish uncle.

PART II

Chapter Twenty-One

What kind of a Christmas would they all have this year, Ellen wondered sadly as she came home from St John's Market on a raw December evening. She'd never enjoyed a Christmas since Da had died and she couldn't rejoice as this one approached. Oh, things had worked out quite well and Con had had only a couple of lapses with the drink and the betting. Tessie kept her well informed about the latter. There had been fierce rows on both occasions but she'd stood up to him, even picking up the poker the last time. But she'd made no attempt to hit him for she hadn't had that terrific surge of blind fury that she'd experienced the first time.

This Christmas there'd be no Mam, no Da and no Eddie. She hated all the bustle and cheerfulness, but she was determined to make an effort for the sake of Tom and Bernie. Bernie was really working hard at school and there was talk of him going to a Technical and Mechanics School when he was fourteen, if she could find the money. That was something she was determined to do. Bernie's future would be very different from Eddie's or Tom's. They had both left school at fourteen and neither of them had wanted to stay on. She'd had one letter from Eddie and she'd near broken her heart as she'd read it. It had come from the Canary Islands, the first stop of the voyage, but obviously not a big enough place to have an agent, or maybe they'd just not bothered to tell him about Mam. His letter was full of the new, interesting and exciting things he'd done and seen. He was obviously enjoying life at sea and she knew she could never ask him to give it up, unless he wanted to. As she'd told Con, there were many men who would work for them.

She'd put the shopping away but of the tea she'd bought there was no sign. She cursed herself; she must have left it on the counter. Now she'd have to go to the shop on the corner. The first thing everyone wanted when they came in, including herself, was a cup of good hot strong tea.

She took her purse and wrapped her shawl around her tightly. She'd go the back way, it was quicker. In the street you always met someone who kept you talking and she had a meal to prepare. They'd all be in soon, as would all the other men in the street – providing they'd had work.

She closed the yard door behind her and stepped into the entry, peering down to avoid standing in the sodden rubbish that clogged it. So intent was she that she didn't hear the sound at first. Then she stopped and listened. Someone was crying. It sounded like a child. As her eyes became accustomed to the darkness she saw a girl huddled against the opposite wall, weeping. She quickly went over and touched the thin shoulder.

'What's the matter? Who is it? What's happened?'

The girl turned towards her. 'Lucy! Lucy, whatever's

the matter?' The youngster's pale face was streaked with
dirt and blood. 'Lucy, what's happened? You've got to tell
me, luv!'

The child shook her head, seemingly unable to speak.
Ellen put an arm around her shoulder and guided her
gently into the house. She sat her down in front of the
range and turned up the gas light.

'Lucy! Oh, has he hurt you? Has your da done this?' In
the light she could see that the poor thing had been beaten.

Lucy just nodded. She couldn't speak.

'What about your mam?'

Fresh sobs racked Lucy and Ellen's anger began to rise.
She, like everyone else in the street, had no time for John
Meakin.

'I'll make you a cup of tea, luv—' Damn! She had none.
She'd have to go to Gussie.

'Just sit there, Lucy, I've run out of tea so I'll go in to
Mrs Cooney. I won't be long, I promise.'

Gussie came back with her and, as always, Tessie had
been sent for too.

'Make that tea, Ellen, while I see to her.'

As Ellen busied herself the child sobbed out to Gussie
the terrible beating her da had given her mam and how
she'd tried to stop him but he'd turned on her, so then
she'd run out.

'Where is yer mam now?' Gussie asked.

'She . . . she's lying on the floor. Da's gone to bed.'

'Has he then. Well, he won't be there for very long!'
Tessie said ominously.

Then Gussie and Tessie left to go and see what they

could do for poor Maggie Meakin.

Lucy seemed a bit calmer. 'Will . . . will . . . the scuffers come?'

'I suppose they will, Lucy.'

'Will he go to jail?'

'Yes, probably, for at least a couple of weeks.' That seemed to be the usual length of sentence doled out by the magistrates for wife-battering.

'Weeks?' The child started to tremble again and Ellen put down her cup and took her in her arms.

'I don't want to go back! I never want to go back! I hate him. I know it's wrong, but I hate him! I don't want to see him again. He . . . makes me do . . . things.'

Ellen looked into the girl's face. 'What things?'

'Secret things. He says it's our secret and . . . and if I tell . . . even Mam . . .'

Horrified thoughts were taking shape in Ellen's mind. 'What "secret" things? You can trust me. Now tell me the truth, Lucy, has he . . . touched you? I don't mean hit you or anything like that.'

Lucy nodded. She was really past caring about not telling anyone, not after what he'd done to her mam.

In halting words interspersed with racking sobs she slowly told Ellen the things her father had made her do. Ellen felt sick. The man was a monster. A monster who had been responsible for her own da's death. A monster who had put this child through hell. She could feel the rage mounting inside her. This time there would be no reprieve for him. She wasn't like her mam in this respect. The man couldn't be forgiven or excused.

She was still cradling and rocking Lucy in her arms when both women came back with faces like thunder.

' 'E's 'alf killed 'er! It looks ter me as if 'e's broken every bone in 'er body. Oh, 'e'll pay for this! Our Mary 'as gone for the tanner doctor.'

'We should go for the police as well!'

'We don't need them, Ellen,' Gussie said firmly.

'We will when I . . . I've told you everything. Lucy, luv, I want you to go upstairs and lie down on my bed. Pull the quilt around yourself and try and get a bit of sleep. You'll be safe. He . . . he won't come here and we'll all see to your mam. She'll be all right, Lucy, I promise.'

Lucy left the room and chokingly Ellen informed the two women of what the child had suffered.

She'd never seen either of them look so angry.

'I'll kill the dirty bastard with me own two 'ands, so 'elp me God!' Tessie fumed.

'So, you see we do need the police.'

'This is more of a reason not to go for them, Ellen. That poor woman might not know 'erself and would die of shame – if she doesn't die from what 'e's done to 'er – if all . . . that came out and was splashed across every bloody newspaper . . .' Gussie shook her head.

'An' 'ow would it affect the poor child? Everyone knowin' an' all? At school even. Kids are terrible cruel. No, Ellen, let the men deal with that bloody evil monster! That's what 'e is. Bloody evil. I've never 'eard the like in me life. It makes me sick to me stomach.'

Reluctantly Ellen agreed.

'I'll keep her here with me. Will they take Maggie to the hospital?'

'They will. But I want the fellers ter get their 'ands on 'im before the doctor arrives because *'e'll* call the scuffers. We'll 'ave to tell Dr Jenkinson that that pig has done a runner.'

'I'll go up and see to her. See if I can get her to eat something and then sleep. Do you think you could ask Dr Jenkinson to call and take a look at her? She just seems to have cuts and bruises but maybe he can give her something to make her sleep.'

'Aye, I'll do that, Ellen, and I'll be back, don't worry.'

'Thanks. I'll go up now. Oh, it's too sickening to think about.'

Barely five minutes later a group of men converged on the Meakins' house. A couple of them looked at the state of Maggie, still lying on the floor in a pool of blood, with Tessie kneeling beside her, afraid to move her until the doctor arrived. Then they went upstairs. Tessie nodded grimly as she heard John Meakin's shouts and yells that continued down the stairs, through the kitchen and scullery and out into the yard and entry.

'Yer dirty bloody bastard!' Ozzie snarled before punching the man in the stomach.

George McFadden seized him by the throat and brought his knee up sharply and Meakin screamed in agony. 'Yer own kid! You're scum, do yer know that? An' this is 'ow we treat scum in this street!'

The entry resounded with cries and screams. And then there was silence.

Ozzie poked at the prostrate, barely recognisable form with the toe of his boot.

' 'Ave we done fer 'im?' Wilf Henshaw asked grimly.

'Yeah. The world's a better place without the likes of 'im!'

' 'E'll not touch anyone else an' I 'ope 'e's roastin' in 'ell!' Ozzie added.

'The doctor will call the scuffers. What'll we do with 'im in case they search?' Georgie asked.

Ozzie looked thoughtful. 'We'll take 'im to the Swan and dump him down in the cellar. Shove 'im down the barrel chute until later. They won't look for 'im there. The scuffers don't make too much fuss anyway, what with 'alf the fellers in the bloody neighbourhood beltin' their wives. Then we'll get 'im down to the Landing Stage. The undertow's strong, 'e'll 'ave gone in seconds an' by the time they find 'im there won't be much left fer anyone ter identify!'

The others all nodded their agreement and between them they dragged the broken, lifeless body of John Meakin down towards the pub's outbuildings. Then they went home to clean themselves up and report that justice had been done. The type of justice no court would recognise but one which everyone believed was right.

Tessie was still with Maggie when the doctor arrived. As soon as he saw the state the woman was in he was consumed with fury. He'd seen women who had been beaten by their husbands many times, but never as badly as this.

'Where is he?' he thundered.

'Done a runner, sir, God knows where he is. Is she bad?'

'Yes. I'll be honest, she'll be lucky to come through this.'

'God 'elp 'er, a quiet, timid little woman. Wouldn't say boo to a goose, sir, an' always scrubbin' an' cleanin'. 'E's always been a birrof a swine, but ter do this, he must be mad. Stark raving mad.'

He looked up at the big, red-faced woman and thought that no one would tangle with her and get away with it.

'Will you send someone for the ambulance? And go to the police station and tell one of that lot to come down here quickly.'

'I will, sir, but why do we need the police?'

'To start a search for him. He'll not get away with this! He'll hang if she dies and he'll be thrown into jail for the rest of his life for attempted murder if she doesn't. I'll make bloody sure of that, if you'll excuse my language, Mrs Ogden.'

'There's no need ter apologise. St Peter'd swear iffen he saw the state of 'er. An' there's more, sir. 'E's been doin' things ter that poor little Lucy that'd turn yer stomach. I can't even bring meself ter tell yer.'

The doctor's face went puce as he tried to stay in control of himself. Incest wasn't unknown, but certainly he'd never heard of anything much around here. The Church held more sway than the police and such abuse was abominated. The men meted out their summary justice in such cases. He realised suddenly the men wouldn't be standing idle now. Something was obviously happening.

I hope they kill the bastard, he thought. It was a wish

that went against the very oath he'd sworn, but sometimes official justice wasn't enough.

'Will yer leave somethin' fer the child, sir?'

He nodded. 'Is she badly hurt?'

'I don't think so.'

'Then I'll call and see her in the morning. Where is she?'

'With Ellen Ryan.'

'She's in good hands.'

Chapter Twenty-Two

The police were the first to arrive, in the form of a huge middle-aged constable with a chest the size of a barrel who the doctor judged to be well over six foot. He bent down and looked at Maggie and shook his head. Then his gaze met that of Dr Jenkinson.

'This is as bad a case as I've seen and I'm up for my twenty-five years' service medal next month. The husband, I presume?'

Dr Jenkinson nodded grimly. 'Apparently he's gone missing—'

'Done a runner,' Tessie interrupted. 'Probably shit scared, if yer'll forgive me swearin'.'

'He's right to be shit scared, the bloody coward! I'll bet he wouldn't try to do this to a man. What's his name and what does he look like?'

'John Meakin's 'is name an' 'e looks like a bloody ferret. Evil little gobshite, if yer'll both pardon me again.'

'I'll need more than that to go on, Mrs . . .?'

'Ogden.'

The constable looked at Tessie with interest. 'Really? Not the wife of one Oswald Ogden?'

He was annoying Tessie with all this idle chat. Poor Maggie was lying there, half dead, and he was more interested in Ozzie. 'Yer can cut that out an' all! Drunk and disorderly but nothin' worse,' she snapped.

'For God's sake, we don't need to go into anyone's background or history,' Dr Jenkinson interposed irritably and Tessie nodded in agreement.

'That feller Meakin is small and wiry, with dark brown hair, small beady eyes and thin lips,' Tessie said grimly, reminding herself to thank the doctor later for changing the subject.

'Any idea where he works, where he drinks?'

'He doesn't drink an' he works at Crane's Buildings. 'E's a caretaker but yer'd think 'e was in charge of the flamin' City Council, the carry on out of 'im!'

It was all written down carefully in a black bound notebook.

Dr Jenkinson was pacing the floor with impatience. 'Where the hell is that ambulance?' The poor woman was unconscious and if he didn't get her to hospital soon she'd have no chance at all.

'But yer don't know the 'alf of it,' Tessie informed the constable, lowering her voice. 'I'd sooner tell yer in the lobby, just in case she can 'ear, like.'

The policeman was reluctant.

'It'll only take a few seconds,' Tessie said emphatically. Both men followed her into the lobby.

Tessie's cheeks turned a deeper red with rage and embarrassment. She was mortified to have to speak of Lucy's suffering. 'I don't even know 'ow ter begin ter tell yer. What that swine done to 'is own daughter and her only twelve!' She looked to the doctor for help and found it.

He looked at the constable. 'Incest,' was all he said.

The other man's face flushed as anger began to surge in him.

'Well, when we get him, and we will, he'll be behind bars for a very long time and when the other inmates find out what he did to the child they'll half kill him. And I don't blame them.'

Tessie said nothing. They wouldn't catch him and Maggie would be spared seeing her husband's name, her own and Lucy's, plastered over the front page of every newspaper.

The doctor nodded at the policeman's words. In prison anyone jailed for abuse of any child would have a very hard time of it indeed. Then he heard the clanging of an ambulance bell.

'Thank God for that!'

'Who'll go with her, doctor?'

'I will.'

'Please, sir, iffen yer don't mind, can I cum too? She 'asn't gorranyone ter see ter 'er.'

'It's highly unusual but I suppose in the circumstances . . .'

'Where is the child?' asked the policeman.

'With a neighbour. She's in safe hands, I can promise you that.'

'Right, I'll go back and get this description out to the lads and when we find him, he won't be handled with kid gloves, you can be certain of that.'

With the help of the doctor, the ambulance crew moved Maggie's inert form on to a stretcher, watched by a small crowd of neighbours alerted by the clanging bell of the ambulance.

The ambulance driver hesitated, looking at Tessie. 'Is she family, sir? You know what they're like!'

'No, she's a neighbour but she's coming just the same. There are no relatives.' And after giving Tessie a hand up he got in himself.

Gussie had sent all the kids upstairs with the threat of dire and terrible punishments if any of them moved or started arguing and fighting. She had the kettle on when Artie came home.

'So, it's sorted then?'

Artie nodded.

'Get in that scullery and get washed. Then give me those clothes, I'll wash them as soon as I can.'

He did as he was told and when he came back into the kitchen she held out a clean pair of trousers and a collarless flannel shirt. Then she made him something to eat.

'So, what will you do with him? Bury the bastard?'

Artie shook his head. 'No, the river. The Landing Stage – there's a fierce undertow.'

' 'Ow are yer goin' ter get 'im down there? Where is 'e?'

'The pub. In the cellar. Later we'll use Con's cart.'

'God, 'ave yer no brains! They're out lookin' fer 'im already, yer'll be stopped and searched and then yer'll all swing and for the likes of . . . *him*!'

Artie looked thoughtful. She was right.

'Get yerself down to Clarkson's an' ask 'im for the loan of 'is 'andcart. It'll be quieter than an 'orse an' cart. 'Orses 'ooves make a terrible clatter on the cobbles an' so do them iron-rimmed wheels. Clarkson's sound, 'e'll ask no questions. If yer go the back ways no one will see yer, and then go to the very far end. Don't go an' try to dump 'im in where the ships tie up.'

'I'm not that thick!' he replied, stung.

'Okay then. I'm goin' in ter see Ellen.'

She found Con sitting at the table but of the two young lads there was no sign at all.

'Where's Ellen?' she demanded.

'Upstairs with the child.'

Gussie nodded briefly. He'd been with the others but there wasn't a stain on him at all, at least nothing she could see.

'Where's yer jacket?'

'Isn't it on the peg, like always, and no, there's nothing on it at all, didn't I check that as soon as I came in.'

'Why don't yer go down ter the pub with the rest of them?'

Con needed no second telling. 'I'll do that, it's a good alibi.'

Gussie found Ellen sitting on the bed, a blanket around herself and Lucy. She was gently rocking the child back and forth, singing softly to her.

'How is she, luv?' Gussie whispered.

'Almost asleep,' Ellen whispered back. 'Dr Jenkinson left medicine and sent word with Tessie's Mary that he'd come tomorrow morning. That was before he went in the ambulance.'

'Come down the stairs, I've told meladdo to go to the pub with the rest of them.'

Gently Ellen laid the drowsy child down and covered her with blankets and the quilt and followed Gussie down.

The kitchen was blessedly warm and they both sank down on the sofa.

'God, what a night it's been.' The older woman passed a hand over her forehead. She had a thumping headache.

'I just can't help thinking of what he did. It's . . . it's so horrible, I really feel ill, and when I look at Lucy I feel even worse.'

'Ellen, girl, yer've got ter put it out of yer 'ead or yer'll go mad, an' I mean it. Yer can tell the poor little thing upstairs that she'll never see 'im again! 'E'll never be able to 'arm 'er again!'

'Did the police . . .?'

'No, they didn't. Oh, they're out lookin' fer 'im, but they won't find 'im.'

'Are you sure? I can't tell her she'll never see him again if there's a chance in the future . . .'

'There won't be, Ellen. Where 'e's gone no one will ever find 'im.'

Ellen's hand went to her throat. 'Do you mean . . . have they . . .?'

'The less you know, luv, the better. You can answer the scuffers' questions truthfully. But Con was with them, I know that.'

Ellen stared at Gussie. She couldn't believe it. The woman was telling her that John Meakin was dead. That the men had killed him. They had *murdered* him. It was no more than he deserved but it was still a shock to learn that these people who had treated her so kindly over the years could do such a terrible thing – and risk their own lives into the bargain.

Gussie stayed with her for she could see Ellen was really upset. No girl of Ellen's age should ever have to hear such appalling things, any more than she should be told that the men who had been her father's friends were capable of such revenge.

' 'Ave some of that medicine yerself, Ellen.'

'No, no. If she wakes, she'll be frightened and I don't want to be sound asleep. I have to be there to comfort her. It's all I can do.'

'You're right, luv, she must be exhausted but you never know. It'd be enough ter give yer the 'orrors, God 'elp her.'

'Now we all know why she was never allowed out to play with the others. Why she always looked pale and scared and why she was crying in the jigger. Oh, I wish I'd taken more notice of her.'

'Don't we all, luv, we could 'ave put a stop to it years ago.'

Ellen went up to check on Lucy every half-hour. It was after eleven before Con came into the kitchen. Surprisingly he was fairly sober, Ellen thought. But was he really capable of murder? She doubted it.

'Well?' Gussie queried.

'It's all been taken care of but the place is coming down with the police. We'll all have to say we were at home and then met up in the pub as usual.'

Gussie nodded her agreement, thankful for once for the time they all spent in the Swan.

'Right then,' Con finished, 'I'm off to my bed. I've work in the morning.'

'And isn't he the lucky one!' Gussie remarked sarcastically after he'd left the room. She didn't like the man at all. 'Will I make more tea?'

'Do make it for yourself, but I'm awash with it. I don't think I could drink another cup for a month,' Ellen replied, so the older woman sat down again.

Fifteen minutes later Tessie walked into the kitchen. They both stared at her, not daring to ask the question.

'It's all right, she's not dead. And she's not going ter die either.'

'Oh, thank God for that!' Gussie exclaimed.

'Get that kettle on, luv, I'm worn out and yer'd get nothin' out of that lot up there! Wanted me ter stay outside the bloody 'ospital doors, in the street, until the doctor insisted I come in. Say what yer like about 'im but 'e's a kind man. 'E treats yer like you were somebody instead of a pig-ignorant slummy.'

'He *is* a good man,' Ellen agreed.

'So, 'ow is she, what's wrong and 'ow long will she be in there?' Gussie demanded.

'Give us a minute, will yer, while I 'ave a sup of this.' I'm froze ter the marrer!' Tessie sat down heavily at the table. 'I got the last tram 'ome an' so did the doctor. There was no fancy motor car or even a cab. I think 'e wanted ter see iffen *I* was all right. It was shockin' seein' 'er like that.'

'Never mind you or 'im, 'ow's Maggie, fer God's sake?'

They both waited, anxiety all over their faces.

'When they cleaned 'er up and washed off all the blood she didn't look so bad. 'Er face is a mess, though. They had to stitch 'er a lot an' she 'ad a little cut an' a lump on 'er 'ead from when she fell but that'll go. That swine really battered 'er. She's got a broken jaw and nose and ribs, a broken arm, and 'er shoulder was out of joint. They called it somethin' fancy that I didn't understand, but Dr Jenkinson said it were out of joint. 'E's broken 'er right leg an' they 'ope there's no damage to 'er kidneys. He must 'ave kicked 'er all around the floor like a bloody football.'

'Jesus, Mary and Joseph! 'E deserved all 'e got. 'E'd 'ave known what it were like ter suffer like 'er before he died and I'm glad,' Gussie cried.

Ellen had to agree. It must have been a terrible beating, and simply terrifying for Lucy to have to watch it and be unable to do anything to stop him. Oh, what a really dreadful life poor little Lucy had had.

'Did she know yer, Tessie? I mean, was she awake, like?' Gussie asked.

'Not ter start with but then she opened 'er eyes an' I took 'er hand, gentle, like, an' said she were safe an' then she tried ter smile. I said we'd go an' see her termorrer. I told 'er Lucy is safe too.'

'What are we goin' ter tell 'er about what that swine did ter Lucy?'

'She won't be strong enough ter cope with that yet, Gussie.'

'Why do we have to tell her at all? Why don't we let Lucy decide when the time is right for them both?' Ellen said.

Gussie nodded her head. 'Yer might be right there, Ellen. There's no need for explanations of any kind yet. Except of course about *'im.*'

Ellen was startled. 'You'll tell her . . . that?'

'Why not? She'll be glad she's shut of him once an' fer all. She's 'ad years of bein' belted, an' never once would she ask for 'elp. Said it would only make 'im worse. We should 'ave took no notice of her. No wonder that poor child was always cryin' in the jigger. It might even 'elp 'er ter get better.'

Ellen wasn't sure about this at all but she said nothing and when the two women had left, she went to bed weary, shocked and nauseous.

Lucy stirred when Ellen got into bed, so she took the child in her arms and sat up, leaning her head on the iron headboard. If she had to sit like this all night she'd do so. This poor child deserved some loving care after what she'd been through over the years.

It was a long night and by morning Ellen was still tired and stiff. She had had to force herself not to allow visions of the girl's suffering to take control of her. Lucy had woken once in the night and had cried for Maggie, screaming in memory of some terrible ordeal. Ellen had held her tightly and stroked her hair until the child had settled again.

Now she eased the girl down and covered her with the quilt, shivering as her bare feet touched the lino. At least it would be warm in the kitchen.

It was and she found Con sitting at the table with a doorstep of bread and cheese and a mug of tea.

'How is the child now?'

'Sleeping peacefully. I wish I could say the same for myself. I sat up all night with her asleep in my arms. I'm as stiff as a board.'

'I'm after thinking that the police will call today.'

'I know and I'll say nothing except I found Lucy crying in the jigger and sent for Gussie Cooney. She and Tessie went and found Maggie and called the doctor. Maggie went to hospital, I kept Lucy here. You went to the pub as usual, with the rest of them. I know nothing more than that.'

He nodded. He knew he could trust her but he wished now he hadn't been dragged into it. Meakin deserved it, but it was a desperate thing to do; murder sat ill on his shoulders. It had been Ozzie's fault, but how could he have refused to go with the man? The things they said that little weasel had done were dreadful enough. Ah, still, Meakin was well and truly gone now, straight down to where they would be stoking up the fires to receive him.

'Right, I'm off to work. If anyone wants to speak to me, tell them I'm on my rounds and you don't know what time I'll be back. It's the truth anyway.'

'I will,' she answered.

She'd cleared the kitchen and sent Bernie to school and Tom to work, both of them quite shaken. There had been no arguments this morning: they knew about Maggie. Ellen had told them but only that John Meakin had beaten Lucy too and now the police were looking for him because Mrs Meakin had been at death's door.

At half past ten she answered the door to Dr Jenkinson who still looked grim and angry.

'So, how is she today, Ellen?'

Ellen took off her apron. 'She's sleeping now, sir. Her sleep was a bit troubled and once she screamed as if she were having a nightmare.'

'Her whole life must have been a nightmare!'

'I think you're right.'

'I won't wake her but can you tell her she won't be able to go into the hospital to see her mother? No children at all, they're very strict about that.'

'That's a shame but I'll keep her here with me. I'll try and keep her mind off . . . things.'

'Are there any relatives at all?'

'None that I know of. We . . . nobody really knew much about them. They kept themselves to themselves.'

'I can understand why,' he replied tersely. 'Have the police found him yet?'

'Not as far as I know, sir, but he might have gone anywhere. Jumped a ship even. Gone to Ireland or the Isle of Man, maybe.'

He looked at her steadily and saw her colour heighten a little and she looked away. So, they'd found him first, as he'd guessed. It didn't matter now. The police could search until next year and they'd not find him.

'I'll look in tomorrow then, but if you're worried, send for me.'

'I will, sir, thank you.'

He made to turn away but thought better of it. 'How are *you* coping, Ellen? I know your uncle drives the coal cart, and your brother is away at sea. Are there any arguments here?'

Ellen looked at him steadily. 'You mean with my uncle, don't you? We've had a few rows but I . . . I can hold my own with him.'

'I heard that too.' A grim smile hovered around his lips. He'd heard of the poker incident. Half the neighbourhood had, and her spirit impressed him.

'When does your brother, I'm sorry, your stepbrother come home?'

'At the end of this month. Actually, that's what I don't know how to cope with. He'll want to know about . . . Mam.'

She bore a heavy burden on those slender shoulders, Dr Jenkinson thought compassionately, and now it looked as if she had taken poor Lucy Meakin under her wing too. Life was unfair for many people: he supposed it always would be.

Lucy was up and dressed and helping Ellen to prepare the vegetables for their tea when the police called. She'd been very subdued, even after Ellen had told her she was safe now and that her mam was being taken care of and would, one day, come home.

The instant they heard the knock at the door Lucy threw her arms around Ellen's waist and buried her face against Ellen's chest.

Ellen put her arms around her. 'It's all right, Lucy, no one's going to hurt you. Do you want to go upstairs?'

'Yes, please, Ellen.' The girl's eyes were full of tears and her face was as white as a sheet, but she let Ellen go and answered the door.

'You won't need to speak to her yet, will you?' Ellen asked after ushering the two policemen in, while Lucy shrank into the corner.

'Not yet. I can see the state she's in,' the man in the tweed overcoat and bowler hat replied. He was obviously CID and he unnerved Ellen a bit. She'd never had any dealings with them before but their reputation went before them. They were feared by many as utterly ruthless. A law unto themselves, she'd heard said. She watched as Lucy went upstairs, then she went back into the kitchen and sat down, indicating that they sit also. The CID man did, the uniformed sergeant declined.

'So, Miss Ryan. Do you know what happened? I want your version, not hearsay. Just tell me what you know.' Out came the ubiquitous black notebook.

Ellen started shakily but her voice grew calmer as she spoke of finding Lucy, telling Gussie, hearing how bad Maggie had been beaten. Of Tessie going with her to the hospital.

'So, you never saw Mrs Meakin at all?'

'No, sir. I stayed here with Lucy, she was in a terrible state too.'

'Did you know there was a search going on for Mr Meakin?' He almost spat the name.

'I heard that Dr Jenkinson had sent for the police and the ambulance.'

'So, what about your uncle. Conor Ryan?'

'What about him?'

'Where was he last night?'

'He came home from work – he drives our coal cart.' Ellen took a deep breath. 'He had his meal, he got changed and went to the pub, as he does every night after work.'

'What time was that?'

'I'm not sure about that. He doesn't know what time he'll finish from day to day but I think it was about half past six. He helped himself: I'd done a hotpot. I was busy caring for Lucy.'

'And what time did he go over to the pub?'

'I really don't know. She was in a terrible state and so was I after she told me . . .'

'Yes, yes, we understand. But try and remember.'

'Why do you want to know all this?' she asked.

'Because so far, despite a thorough search, there has been no sign at all of John Meakin.'

'And you think . . .?'

'We've got open minds but maybe there's a chance that someone took the law into their own hands.'

'I don't know what you mean.' Ellen tried to look puzzled.

'He means that some of the fellers around here would have meted out their own punishment,' the sergeant interrupted in a tight voice. He for one was certain that that was what had happened. He doubted very much if anyone would see the man again.

'No! No, Uncle Con wouldn't do anything like that. He went for a drink with his mates – he always does. Ask the landlord of the Swan.'

'We have.' Suddenly the CID man stood up. 'Right, that's all for now, Miss Ryan.'

She showed them out and released her breath slowly. She hoped all their stories tied up. She looked up and saw Lucy sitting on the top stair, her eyes – full of fear – enormous in her deathly pale face. Ellen ran up to her and put her arms around her again.

'Don't be frightened. They only wanted to talk to me.'

'What about?'

'Your mam and Uncle Con. They . . . they haven't found your . . . da . . . yet.'

The child began to tremble.

'Hush now. I promised you you'd be safe here. Maybe they'll never find him, Lucy. Maybe he's dead.'

The child gazed up at her with such a look of relief that she repeated the words. 'Maybe he's dead. Maybe he drowned in the river, I don't know. What I *do* know is that he won't come back, ever.'

That evening Tessie and Gussie arrived, dressed for going out.

'We're off down the hospital, Ellen, do yer want ter come with us?'

'Yes. At least I can tell Lucy how her mam is then.'

'Send Lucy inter our 'ouse, yer don't want 'er left 'ere with them lads,' Gussie said. 'Our Sally and Sadie will see to her.'

'All right, wait while I tell her.'

Lucy went quietly into Gussie's and Ellen wrapped

herself in her shawl against the bitter wind as they went for the tram.

It was a cold, windblown trio who arrived at the Royal Infirmary.

Gussie looked around the big, white-tiled waiting room. 'God, I 'ate these places! They 'ave an 'orrible smell.'

'Who do we ask?' Ellen said to Tessie.

'The one over there will do,' Tessie replied, walking towards the desk.

The nurse looked up. 'Can I help you?'

'Yiz can. We've come ter see 'ow Maggie Meakin is doin'. She was brung in last night with Dr Jenkinson and meself.'

'I'll have to ask Sister. *Three* visitors. Are any of you relatives?'

'No, she 'asn't got none, God 'elp 'er.'

The nurse disappeared and returned with the Sister, a middle-aged woman whose iron-grey hair was dragged back into a tight bun beneath the pleated white cap she wore. It was obvious to all three of them that she was going to prove formidable, but the light of battle was already in Tessie's eyes.

'It is absolutely against the Rules and Regulations to allow *three* of you in and I believe none of you is related to Mrs Meakin anyway. Nor is it visiting time. Come back tomorrow – just two of you.'

Tessie drew herself up tall. 'Now youse listen ter me. That woman was beaten to within an inch of 'er life by 'er bloody 'usband – may 'e roast for ever – I cum in with 'er last night with the doctor.'

The young nurse held her breath. No one spoke to Sister like this.

Sister sniffed. 'That is no concern of mine. What the night staff do never seems to be appropriate.'

'Well it bloody should be summat yer worry about!'

'How dare you swear at me!' Sister answered, outraged.

'We're goin' ter see 'er, one at a time if yer want, but we ain't movin' until we 'ave. And yer can call the doctor or the scuffers but they won't be very 'appy, they're all out searchin' for 'er 'usband. An' Dr Jenkinson won't take no lip from youse. Yer gob is as starched as yer apron!'

Sister's face turned red with fury. As she fought a battle to keep hold of her temper she realised the best thing she could do was let them in, one by one, and tell them never to come again.

'Very well. One at a time and this is the first and last time you'll be allowed in here. Nurse, show whichever one of them wants to go first to the ward where Mrs Meakin is.'

'You go, Ellen, then you can get back. I don't think that child should be left anywhere for long,' Gussie urged.

Ellen followed the nurse, whose apron crackled with starch as she walked along the narrow green-tiled corridor and into a small, bare room. When the nurse opened the door Ellen gasped aloud. She could hardly believe that the woman in the narrow bed was Maggie Meakin. She looked so very old. Despite the cuts the bruises and the stitches her face was lined and wrinkled.

'Mrs Meakin! Are you awake? It's me, Ellen Ryan, I've come to see you,' she said softly.

The puffed-up eyes opened slightly.

'I don't want you to worry about Lucy.'

Maggie tried to speak but Ellen quietened her.

'She's fine. She is a bit upset but that's only natural. Dr Jenkinson gave her something and she slept all night and half of the morning. I'm going to keep her and look after her until you come home, so don't worry about her at all. Bernie will take her to school and bring her back. Oh, I know she's not a baby but I'll feel better and I expect you will too, if she's looked after by him.' Suddenly she had a flash of inspiration. 'They won't let her come in to see you, it's the rule, but I know what I'll do. I'll get her to write a letter to you. Would you like that?'

The movement of Maggie's head was very slight but Ellen smiled. It would help them both. She neither saw nor heard her two neighbours approach but she smiled as they came into the room. So the old battleaxe had let them both in. Tessie made her own rules and was more than a match for most figures of authority.

' 'Ow are yer, luv?' Tessie whispered. 'She looks better than she did last night.'

'Holy God! It's going ter take her ages to recover,' Gussie moaned.

'Yiz a right Job's comforter, Gussie. If yer can't say anythin' 'appy, like, then shurrup.'

'I've told her Lucy is fine and that she's going to stay with me,' Ellen said quietly.

'Don't yer try ter talk, luv,' Gussie advised Maggie then she turned to Ellen. 'I think yer'd better go now before the one with the starched gob comes lookin' fer us. She'll 'ave missed us by now and there'll be murder.' She crossed herself. 'Oh, God 'elp us, I shouldn't be sayin' that!'

Ellen leaned over Maggie again. 'Don't forget, she's fine and I'll send in her letter.' She waved as she reached the door in time to see Sister stalk up with a face like thunder, accompanied by the nurse and a man she presumed was some sort of caretaker. Tessie and Gussie wouldn't be long in there. She'd wait for them in the hallway.

'Yer don't need ter worry about *anythin'*, Maggie, luv. Not a single thing. Everythin' is taken care of. You just get yerself fit an' well ter come 'ome.'

Tessie leaned over her. 'An' yer won't ever fear *'im* again either. That's taken care of too. There's terrible strong tides an' currents in that river. Especially near the Landin' Stage. Iffen anyone was ter fall, like' – she shrugged – 'well, yer know what I mean.'

Maggie just had time to nod and try to smile with relief before Sister and the deputation arrived.

'There's no need fer youse ter come in 'ere mob-'anded. We're just leavin'. Tarrah, Maggie. Take care of 'er,' Tessie said with a venomous look at the Sister.

Chapter Twenty-Three

Maggie steadily improved. There was nothing or no one to fear now and although she was in terrible pain the thought of a life free of constant terror for herself and Lucy gave her something to cling to, to get well for.

She had been moved out of the room when it was realised she was in no danger of dying. Now she lay in a big ward in the centre of which was an iron stove for heating. It wasn't very efficient as the ward was large. The walls were white tiled from floor to ceiling and the windows were high up in the walls so there was nothing to see but the sky. But Maggie found the movements of the clouds very restful and the women around her were friendly. She couldn't speak very well for her jaw had been wired but the doctors all told her it was for the best. It would help the broken jaw heal quickly.

The days went slowly for visiting was only allowed once a day, for half an hour in the evenings, only two people were allowed in and all visitors had to be out of the wards on time. It was a bit like prison, she thought, although she had no idea what life was like in one of those institutions. But she looked forward to the day when she would go home. She missed Lucy so much, although she'd had two letters which had been cheerful and when Ellen came to visit she told her how Lucy was changing from a quiet, timid little thing into a rosy-cheeked girl who laughed and played like other children of her age. That was something Maggie couldn't wait to see. She'd tried her best but she'd been no match for *him*. But he was dead and now the years ahead looked rosy. She knew she shouldn't feel like this, but she did. Her married life had been tortuous.

It was Ellen's day for visiting and Maggie was looking forward to the time when, after a thorough check by the staff nurse that everything was tidy, the ward doors would be open and the visitors stream through.

Ellen had another letter from Lucy to deliver and she was thinking of how well her protégé was doing as she stood waiting in the corridor. There were the usual mix of visitors of all classes (except the very well off), but one in particular stood out as he towered head and shoulders above everyone else. You couldn't help but notice him, she thought. He was quite handsome and decently dressed and was clutching a bunch of flowers which, whenever any of the men looked at him, he tried to hide behind his back. While doing this he caught Ellen's eye and winked at her. The expression on his face made Ellen smile. Then a bell rang and the double doors were thrown open.

Ellen walked down to the end of the ward; Maggie's was the last bed. She smiled as she approached. Maggie's face didn't look too bad now.

'How are you today? I've brought a letter from Lucy, will I read it for you?'

She was surprised to see Maggie looking past her and she turned to see what was capturing Maggie's interest.

'Hello, Auntie Maggie.'

It was the young man she'd seen waiting in the corridor.

Ellen became flustered. 'I didn't think . . . I'd no idea that she had anyone . . .'

'My mam was her sister but she died with my da in a road accident five years ago. And of course *he* kept me away. But I also go to sea,' he informed her. She was a good-looking girl, he thought. Not a raving beauty but lovely in her own way.

'How did you know to come here?' Ellen asked.

'I've been thinking a lot about my aunt lately, and Lucy.' He looked down at Maggie, obviously upset at her injuries. 'Maggie and Lucy are all the family I've got, so I decided to visit. When I called and got no reply I went next door. They told me all about it. I'm Ben Hayes, by the way.'

'I'm Ellen Ryan, I live in Milton Street too.' She looked down at Maggie. 'She can't talk very well, her jaw is wired. He broke it, amongst other things.'

His dark brown eyes became hard. 'I never knew. I never knew what he'd done and had been doing for years. Not even Mam knew. Oh, she called a couple of times but he gave her the height of abuse and Auntie Maggie was so afraid of him that she couldn't hold a proper conversation, or even tell Mam what was going on.'

'He used to hit her where it wouldn't show and Lucy too.'

'Have they found him? Is he in jail?'

'He's not in jail because they haven't found him. Not a trace.'

He leaned over the bed. 'Auntie Maggie, you know that if I'd known I'd have come round and sorted him out. He'd never have raised a hand to you again. I feel terrible seeing you like this and never realising about all the times you've suffered.' There was real compassion in his voice.

Maggie stretched out her good hand and he clasped it in his.

'Well, you're here now and she's delighted to see you,' Ellen said, smiling at him and beginning to feel bashful. 'Would you like to read Lucy's letter to her?'

'If you don't mind.'

'Course I don't. Here.' She handed him the single piece of paper with the childish writing and while he read she found herself unable to take her eyes off him. She looked at him surreptitiously from beneath her lashes. What was so . . . different . . . so special about him? she thought. He looked the same as hundreds of lads his age. He was twenty-one or -two she guessed, more Eddie's age than her own. Although he was so big he was treating Maggie with great gentleness and he certainly read well.

The loud clanging of the bell ended the brief period of visiting.

'We'd better go before the one with the starched face throws us out. They're very strict.'

'Tessie will be in tomorrow,' Ellen informed Maggie.

'And so will I. See you tomorrow, Auntie Maggie.'

They walked out together into the cold dark night. Ellen shivered.

'I'd have killed him if I'd got to him first.'

She looked up at him, suspicion in her eyes. 'What do you mean by that?'

'Ellen, I was born and brought up in the same neighbourhood. I *know* no man in the street would have sat back, leaving her in that state. No, they'd find him and give him hell.'

She nodded and pulled her shawl closer. He was having a very strange effect on her. 'I know she's worried about how she'll manage when she comes out. He had some savings. They'll cover the rent for a few weeks. Tessie, Mrs Ogden, says she could take in lodgers. She and Lucy only need two rooms: a kitchen and a bedroom. She could rent the rest. It's like a new pin, that house, she was always scrubbing.' She looked up at him again. 'I've never seen you around.'

'I told you, I go away to sea, as a stoker with Cunard. I live in digs on the other side of the city.'

'That's probably why I've not seen you.'

'What do you do?' he asked.

'I keep house. I used to work for Tate's until my mam died. My da's dead too and that's another thing we've got to hate Mr Meakin for. He tried to burn my da's yard and everything in it. The coal, the carts, even the poor horses. One had to be shot. I can still remember seeing the poor creature. It was burning all over and was mad with the pain. Da's hands were so burned getting them out that he got blood poisoning and died.'

'Meakin's got a lot to answer for when we finally catch up with him.'

She decided it was now or never. 'No one will ever catch up with him. I mean he's . . .'

He'd thought as much. 'You don't have to say it. I understand, Ellen. He deserved to die.'

She decided to change the subject. 'My stepbrother Eddie is at sea, due home any time now. He's been to Africa on the *Windsor Castle*.'

'The mail boat?'

She nodded. 'Do you like going away to sea?

He grimaced. 'No, I don't like it. I hate it.'

'Why?'

'Because it's hot, dirty, back-breaking work, like being in hell, if you can imagine it: the heat, the darkness, the dirt and coal dust. There's no escaping it and the wooden clogs and canvas mitts we have to wear just make it hotter.'

'Why the clogs?'

'Supposedly to protect our feet. There's an art to being a stoker, especially in bad weather. If you don't get the furnace door closed before the bow rises, the white-hot coals spill out all over your feet and legs. I've seen it happen too often. But it's work, and at least Cunard feed you well.'

'What about the men you work with? Do they feel the same?' queried Ellen. Did Eddie hate his work too, despite the cheerful letter?

'Oh no,' said Ben. 'They're all hard men. They have to be or you'd never stick it. Often there's fights and no one intervenes, they know better. Nearly all the stokers and trimmers are from the Scottie Road area. We're called the Black Gang.'

Ellen stopped walking. 'Well, this is my tram stop.' She

couldn't help feeling a little disappointed that their conversation had to end.

'I'll wait with you, if you like?'

'Thanks.' She was glad, but a little uncomfortable, not knowing what to say next.

'Will you be visiting Auntie Maggie again?'

'Yes, it's my turn in three days' time. Two other neighbours visit, we didn't know . . .'

'How could you? I'm so sorry. I could have prevented it and that's something I'll have to live with.'

'Well, it's all over for them both now. They'll be happy.'

'Will I see you again at the hospital then?'

She smiled. 'Yes. Yes, I'll be there.'

Again she felt shy as the tram stopped and he helped her up the one step to the platform. But she knew she'd like to see him again.

When she arrived home it was to find Bernie, Tom and Lucy sitting in rapt silence listening to a story. And it was Eddie who was telling it to them!

She cried out in surprise and delight. 'Oh, I didn't expect you so soon! Why didn't you send a telegram or a message? Oh, Eddie, it's so good to have you home!' She hugged him tightly.

'I didn't know myself. We made up time because the weather has been so good. No storms or rough seas.' Then he broke off and looked at her with sadness in his eyes. 'Oh, Ellen, poor Ma.'

'We'll talk later about . . . about Mam. I don't want to upset Tom and Bernie again.'

'I understand,' he answered quietly.

She smiled again. 'I just can't believe it, you've been away for so long! This calls for a celebration. Tom, pass me my purse, then you can go down to Murphy's chippy and get chips and spicy meatballs for everyone!'

'No, let me pay for them. I'm flush, I've just been paid off, remember.' Eddie forced himself to smile and joke. The grief and the guilt would wait until later.

Ellen set the table and put the kettle on to boil. She nodded in the direction of the young girl.

'Lucy's staying with us for a bit. Her mam's not well, she's in the Royal.' She lowered her voice. 'I'll tell you all about that later too – and don't ask about her da.'

'She'll be out soon, Lucy, I'll bet,' Eddie said.

The child's face lit up.

Eddie thought he'd never seen her look so happy. Another mystery for later on.

Tom and Bernie came back with the chips and meatballs; Ellen had cut and buttered some bread. She looked around her and smiled. They were together again, sitting down around the table, eating, talking, laughing. A sadness tinged her mood. If only Mam and Da were here. She shrugged the thought off. They were all enjoying themselves.

It was a great evening until Con came in from the pub. 'Ah, I see the wanderer's returned and you've been stuffing your faces,' he growled. 'Where's mine?'

'Er, sorry, but we sort of didn't think,' Eddie said, embarrassed.

'A grand way to treat the head of the family, I must say, especially after I've been working all the hours God sends.'

'We all work, Uncle Con,' Ellen reminded him, 'and we're doing so well that I'm sure we can buy another horse and cart.'

There was always an argument over the money he collected but usually she got most of it. Because she kept lists and books and Eddie always told her the amount of coal they bought and who they sold it to, she knew how much money they had. Of course it meant that Eddie always got caught up in these arguments but he didn't seem to mind too much.

'You're sure we've got the cash, are you? Because I don't see so much of it nowadays.'

'Yes, I am,' she replied confidently.

Eddie looked at her with apprehension but she smiled at him.

After dinner, as per usual, Con went down to the Swan. Bernie was teaching Lucy long multiplication and they settled down together at the table. Tom had gone to see one of his mates from work. They were going to the pictures. Ellen had to admit to herself that Eddie's chosen career seemed to suit him. He was far more confident, more sure of himself.

'I'll be home for a few weeks, Ellen, don't spoil the lad's night out. It's all been arranged and I don't mind, really,' Eddie had pleaded when Ellen had remarked that Tom should stay in.

'Do you intend to get another cart, Ellen? I know it was Da's dream and Ma worked so hard to keep it alive, but . . .'

'Don't worry, Eddie, I'll never ask you to give up the

sea. It's your life now. You're not a kid, you're a grown man.'

Eddie was greatly relieved.

When Tom had gone out and Ellen had sent Bernie and Lucy to bed Eddie looked closely at his stepsister. 'Was it very bad, Ellen, when Ma was dying?'

She nodded, tears stinging her eyes at the stark memories his question brought back. 'I had no way of telling you, you'd only just sailed. She'd kept it a secret, only Gussie and Tessie knew. It was very quick, thank God. She didn't linger but . . . but there was so much blood.' She fought to keep her voice steady. 'She caught it working in the Immigrant House. Dr Jenkinson was so kind and wouldn't take a penny. But I haven't got over it. Even now there are times when I find myself turning round to talk to her, and then remember she . . . she's gone.'

'I couldn't believe it, Ellen. I'd been out with the lads and next day . . .' He shook his head, feeling guilty for his visit to *that* kind of house when all the time Ma was dying. 'When they saw the state I was in and heard . . . they took me out and got me drunk. But all the way home I just couldn't believe it. It wouldn't sink in until I walked up the street.'

'Annie . . . Annie didn't come to the funeral, not even to the Mass.'

'Why?'

'I don't know. Tessie went to see her, to tell her, so she did know. She just never turned up.'

Eddie found his sister's hard-heartedness beyond belief and said so.

'Oh, it's no good upsetting yourself, Eddie, you know what she's like and she never had much affection for Mam. I've been wondering how she is now . . . She must be almost due to have the baby.'

'I wouldn't give her another thought, Ellen. She's not worth it,' Eddie said bitterly. 'What about the two lads?' he asked, anxious to change the subject.

'Tom's doing fine, he wants to be a reporter one day and the first step is to get a job in the office. He's hoping to get that next year. Bernie works hard and he could go to a Technical School, if I can find the money. I've thought about it a lot, Eddie. If we get the second cart, I'd have more money eventually but I'd have to spend most of the savings on a cart and a horse.'

'I'll pay for him, Ellen. I want to. It's what Da would have expected me to do. We'd have one of the family with a good trade and a secure future.'

'All right, that seems fair enough.'

'What about Uncle Con? Any more rows?'

'A couple. He doesn't seem as bad now. He knows I'm not afraid of him and it seems as long as he's a roof over his head, food in his belly and enough for a few jars each night he's happy.'

'Why is Mrs Meakin in hospital and why couldn't I mention *him*?'

Ellen sighed deeply. 'He beat her half to death. She was in such a terrible state even the policeman said he'd never seen anything like it, so I heard. As for poor Lucy, I . . . I can't even tell you, it's so terrible. Ask any of the men in the street. But it's all been taken care of. They'll never see him again, and Lucy will stay with me, here, until her mam comes home. I've been teaching her to cook and Bernie has been helping her with homework. They get on well together.'

'Matchmaking, Ellen?'

She laughed. 'Don't be daft! They're just a couple of kids.'

'What about you?'

'Me?'

'Have you got a lad lined up?'

'I wish I had. I don't get out much either.' She was thinking of Ben Hayes but said nothing. All he'd said was he'd see her at the hospital. There was nothing unusual in that, she shouldn't read anything into it.

Annie was terrified. The pain was so sharp and intense that she screamed and caught hold of the back of a chair. This must be it. This must be the start of her labour and she was afraid, very afraid. Oh, everyone said it wasn't that bad, why would women go on and on having babies if it was that bad? And you forgot the pain, they said, but she wondered how long these terrible cramps would go on for. That was something everyone said you just couldn't predict. Every birth was different. Sometimes easy, sometimes hard. She would soon find out for she was going to have her child here and now.

As the pain slowly eased she looked around at the small room where she'd lived after she left the house in Newsham Park. It contained only the bare essentials. A bed, a chair, a small washstand, a chest of drawers and a gas ring, but at least it was clean now. It had been far from clean when she'd come here and having become used to the better conditions she'd lived in whilst in service she'd immediately scrubbed the whole of it, walls as well. She shared the kitchen and the privy with the other girls. She'd got used to the way of living in time; she was glad to be away from Newsham Park: she'd never settled or fitted in there. After she'd given in her notice she'd seen the looks of scorn and self-righteous smugness that passed between the other girls, from Collins in particular. She had caught them a couple of times whispering and her cheeks had burned at their sniggering but she'd said nothing.

The pain returned with renewed force and she gasped aloud. She'd have to get help. Panic forced her slowly to make her way to the door, open it and yell at the top of her voice for Maisey.

Eventually the woman came upstairs, puffing and panting as she dragged her overweight, overdressed figure up each step.

'For God's sake, Annie, shurrup, you'll put the customers off and that won't do no one any good.'

'The pains, Maisey! The pains have started.'

Mrs Maisey Butler, as she called herself, although she'd never been married, looked at Annie with annoyance. When the girl had found her way to her, pregnant and with no family – or so she said – she'd been reluctant to take her in and had told her so.

'You won't be much use to me, you can't work in that condition, the fellers don't like it. Well, the type of feller we get anyway. There's some that wouldn't be so fussy, particularly the foreign ones off the ships, but I have me rules.'

'Oh, please, please, I'm so desperate? I'll do anything, anything at all. Scrubbing, cleaning, shopping, cooking. I was in service. I'll . . . I'll . . . "work" just as soon as I can.'

'All right then, but you'll have to "entertain", as I prefer to call it, frequently after the kid is born and you'll have to feed and clothe it as well as yourself. This isn't a charity house.'

Annie had been so relieved. 'I will, I promise.' Before then she'd wandered the streets, finding a bed for the night where she could until her money was gone. Being in her condition and showing it, she'd not been able to get a job and although hungry and full of despair she wouldn't entertain the idea of going back to Milton Street. That was why she'd finished up on Maisey's doorstep.

She'd pushed to the back of her mind what 'entertaining' involved. She wouldn't think about it until . . . well, later. The only time she'd felt any shame or guilt was when one of the other girls asked about her mam and da. She'd said they were both dead and she was glad of it. They'd not see the degradation that was now her lot. But then she'd thought that if neither of them had died she wouldn't have been forced into this situation. She was *never* going back to Milton Street to live: she hated that lot.

Now the hours dragged by and she was nearly exhausted. Her nightdress, her hair, her whole body was drenched with sweat. All she wanted was for the pain to go away. To be able to sleep. Not to have to give birth to this child that was making its slow and painful way into the world.

She screamed again but at last she heard Maisey yell, 'PUSH!'

She used up her last remaining energy to do so and felt something come away from her and then the fretful wail of a newborn baby.

'It's a boy,' Maisey informed her. 'You can be thankful it's not a girl. Life's bloody hard on us girls an' women. Fellers get away scot free!'

Annie took the tiny scrap of humanity, wrapped in a sheet, from Maisey and marvelled at the tiny fingers that took such a strong hold of her own.

'What are you going to call him?'

'Daniel.'

Maisey nodded her agreement. 'Oh, aye, Danny's a nice name.'

Annie looked up at the older woman. 'No, I won't have him called Danny, it's Daniel.'

Maisey cast her eyes to the ceiling. 'Oh, God Almighty, would you listen to her. A tart that's insisting her brat be called by his full title. Well, in a couple of weeks you'll have forgotten all about niceties like that. You'll have your work cut out to cope with him and the customers,' she finished acidly.

Annie lay back on the pillow. A tart. That's what she'd become. A common little tart, anyone's for the price of a few shillings, that's what faced her. What kind of a mother would she ever be?

Two weeks later the time had come and afterwards she'd felt so sore, so dirty and so humiliated that she sat up all night crying bitterly, her tears falling on Daniel's downy dark hair as she cradled him in her arms. For hour after hour she'd fought with her conscience. It was the most important and painful decision she'd ever had to make. She wasn't going to bring him up in this house. She didn't want him living in this room, watching, listening to the 'entertainment'. She wanted to give him the world but she couldn't. Not here, not yet. Maybe never. It broke her heart but it had to be done. She held him tightly and kissed his soft rosy little cheek. It was time.

In the kitchen in Milton Street Ellen was darning Tom's socks. 'I've never known anyone to wear out their socks so quickly,' she said to nobody in particular.

Tom was out, as was Con, and Bernie was helping Lucy with her latest letter to Maggie.

Glancing up at the clock on the mantel, Ellen put the sock down. 'Lucy, you should be in bed now, you'll never get up for school in the morning,' she chided gently.

'We've finished but I just need to go down the yard.'

Ellen smiled. Lucy never called it a 'privy' or a 'lavvie'. She said she was 'going down the yard'. No doubt one of Maggie's expressions.

'Well, she certainly looks better,' Eddie commented. 'She's more chatty and she even laughed once. In all the years I've known her I've never seen her smile or heard her laugh.'

'She never had anything to smile or laugh about,' Ellen replied grimly. Lucy still had nightmares and sometimes wet the bed, which she was really ashamed of. But Ellen didn't shout or even mention it to anyone. In fact she was so caring that it didn't happen very much now.

'Ellen! Ellen, come quick!'

Ellen jumped up, the darning forgotten. 'Lucy! Oh, God, what's happened now?'

Both she and Eddie rushed into the scullery to find Lucy holding a bundle, amazement written all over her face.

'What is it?' Ellen asked, full of curiosity.

'It's . . . it's a baby!'

'A *baby*!'

'I found it on the step.' Lucy passed the infant to Ellen who drew the blanket away from the baby's face. It was a very young baby.

'Did you see anyone, Lucy?'

'No, nothing. Nothing at all. I didn't even hear the yard door close.'

'Look, there's something attached to the blanket,' Eddie pointed out.

Ellen went into the kitchen where there was more light and Eddie unpinned the scrawled note.

His name is Daniel. Look after him, Ellen, I can't. Annie.

Ellen looked at Eddie, stunned and confused.

'Why can't she look after him?' Eddie asked.

'I don't know, but I know one thing, we've got to find her, Eddie, she's in trouble. I'm certain she'd never have left her baby if she wasn't.'

Chapter Twenty-Four

Eddie made a grab for his coat and cap. 'I'll start now. She can't have got very far.'

'Hurry then, and if you have to drag her back here then do it!' Ellen urged. Annie must be in a terrible state both physically and mentally. She was certain that her stepsister couldn't be so cold and callous as to just abandon her baby without good reason. Annie wasn't *that* bad.

The baby began to whimper and Ellen instinctively began to rock him in her arms, just as she'd nursed Lucy in those first terrible days and nights. Her behaviour caused Lucy to tug at Ellen's skirt.

'What will happen, Ellen?' she asked quietly.

Ellen could see the child was distressed.

'Annie and the baby will come and live here, with us, Lucy. We'll manage.'

Bernie, who had watched everything in total silence, now got up from the table.

'Is he . . . Annie's baby? Really *hers*, I mean?'

'Of course he is, Bernie, you're his uncle. His Uncle Bernie.'

The lad shook his head and looked confused. He was

too young to be an uncle, surely?

Lucy's eyes widened with fear. 'I . . . I won't have to go and live with . . . that man?'

Ellen was puzzled. 'Which man?'

'The man you said went in to visit Mam. You said he was my cousin.' Lucy's bottom lip trembled. She didn't want to have to live in a house with *any* man again. She just wanted to live quietly with her mam. She'd accepted Tom and Bernie and even Eddie but she was scared of Con and tried to avoid him as much as possible, even though Ellen had reassured her he wouldn't harm her in any way.

'You mean Ben? Ben Hayes?'

Lucy nodded.

Ellen felt a flush come to her cheeks. 'No, of course not. What made you think that? He lives alone, somewhere across the other side of the city.'

'I thought because he's my cousin, I'd . . . I'd have to leave. With Annie coming here to live, you'd not have room for me.'

Ellen reached out with her free hand and pushed back a strand of the girl's hair that had fallen on to her forehead. 'Oh, Lucy. You know I'd never make you go anywhere if you didn't want to. Anyway, there'll *always* be room for you here. Look, let's have a proper look at Daniel. He . . . he's my nephew. We've both found out that we've got more relatives now.'

Ellen pulled the blanket away from the baby's face again. Oh, he was just gorgeous, she thought. He looked a little bit like Annie but she hoped he wouldn't have any of the Raffertys' looks or characteristics.

Lucy, much happier now, was peering over Ellen's shoulder. 'Where will he sleep?'

Ellen thought for a minute then turned to the child. 'Go and take one of the drawers from Uncle Con's chest in his room. Just put his things on the bed. We'll make it into a sort of cot, until we get ourselves sorted out.' For the first time she began to think of where they would all sleep. Tom, Bernie and Eddie shared a room and there was more room when Eddie was away at sea. Con had the front downstairs room to himself, so she, Annie, Lucy and Daniel would all have to share the second bedroom. It would be terribly cramped, maybe she should ask Con to move into their room and they could all have his. For the first time she thought about Con's reaction to the situation. She knew well enough his views on Annie, but she'd do the best she could.

They were just settling the baby in the drawer when Eddie came back, puffed, windswept and worried: no matter what their differences were Annie was still his sister.

'Not a sight nor sign of her, Ellen. I've been up and down every street in the entire neighbourhood. I ran, as you can see.' He hung on to the overmantel to get his breath, his chest heaving with the exertion.

Ellen left Lucy to finish tucking the blanket around the baby and straightened up. 'She must have caught a tram fairly quickly then.'

'She must have run like hell up to the main road and been lucky enough to find one that was just passing. What'll we do now? You know I'm leaving again in a couple of days.'

Ellen was determined. 'We'll keep on looking for her. I'll help.'

'Ellen, this is a big city, she could be anywhere. How many streets, courts and rooms are there? Hundreds, thousands. And if she hears we're searching for her she'll move.'

'We've *got* to try, Eddie. It's all we *can* do. She must be desperate.'

'Who must be desperate?'

None of them had heard Con come in.

'Annie,' Ellen replied, bracing herself for an argument.

Bernie edged his way towards the door as Con's voice grew louder.

'Oh, aye, that's a good word for her, "desperate", that's what she is all right. What's that?' His gaze alighted on the drawer that Lucy had placed on the floor near the range.

Ellen faced him squarely, her chin up, her gaze defiant. 'It's Annie's baby, Daniel. Your great-nephew. Lucy found him on the back step and Eddie went to see if he could find her.'

Con's complexion darkened.

Ellen continued regardless. 'When we *do* find her, she'll live here.'

'No, she bloody won't! And he's not staying here either. You can take him to the orphanage, let them look after him. No father to claim him and his bloody little tart of a mammy doesn't want him so she dumps him here.'

Ellen's eyes narrowed while Eddie clenched his fists and Lucy cowered against the brass fender. 'He's not going to any orphanage. He's family. He's my nephew and Eddie's.

Your flesh and blood too. I'll look after him *and* we'll go on looking for Annie because she must be half out of her mind to have left him.'

'Half out of her mind, is it?' Con yelled. 'What sort of an excuse is that? She's not dumping him on us!'

Ellen forced herself to remain calm. 'I don't see what you're complaining about, I'll look after him.'

'And is it you who'll be providing the money for his food and clothes?'

'I will,' Ellen answered firmly.

'Out of what *I* work bloody hard for.'

'You wouldn't have any work, let alone a business, but for Mam.'

'If there's going to be a row over it, I'll pay,' Eddie intervened. He knew Ellen and his uncle were shaping up for a row and he'd watched Lucy's face grow paler. She was clutching the side of the makeshift cot tightly, defensively.

'Ellen, shouldn't Lucy be in bed now? It's getting late.'

Ellen nodded, not taking her eyes off her uncle's face. Her temper was rising but her voice was calm and steady. 'Yes, it's way past your bedtime, Lucy. Off you go, I'll be up soon.'

She left the room thankfully but not without a last fearful glance over her shoulder at Ellen.

'Lucy, wait. Will you take Daniel up too? Eddie will open the door and help you.' She bent and picked up the drawer and the child took it from her. Eddie opened the door and went ahead. Ellen turned back to face her uncle.

'He goes and that's final,' Con said emphatically. He

wasn't going to have to dig deeper into his pockets for one of the Raffertys' bastards and he was sure that Annie was a streetwalker who just didn't want the responsibility of a child to hinder her career. Ellen was a soft touch when it came to kids and that hard-hearted little bitch knew it. Even if they found her he doubted she'd come back here to live, even if he permitted it.

'*You'll* go before I take him to an orphanage.'

'Oh, so I'm the one to go!' Con laughed derisively. 'And how would you get along with the business?'

'Tom is old enough, Bernie could help—'

'And if it came to the push, I'd give up the sea,' Eddie interrupted, coming back into the room and closing the door behind him.

Ellen cast him a grateful look.

Con changed tactics. She was a stubborn bitch and that temper was really fearsome. 'So you'd deny the lad his career at sea? You'd deny young Bernie his chance at the Technical School and a job for life afterwards and for what? A nephew? He's not even that. He's a step-nephew. And do you think if you find her she'll want to come back here? And if she does she'll be up to her old tricks in no time. Jaysus, Ellen, can't you see what she's done to you – all of you? She thinks you're all eejits.'

'If you'd stop complaining and laying down the law, no one would have to be denied anything. And what's more, does it matter if she does think we're eejits? I don't care what she thinks, it's an innocent baby I'm thinking about and I'm telling you for the last time, he stays!'

Con glared at her. One of these days he'd sort her out.

He'd bring her down off her high horse. But he wasn't going to win this battle now, not with Eddie here too. 'Then you can pay to keep him,' he yelled. 'I'm not giving a farthing!'

'You won't need to. And one other thing: I've not forgotten your part in the "accident" John Meakin had.' She turned away. She'd stoop to blackmail if she had to, to get her own way. 'Eddie, I'll go up to Lucy now.'

Eddie nodded. 'I'll see to Bernie, he looked a bit baffled before he slid out.'

Con swore and threw himself down on to the sofa. He knew she meant what she'd said about Meakin and if she did tell the police he knew he'd have a hard time of it not to bring the other men's names into it, and he'd go down for a long, long time. Maybe they'd even hang him. Damn her. Damn her to hell and back, there were times when he wished he'd stayed in Dublin. But, yes, he promised himself, he'd get even with her sooner or later.

Early next morning, while Daniel and Lucy were still asleep, Ellen went out and, full of a mixture of excitement and determination, bought nappies, feeding bottles and a big soaking bucket.

Nothing more was said about Daniel but after they'd all gone to school or work Gussie, accompanied by Tessie, came into the house.

'We 'eard through the walls last night, Ellen. What's goin' on?' Gussie asked point blank.

'Annie left her baby on the back step.'

Gussie crossed herself. 'Jesus, Mary an' holy St Joseph! What made 'er do that?'

'She must be in an awful state.'

'Yer didn't see 'er then?' Tessie questioned.

'No. Eddie ran after her but couldn't find her. God knows just how we *are* going to find her. I'm worried sick about her.'

Gussie sniffed and crossed her arms across her chest. 'I'd not bother me 'ead about *that* one, Ellen.'

'Look at the way she never even turned up for yer mam's funeral. A disgrace that was. A flaming disgrace,' Tessie added.

'An' now she's just dumped 'er troubles on yer doorstep. The flamin' nerve!'

'I'm trying not to think like that. Maybe she just realised she *couldn't* care for him. I think she wanted to but just . . . couldn't. Anyway, he's the one I'm really concerned about.'

'Give 'im 'ere, luv, yer don't know nothin' about babies.'

Ellen passed a sleeping Daniel over and Gussie cradled him in her arms.

'Well, 'e looks well enough. God, this takes me back.'

'Me an' all, Gussie, though I'm glad it's all over an' done with now. They don't get any better the older they get, mind you. Yer'll 'ave ter give 'im a bottle, Ellen. Yer can't feed him.'

'I know. In fact I'd really be glad of your help and advice. He cried quite a lot last night and I just dipped my finger into some milk and he sucked it off but I knew it wasn't enough. And what do I do if he cries and cries and keeps on?'

'Yer go through a list of things in yer mind. Is 'e 'ungry, is 'e wet, is 'e cold or too 'ot, 'as he got wind or the colic.'

'And what if he has got wind or colic?'

'Gripewater. Yer give 'im gripewater. Nurse 'Arvey's is best.'

'Oh, I think I'm going to need a lot of help. I don't know *anything*.'

'Don't worry, Ellen, yer a natural. Yer'll 'ave it all off pat in no time. It'll be second nature to yer. Don't yer remember when Bernie was a baby?'

'Not much. I was only young and Mam saw to everything like that.'

'Now, are yer goin' ter see Maggie ternight or do yer not want ter bother? She'll understand.'

'I'd forgotten that, I . . . I don't want to let her down but . . .'

'Then bring 'im in ter me, I'll mind 'im while yer go. I think she's glad of yer visits 'cos yer can tell 'er more about Lucy. Was she all right last night? Con was yellin' a bit.'

'She got upset but strangely Daniel seemed to help her get over it. She's fascinated with him – he's so lovely when he's happy. But thanks, I really appreciate you looking after him,' Ellen replied with conviction. Though Daniel was lovely, she wanted to see Ben Hayes again.

She dressed with care, taking time to pin up her hair, something she seldom did. In the past it was enough to just make sure it was tidy. Ben visited Maggie almost every night and on the days Ellen visited too he walked her to the tram stop. At first she'd been shy – she'd never known a lad so well before, but gradually she'd become more relaxed with him. She'd begun to experiment with her hairstyle, take time choosing what clothes she wore – not that she had a huge collection – and each time she saw him she felt a surge of breathless excitement. Today she smiled as she caught sight of his tall figure. He waved and she waved back.

'I didn't know if you'd come,' she said shyly.

'I said I would and I never break a promise, if I can help it. Here, these are for you, the rest are for Auntie Maggie.' He thrust a small bunch of violets into her hand, looking embarrassed. She was taken aback by the flowers. The last time he'd walked her to her tram, he'd held her hand and she hadn't pulled away. She'd gripped it tightly. Her heart had been beating quickly and jerkily and she'd wondered, would he kiss her on the cheek before she stepped onto the platform? He hadn't and she'd felt all the elation drain from her until he'd said, 'Take care, Ellen, you're . . . you're very special to me.'

As she'd sat staring but unseeing through the tram window, she admitted to herself that she was in love.

'How's Lucy?'

'She fine. She got this notion in her head that because you're her cousin she'd have to go and live with you and she didn't want to.'

'Where did she get that idea? I can't blame her for it, of course. It's a wonder she's not scared of all men.'

'She's fine with the lads but she's terrified of Uncle Con.'

'Who is Uncle Con?'

'My da's brother. He came over from Ireland to help run the business. I've had a few rows with him, but I can cope. I think it's just the thought of any kind of row that upsets Lucy and he's the one who causes the big arguments.'

'The poor kid,' he said sympathetically. 'Do you look after all of them?'

'Yes, and we've had an addition since I last saw you.'

'An addition? In what way?'

'My stepsister Annie's baby. She left him on the step and I'm worried about her because I think she must be in real trouble, even though no one else thinks so. Eddie went out to find her, but couldn't. We . . . we'll keep on trying but it's a big city.' She held the violets to her nose, partly to hide her confusion.

'I see. Maybe I can help. I live over the other side, I can ask around.'

She was amazed by his reaction. She'd expected shock and denunciation.

'Would you really? Her name is Annie Ryan. She's not as tall as me but she's much prettier. She has blonde hair and deep blue eyes.'

'With that description I don't think I'll have much trouble.'

Maybe she'd given him too much of a description. She just prayed Annie hadn't forgotten her upbringing and wasn't doing something 'desperate' as Con would put it.

'Cheer up, Ellen, things have a way of working themselves out.'

'Oh, I hope so.' She smiled, and with him by her side she began to feel that one day they might.

★ ★ ★

They both found Maggie in better spirits. She'd been so delighted to have contact with her sister's son again. She didn't feel so alone in the world now. She knew he wouldn't have stood by and let her be beaten, if he'd known. Ellen, Tessie and Gussie were so good, so generous, but of course she'd never known that before. *He'd* never let her associate with them. Dirty slummies, he'd always called them. She looked at Ellen and saw something different about her and she smiled to herself. Ellen was obviously taken with Ben and as she watched them she knew the feeling was mutual. When she got out of here she'd ask him to come and live with herself and Lucy. He'd be able to see more of Ellen then.

During Ellen's next visit to the hospital she found it hard to concentrate and she barely looked at Ben. She'd give herself away if she did and she wasn't completely sure of her feelings yet.

'I thought she was looking much better tonight.' Ben said as they crossed the road.

'So did I. Sort of happy and excited. She'll be out soon and I think she's really looking forward to it. But she kept staring at me oddly and I don't know why. Maybe because she's thinking about Lucy, and Lucy's with me.'

'Or maybe it's something else.'

'Like what?' she asked, puzzled.

He looked down at her. 'Like . . . us? Do you think you could ever . . . well . . . like me, Ellen?'

She was first startled and then full of pure happiness.

Her feelings were so intense that she shivered. 'I . . . I . . . of course I *like* you, Ben.'

'I know we haven't known each other long, you hardly know anything about me, but as soon as I saw you I knew . . . something . . .' He looked down at his boots, confused and apprehensive. What if she gave him the brush off? What if she laughed and made fun of him? Told him she never wanted to see him again? Well, he'd find out now. Nothing ventured, nothing gained. He was surprised and heartened to see that her eyes were shining as she looked up at him.

'I just *knew* that too. I more than like you, Ben.' She felt jittery and nervous yet elated.

'Ellen, I know it's not the time and place, but . . . well . . . I love you.'

'Oh, Ben, I think I . . . I've loved you from the first time I set eyes on you.'

He gathered her in his arms. She made no attempt to pull away. She felt that this was exactly just how it should be.

'Oh, Ellen, I've never stopped thinking about you. It's crazy, it's foolish, it's . . . Oh, I don't know.'

She reached up and stroked his cheek. There were tears in her eyes. Tears of pure joy. 'It's not crazy or daft, we were meant to be together.'

'I sail in two days. Can I see you before I go?'

'Yes, every day, please.'

'Will you . . . I mean . . . will you wait for me, Ellen?'

'I'll wait for ever, I promise.'

'I haven't got much to offer you. I've nothing really, I'm just a common labourer.'

'No, you're not. You told me yourself it's a skilful job being a stoker.'

'I've no home to offer you, not even a single room.'

'I don't care, Ben, I just want to be with you, that's if . . . if . . .' A thought flashed through her mind. Oh, what if she was reading too much into his words? What if he only meant . . .

He saw her confusion. 'Ellen, when I get home next will you marry me? I'll always look after you but I'll understand if you want time to think.'

She didn't need time to think. 'Yes, of course I'll marry you, Ben.' She'd never felt so happy in all her life. Over the next two days they'd sort everything out. The family, his job, where they would live. So much to do in so short a time. He'd be home again in two weeks, the Cunard ships were fast. 'Ocean greyhounds,' she'd heard them called. She felt swept up in a tide that raced along, carrying her with it. She *knew* it was right. They were *meant* to fall in love and marry. She *knew* that Mam and Da would have approved.

He held her closely and kissed the top of her forehead. 'I wasn't expecting you to come rushing off with me to the church, but . . .'

She raised her lips to his and he forgot the rest of the sentence.

She was reluctant to board the tram when it arrived so he got on with her.

'I'll see you home.'

'Thanks.' Her eyes were shining and she wanted to tell

everyone on the tram that she was in love and would be getting married soon. But she didn't, she just sat quietly, holding his hand.

When they reached Milton Street she turned to him. 'I wish I could ask you in, but . . .'

'Ellen, I understand. You need time to tell them. On your own, not with me around. They'll be a bit surprised, shocked even.'

She nodded.

'So, I'll see you tomorrow afternoon? Will that be all right?'

'Yes. Everyone will be out, there'll be just Daniel and me.'

He took her in his arms again and kissed her, then he pulled away. 'I'll see you tomorrow.'

She watched him walk away. Yes, tomorrow they'd sort everything out. But she knew of at least one person who wasn't going to be happy at all. Uncle Con.

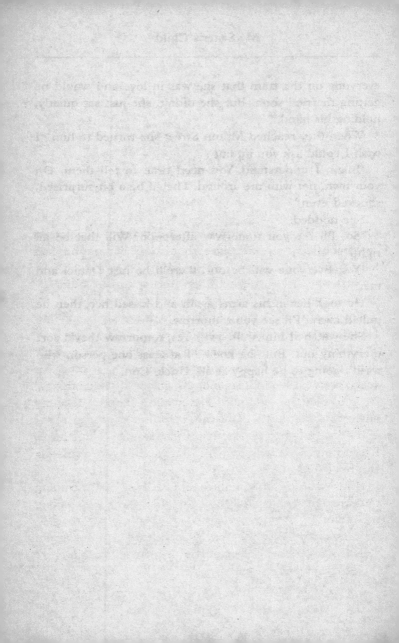

Chapter Twenty-Five

Gussie, who had been sitting with Lucy and Daniel, could see by Ellen's shining eyes that something good had happened.

'Just what are yer up to, Ellen? Yer look fit ter burst.'

'I've met someone and I'm going to get married.'

Gussie was visibly startled. 'Jesus, Mary an' Joseph! Who? How long have yer known 'im? What's 'is name?'

'He's Maggie's nephew, Ben Hayes, and I know you'll think I'm crazy because we haven't known each other for years, been engaged for six months, any of the usual things.'

'You're off yer 'ead, girl! Never mind "crazy". Take my advice an' go slowly. 'Ow can yer know someone if yer don't really know 'im? Not that 'e isn't a nice enough feller. I seen him in the 'ospital with Maggie. 'E looks a fine big lad, but . . .'

'I just *know* he's the right one, I really do. He's coming tomorrow afternoon so we can sort things out. He's sailing very soon.'

' 'E's a stoker, isn't 'e? God, Ellen, be careful. Think again. Them Black Gangs is shockin' fer drinkin' an' fightin'.'

'Oh, he's not like that.'

''Ow do yer know what 'e's like when 'e's away?'

'I don't, but I'm going to marry him because I love him.'

'Ellen, if yer poor mam, God rest 'er, were here she'd go mad. I know she would. At least she'd insist yer wait. Get engaged fer a year, do things proper, like. Fer God's sake, girl, don't go in like a bull in a china shop because it could all end with a broken heart – yours.'

'It *won't*! I *know*! I really *know*!'

Gussie sighed and shrugged. 'Well, I know someone who won't be very 'appy an' could even put a stop to it altogether.'

'Uncle Con can't stop me!' Ellen cried as the meaning of the older woman's words sunk in.

'You're not twenty-one yet, Ellen, an' I suppose yer could call 'im yer guardian.'

'Then I'm not going to tell him at all.'

' 'E'll find out one way or another.'

'No, he won't. I'll just tell him I've met Ben and he's asked me to walk out with him, that's all.'

Gussie took note of Ellen's obstinate expression. 'Well, if yer mind's set on it . . .'

'It is,' Ellen replied firmly.

'Then I'll gerroff 'ome before meladdo comes in from the pub. 'Oo are yer going ter tell?'

'Eddie, Tessie, the lads and Lucy but I'll swear them to secrecy.'

'Well, let's 'ope they can all keep their traps shut. At least Eddie won't be around for much longer. I 'eard he's sailin' soon.'

Ellen nodded, thanked her neighbour again and sat down

before the fire. Her neighbour was one of the worst gossips in the street but she knew at least she could be trusted with this news. Gussie was right, Con could prove a serious threat. She'd go to bed before he came home, even though she knew she wouldn't sleep. She was too excited.

She'd tidied up all morning then put on her best blouse and skirt and fiddled with her hair until she was satisfied that it looked becoming, in a softer style than usual. Gussie had taken baby Daniel into her house for the afternoon. Gussie had informed Tessie of the news and she was of the same opinion as her neighbour that Ellen was mad. Ellen hadn't had time to tell the rest of the family, except Eddie. She'd had to ask him to go out for the afternoon.

He was astounded. 'Ellen, you don't mean it? You *can't* mean it!'

'I do mean it. I love him. When you find the right girl you'll know it, you'll know just how I feel right now.'

'But he's one of a Black Gang. They're terrible, Ellen. They've been known to kill each other in drunken fights. No one tries to stop them, not even the officers.'

'He's not like that, Eddie. He really isn't.'

Eddie shook his head and looked very perturbed. 'I can see it's no use trying to talk you out of it. When are you going to tell Uncle Con?'

'The night before I get married.'

'I don't blame you.'

'I do have plans, Eddie. Ben won't have to be part of a Black Gang for ever.'

Eddie had looked doubtful. 'I hope you know what you're doing, Ellen.'

Now she felt nervous and her hand trembled slightly as she pulled the curtain aside to try to see if he was coming down the street. She let it fall into place as she caught sight of him. Giving her hair a final pat, she went into the lobby to wait.

'Come in, Ben,' she said, smiling, as she opened the front door.

'You look lovely, Ellen. Here, these are for you.'

She smiled at him. 'Oh, you and your flowers. Don't let your mates hear about it. Still, I think I'll always love violets.'

She put the flowers in a small glass jar and made a pot of tea. He watched her. He was even more certain that he loved her and he didn't intend to let her slip away from him. He wished he could offer her more than the few pounds he'd managed to save by not going on a drinking, gambling and womanising shore leave like most of the men he worked with. He did have a drink – God knows he'd earned it – but he never let himself get completely broke like most of them.

'I've been awake half the night, Ellen, thinking, planning,' he said, taking the cup from her.

'So have I, Ben.'

'I thought that after we're married we could live in Auntie Maggie's house until she comes home. She wouldn't mind, I'm sure, and I'd pay her rent. We'd be lodgers. Well, not quite, we'd really be more of a family. I'll be away a lot, will you mind that?'

'I . . . I was thinking about that and of how you said you

hated going to sea and I thought, if you don't mind, that if I bought another horse and cart you could become part of the business. I intended to get a second cart soon anyway.'

He looked taken aback. Part of a business. Working for himself – for her, that was something he had never in his wildest dreams envisaged.

'It's not . . . charity, Ben. You'll *be* part of the family. It was Da's dearest wish: "a family firm", and Mam tried her best to keep it going, but Eddie loves the sea, Tom wants to be a reporter and Bernie will be going to a Technical School. So you see we need help with the business; you'd be part of it, a really important part.'

'What about your uncle?' he asked. 'How will he take it?'

'I've not told him yet and I don't intend to until the night before we get married. You see, I'm not twenty-one and Mrs Cooney said he could stop me getting married because he's my guardian or something.'

'The more I hear about him, the less I like him, Ellen.'

'Oh, I'm sorry Mam ever asked him to come to Liverpool to run the business. Almost since he arrived we've been terrified that one day he'll sell everything and go back to Ireland with the money.'

'Not if I have a say in it he won't.'

'Oh, Ben, I'm so relieved.'

'We'll have to get a special dispensation from the church. They usually have to call the banns in both parishes.' He took her hand. 'I'll go and sort that out, Ellen. Will you still want to live here?'

She nodded. 'I have them all to see to: Lucy, the lads

and now Daniel. It'll be a bit cramped to say the least but I'll live in Maggie's house if you really want me to.'

'It's what *you* want, Ellen,' he said earnestly.

'Well, let's see what happens. I'm a bit concerned about Lucy.'

'She'll get used to me in time, I know she will.'

Ellen smiled at him. 'So, will you become part of the business?'

'Try and stop me! My own boss, no slaving in a place as hot and dangerous as the hobs of hell! I'll never be able to thank you, Ellen.'

'You won't need to. I won't have you beholden to me like that. You'll be working – working for *us* – and working hard, out in all weathers.'

He took her in his arms. 'I'll love it. Life has just become so . . . so wonderful. I love you so much, Ellen Ryan.'

'In a couple of weeks it'll be Ellen Hayes,' she said, her cheeks flushing with happiness.

'That's right. Mrs Ben Hayes – for ever.'

The rest of the family took the news in different ways. Tom and Bernie seemed only interested in how much these changes would affect their lives. Eddie was dubious but relieved he would be away and would never have to give up the sea to work in the business. Lucy went very pale and quiet until Ellen had explained everything in great detail and with firm reassurances that her mam would be home soon and they really hadn't decided where they were going to live yet.

Gussie and Tessie were both going into town with Ellen

to choose something to wear for her wedding. They'd both
gone with her to see Father Healy too, and lent their
support, grudgingly. Ben had gone to the Register Office
in Brougham Terrace for the special licence before he sailed.

She wasn't having the traditional long white dress and
veil, there wasn't the time or the money, nor could she risk
Con finding anything out.

'Just a nice dress and hat, that's all,' she'd told both her
neighbours.

'I don't know if yer mam would 'ave approved of it all,
Ellen, but we'll be glad ter cum, like. Sort of in 'er place,'
Tessie had replied when she and Gussie had been asked.

'Blackler's, Frisby Dyke's, Sturla's or Frost's?' Gussie
asked.

'Blackler's. I don't want to pay too much so Frisby
Dyke's is out and the other two are a bit . . . well . . .'

'Ordinary?' Tessie had finished.

Once inside the department store they all looked around.
'Yer know it's ages since I've been in 'ere. God, would yer
look at the style of the place,' Gussie said in almost
reverential tones. Her family clothes were almost always
bought second-hand so there were few occasions when she
ventured across the doorsteps of the big shops.

Tessie gazed up the well of the staircase. 'Am I seein'
things or is that a parrot up there?'

'Fer God's sake, Tessie, don't show yer ignorance.
They've 'ad that parrot fer years.'

'It can't be the same one! 'Ave they 'ad it stuffed, like?'

' 'Ow the hell should I know?'

Two sales assistants were approaching.

' 'Ere comes the 'eavy mob!' Tessie muttered.

'Well, we're here to buy an' our money's as good as anyone else's!' Gussie said emphatically.

'May we help, er . . . ladies?' the older of the two asked. They both wore the uniform of all shop assistants: a plain black dress with detachable white collar and cuffs, the ankle-length skirt revealing polished black button boots.

'Yer can. She's lookin' fer somethin' special, like, fer 'er weddin'.'

'But not a proper wedding dress,' Ellen interrupted hastily.

Seeing that their intention was actually to buy and not just wander around doing God knows what, the elder of the women moved away. The younger one was more Ellen's age.

'What about something in pale pink or peach?' she suggested.

'Well, maybe peach. Pink is a bit . . .'

'Washed-out-looking,' the girl replied, smiling. It wasn't often that she was left on her own to attend to customers. She'd only been there for two months, and the girl was young – about her own age. She wondered which of the old battleaxes was the mother and which the future mother-in-law.

She disappeared and Tessie and Gussie wandered around looking at the price of the dresses.

'God, would yer look at the price of this, Tessie? An' it says "Economically Priced" on the ticket! I don't call fifteen and six "Economical" at all. Yer could rig out the whole family fer that!'

Tessie sniffed her agreement. 'They 'as no idea 'ow the rest of us live. That's a man's flamin' wage, if 'e's lucky enough ter get work. We'd best get back before they sell Ellen somethin' she can't afford and won't wear again. Oh, I know these types,' Tessie finished, although she knew she knew nothing about 'these types' at all.

The assistant had reappeared with two dresses draped over her arm, one of peach taffeta trimmed with cream ribbons, the other cream trimmed with peach ribbons and buttons. She held them out for Ellen's inspection.

'I think I like the peach one better.' She'd never owned a dress in her life. It had always been blouses and skirts. This looked a dream.

'Then we'll try it, if you'll come with me?'

Tessie and Gussie had another opportunity to search and remark about the scandalous prices but when Ellen appeared they both gasped and clasped their hands.

'Oh, Ellen! Yer mam would 'ave been over the moon ter see yer.'

'Yer look gorgeous, luv. 'E'll be delighted with yer.'

Ellen flushed with pleasure. When the dress had been carefully lifted over her head and she'd looked at herself in the long mirror it was just as if a miracle had happened. She was transformed. The dress had a high collar and leg-o'-mutton sleeves; the deep cuffs were fastened with tiny pearl buttons. Narrow bands of cream satin ribbon ran in rows from the collar to the edge of the bodice. The skirt was full, longer than she usually wore and made her waist look tiny.

'It's a bit tight,' she'd said as the assistant fastened up

the row of buttons at the back of the bodice.

'It's the boning. Have you never worn a corset?'

'No.'

'I wish I hadn't but in here they insist! Miss Harper – the other one – has hers laced so tightly I wonder she can breathe, let alone eat!' the girl whispered conspiratorially. 'There.' She stood back after puffing out the skirt.

'Is that really *me*?' Ellen had gasped.

'It is. Would you like to show the other . . . ladies?'

'Oh, yes please.'

Their astonished reaction made her want to pinch herself. Surely she was dreaming – she felt happy and sad at the same time.

'Now for a hat, miss.' The sales girl had really entered into the spirit of the thing, especially as her superior had left her alone.

'Oh, she's gorra 'ave a dead posh 'at,' Tessie enthused.

'Just excuse me while I go and fetch a couple from Millinery.'

' 'Ow much is it, Ellen? It's dead gorgeous but I mean can yer afford it?'

'I can afford it.'

Gussie was inspecting the back and found the price ticket. 'It's twenty-one shillin's. I don't suppose it's bad, not when you consider them "Economical"-priced ones.'

'It's a bit tight. She said it was the boning and asked did I never wear a corset.'

'Yer've no need of one of them things, Ellen, yet. I wore one once. When I was first married, like, but after I 'ad our Mary I give up on it. I was crucified with the damned thing and 'avin kids ruins yer figure anyway.'

'An' who 'as time ter be messin' about lacin' the flamin' things?' Gussie added.

The assistant returned with two large peach and cream picture hats trimmed with bows and artificial flowers.

Ellen tried them both but settled for the less fancy one.

'All yer'd need on the other one is a stuffed bird an' yer'd 'ave the lot. Feathers, flowers and flounces, as me mam used ter say,' Gussie whispered.

When everything had been wrapped and paid for and the assistant thanked they left. She watched them go with some regret, wishing she were getting married. Still, it was a good sale and she'd enjoyed it.

'Will we go for a cup of tea?'

'Can yer afford one, Ellen?' asked Gussie doubtfully.

'I think so. The hat was a bit more than I intended to pay but . . . oh, you only get married once!'

'Hopefully, but look at 'er in number fifty. Three times a widder, that one.'

'Oh, fer God's sake, Gussie, purra sock in it, will yer? I'm wore out an' I just 'ope your Mary is lookin' after that baby properly.'

'One cup of tea and then home,' Ellen pronounced firmly.

They made their way to Lime Street where there was a small café where you could get a pot of tea and a scone for sixpence.

'The perfect end to a perfect outin',' Tessie remarked as she pushed open the door. Ellen, however, didn't go in; she was standing looking across the street towards the station concourse.

'What's up with yer?' Gussie demanded, looking closely at Ellen for her cheeks had lost the flush of excitement and her eyes their sparkle.

'Nothing. It's just that I thought . . . I thought I saw Annie across the road, on the station steps.'

'Where?' Tessie demanded, stepping on to the pavement again.

'She's gone now, but I'm sure it was her and she was all dressed up too. Really dressed up. A hat and gloves and handbag too.'

The two older women exchanged glances and pursed their lips.

'It can't 'ave been. Your Annie was never dressed up like that in 'er life. A hat! Gloves! A handbag! No. Let's get that cuppa, I'm spittin' feathers.' Gussie gently pushed Ellen into the café. It very probably was Annie Ryan. She had the looks and the barefaced cheek to be strutting up and down Lime Street at this time of day. Maybe the hat and gloves were to fool the scuffers for it wouldn't be long before she was arrested. Common little tart.

Chapter Twenty-Six

Annie hadn't been looking across the road. She was intent on searching the faces of the crowd, eagerly waiting for Juan Caballe. He had promised to meet her here. She adjusted her hat a little so more of her face was visible. She had been so lucky to meet him, she thought. Oh, she'd been heart-broken and half demented that night and she'd been so fortunate that just as she'd got to the main road a tram was at the stop. The driver had waited for her.

'God, girl, yer look awful, are yer ill?' he'd asked with concern.

'No, just a bit out of breath. I'll be fine when I've sat down for a few minutes,' she'd answered.

She'd felt weak and sick and tears were welling up in her eyes. She must have looked terrible.

Now she fiddled with her soft leather gloves. She still couldn't get used to the feel of them. She'd never worn gloves before.

He'd saved her from a life at Maisey's. She'd never felt so depressed or full of self-loathing in her life before but then she'd met the tall, handsome first officer of a Spanish cargo ship. He'd been gentle and he'd been kind. So kind that he'd insisted on her leaving Maisey's, promising he would find a couple of nice rooms. He seemed besotted with her. He'd showered her with gifts. Everything she now wore he'd bought, even her underwear, the silk stockings and dainty shoes. Things she'd never had in her life before. And he treated her like a lady, someone of worth. Her first couple of 'clients' had treated her as if she were not a person at all, just an object to satisfy their needs, a common whore. But she wasn't a whore, she told herself. Freddie Rafferty had taken advantage of her.

She looked askance at a police constable who was patrolling the station. Well, if he approached her she'd tell him she was a respectable married woman waiting for her husband. Was that a crime now? Again she patted her hat and peered up the street. Then she smiled as she saw him approaching.

'Did you find somewhere?' she asked, her deep blue eyes sparkling. Her eyes were one of the things that he found most attractive about her. That and her youth, fair soft skin and the abundance of curly blonde hair which when loose fell to below her shoulders.

'Yes, I think so. Two very nice, clean rooms and I will buy furniture. What was there was not suitable.'

'Oh, Juan, where are they? Can we go and see them now?'

He smiled. 'Of course, my little English rosebud!'

Annie laughed. She was fully aware of what attracted him. She was also aware that back in Valencia there was a Señora Caballe and four children. He had answered her questions truthfully. He'd not even tried to evade them.

'There is not much to tell,' was how he'd answered. 'Ana is a good woman, a good mother. I don't see much of any of them and she has accepted that. It is part of my career and they are well cared for. I don't think she misses the passion that there once was between us.'

She took the slip of paper from him. 'Number six, Neston Street,' she read aloud. 'That's off County Road in Walton. It's a nice part of the city.'

He tucked her arm through his and they walked to the tram stop.

All the way there Annie's thoughts were racing. He'd promised to give her money for a decent roof over her head and clothes on her back and so far he had. He was away for almost two months at a time, so she could go and get her baby back. She would explain fully about Daniel and that little rat Freddie Rafferty. She would make him see she wasn't really a whore. That she'd been brought up decently. She'd made one mistake, only one, but it had totally changed her life. And now, dressed as she was, wouldn't she just love to see the faces of Ellen, Gussie Cooney and that loud, common Tessie Ogden?

The rooms were on a quiet road of red-brick Victorian terraced houses. There wasn't one building that looked dirty or run down. All the paintwork was fresh and bright; there were no dirty grey-looking cotton curtains at the windows, all were pristine white. Number 6 had a smart dark blue front door and, as he opened the gate that led to a short pathway, she noticed the curtains twitch in the house next door.

'They're watching us. Seeing if we are respectable enough,' she whispered.

'And are we?' He spoke perfect English. So perfect that sometimes he didn't understand what she said, for her accent was so strong.

'We are indeed.' She raised her chin as he knocked.

'Ah, good day once more, Mrs Coleman. I have brought my wife to see the accommodation, as I promised.'

The woman took one look at Annie and knew she was definitely not his wife. But he was paying over the odds, he had told her he was an officer and up to now he seemed to be a gentleman as well. The girl was well dressed and very pretty.

'Please do come in,' she replied with a light smile.

Annie smiled back as she was ushered into the hall and her landlady opened a door on her left. Annie bit back the cry of surprise and joy. She had never seen a room like this, not even in Newsham Park, although she'd never got beyond the kitchen while she was there. It looked as if it had recently been decorated. The pale blue wallpaper matched the curtains. There was a carpet on the floor, a good one. Over the fireplace was an ornate gilt mirror and on one wall was a picture of a garden in summer. She couldn't see what was wrong with the furniture.

'It's . . . it's very nice,' she managed to say calmly as if she'd been used to living in houses like this.

'As I explained, madam, the furniture will not do.'

'But it will be fine until we can choose something else,' Annie interrupted.

She caught the smile that hovered on the woman's lips as she opened the door again.

'Now the bedroom.'

Again it was nicely decorated, the rug was good and the floorboards had been varnished. Once again she could see nothing wrong with the furniture. There was a marble-topped washstand, complete with a china jug and bowl set. The bedspread and eiderdown looked a little faded but she could see they had been expensive when new.

'I . . . I think it will suit us well, Mrs Coleman.'

'You'll have to share the kitchen with us but I'm sure we'll work that out. I'm only renting out because I've been widowed fairly recently.'

'I'm sorry to hear that, madam,' Juan said deferentially before continuing. 'And the other . . . amenities?'

'In the yard. All very clean. Scrubbed and disinfected every day.'

Annie looked up at him. All her life she'd had to share filthy stinking privies. 'I'm sure we can take Mrs Coleman's word for that.'

'You like it? You are happy with it, Anne?' he asked.

It was a little off-putting to be called by her proper Christian name and she had to shake herself mentally to remember that. 'Oh, I'm very happy with it, Juan.'

'Good. Then here is two months' rent plus a deposit.' He counted out the notes.

'Well, I'll leave you to get . . . used . . . er, accustomed to it.'

'Our personal things and clothes will be brought later on,' Annie said.

'I'm sure they will.'

As her new landlady closed the door behind her Annie threw her arms around him. 'Oh, Juan! It's . . . it's . . . perfect.'

'Then you can show me how much you approve of this "perfect" choice.'

'Shall we start "approving" the bedroom?'

He took her in his arms. 'I think that would be a good place to start.'

She hadn't found the right moment to mention Daniel. In fact she was a little dubious about it. She didn't want to lose everything. He'd be sailing in two days and she wouldn't see him again for two months so she'd go to Milton Street and then bring Daniel here. When Juan came to Liverpool next he would be desperate for her and then she would tell him and Daniel would be two months older and . . . oh, he was sure to understand her predicament.

She'd spent a happy couple of days choosing furniture which was to be delivered and her landlady had said she would remove all the existing furniture into storage. She had advised them to shop at Hiller's on County Road. As a leaving gift he'd bought her a gold locket on a chain with a photograph of himself in it.

'Now you will be able to see me every day, and you must have a photograph taken and put it in the locket too.' He'd laughed when she'd finished kissing him. 'You do love me, Anne?'

'Of course I do. I've told you, you are the first person to treat me so . . . so well.'

'And you'll be waiting for me?'

'I'll check *The Journal of Commerce* every week to see exactly when your ship is due in and I'll be at the dock gate.'

'Oh, Anne, I just wish I'd met you fifteen years ago, when I was a young and free man.'

'So do I, but to me you are still young and there's nothing we can do about . . . about you being free. I love you just the same.' She meant it. At least she thought she loved him. But what was love really? She'd loved her mam and da but that was a different kind of love. Now she was secure, well cared for, well dressed and he'd given her money to live on. What more could she ask? Yes, in her way she loved him.

Next morning he was packed and ready to go and so was she. She felt a little depressed at the thought of the future: she'd have no one to talk to. But then she cheered up. This afternoon she'd have Daniel back with her.

He didn't take her aboard his ship, which was tied up in the Hornby Dock; instead when they reached the dock gate he took her in his arms and kissed her.

'I'll write to you and please, Anne, take care of yourself.'

'I will, I promise,' she said, smiling up at him.

He turned away and began to walk towards the *Maria Antonia*. She watched him and when he reached the gangway he turned and waved. She waved back then turned away to get a tram to Milton Street.

Everyone was out at work or school and Ellen was doing the ironing with Daniel asleep in his makeshift cot in front of the fire. He was a beautiful baby, she thought. Already he was so much a part of her life. She couldn't believe just how happy she was nowadays. She could barely hide her excitement. Not long to wait now and she would be married. It had upset her terribly when Ben had sailed but she took comfort from the fact that it was for the last time. Her dress was hanging behind the bedroom door, covered with an old sheet and her hat was in its box under the bed. Mary Ogden and Sally Cooney had told her they would get her a small posy of flowers as a sort of wedding present. They were both the same age as her and as neither had a steady boyfriend, were a bit envious. Everyone was sworn to secrecy in case Con found out but she thanked God that he didn't appear to notice anything different about her demeanour.

When she heard the knock on the front door she was irritated. Who on earth was this and why knock? The door was open. She put the flat iron back on the hearth and went into the lobby.

Her eyes widened as she saw the figure on the step. 'Annie! Annie, is that you? And all dressed up?'

'It is. Can I come in?'

'Of course, this will always be your home.'

'No it won't,' Annie sniffed. 'Besides I have a home of my own now.'

'Come in and I'll put the kettle on. We were all so worried about you.'

'I'll bet you were,' Annie answered sarcastically.

Nothing much had changed, she thought as she followed Ellen down the lobby. God, the place really was a pigsty, despite the fact that Ellen did her best. How had she stuck it for all those years? Annie was used to better things now. Even when she'd been at Maisey's it was better than this. Ellen didn't seem to have changed much either. The same clothes, the work-roughened hands, but her hair was different. The style was softer and when she looked really closely at her stepsister she realised there was something about Ellen that she couldn't quite put her finger on.

'You look well, Annie,' Ellen said. 'Those are beautiful clothes.' They looked to be even more expensive than her wedding outfit.

'Thanks.' Annie's eyes were fixed on the drawer where her baby lay asleep. She wanted to scoop him up in her arms. She'd really missed him.

Ellen noticed and felt her heart drop like a stone, but she busied herself with the kettle.

'Why didn't you come to Mam's funeral?'

'I couldn't and you know why. You wanted everyone to see my . . . my condition.'

'That's not fair, neither is it right. I *did* want you to come.'

'Well, I've not come here for an argument.'

'What have you come for?' Ellen asked, although she already knew the answer.

'For my baby. For Daniel.'

'You left him here, Annie, you just dumped him. You could have come in and explained, asked me to look after him.'

'Oh, yes! We could have had a nice chat about things over a cup of tea! Grow up, Ellen!'

Ellen's temper was rising. 'We *could*. You never gave me the chance. You've always resented me, Annie, but what for, God alone knows.'

'Well, I've come up in the world now. I've a decent home for him and money to give him everything you can't.'

Ellen nodded slowly. 'I knew that's what you'd come for.'

'And so did I,' Gussie said coming through the scullery. 'All done up like a fancy lady, walkin' down the street slowly so everyone would get a good look at yer, then knockin' on the door. The bloody nerve! Yer might 'ave expensive clothes but you're still a tart! Who paid for that get-up? A dozen or more fellers, or 'ave yer struck it lucky? Found yerself some old fool who doesn't want too much for 'is money!'

Annie rounded on her. 'I'm not a tart! And where I got the money and the clothes is nothing to do with you, you nosy old cow!'

'A nosy old cow, is it! I can tell yer a few home truths, yer little slut! Yer didn't even go ter yer ma's funeral then yer dumped that baby on the back step, without botherin' to find out what kind of a state things were in in 'ere. Yer didn't bloody care. All yer've ever cared about is yerself an' it's you that's the bloody cow. You're not fit ter bring up that child.'

'He's *my* child.'

'He's Freddie Rafferty's bastard an' with you fer a mam, he'll probably be flung inter jail as soon as he's old enough ter go thievin' and fightin',' Gussie shouted.

'He'll grow up to be a gentleman!' Annie yelled back.

'A gentleman! Will yer bloody listen to 'er? 'Ow long do yer think yer fancy man will last? Does he know about the child?'

'Of course he does!' Annie snapped back.

'No 'e doesn't, I can see it in yer eyes!'

'Oh, please stop it, both of you. It's not doing any good and now you've woken him.' Ellen bent and picked the baby up, rocking him in her arms to try to hide the tears that had sprung into her eyes. He *was* Annie's baby. She had every right to take him to live with her and bring him up, but Ellen had grown to love him so much that it was tearing at her heart to admit those things.

She handed him over to Annie with bitter reluctance. Would she ever see him again? Annie wouldn't bring him down to Milton Street. She'd make sure Ellen saw as little of him as possible. She'd never see him take his first steps, cut his first tooth, utter his first word and she wanted so much to experience all those things – and more.

She fought down the sobs. 'I'll get his things together.'

'Don't bother, I'll buy him new ones on the way home and I'll have a proper cot delivered. He's not going to have to make do with that.' She indicated the chest drawer with her head.

'Can I . . . can I see him? I mean come to your house?'

'What for? Just to spy and then come back and gossip about what I have or haven't got? No, it'd be better if you never saw him again.'

'Yer hard-hearted, selfish little bitch. Ellen 'as done everythin' fer 'im and she fought with Con over keeping him. That feller was all set ter take him ter an orphanage.'

Annie ignored her and took the paper bag in which Ellen had packed his few things. 'I'll be going now, and don't try to follow me or find me!'

The front door slammed shut and Ellen sank on to the sofa and began to cry softly. She thought her heart would break.

'Ah, cum on, luv. Yer did yer best, there's nothin' else yer can do. The courts would never let yer 'ave 'im.'

'Oh, I know, Gussie, but . . . but . . . what will happen to him?'

'Don't worry, luv, she's a born survivor, is that one. She'll always 'ave money and I think she meant it when she said 'e wouldn't go short.'

'Oh, I hope you're right, I really do. I'm going to miss him so much.'

'You're bound to, Ellen, but look on the bright side, yer'll be married yerself soon and one day yer'll 'ave yer own babies.'

Ellen wiped her eyes. Gussie was right. She would just have to concentrate on her own wedding. But she couldn't believe she'd ever forget about Daniel; he'd been a bright ray of light in her life and now that light had gone, possibly for ever. She just hoped and prayed Annie would look after him as she'd said she would. That was all she could do for him now. She felt helpless and bereft, and longed for Ben's comforting arms more than ever.

Chapter Twenty-Seven

Somehow everybody had managed to keep Ellen's secret from Con and on the Thursday night when the *Carpathia* was due to dock there was a much-needed, welcome surprise waiting for Ellen when she went into the hospital to see Maggie.

Ellen thought how much younger Maggie looked and how much colour her cheeks had in them now. Even the scars were beginning to fade. She looked so different to the broken, bloody woman she had once been.

'I'm going home tomorrow. I'll be home, Ellen, in time for your wedding.'

'Oh, that's great, it's really great! And Lucy will be over the moon. She's missed you so much.' Missing Daniel had brought home to Ellen just how hard it must have been for Maggie and Lucy to be apart.

'Oh, I know and I've missed her but you've been so good to her, Ellen. I knew she'd be well cared for.'

Ellen smiled. 'What else could I do? She's been happy with us—'

'Yes, for the first time in her life she's been really happy,' Maggie interrupted with bitterness in her voice.

'All she wants now is to go back home and live with you. We'll still see a lot of her, you know what Milton Street's like.' Ellen laughed.

'I don't really, Ellen, and I've lived there all my married life. But I'll find things out for myself now. Things that I never knew. Like how good and generous people like Tessie and Gussie are. We'll both be really happy, Ellen, with the house to ourselves.'

Ellen took her hand. 'Of course you will.' She would rather die herself than tell this still frail woman what her now deceased husband had done to the daughter Maggie loved so much. She was certain Maggie knew what had happened to *him* but she never ever mentioned his name and police inquiries had stopped. They had better things to do with their time than carry on looking for the likes of John Meakin, who by now could be anywhere in the world. Liverpool was a busy, thriving port.

'Will you come to the church?'

Maggie's brow creased in a frown. 'I don't know how strong I'll be.'

'Let's just wait and see. If you're not up to it I'll understand.'

The frown disappeared. 'Just think, Ellen, you'll be family. Ben's a good lad. I only wish I'd seen more of him and his mam and da. They were good people too.'

Ellen nodded. 'Don't fret about it, it just wasn't possible. But I know he's good – I'm so lucky.'

'And you met him in here so a little bit of good has come out of . . . of what happened to me.'

'I wish it had been different, for your sake.'

Maggie smiled. 'Don't worry about me. I'm looking forward to a different life now. A happy one. Go on, get off to meet him and I'll see you tomorrow.'

'Do the others know you're coming home? Tessie and Gussie?'

'No.'

'I'll make sure they do, tonight, as soon as I get home.'

'Go on, luv, or you might miss him.'

All the way down to the docks on the tram Ellen's heart was beating faster and faster. He had only been away two weeks but she had missed him so much. It was a cold, clear night and the Dock Road was busy.

As she got off, the *Carpathia*'s funnels, rigging and portholes were all lit up and she quickened her steps. The passengers would already have disembarked at the Pier Head with their luggage, and now it was crew who were coming down the gangway. A small group of women of all ages stood at the gates. A little of her euphoria disappeared. She didn't want to have to wait here with them. They were only here for one purpose. To get as much money from their husbands as possible before it was spent in the dozens of pubs on the Dock Road.

'Can I go through and meet my . . . my fiancé, please?' she pleaded with the policeman on the dock gate. 'I know it's not really allowed . . .'

He looked at the group of women. 'It's not. I'd have every wife, mother and daughter down here. There would have to be at least three of us.'

'Oh, please? I won't be down here again, it's his last trip.

We're getting married on Saturday.'

He grinned. 'Go on then, girl, and the best of luck to you. I'll deal with this lot, they won't be very pleased but . . .' He shrugged.

'Thanks!'

As she walked across the cobbles towards the ship she searched the faces of the men who were coming ashore in ones and twos and then she saw him. Her heart leaped and she began to run.

When she reached him, he flung his arms around her, lifting her off her feet, and kissed her, to the resounding cheers of his fellow shipmates.

'Aye, Ben, purrer down, yer don't know where she's been, la!' someone shouted and they both laughed.

Ellen looked up at him, her eyes shining as he put his arm around her waist. 'Oh, it's been so hard, just waiting. I could never be the wife of a seaman. I don't know how they do it.'

'All that's kept me going is the thought of getting back to you and leaving the stokehold for good.'

'No, you'll *never* have to work like that again. I was up at the hospital. Your Auntie Maggie is coming home tomorrow!'

'That's great news.'

'It is, Lucy will be so pleased.'

'Did they . . .?' The question hung in the air.

'No. Not a sign. The police have stopped looking.'

'Good. Now we'll have to sort out where we're going to live. I'll take you for a drink and we can talk.' Seeing her anxious expression he hurried on. 'No, I don't mean any of the alehouses most of this lot are heading for. The Pen and Wig is respectable and they have a lounge bar – or would you prefer the snug?'

She relaxed. 'The snug, it'll be more private.'

It wasn't far to walk and as she looked around she saw that it *was* a decent pub. The snug, which fortunately was empty, even boasted a rug on the floor and fancy glass mantles on the gas jets.

'What will you have?'

'I don't know. I've never had a drink before. Not a proper one.'

'A sweet sherry?'

She nodded and watched him approach the hatch that opened to the public bar and knock loudly on it. Could she really feel any happier than she did now? Her heart felt as if it was going to burst.

He returned and put two glasses down on the table. 'So you've not told your uncle, I take it?'

'No, I'm going to tell him tomorrow night.'

'I'll come round.'

'Come later on, Ben, let me tell him alone. Besides, everyone will be having a bit of a drink. When I tell Tessie and Gussie there'll be a whip round for a little do to welcome Maggie home.'

'If you're sure.'

'I am. I can cope with him.'

He smiled. Two do's in two days!

'So, have you decided yet where we're going to live?' Ellen asked.

'I thought we'd have a couple of nights away.'

'A honeymoon?'

'I wish it could be a proper one, somewhere foreign maybe, but will Llandudno or Colwyn Bay do instead?'

'I don't care where we go, just as long as you're with me.'

'Then I'll sort it out tomorrow.'

Ellen sipped the drink and found she liked the taste. 'Will it be all right if we stay in my house for a while? It will mean Maggie and Lucy can have some time together and will sort of let me organise things. It's difficult being the only girl, I've had to take Mam's place. We'll wait to move in with Maggie until our Bernie goes to the Technical School. I'll still do the cleaning, washing, shopping and cooking and Gussie will keep her eye on them all, and I'll only be across the street. The only thing I'm worried about is how you and Uncle Con will get on.'

'Leave him to me, Ellen, you'll not be having to put up with rows and fights every day. I'll tell him straight that we won't be living there for ever so he can just put up with it. Auntie Maggie's got a nice home.'

'I know. Oh, Ben, I'm so happy. Everything good is happening at once. I'm the luckiest girl in the entire city.'

He took her hand. 'And I'm the luckiest bloke.'

As soon as Gussie and Tessie knew that Maggie was coming home next day, as late as it was, they launched into plans for a 'welcome home' do.

' 'Oose 'ouse will we 'ave it in?' Tessie asked.

'What about 'er own 'ouse?'

'Don't yer think she mightn't like everyone messin' the place up?'

'There won't be no "messin'" up! I'll see ter that,' Gussie said grimly.

'Fine, now what about food an' a drop ter drink?'

'You take one side of the street, I'll take the other. Ask them for anythin' at all, even farthin's,' Tessie said.

'I'll call in the Swan an' see what 'is nibs will cough up with.'

'Could we . . . could we put some sort of . . . decorations outside?' Lucy ventured. She had burst into tears of joy when Ellen had told her and her eyes were still shining.

'A banner,' Ellen suggested. 'We could make a banner. Mr Clarkson will give you an old sheet and you and Bernie and a couple of the other kids can write "Welcome Home" on it in big letters. Very big letters. Then one of the men can hang it between the two bedroom windows. Yours and Mrs Stanford's. You'll have to do it after school and be quick about it. Oh, Lucy, tomorrow is going to be great and Saturday is going to be even better!'

'Will Mam be able to go and see you, Ellen? You and Ben?'

'If she feels well enough, Lucy.' She hadn't failed to notice how easily the child had spoken Ben's name. She was obviously losing her fear of him and hopefully by the time they moved in with Maggie she would have accepted him. They'd all be happy from now on.

When she went to bed she couldn't sleep, she had so much going on in her mind. In all the hasty arrangements she'd neglected to ask her uncle for a contribution, but she'd do that tomorrow. She let her eyes roam over the darkened room. In two nights' time, Lucy would have gone home and she would be lying in a strange bed in a strange house in a Welsh seaside town and Ben would be lying beside her. If only she could have kept Daniel, then she'd consider life to be perfect. She missed him so much. But as Gussie had said, she'd have her own babies.

She was ready, dressed in her best skirt and blouse. She'd already sent Bernie and Lucy over the road and Tom had just followed them when Con came in and she asked him for a contribution.

'Is it made of money those bloody women think we are. Why all the fuss?'

'Because she deserves a bit of fuss, that's why. All her life she had to put up with . . . *him*.'

'Ah, sure, that's no reason at all.'

'Well, I expect you'll still take a drink.'

'I will so, because I'm paying for it.'

'Have your meal and get washed and changed. The kids have made a banner – perhaps you'd give Mr Cooney a hand to put it up.'

'Haven't I been out all day working? Let one of the others do it. Tom Stanford from next door to them, he's had no work to go to today.'

Ellen raised her eyes to the ceiling as Con slammed out. She was trying to stay calm but it was impossible. She was excited one minute at the thought that by this time tomorrow she'd be Mrs Ben Hayes, then apprehensive the next about telling Uncle Con she was not only getting married, but that Ben would now be a partner in the business. She would have felt less nervous if Eddie had been home but he'd had to sail.

Con reappeared in his Sunday suit and white winged collar which he was fiddling with.

'God, isn't it a bloody trial to have to wear this thing? Isn't it bad enough on Sundays? It has me nearly choked.'

'Before we go over the road there's something I've got to tell you.'

'There is?'

She nodded, feeling her stomach contract with nerves. 'Yes. Ben . . . Ben Hayes and I are getting married tomorrow morning and he's not going back to sea. He'll be family, so he's going to drive a second cart.'

Con stared at her, unable to take it in for a few seconds. Then his temper began to boil up. That big eejit of a gossoon! That feller fit only to work in a Black Gang? He was about to walk in here and take over? The silly little rossi had only known him a few weeks and she was going to marry him and give him a share in the business that he now considered his own. He was the only one in the family who humped sackfuls of coal around all day and in all weathers, and now . . .

'Are you out of your mind, girl?' he roared. 'Haven't you only known the big thicko a few weeks and—'

'He's not a big thicko!'

'He is so. What bloody lies has he told you?'

'None. He's good, he's kind and I love him! Now Lucy's going home we'll live here for a while—'

Con exploded. 'Jaysus! Over my dead body you will! If

you think I'm going to stand by and let him walk in here, you're mistaken, girl, and you're not even of age. *I'm* the one who says who you can or can't marry until you're twenty-one.'

'I don't give a fig about that! You came here with nothing. Mam gave you a roof over your head, three meals a day. A home and a position in life. You're forgetting all that and now you think you're head of the family. Well, you're not and you never will be! It was your gambling and drinking that forced Mam to get that job. The job that killed her! You were partly responsible for killing her!'

Con was nearly dancing with rage. She was asking for it! She'd always been a thorn in his flesh and he'd vowed to make her pay and that's just what he intended to do now. His gaze alighted on the horsewhip leaning in a corner. He'd forgotten to leave it behind when he'd settled Betsy. He seized it and advanced towards her.

'I'm going to show you who's the boss in this family! Me! You've been asking for this for months, you bold, bossy, contrary little rossi!'

Ellen was so surprised that she made no attempt to defend herself and the long thin leather lash caught her across her shoulders. She screamed in agony and fright and tried to grasp the end of it but he'd already pulled it away. She put her hands up to protect her face and had half turned away when the second stroke caught her, tearing the material of her blouse and biting into her skin. Again and again the lash descended, as if a red-hot knife were cutting into her. She screamed again and again, begging him to stop or he'd kill her. He took no notice. She was going to die! He was going to kill her for humiliating him!

She couldn't do a thing to fight back. She was on her knees now, her arms still wrapped around her head. She fell forward on to the floor. Shaking all over, terrified, in unbearable pain, suddenly she realised he'd stopped. Slowly she took her hands away from her face and looked up. Ben was standing over her, the whip clutched in his white-knuckled hands. She began to sob with relief.

'You bastard!' Ben roared. 'You yellow-bellied bastard! I'll kill you for what you've done to her!'

Ellen heard her uncle's yells of pain and the hissing, almost whistling sound of the leather thong. It was Con now begging for mercy.

Suddenly the room was full of people and noise and Gussie was lifting her up.

'Jesus, Mary an' Joseph! 'E's 'alf killed 'er, Ben! Look at the state of 'er! By God, I'll swing fer yer meself, yer get!'

'No one's going to swing because of him!' Ben shouted, 'Get your things together before I kill you. You're leaving Liverpool – now! I'm putting you on the bloody ferry myself even if I have to drag you all the way down there! You can get the hell out of here and never come back.' The final words were bellowed with such force that everyone in the room fell silent.

Then Ellen heard Ben push Con whimpering like a baby into the front room.

'God Almighty, he means it!' Tessie said in a hushed voice.

'Well, it'll be good riddance ter that feller! 'Is gamblin' an' drinkin' cost poor Molly 'er life! 'E'll be no loss.'

Ellen was sitting up, her head resting in Gussie's lap when Con was dragged back into the kitchen by the collar of his jacket. In one hand he carried an old carpet bag, in the other his cap. The livid red weals stood out against the deathly pale skin of his face.

Ben turned to Tessie. 'Start the party without us! I won't be long! I've a bloody mind to chuck him in the river.'

'And finish up like someone else we knew!' Tessie growled. 'You're gettin' off light, Con Ryan.'

'Will you see to Ellen, please?' Ben paused to beg the two women who were crouched down and supporting Ellen.

'Of course we will, lad. Just gerrim out of 'ere before I belt 'im meself,' Tessie said with venom. Ben looked down at Ellen, the fierce tide of anger still flowing in his veins.

'I'll be back as soon as I can, Ellen. Will you be all right?' She nodded slowly and Con was dragged through the door.

'Oh, I thought he was going to kill me, I really did. I asked Ben not to come too early,' Ellen sobbed.

'It's a good job 'e didn't take any notice of yer, Ellen. Gussie, what can we do about the mess 'e's left 'er in – an' 'er weddin' day termorrer an' all?'

'I'll send our Teddy for Dr Jenkinson. 'E'll be able ter give 'er some cream or lotion. 'E's another one who'll be glad to see the back of that feller.'

'It's such a shame ter spoil Maggie's do,' Tessie said sadly.

'She won't mind. She'll just be glad ter be 'ome an' there's enough people over there anyway. We'll go over later, Tess.'

Dr Jenkinson arrived and looked with horror at Ellen's back, shoulders and face.

'Who did this? All I could get out of the lad was that someone had taken a horsewhip to her.'

' 'Er flamin' uncle. That Con Ryan feller.'

'Where is he?'

'Gone! Ben Hayes, Maggie Meakin's nephew an' the feller Ellen's goin' ter marry termorrer give 'im a taste of the whip an' he's dragged 'im bag an' baggage down ter the Dublin ferry.'

Dr Jenkinson looked at Ellen with pity. She'd suffered so much in this last year.

'I'll leave you some lotion. It'll sting, Ellen, I'm afraid, but it will be a help. I'll also leave something to calm you down. Will you still go ahead with the ceremony?'

Ellen tried to smile. 'Yes.'

'It would be better to postpone it.'

'No. I . . . I'll manage. It'll be better by then.'

'Not much but you're determined, I see. Well, good luck, you deserve it.'

'Doctor, will yer . . . well, would yer like ter just go an' see Maggie . . . Mrs Meakin before yer go. We've give 'er a birrof a do, like. She'll be dead pleased ter see yer.'

'I will.' He looked around at them all. 'There's been far too much violence in this street. Let's hope this is the end of it.'

'Amen ter that, sir.'

'I'll go and see Mrs Meakin and then I'll come back before I go home.'

'You're a saint, sir, yer are. There's not many who'd be

as kind an' good ter the likes of us. We're poor an' 'ave hardly any education and the fellers often 'ave no work and people look down on us as dirty, common slummies, but we can't 'elp that, so when someone like yerself, sir, 'elps us, we really appreciate it. God bless yer fer the proper gentleman yer are.'

He felt humbled and yet satisfied too. This was the very reason he'd become a doctor and why he preferred to be a Dispensary doctor instead of working from a grand Georgian house in Rodney Street.

'Thank you, Mrs Ogden. It makes my job worth doing. I'll see you a little later on.' He left, smiling to himself, to join the underfed, ignorant, grimy crowd in Maggie Meakin's house.

When he returned, after accepting two pints of beer and making a point of speaking to almost everyone in the house, Maggie and Lucy particularly (although he realised his presence made them all uneasy), he found Ellen in the arms of a very tall young man.

'Ah, I presume you're the bridegroom?' he greeted Ben, whose eyes were full of concern for Ellen.

'I am. That man'll not touch anyone again, it's back to where he belongs.'

'Indeed.' The doctor thought he wouldn't like to get on the wrong side of this man. 'Good luck to you both. Take good care of her.' He dug into his pocket, pulled out a white five-pound note and pressed it into Ellen's hand. 'A wedding present. Buy something that will remind you of me. Now I'll be off home. The party is going very well and Mrs Meakin looks well too.'

'That's very kind of you, sir,' Ben said. 'We *will* buy something. Something fancy that we would never have thought of buying.'

'Good night then. I'll let myself out.'

Tessie and Gussie had both gone over to Maggie's and they were alone.

As he left, Ben crouched down and touched Ellen's face gently. 'I . . . I should have killed him! I love you so much, Ellen, that I regretted not doing so all the way back from the docks. Shall we postpone the wedding?'

'No! No, Ben, I'll manage. Tessie has put that lotion on. I . . . Will you carry me over to see your Auntie Maggie, please?'

He gazed at her adoringly. 'Ellen, I'd carry you to the ends of the earth if you asked me.'

Chapter Twenty-Eight

1914

It was so hot, Ellen thought, wiping the beads of perspiration from her forehead with the back of her hand. Well, at least the washing would dry. It was more than three years since Tessie had, with all the gentleness she possessed, helped her into the peach and cream dress and young Lucy had put her hat on for her as she couldn't raise her arms. She had then stood beside Ben at the altar rails and made her vows to love, honour and obey him for better or for worse, in sickness and in health, for richer or poorer until death would part them. It had been the happiest day of her life, despite the pain. And the past three years had been the happiest she could remember although the summer months, particularly August, were hated by everyone who lived in the slums. It was a time of increased smells, flies, vermin and disease, but this year it was all that and more. There was so much unrest in the world and people were saying there'd be a war soon. She dreaded the word even though every man and boy she knew actually seemed to be looking forward to it.

'They're as thick as planks, the bloody lot of them!' Tessie had pronounced only last week.

'Well, yer've got ter admit, Tess, it's fer King an' Country. It's fer all our pride, we's gorran Empire. That's what Artie says anyhow.'

'They're too old fer the bloody army an' navy. Ozzie says if war comes workin' on the docks will be a "special job", like. It'll be the only time *that* feller will put 'is back into a job since Adam was a lad!'

'They'll 'ave ter "keep the 'ome fires burnin' " like that song.'

Ellen had felt uneasy. Ben wasn't too old and neither were Eddie and Tom. Bernie was only seventeen and surely that was too young. He had another year at the Technical School and then three more years as an apprentice tool-maker: a much-sought-after trade and a good steady job with a pension at the end of it.

She plunged her arms into the tub of hot water again, but felt faint. She'd have to sit down, she felt very queasy.

She went inside and lit the gas ring, filled the kettle and placed it on the gas. It was like a furnace in the room but there was nothing she could do about that. Every window and door in the house was open and she'd hung sticky strips of brown paper from every protruding object to try to keep the flies down. Every bit of food that wasn't in the mesh-fronted food press was covered with muslin. She caught a glimpse of herself on the mirror over the mantel-shelf. Her face was scarlet, wisps of hair clung damply to her forehead and cheeks. She had smudges on her nose. In fact she looked a complete fright. She'd have to clean herself up before Ben came home. They hadn't gone to live with Maggie in the end. After Con had gone the place seemed more spacious and Maggie had taken in a boarder to help out with expenses.

She and Lucy were two completely different people now, she thought. Maggie had put on weight. The pinched look had gone. Her eyes were bright and enquiring and she laughed and gossiped with everyone else. Lucy had changed too, beyond belief.

'God it's 'ot. I see yer've started on the washin', Ellen. I was comin' in ter ask yer if yer was goin' ter the bag wash. It'll be swelterin' down there but at least yer can gerrit all done an' mangled, like.'

'No, I've not got a lot, except for Ben's work clothes. I've got them soaking. With this heat everything will be dry in no time. I might even get it all ironed tonight when it's cooler.'

'Now don't be goin' mad, Ellen, yer look wore out now.'

'I felt sickly so I came in, though it's just as hot in here.'

'It's the 'eat that's made yer feel sickly, luv. I 'ope this flamin' weather breaks after the Bank 'Oliday, like.' Tessie sat down at the table thankfully. 'Are yer goin' anywhere?'

'Ben said we could go for a sail to New Brighton and take Bernie and Lucy, if they want to come.'

'He's as mad as you. The ferries will be packed all day an' so will the beach and draggin' them two with yer will wear yer out.'

'But it'll be a day out and it will be cool on the ferry going across and back.'

'Well, I'm goin' ter take things easy. Put me feet up and let them all wait on me fer a change. Do yer know what I caught Teddy Cooney doin' last night?'

'No. What?' Ellen asked. Young Teddy was still the bane of Gussie's life even though he was now seventeen.

'Purrin' bottle tops on the tram lines ter flatten them so 'e can use them in those penny chocolate machines, an' the age of 'im too! I give 'im a right clock around the ears, I can tell yer, and then I told Gussie so he got another belt!'

Ellen smiled. 'They never grow up, do they?'

'They don't, luv. In fact the older they get the worse they are. What time will Ben be in?'

'Oh, some time this afternoon, there's not much coal needed in summer, it's always the same. Sometimes I wonder about the wisdom of getting that second cart, we still have to pay Joe Larkin wages even when we're not busy.'

'Well, it can't last fer much longer now an' September can be chilly an' damp. Are yer sure you're all right? Yer've gone a funny colour.'

Suddenly Ellen felt the bile rising in her throat. She ran into the scullery and was sick.

Tessie put a damp cloth to her forehead. 'Go an' sit down, luv, I'll clean this sink up.'

Thankfully Ellen did so, feeling weak and clammy. She prayed she wasn't sickening for something.

'Yer can leave that washin' alone, yer'll 'ave ter take things easy now in your condition.'

'What condition?'

'Don't tell me yer don't know.'

Ellen stared at the older woman in amazement. 'Do you mean . . .?'

'Of course I do. You're pregnant.'

Ellen placed her hands on her cheeks as a sense of wonderment crept over her. At last! At last she and Ben were going to have a baby. She had been getting worried that she might not be able to have children and that always made her think of Daniel. Barely a day passed when she didn't remember him. She longed to know just how he was getting along. She'd neither seen nor heard anything of him and Annie for years. He wouldn't be a baby any more. He would be talking and walking. She hoped desperately that Annie was looking after him.

'It never occurred to me! Oh, Tessie, I'm so thrilled. Will you keep it to yourself though until I've told Ben?'

'Of course. You get yourself round ter see the doctor, just to make sure, like.'

'But I've shopping to do, a meal to make.'

'Gussie an' me will see ter all that fer yer.'

'A baby! A baby! I can't believe it.'

'Oh, you'll believe it all right when you're draggin' yerself around, tryin' ter stay awake because yer've been up 'alf the flamin' night with it.' Tessie's tone was sharp but her smile belied it. 'Go and sit on the front step this afternoon. The sun's gone off it by then, and it might be a bit cooler there.'

'I will. Oh, I can't wait to tell Ben.'

* * *

367

She had taken Tessie's advice. She'd been to see Dr Jenkinson who with a smile confirmed she was indeed going to have a baby. Now she was sitting on the top step, her head resting on the doorframe when she saw Ben coming up the street, and with him was Eddie. For a brief second she thought of her mam and da. She got to her feet. Despite her preoccupation, how on earth could she have forgotten that today was the day her brother was coming home?

'There she is waiting for us and isn't she a picture, all pale and cool looking?' Ben said to Eddie, the smile lighting up his coal-blackened face.

Even covered in coal dust he was still handsome, Ellen thought, and she loved him more with each day that passed.

'Eddie, it's great to see you.' She hugged her brother who was now a seasoned sailor and had graduated to the position of pantry boy on the *Olympic*, a White Star Line ship. 'Did you have a good trip?'

'I did, thanks, Ellen, but it might be my last.'

'Your last?'

'Come on in. I'll get washed and changed and you make us some tea, please, luv. Then we'll talk about it.'

As she made tea Ellen kept glancing at her brother. What did he mean? Was he giving up the sea and getting a shore job? And if so, why? He loved the sea and he'd been to an awful lot of different countries – she had the souvenirs to prove it.

'Well, are you going to tell me now or shall I tell you my news first?' she asked Eddie as Ben emerged from the scullery.

'What news?' Ben demanded.

'No, let me tell her mine first. Get it out of the way.'

Ellen sat down. 'Fire away then,' she said, not knowing how close to the truth she had come.

'Ellen, I'm going to join the Royal Navy,' Eddie said.

'The Royal Navy? Why?'

'Because there's going to be a war, Ellen, I'm certain of it. In fact I think they're going to have a hard time getting a crew to sign on again and that applies to all the lines.'

Ellen gasped. 'No. No, it can't be true. Not so soon.'

Ben leaned across the table and took her hand.

'Ellen, it *is* coming and within the next few days, I'm certain of it. All the men in the Royal Naval Reserve have been called up and will be leaving soon for Chatham. In fact, well . . . in fact I'm going to join up myself. Business is slack and it'll all be over by Christmas – if it even lasts that long.'

She didn't know what to say. Ben was going to join up and leave her? When she was about to tell him that he was going to be a father?

'Ellen, what's the matter? Honestly, it *will* all be over in a few months, we might never see any action. We've got the biggest and best fleet in the world. The Kaiser's been building his up but the song's right. Britannia *does* rule the waves and always will.'

'Ben's right, Ellen. I bet our Tom and Bernie will join up too.'

'No! Not Bernie! He's too young, he's only seventeen.'

Ben frowned at his brother-in-law. 'They won't take anyone under eighteen, Ellen, so don't worry about meladdo.'

She brushed away a tear with the back of her hand. 'It's not that. Really it's not. It's just that . . . well, I didn't want to tell you my news like this.'

'What's your news, Ellen? I'm sorry if we've upset you.'

She smiled at her husband and squeezed his hand. 'We . . . we're going to have a baby. I only found out today. I went to see Dr Jenkinson earlier this afternoon.'

Eddie grinned from ear to ear but Ben just stared at her, his mouth open.

'Well, haven't you got anything to say, Ben Hayes?'

'Oh, Ellen!' He swept her up in his arms and hugged her to him. 'Oh, Ellen, I'm so delighted and happy! I love you so much and I'd begun . . .'

'I know, Ben, I was getting worried myself, but—'

'So, when's the happy event then?' Eddie demanded.

'Next May. I hope it's a boy, a son, to carry the business on. Mam and Da would have been so proud.'

'I don't care whether it's a boy or a girl.'

'Ben, are you really happy?'

'I am! How can you even ask?'

'You can see now why all the talk of war was upsetting me.'

'Well then, there'll be no more gloom and doom. We'll have to celebrate this.'

'Oh, I couldn't stand all the fuss of a do. Why don't you and all the men have a drink in the Swan?'

'I want to celebrate with you.'

'You can do that later on,' she laughed.

It wasn't long before the whole of the street knew but the

subject of war was hard to keep out of conversation.

Lucy had come over to take her to Maggie's house for a small celebration. Ellen smiled at the girl whom she now looked on as a younger sister. At sixteen Lucy was a quiet, pretty girl. Her quietness wasn't the same as it had been when her father had been alive – she laughed and smiled all the time – but now she was just naturally unassuming and a bit shy. She and Bernie were close friends and Ellen often wondered if they would marry – in time? All Lucy's fears and apprehension where men were concerned seemed to have disappeared and she'd never told Maggie a single thing about what John Meakin had done to her.

When she arrived they were all there: Tessie, Gussie, Maggie, Mary Ogden, Doris Henshaw, Mrs Stanford from next door and other women and girls she knew.

'Oh, if I'd have known you were all here I'd have panicked.'

Maggie smiled at her. 'I know, that's why we didn't tell you.'

'God luv yer, Ellen, we thought yer were never goin' ter get started,' Tessie laughed.

Gussie produced two bottles of cheap sherry that she'd got from the pub. 'Maggie, 'ave yer got enough glasses an' cups so everyone can 'ave a little swig, ter toast Ellen?'

'I have, because nearly everyone brought their own.'

'Come on, Maggie, girl, giz a drop in 'ere. Then 'ere's to yer, luv, you an' Ben,' Gussie said, holding up a mug.

'God bless the pair of yiz an' the baby,' Tessie said solemnly.

'It's a pity about all this war talk,' Vi Stanford said, looking her usual gloomy self.

Tessie instantly rounded on her. 'Trust youse ter put the mockers on things! I'm fed up ter the back teeth 'earin' about bloody war. We're 'ere ter 'ave a birrof a drink an' congratulate Ellen, not be talkin' of a damned war.' Then she addressed her eldest daughter. 'Mary, gerrup an' ask yer da ter give yer the money for another couple of bottles of this stuff.'

'Ah, Mam, he'll only moan.'

'I don't flamin' well care, 'e's got money. I know it fer a fact. 'E won a few bob on the 'orses and they'll all be knockin' back the ale an' won't come 'ome until the money's run out, or Ernie Bradshaw chucks them out, whichever is first. Go on, girl.'

Mary went with a bad grace.

'That one'll be the death of me. Still single at 'er age. I 'ad 'er an' our Martin at 'er age an' she's not even walkin' out. I've told 'er she'll be an old maid if she doesn't shift 'erself! With all these young fellers dashin' off ter the Recruitin' Office there won't be anyone fer 'er ter find soon.'

'Oh, let 'er alone, Tess, she's not a bad girl, she'll find a feller soon enough,' Gussie reprimanded her friend.

'I suppose you're right. Well, that's enough of our Mary. Is anyone goin' on an outin', like, fer the Bank 'Oliday?'

In seconds the noise level in the room rose in a crescendo as plans and outings were discussed. Ellen looked around happily. She couldn't have wished for anything more.

Chapter Twenty-Nine

Despite the ominous atmosphere they all went to New Brighton on the August Bank Holiday Monday.

'Gussie said the ferries would be packed,' Ellen said, hanging on to Ben's arm as the press of people surged forward to board the *Iris*. 'Bernie, keep hold of Lucy or you'll get separated. If you do then we'll wait by the Tower for you.'

Everyone was in a holiday mood and it was a perfect day to go to the seaside. The sun in its brazen glory beat down from a clear azure sky. It was strong even though it was only nine o'clock in the morning. The waters of the Mersey, normally grey and turgid, appeared blue as they reflected the colour of the sky, and the wavelets were touched with gold and shimmered.

Lucy looked up at Bernie trustingly and he took hold of her hand. They'd been close ever since Lucy had come to live with them, and even after she'd gone home Ellen said she spent more time with them than she did with Maggie. Now he was sure she looked on him with more than just friendship and affection and he felt the same way. It was just that they hadn't told each other yet. But did they need to at all? Suddenly the rush for the gangway put a stop to Bernie's reverie.

It was a terrible crush but mainly due to Ben's size and determination they all managed to get a place on the upper deck. All the seats, which were in fact folded life-rafts, were taken, so it was standing room only.

'Never mind, at least we've got the rail to lean on,' Ellen said, looking up at her husband and smiling. She still couldn't really take it in. She didn't *feel* any different and she didn't *look* any different. Last night when she'd washed and put on her nightdress she'd gently run her fingers across her stomach. There was a baby in there – growing. 'It's . . . it's like a miracle,' she'd said with awe.

Ben had put his arms around her. 'It's *our* miracle, Ellen,' he'd said, holding her tightly.

Bernie spent the whole trip pointing out the ships and which shipping line they belonged to to Lucy and the group of people nearest to them. Other groups were doing the same thing. Liverpudlians were fiercely proud of their port and the River Mersey.

Once they reached New Brighton they all found a space on the crowded beach and Ellen sent Lucy and Bernie to the café which did a roaring trade providing pots of tea and mugs for sixpence, threepence of which was a deposit on the mugs and pot.

There were all kinds of things to do: go up the Tower; listen to the organ in its ballroom; dance even. There was the fun fair and the amusements; you could walk out to the old fort built to defend the Mersey estuary and see the cannons; or you could watch the one-legged diver.

When they'd all had a refreshing mug of tea Bernie and Lucy announced that they were going to paddle. Ellen watched them with affection as they threaded their way over the crowded beach between families enjoying the sun and kids trying to make sandcastles with buckets and spades, sticking little paper flags on the sandy turrets. She smiled as Lucy held up her skirt at the water's edge, then squealed with mock anger as Bernie splashed water over her.

'They look like two big kids,' Ben remarked.

She leaned her head on Ben's shoulder. 'They are, but I was thinking . . .'

'You're match-making,' he laughed.

'Well, they get on so well together. He'll have a good job and she's such a sweet little thing.'

'You can't push them together, luv, you have to let them live their own lives.'

'I know, but everyone would be so pleased, especially Maggie.'

He tilted her face and looked into her eyes. 'We'll have our own child to think and worry about.'

'But they're so well suited!'

'No more speculating. Let's just enjoy ourselves,' he said firmly. He wasn't going to spoil the day by thinking too hard about the future. War couldn't be far away now. An ultimatum had been given by Mr Asquith, the Prime Minister, demanding that Belgium's neutrality be respected as agreed in the Treaty of 1839, a Treaty the Kaiser was giving no signs of sticking to. Britain, France and Russia had all pledged to do just that but already war and wholesale slaughter was raging in the Balkan states.

They were all tired when they got home. It had been so hot that Ellen insisted Lucy should not take off her hat, the straw boater trimmed with a blue ribbon.

'You'll get sunstroke. I'm just as hot, but I'm not taking mine off,' she'd replied to the protests.

She had managed to get a seat on the ferry home and she was so thankful for it. Ben had elbowed and shoved his way ruthlessly forward to secure it.

As they walked up the street, most of the neighbours who hadn't gone anywhere were sitting on their doorsteps.

' 'Ave yer 'ad a good day then?' Gussie asked them as they neared home.

'It was great. I really enjoyed it.'

'And so did I,' Lucy added.

'We were packed like sardines on the ferries. It's a good job it's not a long journey,' Ben added.

Gussie looked at him closely and he met her gaze with steadiness. He realised she knew something. 'Artie an' Ozzie an' most of the fellers is in the pub. Why don't yer go an' join them? I bet yer could murder a pint.'

Ben nodded. He was right. She knew.

'Can I come with you?' Bernie asked. He'd sensed the change in mood and he knew all about the impending war: Tom always brought home a copy of the *Echo* on which he was now a very junior reporter.

'No, you can't, you're too young!' Ellen retorted.

'Let 'im go, luv, 'e can have a lemonade shandy and I don't think that either Ernie Bradshaw or the police will have under-age drinking on their minds. Our Teddy's over there, it might keep 'im out of bloody mischief. 'E'll be the death of me, will that lad! Come on in, Ellen, I'll put the kettle on.'

'No, come to me, I've the gas ring. Are you coming, Lucy, or will you go straight home?'

'Will I go and get Mam?' Lucy asked. There was something strange going on and she wanted to learn more about it.

'Yes, and knock on Tessie's door too, she must have given up and gone inside,' Ellen added for there was no sign of her.

'Mrs Ogden's out somewhere,' Lucy announced as she came back. 'But Mam's on her way.'

'Tessie's probably down the pub. She said ter me that iffen their Ozzie can afford to 'ave a drink, then so can she. Their Mary and Sal, Johnnie, Vic and Ken are all out fer the day an' although she's always complainin' about them bein' under 'er feet, I think she got fed up of 'er own company.'

'Did you hear that Vera McFadden is getting married next month?'

'No. So 'e's finally got around to it. They've been engaged for six flamin' years. Mind you, that was his mam's fault. Bad-tempered interfering auld bitch! Well, that's a turn-up for the book. He must 'ave a few bob saved up by now. Do yer know where they're goin' ter live, Ellen? Not with his mam, I 'ope, or there'll be skin an' 'air flyin'.'

'I don't know. It was Mary Ogden who told me.'

'Oh, God! Tessie'll be goin' on at 'er again. I said to 'er, Tess, leave that girl alone. If she finds the right feller in time so be it, if she doesn't she doesn't. Better than 'avin' an 'usband who drinks, gambles, wastes money on fancy women or bel—' She stopped, remembering Lucy's childhood years. 'Besides, I said she'd be able ter look after 'er in 'er old age.'

'An' didn't that go down a treat an' all!' Tessie said, coming in, her face scarlet with the heat.

'Did yer tell 'er that?'

'I did an' what did I get for me trouble? "Mam, I'm thinkin' of emigratin'." EMIGRATIN'!'

They were all surprised.

'Where the hell to?' Gussie demanded.

'Australia, no less! The other side of the flamin' world!'

'On her own? All that way?' Ellen asked in amazement.

'It seems as though she'd rather do that than look after 'er da an' me.'

Ellen recovered herself. 'That's a bit drastic, isn't it?'

'Maybe she thinks she'll stand more of a chance finding an 'usband out there. I think there's a shortage of women an' girls. I can remember Eddie saying something about it.'

'Well, I'm washin' me 'ands of the whole thing. Let 'er go, I said ter Ozzie. Let 'er go an' ruin 'er life!'

'Oh, Tessie, I'm so sorry,' Maggie said, thinking how it would break her heart if Lucy should ever decide to do anything like that. It was an awfully big step to take.

'Ah well, she might 'ave ter stay put if there's goin' ter be a war,' Tessie finished smugly.

They nodded their agreement but remained silent.

* * *

Ben had to wake Ellen next morning.

'What time is it?' she asked, rubbing her eyes.

'Ten o'clock.'

She sat up. 'TEN o'clock! Ben, why didn't you wake me earlier? I've nothing prepared and I'll never catch up on the chores. Ten o'clock! Why haven't you gone to work?'

He sat down on the bed and took her hands. 'War has been declared and . . . and I'm going down to the Recruiting Station with Eddie and Tom and most of the lads in the street.'

She was horrified. 'Oh, no! What . . . what will happen, Ben? Will you have to go away today? What'll happen to us, the baby, the business . . .'

He took her in his arms. 'Nothing's going to happen right away, luv. I told you it will all be over in a couple of months. Germany and Austria can't take on France, Russia and our Empire and win. We'll have troops from Canada, Australia, New Zealand, South Africa and God knows what other part of Africa, then there's India, Hong Kong, Burma, that's nearly the whole of the world. They won't have a cat in hell's chance of winning. And don't worry, I'll sort everything out here. Now I'm going to bring you a cup of tea and if you feel like a bit more sleep go ahead.'

'I won't be able to sleep, Ben. I'll get up.' She wouldn't be able to sleep much at all from now on, worrying about what would happen to them all. Ben and all her brothers.

Annie had slept late too. She'd tossed and turned all the long, hot and humid night. In the end she'd got up and gone into the living room so as not to disturb Daniel. She felt terrible. Shocked, unable to think clearly, sick and trembling all over. Her nightdress was sticking to her with sweat. Oh, what was she going to say to Juan? It was his fault, it *had* to be! She had never even gone out with another man. And why now? Daniel was such a beautiful child and she loved him dearly. In the months Juan was away she spent all her time caring for him, playing with him, taking him for walks. Juan left her a substantial amount of money each time he came to Liverpool and she was careful with it for she'd known poverty. It was too precious to squander. She even had some savings.

After her initial shock and anger that Annie hadn't told her about the baby, Mrs Coleman herself had become quite fond of Daniel and often walked to the park with Annie.

She sat there dazed until the first fingers of dawn crept across the sky and the pale rim of the moon disappeared. She'd dozed and it was Daniel's demands to be lifted out of his cot that had woken her.

She got up and went through into the bedroom. 'Oh, come on to your mam. Let's get you washed and dressed and have some breakfast. Mam's sorry she wasn't here. I was only in the living room.' She lifted him out of the cot and held him tightly. What would happen to him? Oh, God, what would happen to her child? It was all too terrible to contemplate.

She tried to pull herself together and somehow she'd washed, dressed and fed both herself and her child when Mrs Coleman knocked on her door.

'Oh, this heat is wearing me out! Did you manage to get much sleep?'

Annie shook her head.

'And what about Daniel? It's much too hot for the little ones and they don't know what ails them.'

'Oh, he slept through.'

'Well, that's a blessing. Is it today that Señor Caballe is back?' She didn't say 'home'. She'd realised long ago that this certainly wasn't his home, but Annie didn't behave like a tart or a fancy woman and gradually she'd forgotten that Annie wasn't married.

'Later tonight.'

'Will you be going down to meet him?'

'No. No, it's too late for Daniel.'

'Don't worry about him, Annie, I'll see to him. Go and have a drink or something. You never go out, even when he's home.'

Annie thought about it. Maybe it would be better to tell him somewhere else other than here. God alone knew how he would react.

'If you really don't mind?'

'Of course I don't, he's a little luv.'

Later that day, when the warm, heavy dusk was falling, Annie dressed with care. Her pale blue-and-white-striped shirt-style dress was fresh and crisp, her blue-and-white straw hat was trimmed with a blue ribbon and a large white daisy. She had short white gloves, a white purse and white button boots and silk stockings. She was on the point of tears as she looked at herself in the mirror. She remembered how annoyed he'd been with her when he'd come home the first time to find she had a baby, but he'd quickly got over it and was kind and generous to the child. Would he shout tonight the way he had done then? Rant in Spanish, waving his arms in flamboyant gestures? She hoped not, but it ought to be herself doing the shouting. Oh, God, everything was such a mess!

It was still very warm, she thought, as she waited by the dock gate. She didn't look at or even see the girls and women hanging around. They were always there, tarts hoping to get their hands on the money of the Spanish sailors. Unlike them, she was respectable and the dock policeman knew it and sometimes let her through to wait on the other side of the gate.

It wasn't long before she saw him walking towards her.

He was never demonstrative before members of his own crew. He never held her and kissed her, just gave her a peck on either cheek. It was different when they got home, of course. Tonight for once she didn't mind this formality.

'Anne, you are well? You look so cool and lovely.'

'Thank you,' she replied in a tight voice.

'How is Daniel?'

'He's well. Mrs Coleman is looking after him. Could we go . . . somewhere?'

He looked down at her. Something was wrong. He could see it in her eyes. 'Of course. Where?'

'Somewhere private.'

'The lounge of an hotel?'

She nodded.

He hailed a passing cab and helped her in. 'The Stork Hotel, if you please,' he instructed the driver.

They didn't speak until they reached the hotel in

Williamson Square and he had paid the cab, escorted her into the lounge and ordered two drinks.

Her stomach was churning. Why was she feeling like this? He was the one who should be upset.

He looked at her with concern. 'Now, what is it, Anne?'

'I . . . I'm ill and it's . . . your fault.'

He looked at her quizzically. 'What is all this about?'

Her voice rose a little. 'I told you I'm sick. I . . . I've been to a doctor and I've got . . . syphilis and the only person I could have caught it from is you!'

His expression changed. His dark eyes narrowed as he glared at her.

'Well, aren't you going to say anything? You know what happens if you get the syph. You—'

'Your body rots away. Even your face is eaten away and you die! And this is what you are saying *I* have done to you?'

'Yes. There could be no one else!'

He was seething with anger and his eyes flashed danger-ously. She was a whore after all. A whore who'd no doubt become bored while he was away.

'I have transmitted nothing! Nothing, do you understand me? I do not believe you. You are a whore! Who else have you been offering your body to while I have been away? I gave you everything! I took you from that . . . that whore-house . . . and gave you everything but obviously it was not enough! Now you have the . . . the audacity to blame *me*!'

Annie too was shaking. 'I'm *not* a whore! I've been with no one. I never even go out! It's *got* to be you! How many other girls do you have in other ports? Is that where you picked it up? Have you given . . . *it* . . . to your wife?'

'Don't you even dare to utter Ana's name! She is the mother of my children and there are no other women.' Not on a permanent basis, he thought. Oh, he had occasionally visited brothels, but he'd been careful. There was definitely nothing wrong with him.

Annie was now very near to tears. She hadn't expected this.

'You even have another man's child! A man you said took advantage of you one night! Excuse me for my amusement but one night! Do you think I am a fool? It takes longer than that to conceive!' He stood up.

'What are you doing? Where are you going? You can't leave me like this!' she cried.

'It is quite simple. I am returning to my ship. I am not responsible for you. Despite everything I have given you I was nothing but a fool. I owe you nothing. You can go back to earning your living the way you used to do. War will be declared any day now and therefore it will be dangerous for foreign ships to use this port. There will be mines and submarines. I will never see you again and I will not be unhappy about that. Goodbye, Annie!' he spat contemptuously using the slang version of her name for the first time.

Stunned, she gripped the stem of the glass so hard that it broke. Blood began to drip on to her skirt but she didn't even feel the cut. He'd gone! He'd left her! She would never see him again – but it *wasn't* her fault. Could she have caught it from those few times when she was at Maisey's before she'd met him? No, that was four years ago. She'd have known before now, surely?

'Excuse me, madam, but may I help you? Your hand is bleeding.'

She looked up at the waiter through eyes swimming with tears. 'Oh . . . I . . . thank you.'

She watched, completely numb, as he took the glass and used his own handkerchief to bind up the cut.

'You must look after it. Keep it clean. Are you feeling sick?'

She couldn't answer him.

'Shall I get you a cab?'

She nodded. She couldn't face the journey home by tram. It was expensive but it would be the last extravagance she'd indulge in. She would have to go back to that house and face what future she had left. What would happen to them? What would happen to Daniel? She'd have to move, she couldn't afford the rent. She'd have to get work but who'd take care of Daniel?

All the way home she sobbed. There was nothing else to do but go back to Maisey's. Could she stand it? She'd have to. She had to earn some kind of money to pay someone to look after her child when she was too far gone to work, and after . . . oh, she couldn't think about death. It was too horrific. If it wasn't for Daniel she would kill herself now, this minute.

Chapter Thirty

The war news was all depressingly bad. In early September last year the whole country had been alarmed when the British Expeditionary Force had had to retreat to Mons as the German army pushed rapidly forward. The Government had called for five hundred thousand more men but by December there were a hundred thousand men and boys dead and people had stopped saying it would all be over soon.

In late September Ellen had been horrified to learn that German submarines had sunk three British cruisers off the coast of Holland.

'It's not a fair way of fightin', isn't that. It's low an' sneaky,' Gussie had said bitterly.

'But we've got a much bigger fleet,' she had cried.

'Now don't get upset about it, Ellen, we don't know the names of the ships. All our lads are on *Indefatigable* and *Invincible* an' they're not cruisers,' Gussie had tried to comfort her. 'Don't you fret, not in your condition.'

But she'd found it very hard to put the incident out of her mind.

She wished the baby would come soon; it was May and

she was so big and awkward and tired. She eased herself down into an armchair. Her feet and ankles were swollen and she looked a mess, she thought. Still, even in this state, she wished Ben were home. She missed him so much. He wrote, of course, but the letters were infrequent as they were posted whenever the ship docked, which wasn't very often. It seemed an age since they'd all gone to Lime Street Station to see the lads off. The station had been crowded with families of men getting ready to board the special trains. So many of them were so young. They couldn't all have been eighteen. There'd seemed to be an air of excitement still, just as there had been last August on the day war was declared.

Later on hundreds of people had lined the streets all the way from the south end of the city to Lime Street when Lord Derby had taken the salute on the steps of St George's Hall. The columns of marching men, clad in khaki, had seemed endless. They had been the men of the 1st, 2nd and 3rd King's Liverpool Regiment, volunteers all of them and they'd been cheered loudly. Young lads had hurled their caps in the air, women had been crying with pride. And now . . . she didn't think there was anything exciting at all. Too many men had been killed already and it was far from over. In fact it looked as though it had only just begun.

Bernie came in from work, looking disgruntled. He was worrying her now. He was mad keen to go and volunteer.

'There'll be holy murder now, Ellen,' he announced.

'Why?'

'One of those damned submarines has sunk the *Lusitania*

and there were a lot of women and kids on board, mainly American, but the crew were mostly Scousers, and she was a merchant ship, not a warship!'

Ellen's hand went to her throat. 'Oh, God help them all! That's wicked, downright wicked!' she cried.

'Well, it might get the Yanks to join the fight.'

She shook her head sadly. 'Fighting and death, that's all I seem to be hearing now.' She grimaced as she felt a short, stabbing pain in her back. It wasn't serious; she'd had it before.

'But don't you see, Ellen, now I've *got* to enlist.'

'No! Isn't it enough that your brothers and Ben are out there somewhere, risking their lives?'

'Ellen, this is war and from what I've been reading it's not going our way at all. Don't you remember that in April hundreds of thousands of men were killed at Ypres? I *have* to go!'

'No, you don't,' she argued.

'Ellen, I'm eighteen! Teddy Cooney has enlisted in the navy.'

'I don't care what Teddy Cooney's done, he could fly to the moon for all I care, you're not going.'

He slammed out, surprising Lucy as she came in the back way.

'What's the matter with him, Ellen?'

'They've sunk the *Lusitania* and he wants to enlist but I've forbidden him to. Oh, Lucy, how will we manage if he goes? I can't drive a coal cart. I can't do *anything* like this.'

'I've already begged him not to go but he's determined.' Lucy looked pleadingly at Ellen. 'I don't want him to go either! I don't want him to be killed or maimed like George Pringle and Frank Wilson from further down.'

Ellen took Lucy's hand and managed a smile. 'I know, Lucy. I know. If I've got anything to do with it he won't go anywhere. Now come and tell me if you've made any plans. He was only in for a few minutes and didn't say anything.'

Lucy smiled. 'I'll put the kettle on, I can see you're tired and upset. We finally have. We're going to get engaged in September, but he'll have to finish his apprenticeship before we can think of getting married.'

'That's the best news I've heard for ages. Have you told your mam?'

'Yes. She's made up. She says we can live there.'

'What about the Fittons?'

'He's gone off to the war and she's always complaining about the rent money. I think they'll move out eventually. But what about all those poor people on the *Lusitania*? It's . . . it's just too bad to think about. They never had a chance. It said in the paper that she sank in fifteen minutes. Little children and old ladies. It's . . . awful!'

'I've just said that to Bernie. They were nearly all American, he said, so no one is safe. Oh, Lucy, what'll become of us? They've already sent some kind of rocket or bomb over to London, killing innocent people in their homes.'

'I know. It's terrible. But what I came to tell you, as well as our engagement, is that from Monday I'm going to be a conductress on the trams.'

'Good grief!'

'Ellen, all the women are doing the men's jobs now. All

girls and women have to help unless they've got families or are, well . . . like you.'

Ellen frowned. What had things come to?

'All women and girls? Have so many men gone?'

Lucy nodded. 'They'll even work on the docks. Mary Ogden is complaining that she'll be lifting coal sacks and that it's not right. The work's too heavy.'

Ellen looked at her thoughtfully. 'Do you think they'd let her work for me? Drive the cart?'

'I suppose she could. Someone's got to do it, but who would hump the coal?'

'Wally Perkins. He's a big lad for his age.'

Lucy put down her teacup. 'Will I go and ask him?'

'No, I'll get Bernie to do that, when he comes back! You could go and ask Mary for me though.'

Lucy nodded. She was a bit afraid of working on the trams but she'd get used to it. She'd have to and it was one of the easier occupations. She could be working in munitions, down at the docks, or driving a coal cart like Mary Ogden was presumably going to do. She prayed things wouldn't get any worse and that it really would be over soon.

Maggie came over to see her, bringing a few fairy cakes she'd made.

'I thought you might have a fancy for a bit of cake.'

'That's so kind of you. What do you think about Lucy, and Bernie?'

'I'm so pleased, Ellen. They were made for each other and I'll never forget how good he was with her after . . . well, after.'

'And she's going to work on the trams.'

'I know. Things are in a desperate state. Did you hear about the *Lusitania*?'

'Yes, Bernie told me. God help them all.'

'There'll be trouble over it.'

'And so there should be.'

'Is there anything I can do or get you, luv?'

'No, but thanks. I just wish this baby would stir itself, the waiting is endless.'

'Yer can say that again, Ellen,' Tessie said, coming in the back way as usual. Most of the time Ellen thought she came just to get some peace and quiet, away from her own brood. 'I've cum ter tell yer that there's all kinds goin' on on Scottie Road!'

'Like what?' Maggie asked.

'Well, any shop with a German name is being smashed up. Reigler's, the pork shop, was the first to have its window smashed. People are so mad about the *Lucy* there'll be real trouble soon. Riots, I shouldn't wonder.'

'Oh, my God!' Maggie cried. She was terrified of any kind of violence.

'Won't the police do anything?' Ellen asked.

'I suppose they'll 'ave ter put on a birrof a show, like, but their 'earts won't be in it. Half the crew were Scousers.'

'It's . . . it's . . .' Ellen never finished her sentence as a pain gripped her and she cried out.

'Jesus, Mary an' Holy St Joseph! She's started.'

'Will I go for Gussie?' Maggie asked.

'Yes, an' tell 'er ter bring some newspaper an' rags and be quick.'

Pain tore again through Ellen's body.

'Hang on ter me, luv, you're in safe hands, we've all been through it,' Tessie said comfortingly while exchanging a quick glance with her neighbour.

Gussie arrived, panting, laden down with newspapers she'd been collecting and some old sheets, torn into smaller pieces.

' 'Ave yer got all yer stuff tergether, Ellen, luv?' she asked.

'Yes. The papers and rags are under the sink in the scullery and the baby's things are in a drawer, in the ... Oh, God!' she ended in a scream.

For hours on end Ellen strained and screamed in agony. Maggie's hand was nearly broken but she wouldn't pull it away, Ellen needed her to hang on to. She could remember how she'd hung on to her own mam's hand when Lucy had been born, but Ellen had no mam so it was even more important that she gave Ellen what support and comfort she could.

Tessie had had enough kids herself to know something was wrong. None had taken this long.

'I think yer should go fer the doctor,' she whispered to Gussie.

Gussie nodded. 'I'll send our Sal, she's the only one with a bit of sense.'

Ellen was exhausted. She was drenched in sweat. Everything was sticking to her and her head felt as though it would explode. How much longer could this go on? How much longer could she stand the terrible pains? Then thankfully she saw the familiar face of Dr Jenkinson and felt so relieved.

'Right now, Ellen Hayes, let's see what's going on.'

Ellen didn't remember much. Occasionally chloroform on a cloth was pressed to her nose and then she felt drowsy and the pain wasn't so bad.

She was unaware of the anxiety of everyone in the room which was in semi-darkness for privacy. She was so tired that she wished they would leave the cloth over her nose completely and let her drift into sleep.

At last there was a spasm of pain even more violent than the others and the urge to push and then, faintly, she heard the cry of a baby. She sank back on the pillow and her tiredness slipped away as Maggie held out her child to her, wrapped in a sheet.

'It's a girl, Ellen, and she's perfect.'

Ellen took her baby in her arms and an enormous wave of happiness washed over her. She'd never felt like this before. She was filled with pure joy and tenderness.

'Congratulations. What are you going to call her?' Dr Jenkinson asked, washing his hands in the bowl of hot water Maggie had brought in.

'Mary, after Mam.'

'Yer mam's name was Molly,' Gussie said, confused.

'I know. Molly is a sort of nickname for it. Her second name will be Elizabeth after Ben's mam.' Oh, she wished he were here with her, with them, a real family now, but he was on the sea – God alone knew where.

'Now let us take her and wash her then you can feed her and we'll clear up. You need sleep, girl, after what you've been through. There were a few anxious minutes, I can tell you.'

But it was all worth it. Ellen smiled at them all. 'What would I do without you all? I've got three mams and she'll have three grannies.'

They all surreptitiously wiped their eyes. Mary Elizabeth Hayes would always hold a special place in their hearts.

When Bernie reached Scotland Road it was more crowded than he'd ever seen it before. People were shouting, yelling, screeching and he could hear the sound of breaking glass and cries of terror and outrage. What the hell was going on? It was far more than a fight outside a pub.

He caught the shoulder of a small scruffy lad. 'Here, lad, what's going on?'

'Ain't yer 'eard? The Hun's sunk the *Lucy* an' me da was on her and me mam's screamin' and cryin'.' The lad's eyes were suspiciously bright.

'I know all about that but what's everyone doing?'

'Gettin' our own back. Anythin' with a German name gets smashed up an' yer take what yer can.'

Bernie leaned against the wall of a pub and tried to think clearly. The way things were going there would be wholesale rioting before long and it wouldn't totally be for the sinking of one of Cunard's big new liners. The *Lucy*, as she was affectionately called in Liverpool, was the sister ship of the *Mauretania*. Between them they crossed the Atlantic like express trains, the *Maury* holding the Blue Riband for the fastest time. But you couldn't blame these people: their fury and grief were spurring them on. There would be many new widows and orphans in the city tonight. No, not all the looting would be motivated by anger. Most of the Liverpool men on the *Lusitania* worked in the stokehold and wouldn't have stood a chance. Neither would many of the other ranks. Suddenly he made up his mind.

He couldn't stand by and let things like this happen, he had to do something. He'd go to the Royal Navy Recruiting Office now. He was eighteen and wouldn't even have to lie about his age like many did. He *had* to do something. How could he stay here while innocent women and children were being killed without mercy on the high seas? No one lasted long in the cold waters of the great western ocean.

He fought his way through the crowds until he at last reached Byrom Street. Some semblance of order had been restored now, but it had been an ugly scene until a few minutes ago: half starved, ragged men, women and kids screaming abuse and grabbing anything they could, heedless of the broken glass under their often bare feet.

One old woman had approached him, her grey hair hanging down, her shawl full of holes, in her hands a ham joint and about two dozen sausages. 'We'll teach them ter sink the *Lucy*!' she'd screamed at him in a voice like that of a scared crow.

The talk on the tram was all the same. Everyone was shocked and angry. It made him even more determined.

He was given a perfunctory medical, asked his name, age, address and then was told to sign on the dotted line. He felt so much better when he came out. All he had to do now was pick up his uniform and go home and tell Ellen.

She would be furious but there was nothing she could do about it now.

As he walked up Milton Street he met the doctor coming down.

Dr Jenkinson smiled at Bernie and stopped. 'Well, your sister's had a beautiful baby girl.'

Bernie stared at him in confusion. 'What . . . now . . .?'

'About half an hour ago. You're an uncle. Congratulations.'

'Thanks. I . . . I don't know how she's going to take what I've done.'

'What *have* you done?'

'Joined the Royal Navy. I go to Chatham tomorrow for training. She . . . she didn't want me to go but after what they did to the *Lusitania* I've *got* to do something, sir.'

Dr Jenkinson nodded grimly. 'I'll be going to France myself soon. They need all the doctors they can get, even old ones like me. Good luck, lad. Take care and give a good account of yourself when the time comes,' he said before resuming his journey.

He'd fought in the Boer War and knew what lay ahead of them all. Dirt, flies, vermin, bloody and broken bodies. Wounds that would fester and become gangrenous and limbs that would have to be amputated. The screams and sobbing of fatally wounded men and boys. He had never joined in the cheering and patriotic singing. There was nothing glorious or exciting about war – particularly this one. Wholesale slaughter; the use of gas. Man's inhumanity to man seemed to know no bounds.

'Oh, so you've come home,' Tessie said as Bernie came

in. She was stuffing the blood- and sweat-stained news-papers into the fire.

'I've just seen the doctor. I didn't know.'

'She's fine, they both are, but little Mary Elizabeth took her time all right.'

'A girl?'

'A fine healthy one and a good weight too. Six pounds seven ounces.'

Bernie didn't answer and Tessie looked at him closely.

'What's up with yer? I can see there's somethin' on yer mind.'

'I don't know if I should tell her . . . Ellen. She didn't want me to go.'

'I thought so. You've joined up. Well, is it the army or navy?'

'The navy. I go tomorrow.'

'Well, she's asleep now but I'll tell her later, if yer want.'

'Thanks. I'll go and tell Lucy. I know she'll be upset.'

'Yer'll 'ave ter go, lad, sooner or later. It's not goin' well at all, but yer'll be a bit safer in the navy. There's not much happenin' to them.'

He nodded his agreement and turned to go.

'Bernie, when yer get down there, ask them ter put yer on the same ship as yer brothers, if yer gerra chance, like,' Tessie called after him.

Chapter Thirty-One

Annie felt really ill and she could no longer look at herself in a mirror. She was now just skin and bone. There were times when she thought she could almost feel the disease eating away her insides, usually at night when darkness brought all her fears crowding into her head. On such nights she suffered terrible torments and dreams. She looked across the small, bare room where Daniel was asleep. Oh, God, did I really deserve this? she pleaded silently, the tears falling down her cheeks. One night with Freddie Rafferty, a night she couldn't even remember, a night that had shattered her world and changed her life and now . . . this. This terrible disease that was killing her slowly.

She'd moved from the house in Walton last year. She'd been honest with the woman. She just couldn't afford the rent any longer.

'What about Señor Caballe?'

'Señor Caballe won't be coming to Liverpool any more. It's the war, you see. The submarines and mines.'

'Oh, I'm sorry,' Mrs Coleman had replied, but she couldn't afford to keep them out of charity, much as she'd wanted to.

When she'd gone back Maisey had been sarcastic, as
had the other girls.

'Oh, Miss High and bloody Mighty then, weren't you?
You said hell would freeze over before you crossed this
doorstep again,' Maisey had reminded her.

'I know but . . . things change.'

'You'll have to work.'

'Oh, I intend to, believe me,' she'd answered with a
confidence she was far from feeling. She'd felt sick at the
thought of what she would have to do but she couldn't
afford to be squeamish. She didn't dare tell Maisey about
her illness. She'd have been thrown out on the streets and
Daniel with her.

She turned her face to the wall that was covered in
patches of damp. Oh, Holy Mother of God, what would
happen to her boy?

She was too ill to work now and she'd have to tell Maisey
soon. When she took her clothes off she could see the
disappointment in her 'clients'' eyes. It had already started
to attack her face, but she'd managed to disguise it so far
with her hair. Yet it would only get worse and she would
soon look hideous, like a leper.

Daniel woke and stood up.

'Mam, me want out.'

She slowly dragged herself upright. 'All right, Mam will
see to you now.' She could have cried at the thought of all
the lovely things she'd once had to dress him. Now he wore
second-hand stuff and she couldn't afford to keep him in
boots.

The room was becoming dirty, she hadn't the energy or

the enthusiasm to clean, even though she spent much of her time in here now. There was only half a loaf, some dripping, a few ounces of tea and a half-bottle of sterilised milk to last the week after what she paid Maisey. Despair swamped her. She dropped her head into her hands. There was only one thing left to do. She'd write to Ellen. Ellen would love Daniel. She'd been cruel to Ellen and now she regretted it so much. She prayed that her stepsister wouldn't harbour a grudge and refuse her.

Ellen read the badly written, misspelt letter and it tore at her heart. Oh, why, why hadn't Annie let her know she was ill? She would have looked after her and Daniel. Gussie had brought the letter in. Ellen was still confined to bed and would be for another week although she felt fine. When she'd told all the other women this they'd instantly ordered her back to bed, scandalised. Two weeks in bed at least was the usual length of recovery.

'So, who's it from?' Gussie asked. 'I know it's not bad news – it's not one of them brown envelopes they send those damned telegrams in.' There had been too many of those of late.

'Annie.'

'ANNIE! That hardfaced little bitch!'

'She's ill, very ill. She wants me to take Daniel and look after him.'

'She's changed her tune.'

'I think she really *is* ill. I'll go and see her.'

'Oh, no, yer won't!'

'But I've got to help her,' Ellen protested.

'When did she ever help you?'

'Oh, that doesn't matter now.'

'Well, you're not going. Where is it she lives anyway?'

'In a room in number forty, Mann Street, off Stanhope Street, near to Coburg Dock.'

'Well, you're certainly *not* goin' there. God, what a place ter end up in. Yer mam and da must be spinnin' in their graves!'

'I have to!'

'I'll go. You're not fit an' it's no place for yer with all them foreign sailors an' the alehouses full of crimps an' whores. It's Maggie May land down there. In fact I'll take Tessie with me, it's that bad.'

'Don't be too hard on her, please. For my sake and Mam's and Da's too. She wasn't really bad.'

'If you're not really bad you don't end up in places like where she's livin' now.'

'Please?' Ellen begged.

'Oh, I'll see, but iffen she starts givin' us cheek then . . .'

'I think she's too ill.'

'What's the matter with her anyway?'

'She doesn't say.'

'No, and I've a good idea why,' Gussie said grimly, taking the letter from Ellen.

When she reached Mann Street, Gussie was glad she hadn't let Ellen come. Glad, too, that she'd asked Tessie to accompany her. 'This lot'd slit yer throat as soon as look at yer,' Tessie had remarked grimly as they marched on. Oh, some of the tarts that hung around may be better dressed than them but she and Gussie were God-fearing, respect-able women and they held their heads up and glared right back when the whores stared at them.

' 'Aven't yer seen respectable women before?' Gussie shouted to two who were propping up a lamppost.

'A pair of auld slummies is what I'm lookin' at!' one yelled back.

'Yer 'ardfaced bitch, I'll tear the 'air from yer 'ead if there's any more of that, an' don't think I wouldn't!'

The door of number 40 was closed so Tessie hammered on it.

It opened and a small, fat woman in a gaudy yellow, orange and black dressing gown opened it. Gussie was glad she had to look down on the woman. It gave her the advantage.

'What the hell do yer want, hammering on me door at this hour of the day?'

'It's bloody nearly dinnertime, yer auld tart. We want ter see Annie Ryan,' Gussie demanded.

'What for?' Maisey asked, fishing a packet of Will's Woodbines from out of a pocket, along with some matches.

' 'Er stepsister 'ad a letter from 'er this mornin' sayin' she was ill an' would Ellen mind Daniel.'

Maisey inhaled deeply and viewed them both with suspicion, although she really wouldn't like to cross either of them. 'How ill? She's never said nothing to me. But then she keeps herself to herself. Thinks she's a cut above us.'

'I can't say I blame 'er fer that, judging by the get up of youse. 'Ow long 'ave yer 'ad this whorehouse then?'

Maisey threw away the cigarette. 'Listen, youse, I'm not

standing here being insulted by the likes of you. I keep a good house an' my girls aren't trash.'

'That's a matter of opinion! Well, does she live 'ere and can I see 'er?'

'She does. Go up the stairs an' it's the third door along, an' you can tell me what's up with her, after you've seen her. I've a right to know.'

'You can go ter hell!' Gussie shot back at her.

Both women were horrified when they saw Annie.

'Christ Almighty!' Tessie said. They had both had a fair idea of what was wrong with Annie but neither of them had thought it would have got so far.

'Oh, my God, Annie!' Gussie said, shaking her head.

'Where's Ellen, please?'

'She's still gettin' over 'avin' Mary. It were an 'ard an' long labour. We cum instead.'

'Don't start on me, please? I know . . . I'm . . . what I am and what I've got . . .'

'I'm not goin' ter start on yer but I will on that one downstairs for lettin' yer get like this!'

'She . . . she doesn't know. I didn't get it here. A Spanish officer I lived with gave it to me and then . . . and then . . .' She broke down.

'Well, it doesn't matter now. Get yer things tergether an' his, you're going home.' Tessie was reminding herself how Molly would have acted if she'd been alive. She couldn't leave either of them here in this stinking room.

'Doesn't she ever clean up?' Gussie demanded, while Tessie gathered up the few bits and pieces Annie had.

'No. You have to do it yourself and I . . . I haven't been

able to do it properly for weeks. It was all too much,' Annie said through her tears.

'Ah, come on, luv,' Gussie said, putting a stout arm around her. 'We'll all do what we can fer yer, fer Molly an' Jack's sake.'

Annie had been too weak to get the tram so Gussie got a cab, after getting Maisey to cough up a shilling.

'It's the least yer can do, yer auld trollop!' she said scathingly. 'So much fer yer "respectable" 'ouse! How many more 'ave got the syph then?'

Maisey had looked blankly at them for a few seconds. 'Is that what she's got, the dirty little whore?' she screamed. 'She never got it here! An' how many fellers has she give it to? I'll lose custom now!' Maisey had screamed abuse after the cab but they all ignored her.

'Oh, Annie! Oh, my God!' Ellen got up and put her arms around her stepsister, pulling her down on to the bed beside her. 'What is it?' She looked up, mystified, at the two older women.

'Syphilis. She's goin' ter die. God knows just when, we don't, but that's the truth.'

Ellen held her stepsister tightly. She was all skin and bone and her hair had been pushed back, revealing the disfigurement of her face.

'Take Daniel, Ellen,' Annie begged, when she could finally speak.

'Of course. You know I will. Oh, Annie, let me help you. You're the one who should be in this bed, not me.'

With the aid of Gussie and Tessie, they got Annie into the bed and had managed to get some broth down her.

Ellen held out her arms to the child she had loved so much. 'Daniel, come to me. I'm your Auntie Ellen, but you won't remember me. I looked after you when you were a baby but you're a big boy now. You've grown up.'

The child held back, suspicion all over his grimy face and his unkempt hair fell into his eyes. Eyes that regarded her nervously.

'There's no need to be frightened of me. Come and give me a hug.'

Reluctantly he came closer and Ellen held him tightly, her heart full of love and pity for him. He was undernourished, dirty, his clothes little better than rags and they smelled. Probably his hair was full of lice but despite all that, he was still the child she'd loved and lost. But all that was over now. She brushed the dark hair out of his eyes and kissed his cheek. 'You've come home now and we all love you,' she said through tears of mingled happiness and sorrow for Annie's fate.

'Right, meladdo, let's get all this stuff offen yer an' give yer a bath,' Gussie said determinedly, prising him from Ellen's embrace. He'd been bathed, something he wasn't used to, and he screamed and kicked and cried for his mam, but he quietened down when Ellen fed him and sat him on the bed beside his mother.

'Ellen, she's goin' ter need nursin' and he's a right little handful. God knows how he's been dragged up.'

'I know you're right, but how long before . . .' She couldn't finish.

Tessie shrugged.

'Send for the Dispensary doctor. Oh, I wish Dr Jenkinson were still here.'

Gussie agreed. 'Amen ter that. This feller's not the same at all.'

'He'll have to do, I'm afraid.'

The new doctor's manner was far different from Dr Jenkinson's. He was brusque and looked down his nose at them all, particularly when told what was the matter with Annie.

'How long has she had it?'

'I don't know, but it must have been some time.'

'Do you know where she caught it or rather from whom?'

'She muttered something about some foreign ship's officer.'

He didn't reply.

'So, 'ow long?'

He shook his head. 'Hard to tell. Some go quickly, some slowly. It could be a month or a year.'

'Is there anything you can give her? I'll pay,' Ellen begged him.

'Not really. A bottle of laudanum, I suppose.'

He left a small black bottle, took his fee and left.

'A fat lot of use he was an' he took more than sixpence. He's no tanner doctor, 'im. 'E should be reported.'

'Oh, what will we do?'

'As much as we can, Ellen.'

'At least she's home. She won't suffer and . . . die in *that* place.'

'See if she'll talk to yer, Ellen. Just in case there's anyone, a feller, who should know. I'll 'ave ter go now, luv, I 'aven't done a tap all day.'

Ellen sat in the chair beside the bed, Mary alseep in the crook of her arm and Daniel, with his thumb in his mouth, curled up on the bed beside Annie.

'You're so lucky, Ellen.'

'Compared with you I am. Oh, Annie, what happened? How did you end up like this?'

Slowly and with bouts of racking sobs Annie told her.

Ellen shook her head in pity at her stepsister's story. 'You should have come home after he left you high and dry.'

'I couldn't have just turned up here with Daniel and having to tell you all . . . especially Uncle Con, he always hated me.'

'He'd gone back to Ireland and you wouldn't have had to tell us *all*. Not outside the family – and you *are* family, Annie.'

'I always treated you badly, Ellen. I missed my mam so much, and Da. Oh, I'm glad they're not here to see . . . me.'

'If they were here you wouldn't be like this.'

'What did he say, the doctor?'

'Not a lot. He was pretty useless. He left some laudanum and said he didn't know how long . . .' She couldn't say it. 'But you're not to worry. You'll be taken care of, I promise.'

Annie squeezed her hand. 'Eddie, Tom, Bernie?'

'All in the navy. I tried to stop Bernie but I couldn't. When the *Lusitania* went down he enlisted.'

'Are they . . .?'

'So far, thank God, and Ben is in the navy too. He and Eddie are on the *Indefatigable*. Tom and Bernie are on *Invincible*. I pray for them every night and so far they've all been lucky. Not like the men in the army. The whole city seems to be in mourning. But that's enough of that. Try and rest, you're both safe now.'

'I . . . I . . . don't deserve to be treated like this.'

Ellen interrupted. 'You do. You *are* a good girl, Annie. Your only fault was your pride.'

'I know and it's killed me,' Annie replied. Tears oozed once more from her closed eyelids and slid down her disfigured face. Ellen covered her own eyes with her hands. It was a horrible death and so much more so for Annie because she had been such a pretty girl. She'd get some muslin and make a short veil that would hide Annie's face until the end came.

Chapter Thirty-Two

1916

Annie had lingered on and in one way Ellen was glad, particularly when she watched her with Daniel. Annie really loved her son and she'd taken care of him as best she could. Now they were both cared for. There were days when he was too boisterous for her, but then Ellen took him out with Mary Elizabeth who had just celebrated her first birthday.

She'd had a photograph taken of herself and Mary Elizabeth and sent it off to Ben via the Admiralty's postal service. Each letter from him she cherished, thankful that so far none of her menfolk had seen any action. She prayed each night that they would all come through and that it would end soon, although from what she read in the newspapers there didn't seem much hope of that. The news from Flanders was terrible; more and more women and girls were wearing black. In fact sometimes she felt ashamed of wearing light colours.

Gradually everyone in the street had learned of Annie's plight and when they spoke to Ellen it was with sympathy now. Just after Christmas she had been able to tell Annie that Freddie Rafferty, the cause of all her trouble, was dead. He'd been shot trying to desert.

'So you see, he wasn't even brave enough ter carry on. His mam's got nothin' to be proud of. There'll be no medals goin' to that house,' Tessie had pronounced with grim satisfaction.

Annie was past caring but she'd tried to smile.

When she'd first come here, just a year ago, she'd felt so relieved that she had felt an easing in her body and her mind. Now she drifted in and out of a drug-induced sleep. She'd confessed her sins and Father Healy came to the house to give her Communion every Sunday afternoon. Daniel had quickly become part of the family. He was too young to remember his life either in Walton or Mann Street.

'Ah, Ellen, this house has seen too much sorrow and grief,' the parish priest said as he was leaving on the last Sunday of the month.

'I know, Father, but now we are not on our own. We're getting food and supplies from America and surely that will make a difference.'

'I hope it will. I have heart-broken mothers and wives on my doorstep every day of the week and still the slaughter goes on. But God must have a purpose for it.'

She'd said nothing. She'd seen Dr Jenkinson when he'd been home on leave and she'd been shocked. He looked like an old, old man. His shoulders were hunched and bitterness and anger were etched into every line on his face. He'd denounced God and she'd been even more shocked. But after he'd described the conditions to her, she'd looked on him with pity. He'd called and he hadn't condemned Annie.

'She's paying a heavy price for her mistakes – because that's what they were, Ellen, mistakes. She was a good girl at heart. Headstrong and stubborn, I know, but not bad. Send for me if you need me, if I'm still home,' he'd said, but he knew in his heart he wouldn't be going back to France. There were times when he wished he could believe there was a God. Believe and hope the way most of the men he'd tried to patch up did. It might have been some comfort. But the carnage out there was too great and the conditions too horrendous and he couldn't face it again. He was too old and worn out.

Ellen had sent for him at the beginning of May but Annie had rallied. Ellen wouldn't even let the doctor see what was left of her stepsister's face. He'd protested that he'd seen far worse but still she'd refused. It would turn even his stomach. She was insistent that Annie should be left with a little bit of dignity.

It was hard to believe it was summer, Ben thought, watching the misty grey horizon merge with the cold grey waters of the North Sea. It was hard to believe that a war was raging, that men were dying in their thousands in Flanders. He'd seen no action at all. There had been skirmishes at Heligoland, Coronel and the Falkland Islands in the South Atlantic, but they'd seen and done nothing.

Life was a boring routine and he wondered why some of

them couldn't go on leave. There had been none since he'd sailed two flaming years ago. He was cold and wet stuck in the forward gun turret with Eddie and Charlie Meadows, an older regular navy man from Anfield.

'I wish they'd come out and bloody fight,' Eddie said gloomily.

'No you don't, lad. If one of their shells didn't kill you, the bloody sea would. You'd not last five minutes in that water.'

Ben said nothing but gazed out over the endless stretch of grey ocean. He turned his head and could just make out the long columns of warships. The entire Grand Fleet and the Kaiser's High Seas Fleet could be out there shrouded – as they were – by damp drifting mist. He thought of Tom and young Bernie on *Invincible* and then of Ellen. He thought about her and Mary Elizabeth all the time. He hadn't even seen his daughter. Oh, the cherished photo was in his inside pocket, but it wasn't the same as being able to touch them and hold them. He prayed the war would be over soon.

'Do they have *any* summer up here?' Eddie asked Charlie.

'Oh, aye, it can be lovely. It's not all snow and ice. Sometimes in summer it doesn't go dark at all and you can see the Northern Lights. Aye, that's a sight you don't forget.'

Eddie looked bored. 'Why don't they come out and fight?'

'Would you if they had twice as many ships as us?' Charlie said dryly.

'They'll have to come out soon or they'll be a laughing stock. Kaiser Bill and his toy boats. He's just got a bigger bath tub to sail them on. He only wants them to show off, not to fight – by the look of it,' was Eddie's reply.

'Maybe they're out there now and we can't see them? Why else would the old man have us racing out of Rosyth?' Charlie mused.

'I heard a rumour that we're joining Jellicoe. His lot left Scapa ahead of us.'

'He wouldn't take the whole bloody fleet on manoeuvres, would he?'

'Where do you reckon we are?' Ben asked Charlie. 'You've had years of experience.'

'It's a wild guess but I'd say Norway, Jutland maybe.'

They fell silent again, all taking turns in scanning the grey misty waters.

'Nothing. Not a damned thing,' Eddie said with disgust.

'You don't have to see them,' Ben said.

'God! I'd forgotten that. Their bloody submarines.'

They all shivered.

For another hour they scanned the sea and horizon and Eddie was about to launch forth with his usual tirade when the klaxon for Action Stations blared out.

'Christ Almighty! Has he gone mad? I can't see another bloody ship!' Eddie shouted.

'Well, obviously he can. Get to your stations!' Charlie ordered.

With battle ensigns whipping out from their jackstaffs, the two lines of ships charged along at full speed, until Admiral Beatty was within range of Admiral Hipper's squadron. In minutes they were all wreathed in smoke and shell splashes.

Aboard *Indefatigable* it was all noise and action. Sweat poured down the cordite-blackened faces of Ben, Eddie and Charlie as the guns came into play. Between loading, firing and loading again, through eyes smarting with heat and smoke, they caught glimpses of each dull red glow that proclaimed a hit. They were all soaked to the skin by the great geysers of water thrown up by the near misses but they hardly noticed.

Suddenly they were all flung to the deck, slipping and swearing as *Indefatigable* was hit in her midships turret and heeled dangerously to port. Quickly Ben and Charlie got to their feet, ignoring the small cuts and bruised bones. Eddie remained on the deck in a crumpled heap. Ben bent down and shook him.

'Eddie! Eddie, get up! For Christ's sake, get up!'

'He's dead, lad,' Charlie yelled amidst all the noise and confusion. 'Leave him, we've got to save ourselves. Try and—'

The rest of his words were lost as an enormous explosion shook the ship. Then there was another and a solid sheet of orange flame and dense gusts of black smoke enveloped everything and Ben was hurled fifty feet into the sea. When he shook the water out of his eyes he couldn't believe what he was seeing. *Indefatigable* blew up, her steam packet boat danced two hundred feet into the air, then she was gone, swallowed by the cold, grey water, taking a thousand men with her.

From their position on *Invincible* Tom and Bernie looked in horror at the empty surface of the sea. One mighty explosion, followed by another, then the flames, the smoke and then . . . nothing.

'God have mercy on them all,' Tom heard an older man behind them say in a hushed voice.

He turned. Bernie's eyes seemed to have sunk and his face was grey. 'Eddie! Eddie and Ben . . .'

'You knew lads on her?'

'My brother and brother-in-law. Do you think . . .?'

'Not much of a chance, lad, I'm sorry. I've never seen a ship go down so fast.'

There was no more talk, the battle continued as Admiral Beatty ran north towards Admiral Jellicoe's ships and the main fleet. It seemed hours and hours before they saw Jellicoe's ships and then as the German fleet steamed out of the mist Tom felt the hatred and bitterness rise in him. Revenge. That was all he wanted now. Revenge for all the men of *Indefatigable*, especially Eddie and Ben. There was no escape for the German fleet now. They faced a huge arc of battleships that stretched from horizon to horizon. The arc opened fire simultaneously so that the leading German ships were engulfed in smoke and shell splashes.

Load! Fire! Reload! Over and over they repeated the action. There was no time to look and see what was going on: there was too much noise, smoke and fire. They worked as one man. For years they'd waited for this, yet there was nothing heroic or adventurous about it. It was sudden, shocking, and inglorious death. It was death without a headstone. A burial without even a proper service.

A deafening roar of an explosion engulfed them all and

then the deck was tilting under them and they were sliding down and down.

'Jump! For God's sake, jump!' Tom could just about hear Bernie's voice but there was nothing he could do. He seemed welded to the burning steel deck that plunged downwards with gathering speed, until they hit the water.

Tears were running down Bernie's cheeks. He'd clawed his way, inch by inch, to the stern where two more men clung on desperately. He grabbed at a piece of twisted metal and gradually twisted his body around it. *Invincible* had been struck midships. Bow and stern were sticking up in the air. She'd been snapped in two like a dried twig. He hung on but waved with the others as HMS *Lion* sailed past them slowly. *Lion* was crippled but would turn back for the survivors. Bernie knew in his heart that Tom was dead and he sobbed like a baby as the smoke and fire of battle swirled and roared in the water around him.

Annie was worse. Ellen had sat up with her for the last two nights and she was tired and heartsore when Maggie came in, a newspaper in her hand.

'Ellen, have you seen . . . this? You look terrible, luv.'

'I've been up with her for two nights. I don't think it can be much longer. What's so interesting in the paper?'

Maggie sat down. 'There's no easy way, Ellen, you'd best hear it from me.'

'Hear what?'

'There's been a big naval battle somewhere off the coast

of Norway. Jutland. It's very puzzling because neither side seem to have won and . . .'

The colour drained from Ellen's cheeks. 'Ben! For God's sake, tell me!'

'Both *Invincible* and *Indefatigable* were sunk. There were other losses but I don't think you'll be interested.'

'No! Oh, no! Did . . . did anyone survive? Did anyone get away in the boats?'

'It doesn't say. Oh, Ellen, I'm so sorry, but maybe tomorrow we'll know more.'

Ellen slumped into a chair. No! *No!* Not Ben and Eddie and Tom and Bernie! It couldn't be! How was she to go on if . . .

Maggie put her arms around her. 'Cry, Ellen, it'll do you good. Many's the time I've cried.' Although it didn't do me any good, she thought bitterly. And then she thought of Lucy. She'd be devastated if Bernie were dead.

Gussie and Tessie came in and took over but Ellen couldn't be consoled. Her husband and three brothers at the same time. Oh, life was so cruel. Her da, her mam, poor Annie and now . . . now . . .

'She'll go out of 'er mind, Tess, I've seen it 'appen. Give her some of that stuff she gives Annie.'

' 'Ere, Ellen, luv, take this. Now don't be worryin', we'll take care of everythin'. You need to sleep, luv. You'll wake with a clearer mind.'

Reluctantly Ellen took the medicine and gradually her sobs decreased and she let herself sink into the darkness that blotted out every single thought.

They were as good as their word; everyone was looked

after and it was Tessie who went to the door next morning and took the telegrams. There were two of them, both addressed to Ellen.

'Oh, God, Tess!' Gussie cried.

'I know. What'll we do? She's still asleep, God luv 'er.'

'I don't think she can take much more, Gussie. Should we open them?'

'Isn't that a crime?'

'To 'ell with it! At least if there's any 'ope it'll cheer 'er up and . . . and . . . if there isn't we'll do what we can to comfort 'er, like we've always done.'

Slowly Gussie opened the first envelope.

'Well?'

'It says, "The Admiralty regrets that A S Edward Ryan was killed in action on June first".'

'Is that it? No more names?'

'No. Then it means Ben's safe. 'Ere, open this one, my hands are shakin'.'

Tessie opened the other. '"The Admiralty Regrets that A S Thomas Ryan was killed in action on June first".'

Both women stared at each other.

'So it looks as though young Bernie got out alive too. Thank God for small mercies. Will I wake 'er?'

'No, leave 'er to sleep. Time enough later.'

Ellen had a dull headache. She felt as though her mind was clogged with cotton wool. 'What time is it?' she asked Tessie.

'Eleven o'clock, luv.'

'In the morning?'

'Yes, in the morning. You needed a decent night's sleep so I left you.'

'What happened? I can't remember. Was it Annie?'

'No, luv.'

'Oh, now I remember! Ben! Oh, Ben!'

Tessie held out the telegrams. 'Look, luv, Gussie an' me, well, we opened them. Ben and Bernie we think cum through, but Eddie an' Tom . . .'

Ellen snatched the telegrams and focused hard on the names. Tessie was right. There was no mention of either Ben or Bernie. Grief suddenly claimed her. Eddie! Poor Eddie who had loved the sea so much. Well, now he was buried in it. The sea had claimed him as its own. And Tom. Earnest and ambitious. Well, he'd be in the newspaper now. The paper he'd wanted to be a reporter for. But there *was* hope for the other two . . .

'Do yer want one of us ter go with yer to the Admiralty place at the Pier Head?'

'Will they know?'

'I don't know but we can try.'

'What about Annie and Daniel and Mary Elizabeth?'

'Maggie will stay with them. She's had a night's sleep. Gussie can go 'ome and get some rest. She's not gettin' any younger.' And neither am I, Tessie thought, but she wouldn't let Ellen go down there on her own.

The place was packed with women, all anxious, white-faced and weary. Tessie pushed her way to the front, dragging Ellen behind her.

421

'We've come about 'er 'usband an' brother. She's lost two brothers already.'

'What name? What ship?' the clerk asked.

'*Indefatigable*: A S Ben Hayes, and *Invincible*: A S Bernard Ryan. Do you know if they're . . . alive? I had the telegrams for my two brothers. Please, please, sir, can you tell me anything?'

He scanned the pages of the large book in front of him and then a long list of names. 'Not Killed in Action or Missing Presumed Dead. I'd say there's a good chance they are both alive. Another ship probably picked them up. The bloke on *Indefatigable* was damned lucky. Not many were saved. We'll have official notification of survivors tomorrow. Come down then.'

Once outside Ellen threw her arms around Tessie.

'Oh, thank God! Thank God! I . . . I don't know how I'd have managed without Ben.'

'Come on 'ome now, I'm wore out.'

Next day brought its relief and its sadness. Ben and Bernie had survived. Both had been picked up and would be on their way home. There was some doubt about their condition though. They might be wounded, the clerk had said. Ellen didn't care. She just wanted them both home. As she walked down the street she frowned, there seemed to be some activity around her own door. She thought of her stepsister. Annie! Annie! She began to run.

'Let me through! Oh, please let me through!'

The people parted and she ran into the lobby.

Maggie caught her arm. 'Quickly, quickly, Ellen! Dr Jenkinson's with her.'

She took the stairs two at a time and burst into the bedroom.

'Thank God!' Gussie said.

'Indeed,' Father Healy agreed.

Ellen sank to her knees beside the bed. Annie was still breathing – just.

She took one skeletal hand in her own. 'It's me, Annie. Ellen. I . . . I'm sorry.'

Annie opened her eyes. She was no longer recognisable as the pretty young girl she'd been just a couple of years ago. She was hideous.

'Daniel.' The word was a whisper.

Ellen got up and leaned over her. 'What about him?'

'Take care . . .'

'Oh, Annie, you know I will! I won't let anything happen to him, I promise.'

'I . . . I'll miss him.'

'No! You'll be looking down on him, on *us* for ever. I love him too and he'll be very special. He's my sister's child.'

Annie closed her eyes and tried to smile. Finally, she had found her family. Still clinging to her hand, Ellen buried her face in the quilt.

'Ellen, luv, there are good things around the corner. Ben and Bernie will be coming home soon and she's out of all pain and heartache now.'

Ellen looked up into the eyes of the woman she had helped all those years ago. 'She is, isn't she, Maggie?'

'I found strength and comfort from all the women in this street and you will too.'

Ellen stretched her arms out to Gussie and Tessie. 'As long as I have all of you, I'll manage. I'll cope.'

'Aye: friendship, love, compassion, generosity. They're qualities you're all rich in and they're things that money can't buy. There's still some hope for the world as long as there're women like you,' Dr Jenkinson said quietly as he pulled the sheet up to cover Annie's face.

Headline hopes you have enjoyed reading MY SISTER'S CHILD and invites you to sample the beginning of Lyn Andrews' heart-warming new saga, THE HOUSE ON LONELY STREET, out soon in Headline hardback . . .

Chapter One

Dublin 1911

'Why do you have to be so nasty to them Da? It's not their fault.' Katherine Donovan's blue eyes met her father's cold, flint-grey ones without flinching. She had never before commented on the way he treated his customers, though many was the time she'd pressed her lips tightly together in mute anger and cast darting, fury-filled glances at him. It was the poorest of the poor who came, filled with abject desperation to 'The Harp and Shamrock', to pledge or sell whatever would raise a few shillings. As well as a pawnbroker, her da was a money-lender, his rates nothing short of extortion. But people were grateful for the cash and didn't protest or argue. Most of them didn't really understand what they were agreeing to, for in the heart of the slums of Dublin, few could read or write.

'I'll stand no more talk like that from you, you bold rossie,' her father growled back. His tone was chilly and bitter. 'And anyway, for your information, they are all eejits, and idlers.'

Now that she'd started, Katherine plunged on, determined to have her say for once.

'They *can't* help it. They're not *eejits*, there *isn't* any work.'

He snorted derisively. 'There's plenty of work for those who want it. They can't pay their rent or feed their families because they're all going on strike by the minute. But more often than not they've the price of a pint of Porter or a packet of Woodbines.'

She turned away from him as he slammed out of the kitchen. What was the use? There wasn't a drop of kindness in him. She would make no apology for challenging him, he deserved neither. At heart she'd known there would be no satisfactory reply. He'd been like this for as long as she could remember. Cold, unbending and relentlessly strict.

'Don't let him break your spirit Katherine, I made that mistake,' her mam had once urged and as she'd grown older she'd understood: her father was a cruel, twisted man. Many people were afraid of him and none had a good word for him, and she had suffered because of it. In all her years at school she'd been taunted and shunned. It had been the same with the kids in the street. They'd never let her join their games and she'd often gone home in tears, to no comfort from her da. Gradually she'd become used to it. She never spoke to those who called her names, she just learnt to hold her head up defiantly.

She could remember quite clearly the only time Mam had ever stood up to him, a week before she'd died. It had been over what poor Joe Hely owed. He'd shouted down Joe's excuses and pleadings and actually struck the pale, stooped man twice before Mam had intervened.

'Leave him, Albert, for the love of God! Don't go taking the debt out of his poor, half-crippled body.'

'You mind your tongue, woman, or it's *your* body I'll go taking the debt from,' he'd bawled at her.

Now, up to her elbows in greasy water as she washed the dishes in the scullery sink Katherine let her mind wander back over those years. Her poor, poor mam. A slave would have had a better life. She'd worked ceaselessly from dawn to dusk every day, including Sundays. By the time Da got up the breakfast was ready, the tea wet and the room warm. After that it was washing, polishing, scrubbing. More meals to cook, bread to make, socks and stockings to be darned, the list was endless. She had never been strong either in body or personality. Her mam had had miscarriage after miscarriage before she'd been born. That in itself had been a disappointment for her da. He had wanted a son and after Katherine there were no other children. It was Da who insisted that she should always use her full name. Kate, Katie, Kath, Kit none of these derivatives were permitted. She was 'Katherine' to everybody. Her da always said it separated her from the illiterate rabble they lived amongst.

Mam must have loved him once, she mused, otherwise she would never have married him. How long had it been before she'd realised she'd committed herself for life to a bully? She wrung out the dish cloth and hung it over the single tap, then taking up the tea towel, she began to dry the dishes. She'd been close to her mam and as she'd grown older she had begun to understand just how she was suffering. Nothing ever pleased Da. Nothing either she or Mam did was right. Much as she'd loved and missed her mam she would never wish her back here to this existence, in this slum; even though they had a comfortable home, good food, decent clothes and occasional treats like a few sweets. Of course she'd never been allowed to choose what kind of sweets. Da just gave her the small paper bag and she'd been grateful for that.

She hated this part of the city. Oh, the public buildings and parks were magnificent and were well maintained, and she'd often stared into the windows of Switzers and Brown Thomas in Grafton Street, especially near Christmas. It didn't cost anything to look or wish. The streets with their rows of once-stately Georgian houses, now referred to as tenements, were home to thousands of people. Whole families living in one or two rooms. Dark, damp cellars with no heating housed the truly destitute. The stone steps leading up to the front doors were all worn and cracked. The doors themselves, warped, their paint was peeling – if there was any paint left on them – were left wide open all year, rain or shine. The fanlights above them were glassless or had jagged, fly-blown shards that time and the elements had not quite succeeded in dislodging. You couldn't see clearly into the halls, but maybe that was a blessing.

Her work finished for the day, Katherine took off her apron and went through to the living room. She permitted herself a cynical smile as her father hastily got up from the table, cramming notes and coins into the old tea caddy.

With his back turned deliberately towards her, he fumbled under the big, heavy basket that held the turf.

She knew where he kept his money. She'd never touch it, he knew that.

'Are you going out, Da?' she asked, although she was certain of the answer.

'I am so. Isn't it Wednesday and don't I always go out?'

Katherine nodded. He didn't drink in any of the local pubs, he would be ostracised, at best, by the other patrons. He took a tram out to Dollymount. In a quiet, respectable pub with a snug he would have three pints of Porter and a small Jamesons. Well, it suited her fine because she was going out herself to a public meeting in Beresford Place at which Mr George Bernard Shaw, amongst other illustrious people, was going to speak. Dublin was in turmoil as one after the other the city's industries were closed down by strike action. She felt great sympathy for the strikers, many of whose wives and mothers were amongst her father's customers. He was always giving out about them, berating, ridiculing them and they could say nothing because they needed the money so badly.

When he'd gone out, she put on a jacket and her hat, a straw boater with a blue and white striped ribbon. As she gazed at her reflection in the mirror she felt overdressed for walking through the streets of decrepit houses, but to abandon the hat in favour of a shawl seemed somehow hypocritical. She sighed heavily. She was eighteen years old and she hated her life. Not one single aspect of it could she point out as satisfying. Many of the girls she'd been at school with were married now, and some even had children.

She wondered would she ever meet someone and fall in love? If she did, she'd have a war on her hands because she knew no local lad would ever come up to Da's expectations.

She'd gone as far as the corner, ignoring the looks of contempt cast by the groups of thin, anxious women whose lined and wrinkled faces were pale with ill-nourishment and constant hunger. Their barefoot children, rickety bodies clothed in what were little better than rags, played in the gutter, faces and limbs already so dirty that the extra grime made little difference. Some of the older ones stared at her and put out their tongues and made monkey-like faces at her. This too she ignored although inwardly their animosity cut deeply. If only there was *something, anything*, she could do to help them. But any help she offered would be refused. They wouldn't take charity handouts from Donovan's daughter.

'Katherine! Katherine, will ye wait for me!'

At the sound of the child's voice she stopped and turned around. She smiled. This was the exception to the rule. This was the one who braved the wrath of the others. Eight-year-old Concepta Healy, or 'Ceppi' as she was known, was like her shadow. She followed her everywhere. Da would't have the child over the doorstep, so Ceppi always waited by the corner.

'Are ye going on a nice outing with the good hat on ye and all?'

Katherine took the grubby hands in hers.

'Well, I don't know if it will be a nice outing. It's a meeting.' She brushed back the strands of Ceppi's tangled copper-coloured hair. 'Isn't this desperate. It's like a furze bush.'

'Sure, we've no comb or brush. Didn't our Annie and Sally break them in the fight they had over them.'

Katherine smiled. 'Never mind, I'll buy you a hairbrush.'

Ceppi shrugged nonchalantly. 'Oh, I'm not troubled at all, anyway me mam would take it offen me.'

Katherine nodded and looked into the grey-green eyes that always seemed to be too huge for the pale, pinched little face.

'Will ye bring me on the outing too? I don't care what it is, really I don't.'

Katherine thought about it. There would be crowds of people and there would also be the police and perhaps even the military. If things started to go wrong . . . well, she was a bit apprehensive herself if the truth be told.

'Please? Please? No one will miss me, no one cares. Except maybe me da.'

Katherine relented. Poor Joe Healy. He was a pleasant man who bore his many afflictions with patience and cheerfulness, despite the fact that Lily Healy did nothing for her husband, or for her eight children who were left to fend for themselves. Ceppi was the youngest. Joe Healy had been born with what everyone referred to as a crooked backbone. Walking was not easy and in his latter years he'd been crippled with arthritis. He had also contracted consumption to add to his misery. He got little sympathy from his wife: she'd once yelled at him she was sure he'd got the consumption to spite her. Everyone said he'd never see Christmas, but seemingly the child didn't know this or was putting a very brave face on it.

'Come on then, Ceppi, keep tight hold of my hand.'

The child grinned. 'Will you bring me on a tram?'

Katherine nodded. 'I will so, we're going up to Beresford Place, to a meeting. A big, important meeting.'

'Sure, what's a meeting? Have I been brought to one before?'

Katherine's explanation lasted until they boarded the tram.

Beresford Place was packed, the crowd thickest at the jumble of half-derelict buildings that used to be the Northumberland Commercial and Family Hotel. The twilight of a day that had taken a long time leaving the sky had finally been blanketed by a heavy darkness. At intervals the flaming, pitch-soaked torches men had attached to the walls of buildings illuminated faces and forms, all pale, all etched with hunger and anxiety. And yet, in their eyes there was a spark of determination and hope.

A double line of grim-faced police officers from both the Royal Irish Constabulary and the Dublin City Constabulary blocked their way to the nearest rank of the crowd. Katherine tapped the shoulder of the officer.

'Would you excuse me sir. I want to get through.'

The constable looked down at her. 'Now why should a respectable girl like you want to come here and join this mob of reprobates?'

Katherine looked up at him warily. He wasn't very old and he was quite good-looking. 'You're R.I.C.?'

'I am so, I'm a Kerry man.' He had an accent as thick as butter.

'I didn't think it would be like this, not as crowded, but seeing as we're here we might as well stay.'

'Would ye look at all the polis,' Ceppi said in amazement. As long as she was with Katherine she wasn't afraid of them. Katherine was chatting in a friendly way to this one. She sensed the excitement. 'Oh, please let's stay?' she urged.

Katherine agreed warily, unable to resist the child's enthusiasm.

'On your own head be it then,' nodded the policeman, 'but if there's trouble get yourselves home immediately. I'll look out for you. Mind yourself now.'

As the joined the main body of the crowd Ceppi tugged at Katherine's skirt.

'Wasn't the polis man a sort of . . .?'

'A decent class of a man. But I'm still worried you won't be able to see anything and you might get crushed.'

'I won't! I won't be after letting them walk on me!' Small and thin as Ceppi was, Katherine knew the child could give as good as she got. She'd always had to, just to exist.

The press of bodies increased as more people joined the crowd. The night air became oppressive and it was difficult to hear all that was being said by the speakers. What she *had* heard she agreed with. Their leader, Big Jim Larkin, had demanded a fair day's pay for a fair day's work and an overtime rate of nine pence an hour. He'd demanded that there be no discrimination against Union Members. He'd already put a stop to stevadores paying the dockers in pubs and exacting a drink for it. There would be no more restrictive practices.

She looked around at the sea of uplifted faces. The torchlight made some of them look grotesque but all showed signs of deprivation. There was something else too, a dawning recognition, and resolve to fight for that 'decent day's pay'.

There was some sort of scuffle going on in the crowd behind them and Katherine began to feel very anxious.

'Come on, Ceppi. I think we'd better go home. I'll buy you a hot pie to eat on the way,' she added, forestalling the child's complaints.

With an effort and the aid of the policeman from Kerry they got through the crowd, and they were even more fortunate to get a tram. The driver told her he was on his way back to Nelson's Pillar in Sackville Street. 'That'll be me lot,' he said. 'We're going on strike and the back of me hand to Mr William Martin Murphy and his Dublin Tramway Company.'

They walked quickly to the O'Connell monument and then along the Quays, noting how many people were out on the streets. As promised she bought the child a pie which Ceppi crammed greedily into her mouth.

As they turned the corner they both stopped. There seemed to be some sort of commotion going on around the shop. The street light was dim. Just one single gaslight struggled feebly against the darkness, creating deep shadows. A figure emerged from the mêlée and she recognised it as Ceppi's brother, Con.

'What's wrong, Con? What's going on?'

Con looked wild and distraught, his eyes wide with some sort of panic.

'Ah, God, isn't it me da and your da and the men from the houses,' he panted.

'What men? What's the matter?'

'Me da . . . me da's dead and it was *your* da what did it!'

Katherine was stunned.

'No! No! In the name of God, he couldn't, he . . .' She was struck for words for a second.

'And now the men are after murderin' *him*.'

'Oh, Jesus!' Katherine's hands went to her cheeks. It couldn't be true. It *couldn't*! Her da couldn't have killed poor Joe Healy.

'Come back with me now, Ceppi,' Con demanded, catching hold of his sister's arm.

She shook it off. 'What'll I do?' she asked, looking up at Katherine wide-eyed and bewildered.

Katherine felt ill. Her imagination was running wild. They'd come for her next! she thought in panic. 'Ceppi go with Con,' she urged. 'Go back with him.'

The little girl stood firm. 'No! I will not! I am staying with you!' Her confusion seemed to have been replaced by a blind obstinacy.

'Ceppi, please?'

'No!'

It was useless and time wasn't on her side. She caught the child's hand. 'Run! We've got to run, Ceppi. Run for our lives!' They both tore out of the small circle of gaslight back into the darkness.

Con watched them disappear, then turned and walked unsteadily away.

The Ties That Bind

Lyn Andrews

Tessa O'Leary – the only daughter in a family of fatherless boys, when her mother dies she's her brothers' lifeline to survival. So for Tessa the privations of war are just another battle to be fought for a young woman who was born fighting . . .

Elizabeth Harrison – oppressed by her shopkeeper mother's snobbish expectations, it seems the coming war offers an escape from her family's emotional ties – but at what cost?

The Ties That Bind – the unputdownable story of two young girls in the slumlands of war-wracked Liverpool, bound together by a friendship that surmounts disaster, poverty and heartbreak . . .

'A great saga' *Woman's Realm*

'A compelling read' *Woman's Own*

'Gutsy . . . a vivid picture of a hard-up, hard-working community' *Express*

'Spellbinding . . . the Catherine Cookson of Liverpool' *Northern Echo*

0 7472 5808 2

HEADLINE

Angels of Mercy

Lyn Andrews

Blue-eyed, blonde-haired, full of smiles and sweetness, even as babies twins Kate and Evvie Greenway captured the hearts of Liverpool's Scotland Road slumlands. But now they are almost adults the two girls find that being pleasant, popular and blessed with a loving family isn't quite enough. For they've both fallen for men who will break their youthful hearts . . .

But these sorrows are nothing to the tragedies that await them and so many others when the Great War breaks out. Determined to do their part, Kate and Evvie sign up for nursing training and are despatched to the Front, a terrible world far from the life-affirming energy of their homes. Can anything, hope, love or the bond that has always united the sisters, survive all that lies in store for them?

An unforgettably moving triumph from a masterful storyteller . . .

'A vivid portrayal of life' *Best*

'Gutsy . . . Andrews paints a vivid picture of a hard-up, hard-working community . . . will keep the pages turning' *Express*

'Lyn Andrews presents her readers with more than just another saga . . . She has a realism that is almost palpable' *Liverpool Echo*

0 7472 5807 4

HEADLINE

When Tomorrow Dawns

Lyn Andrews

1945. The people of Liverpool, after six years of terror and grief and getting by, are making the best of the hard-won peace, none more so than the ebullient O'Sheas. They welcome widowed Mary O'Malley from Dublin, her young son Kevin, and Breda, her bold strap of a sister, with open arms and hearts.

Mary is determined to make a fresh start for her family, despite Breda, who is soon up to her old tricks. At first all goes well, and Mary begins to build up an understanding with their new neighbour Chris Kennedy – until events take a dramatic turn that puts Chris beyond her reach. Forced to leave the shelter of the O'Sheas' home, humiliated and bereft, Mary faces a future that is suddenly uncertain once more. But she knows that life has to go on . . .

'Lyn Andrews presents her readers with more than just another saga of romance and family strife. She has a realism that is almost tangible' *Liverpool Echo*

0 7472 5806 6

HEADLINE

Where the Mersey Flows

Lyn Andrews

Leah Cavendish and Nora O'Brien seem to have little in common – except their friendship. Nora is a domestic and Leah the daughter of a wealthy haulage magnate but both are isolated beneath the roof of the opulent Cavendish household.

When Nora is flung out on the streets by Leah's grasping brother-in-law, the outraged Leah follows her, dramatically declaring her intention to move to Liverpool's docklands, alongside Nora and her impoverished family. But nothing can prepare Leah for the squalor that greets her in Oil Street. Nor for Sean Maguire, Nora's defiant Irish neighbour . . .

'A compelling read' *Woman's Realm*

'Enormously popular' *Liverpool Echo*

'Spellbinding . . . the Catherine Cookson of Liverpool' *Northern Echo*

0 7472 5176 2

HEADLINE